W9-BIQ-558

Date: 8/16/17

**LP FIC NOBLIN
Noblin, Annie England,
Just fine with Caroline**

Just Fine with Caroline

Center Point
Large Print

**This Large Print Book carries the
Seal of Approval of N.A.V.H.**

Just Fine with Caroline

—A Cold River Novel—

Annie England Noblin

CENTER POINT LARGE PRINT
THORNDIKE, MAINE

This Center Point Large Print edition is published in the year 2017 by arrangement with William Morrow, an imprint of HarperCollins Publishers.

The text of this Large Print edition is unabridged. In other aspects, this book may vary from the original edition. Printed in the United States of America on permanent paper. Set in 16-point Times New Roman type.

ISBN: 978-1-68324-277-2

Library of Congress Cataloging-in-Publication Data

Names: Noblin, Annie England, author.
Title: Just fine with Caroline : a Cold River novel / Annie England Noblin.
Description: Center Point Large Print edition. | Thorndike, Maine : Center Point Large Print, 2017.
Identifiers: LCCN 2016048888 | ISBN 9781683242772 (hardcover : alk. paper)
Subjects: LCSH: Alzheimer's disease—Patients—Fiction. | Mothers and daughters—Fiction. | Ozark Mountains—Fiction. | Large type books. | Domestic fiction.
Classification: LCC PS3614.O27 J87 2017 | DDC 813/.6—dc23
LC record available at https://lccn.loc.gov/2016048888

For my mother.

Chapter 1

Caroline O'Conner loved to fish. Her favorite tree sat on the bank of the Cold River, just perfect for leaning against with a fishing pole in her hand. She relished casting a line as the fog lifted sluggishly off of the water.

The best time to fish was during the early summer —when it was already hot, but too early for the summer rush of river rats. She would come in and open up the Wormhole, her family's bait and tackle shop, and then sneak off for an hour or two to visit the river and her favorite tree. In fact, that tree was her favorite spot, not just on the river, but in all of Cold River, the river's namesake and the town where she lived.

Cold River, Missouri, a town of about 8,000 people, was nestled in the heart of an area of the United States known as the Ozarks. At any given time you might hear residents of this southwestern part of Missouri refer to themselves as Southerners or Midwesterners, but neither one was entirely true. The Ozarks, a place of rolling hills and flowing rivers, was a place where a person could disappear for days, months, years, or forever. The rugged terrain was rivaled only by the rugged people living there, a people happy to be tucked away from the rest of the world.

Everybody fished in Cold River.

Caroline's father taught her to fish when she was six. He hadn't wanted to. It had been an argument for days between her father and mother, something that she remembered even at that tender age. Caroline had known, since she was old enough to ask about the "boy in the pictures," that she had a brother in heaven, at least, that's what her mother told her, and her daddy didn't fish anymore. But he wanted to, she could tell. He sometimes looked at the fishing poles in the hallway closet, shoved to the back behind the winter coats. He sometimes pulled a tackle box from off the top shelf and looked inside of it for whole minutes at a time and yelled at her when she asked if she could play with the toys inside.

That was when her mother started asking her father to "please take Caroline fishing."

The first time he took her it had been a disaster. He barked orders the entire time and they didn't even catch a fish. But the next week was different. They caught fish and her father smiled. More fish brought more smiles, and over the years, it became the bond she and her father shared.

She was fishing with her father less and less since her mother was diagnosed with Alzheimer's. Most of his free time was spent taking care of her or taking extra shifts at the free clinic so he could have a break from her. His gear sat dejected in one of the hallway closets, and his waders had long acquired cracks.

Caroline shook her head. It was too early for thinking. And she was starting to sweat. That meant it was time to pack it in and begin her trudge back up to the shop. As she walked, she noticed a car parked out in front of the old Cranwell Station across the road.

The "For Sale" sign had been sitting out in front for months. Over the years, the Cranwell family used the store for many different purposes. It had been a gas station in the beginning, a lively meeting spot for summer visitors to the Cold River during the 1920s. It had also been a beauty salon, a five-and-dime store, a used car lot, and a pet grooming facility. Caroline's parents had owned the little bait shop across the street from Cranwell Station since before she was born, and in the twenty-five years since she'd been alive, the place had been all but empty. There just wasn't enough traffic to the river anymore, especially since the new highway routed most tourists around the town of Cold River completely. When the eldest Cranwell brother died, the building began to sit unoccupied and unkempt, a source of hot debate for the remaining Cranwell family members, all four of them, none of whom wanted the responsibility of maintaining the property. They stayed to themselves down at Cranwell Corner and rarely came into town. Caroline couldn't remember the last time she'd seen any member of that family.

She watched as a man got out of the car and proceeded to walk up to the door of the station. It was a man she'd never seen before. He was wearing khakis and a crisp white button-up shirt that made his dark hair and tan skin stand out against the sunlight even more than they already did. He placed his palm against the glass and began to rub at the thick coating of dirt. After peering inside, he began to pull on the door handle.

Surely he's not trying to break in, Caroline thought. *Who robs a place in broad daylight wearing khakis?* Besides, Cranwell Station looked like it was about to fall in at any moment. Maybe he was just lost and looking for direction. He sure looked like he was from the city, and people from the city began to panic when they cruised outside city limits and towards the river. These two buildings, Cranwell Station and her bait shop, were the last stop before leaving civilization.

She continued to watch him from a safe distance as he walked around the station, kicked at loose boards on the porch steps, and pulled at the door handle some more. Once, he went back to his car and pulled out a cell phone, but realizing there was no reception, shoved it into his pocket and commenced cursing at the air. It wasn't until he picked up a rock and started towards one of the windows that Caroline made a move.

"Hey!" she hollered, charging towards him with her fishing pole. "What in the hell do you think you're doing?"

The man stopped when he heard her voice. He turned to face her, the rock still clutched in his hand. "Who are you?"

Caroline stared at him. He looked familiar, but she couldn't put her finger on it. "Who are *you?*"

"I asked you first."

"Why don't you put that rock down?" Caroline asked. "Ain't nothin' in that place worth stealin'."

"What?" The man looked down at the rock in his hand. He began to chuckle. "It would be hard to steal from myself."

"Are you lost?" Caroline wanted to know. He wasn't making any sense. Maybe the heat was getting to him.

"I don't think so," he replied. His eyes were every bit as dark as his hair. "Not if this is Cranwell Station."

"It used to be."

"Good." The man set the rock down on the porch and stuck out his hand. "In that case, I'm Noah Cranwell."

"Cranwell?" Caroline's mouth dropped open. "You're a Cranwell?" There was no way she could have heard that right. "You're related to the Cranwells who own this place?"

"I am the Cranwell who owns this place," he replied. "But the damn keys don't work."

11

Caroline squinted at him. She'd heard rumors about Noah Cranwell her whole life. Now, here he was, standing in front of her while she pointed her fishing pole at him. No wonder he looked so familiar,

"Anyway, I just flew in from New Jersey."

"New Jersey?" Caroline cut him off. "You're a long ways from New Jersey."

"Don't I fucking know it," he grumbled.

Before Caroline could respond, she heard a snarl and saw a flurry of black-and-tan fur, followed by a ripping sound, and Noah began hollering a string of curse words Caroline had never even heard uttered out loud or together.

"It bit me! It bit me!" Noah said, stumbling back. "That damn . . . *thing* bit me!"

Caroline saw her huge, three-legged Tibetan mastiff in front of her with a piece of cloth hanging from her mouth—a piece of Noah's white shirt. "Yara, NO!"

Of course, it didn't matter how loud Caroline hollered, Yara couldn't hear her. In addition to having only three legs, she was also deaf as a post. Four years ago, Caroline found her tangled in a barbed-wire fence a few miles down the road, filthy and her coat full of mats. It took two veterinarians and a horse tranquilizer to get her cleaned up, and one of her legs had been badly mangled and needed to be amputated. Now she was a 120-pound dog with a serious attitude

12

problem. She barked her indignation at Caroline, and then dropped the piece of cloth at the man's feet.

"I'm—I'm so sorry." Caroline bent down to pick up the scrap of shirt. "She thought you were going to attack me. She's deaf, and she doesn't like strangers."

"I cannot believe I left Hoboken for this," he muttered.

"I'm so sorry," Caroline repeated. "She doesn't have rabies or anything. I mean she's been vaccinated. She's just a big baby!" Caroline never thought she'd see the day where *anything* looked more out of place than her tripod Tibetan mastiff in the Missouri Ozarks, but now here he was—Noah Cranwell in the flesh . . . and khakis.

Noah looked up at her from his tattered shirt. He didn't look angry to Caroline. He looked more amused than anything else. "Well, she's the biggest baby I've ever seen."

"I've seen bigger."

"Who are you, anyway?"

"Oh, I'm sorry, I'm Caroline." Caroline dropped her fishing pole and stuck out her hand. "Caroline O'Conner. My family owns the bait and tackle shop across the road."

"I went over there about twenty minutes ago," Noah replied. "The door was wide open, but nobody was there. I could have robbed you blind."

"I doubt you would have robbed me unless you

wanted a trunk full of night crawlers," Caroline said. "Besides, that's what Yara is for."

"She was in there?"

Caroline nodded. "I admit she's not very good at her job, seein' as how she can't hear a damn thing."

"I beg to differ." Noah pointed down at his shirt. "I guess this means we're going to be neighbors."

"I reckon so." Caroline headed back over to her side of the gravel road, with Yara at her heels. She noticed Noah still watching her as she threw her bait and tackle into the back of the truck.

"You just going to leave that dog on the porch?" Noah called, pointing to Yara.

"I am." Caroline threw a glance back at Yara, who was leaning lazily against one of the posts on the porch. Her tongue lolled in and out of her mouth. "Why? You afraid she might attack you or something?"

"Might?" Noah asked. "Pretty sure she already did."

"She won't do it again," Caroline replied. "She didn't seem to like the mouthful she got the first time."

Noah gave Caroline a wry smile before continuing, "So she lives here?"

Caroline sighed. What didn't he understand? "She lives here," she said. "She won't even get up into my truck. The motion scares her."

"That's an odd dog you've got there."

"I'm aware." Caroline grinned at him. She couldn't help it. There was something charming about his persistence.

"Well, I better, what was it you said? I *reckon* I better head back out to my grandfather's and get this key situation figured out." Noah gave her a wave.

"It was nice to meet you." Caroline locked eyes with him, and it startled her that he held her there just a bit longer than was polite. When he finally broke his stare, he turned and ambled over to his car, started the engine, and roared off, leaving her alone, just exactly as she had been before, but at the same time utterly and completely different.

Chapter 2

It was a twelve-mile trip from the river back into town, and that was just enough time for Caroline to relax before she got home. She'd been making the drive regularly for years, but it wasn't until she moved home four years ago that she began to appreciate the quiet passage into Cold River. Tonight, she was running late. She'd spent too much of her day staring across the gravel road at the newly purchased Cranwell Station.

In truth, she'd been staring at Cranwell Station since before she could walk. The place had an air of mystery that even at twenty-five, Caroline couldn't ignore. Her whole life, rumors circulated about the family and their business, but the Cranwells were notorious for keeping their mouths shut tight and people shut off from Cranwell Corner, the place where all of the surviving Cranwells resided. She tried to remember the last time she'd seen a member of the Cranwell family. It had been a long time, at least a year, since she'd seen hide or hair of any of them. It had been at the free clinic where Caroline's father volunteered. Jep Cranwell came in for his chronic emphysema, which caused him to need an oxygen tank much of the time. She could tell he'd once been a strong and strapping man. In fact, now that Caroline had met Noah, it occurred to her that Noah and his grandfather Jep looked quite a bit alike. But the years had not been kind to Jep Cranwell. Both his body and his disposition had withered. He'd berated the receptionist because he'd had to wait, and then when he'd found out that Dr. O'Conner would be treating him and not his regular doctor, he refused to be seen and stormed out of the clinic, oxygen tank in tow.

Caroline shivered just thinking about it. She wondered how the nice, clean-cut man she'd met at the station today could be related to the likes of Jep Cranwell. It just didn't make sense.

Caroline rested her head against the window as she drove. It would be nice to come home to peace and quiet. Instead, she knew just exactly what she'd find. Her mother's nurse would be frantic to get home to her family and would scold her like Caroline was a child. Then Caroline's father would call after she'd fixed supper and she and her mother had been waiting half an hour for him and say that he'd be another half an hour and to just go ahead and eat without him. Even in retirement, Max O'Conner couldn't slow down. After that, Caroline would spend another twenty minutes convincing her mother to take a bath. Just as Caroline would be settling her mother into bed, Caroline's father would come home and make so much commotion that she would give up on the entire night and retreat to her room, leaving her parents to themselves.

Of course, it hadn't always been this way. Caroline had been referred to as a "menopause baby" her whole life as her mother had been forty-five when she'd given birth. Even as a child, Caroline knew that her parents were older than the parents of her friends, but it hadn't been until an ogre named Alzheimer's invaded the body of her mother four years ago that Caroline truly understood what it meant to be the only child of older parents.

Her father couldn't run his medical practice and the bait shop and take care of his wife, so Caroline moved home two semesters shy of graduating with her BS in History Education at Missouri State University. At first her father had been angry, arguing with her into the wee hours of the morning about the importance of her education, but by now he'd come to depend upon her. Even though he'd retired from his practice two years ago, Max O'Conner was still one of the best doctors in Ozark County, and probably the only one who still made house visits out to the hills and hollers. He worked two days a week, and during the summertime, which was the busy season at the bait shop, a nurse came to look after Maureen O'Conner. So that left Caroline to pull into the driveway of her parents' house on 222 Polk Avenue two nights a week, wishing she could just take a nap instead. She was surprised when she saw her father's truck pull into the driveway just a few minutes later.

"Dad?" Caroline asked. "What are you doing home so early? I haven't even started supper." They both waved goodbye to Allison Hood, Maureen O'Conner's day nurse, as she hurried out the door with a stern look and not so much as a word to either of them.

"I didn't have any appointments scheduled," her father replied, rolling his eyes to Allison's back. Neither of them dared cross her. She was a severe woman in her early fifties with little patience for anyone other than Caroline's mother, which was the only reason Dr. O'Conner put up with her. Allison was from Germany, and with what little English she spoke, insisted upon both

Caroline and her father calling her nothing but "Nurse."

"Hi, honey," Max O'Conner said, bending down to kiss his wife once he and Caroline were inside.

"Hello," Maureen replied. She didn't look up from her knitting.

"I'm fixing your favorite tonight—mashed potatoes and green beans," Caroline said to her mother, also bending down to kiss her.

"And meatloaf for me?" her father asked hopefully.

"And meatloaf for you," Caroline said once the nurse was gone. "Might as well go get cleaned up. It'll be a while yet."

As Caroline turned to walk towards the stove, she felt her father's presence still behind her. He wasn't moving towards her and he wasn't talking to her, either. She turned back around to face him. His face was twisted up, his eyebrows knitted so deeply together that they nearly touched his nose. "Is something wrong?" she asked him.

"Pam Brannan died today," he said. The name came out of his mouth with a rush of air. "She was tired. She was ready to go."

Caroline felt her heart drop into her stomach. "I haven't heard from Court all day." It was the only thing she could think of to say. She'd known this was coming. They all had. Still, she hadn't been ready to hear it. "I need to call him."

"He was with her at the hospital in Saint Louis

when she went. His father called me. Thought we might want to know." Max O'Conner engulfed his daughter in a hug. "Give him some time. You know he's going to need you to be there for him."

Caroline gripped the can of green beans she was holding so tightly that she could feel the metal grooves underneath the paper label. Pam Brannan, Court Brannan's stepmother, had been battling cancer for years. First it was breast cancer. Then last year, it spread to her liver. Caroline was there at the Brannan house when they found out about the breast cancer, almost three years ago.

"I'm sorry, kiddo. I know this is hard for you in more ways than one."

"I should have gone up there to see her," Caroline said, tears welling up in her eyes. She wiped furiously at them. "I should have been there."

"Pam knew you loved her, and you know she wouldn't have wanted you to close the shop or leave your own mother for her."

Caroline nodded, pushing her face further into her father's chest. She'd stopped saying out loud when things weren't fair long ago, but she couldn't stop herself from thinking it. Pam Brannan had been one of the most wonderful women she'd ever known, and she'd taken care of Caroline like she was her own child when she married Court's father when Caroline and Court were in junior high. In some ways, she'd been a better mother to them than their own mothers had, and it just wasn't fair that they were both losing her. "I'm okay," Caroline said, finally. "I've got to get back to supper before it's ruined for all of us."

To Caroline's relief, her mother was eating everything placed on her plate. It had been difficult, even in the beginning, to deal with her mother's illness. But she took pleasure in little things, like the way her mother would still eat three platefuls of mashed potatoes.

"How does it taste, Mom?" Caroline asked.

Maureen looked up from her plate and at her daughter. She smiled. "It's very good. Thank you."

Max O'Conner winked at his daughter. "How was your day, kid?"

"It was interesting," Caroline replied. "We got ourselves a new neighbor."

"Oh really?"

Caroline nodded, her mouth full of mashed potatoes. "Noah Cranwell," she replied once she'd swallowed. "Apparently he's bought Cranwell Station."

"Noah Cranwell, eh?" her father asked. "I don't reckon I've seen that boy since he was a toddler."

"Well, he's not a toddler anymore," Caroline replied. "It was kind of strange to see him, you know, given all those rumors about his mom and dad and, well, his whole family."

"Those rumors are a bunch of poppycock." Her father snorted. "They always were. Nothing but vicious lies to make Nora look bad for leaving town after Alistair Cranwell died."

"Nora is Noah's mom?" Caroline asked.

"And Alistair Cranwell was his father," Max O'Conner finished. "Ali died the way he lived —reckless and stupid. He didn't care for anybody or anything except himself."

"Didn't he die in a duel or something?" Caroline probed. She'd heard lots of different stories about how Alistair Cranwell had died, and she'd always thought the duel rumor was the best one. As a general rule, her parents refused to talk about it, and she'd been shushed more than once out in public when she dared to ask questions about the Cranwell family.

"In a bar fight not two days after he got out of prison," her father said. "There's nothing glamorous or exciting about that and nobody but the Cranwells blamed Nora for getting out of town like she did."

"I don't understand why they would be mad about her leaving." Caroline pushed at her meatloaf with her fork.

Max O'Conner sighed. "Nobody crosses Jep Cranwell. Alistair was Jep's only son, and Noah was, and is, his only grandson. I reckon Jep felt mighty slighted when Nora ran off, warranted or not."

"Then I guess he'll be glad to have Noah back."

"Jep Cranwell is never glad for anything," Maureen O'Conner interrupted, looking up from her plate.

Caroline and her father looked at each other. Sometimes Caroline's mother broke into conversations with astounding clarity.

"How come, Mom?" Caroline wanted to know.

"These potatoes are good. May I have some more?" was all her mother said.

"Sure." Caroline picked up her mother's plate and headed back into the kitchen.

"Don't give me too much now," her mother hollered. "Make sure that you save enough for Jeremy when he gets home."

Caroline's breath caught in her throat. She didn't want to turn around and look at her father because she knew the pain would be written all over his face. "Okay, Mom!" she said, trying to sound cheerful. "I'll make sure and leave enough for Jeremy."

Jeremy, Caroline's older brother, had been dead for nearly thirty years. He'd died in a car accident when he was seventeen, five years before Caroline was born. Lately, Maureen O'Conner talked about Jeremy like he was still alive. Max O'Conner warned Caroline that something like this was likely to happen, but it didn't make it any easier for either of them when it started to become a daily routine, and Caroline's father became sullen, oftentimes retreating to his office to "read a book."

Tonight was no different.

"I think I've had my fill," he said, pushing his chair away from the table. "I'm going to go to my office for a bit." He gave Caroline and his wife quick pecks on the cheek. "Caroline, if you'll just leave those dishes, I'll take care of them later."

Caroline smiled up at him. She knew darn well he wasn't going to be doing any dishes. He wouldn't come out of his room until it was time for him to take his wife to bed. "Okay, Dad."

"Love you, kiddo."

"Love you, too," Caroline replied. She watched him disappear into his office. Then she turned back to her mother who had gotten up from the table and returned to her knitting on the couch. Caroline finished the rest of the meal alone and pretended to be grateful for the silence.

Chapter 3

Caroline was pulling a T-shirt over her head when she heard a knock on her door. It was her father. "Hey, kid," he said from the other side of the door. "You care if I come in?"

"Sure."

"Have you heard anything from Court yet?"

"Not yet. I tried to call him earlier, but it went

straight to voice mail. I don't want to push him if he isn't ready to talk."

"You're a good friend," her father replied.

Caroline looked down at her hands. When she looked back up again she noticed her father was holding something behind his back. "Whatcha got there?"

"I forgot to give this to you at dinner." Max O'Conner produced a small, dusty book. "I got it at the library sale. Thought you might like it."

Caroline took the book and turned it over in her hands. "*The Life and Times of Pretty Boy Floyd*," she read aloud. "I haven't read this one. Thanks, Dad."

"I didn't think you had," he replied. "It's a pretty old book—from the '70s, I think. You probably know everything already, but I couldn't pass it up for a nickel."

"Thanks," Caroline said. She grinned up at him. Her father wasn't often, if ever, emotional. Unlike how her mother had been, Max O'Conner chose his words wisely and preferred to say silent on most matters. Caroline appreciated small gestures such as this. "I don't know too much about Pretty Boy Floyd. He wasn't really part of the Dillinger or Barker gangs, so I haven't read up on him."

"The library didn't have anything on Ma Barker," her father said. "And the one book they had on Dillinger, you'd already read."

"Did they have anything on the Cranwell clan?"

Caroline asked with a wry smile on her face.

"Oh, I think those stories are mostly told in whispers at the back of a smoky bar somewhere," her father replied with a chuckle. "I hope this one will do."

"This is perfect."

"Try to get some sleep," her father said, backing out of her room. "Good night, Carolina."

Caroline settled back onto her bed. She was genuinely surprised that Cold River's little library had a book about one of the notorious Depression era gangsters that she hadn't read, especially one so old. For as long as she could remember, she'd been interested in the exploits of John Dillinger, Ma Barker, and the like. As a kid, she happened upon a book in the library that had accidentally been placed in the children's section. It was a book about the Barker Gang, and told of the murder of a sheriff just a few towns away from Cold River, a murder that was supposedly perpetrated by Alvin Karpis, the real brains behind the outfit, even though the gang was named after its matriarch—Ma Barker.

Caroline's mother hadn't been too thrilled with her daughter's newfound interest, but her father was a bit of a history buff and was thrilled for her to learn about that era, especially if it had anything to do with the Ozarks. She supposed that was why Cranwell Station had always fascinated her. Rumors about Noah Cranwell and his parents weren't the only rumors to circulate around that family—the elder generation supposedly ran the only speakeasy out of Cranwell Station during the Depression, supplying partygoers with their very own brand of Ozark Mountain Lightning. Of course, her father clammed up when it came to the Cranwells. Anytime she asked about them, he made a joke or told her it was impolite to gossip.

My parents weren't the only ones, Caroline thought. Court also hated it. As a sheriff's deputy, he was personally offended that his best friend liked to read about criminals while he fought to apprehend them. It was a running joke between them, and whenever anyone asked why they weren't married, Court told them it was because Caroline liked men on the *other* side of the law.

Of course, that wasn't really true, either. The truth was that Caroline hadn't had much experience with men. She'd had only one serious boyfriend back in high school and dated a few boys in college. Otherwise, the only men in Caroline's life were the paper kind—the kind whose dark eyes existed pressed between the pages of a book.

She opened the book to the first chapter and wondered if she ought to call Court just one more time before she went to sleep. She hated the thought of Court and his father alone in that house, wondering what they were going to eat for dinner without Mrs. Brannan around. Picturing the empty place at the table was almost too much for Caroline, and she felt a tear glide down her cheek and splash onto the book in her hands. She shook her head back and forth, ridding herself of those thoughts, and concentrated on the damp page in front of her.

It was almost 2 a.m. before Caroline felt sleepy. She was just sinking down into her bed when she heard a knock on her window.

The knocking was long and loud. The impatient foot tapping of the person knocking was no softer. Caroline rolled over and opened one eye in the direction of the noise.

"Caroline!" The knocking grew more intense. "Car-o-line!"

Caroline pulled the covers back over her head. "Use your key!" was her muffled response. "Go to the front door!"

The knocking stopped. "I forgot about my key." There was a rustle in the bushes outside the window and then it was silent.

"Did you forget about your manners, too?" Caroline asked when a dark figure appeared in the doorway of her room.

"Hush up and scoot over."

Caroline sighed and scooted over to the edge of the bed. "Don't put your cold toes on my legs."

Caroline's cousin Ava Dawn slid in next to her.

"We aren't in junior high anymore. You don't have to sneak out of *or* into the house."

"Don't you even want to know what I'm doing here?"

"No."

Ava Dawn scooted closer to Caroline. "Have you ever thought about straightening your hair? Curls went out last year."

"Go. To. Sleep."

"I left Roy, Caroline. For good this time. I swear."

"I've heard that before."

"I mean it," Ava Dawn whispered, her voice barely audible. "I filed the papers yesterday."

Caroline sat up in bed, squinting at her cousin. "For a divorce?"

"We had a real bad fight the other night. I just can't do it anymore, Carolina. I just can't."

"Are you okay?" Caroline got up and turned on the lights. "Did he hurt you? Do I need to go get my dad?"

Ava Dawn shook her head, and a mess of blond hair fell into her eyes. "No. He was too drunk."

"That figures."

"I deserve better," Ava Dawn said. She straightened up. "I do, you know?"

"I know," Caroline replied. "I've been telling you that since high school."

"Well, Brother Crow says that I'm on a spiritual journey right now, and I sorta believe him."

"Brother Crow?"

"Yeah, you know, down at Second Coming?"

Caroline knew whom Ava Dawn was talking about. How could she not? Haiden Crow had been the preacher at Second Coming Baptist for the last two years, and he'd just about converted the whole town to his congregation. With his slicked-back hair and even slicker tongue, he reminded Caroline more of a snake oil salesman than anything else, and she didn't trust him. So far, she seemed to be in the minority, and now, he'd even won over her cousin. "How long have you been going there?"

"A couple of months," Ava Dawn confessed. "Brother Crow says Roy ain't spiritual like I am." Ava Dawn looked at Caroline. "He says that's why we won't ever work. You think that's true?"

"I think Brother Crow is saying an awful lot," Caroline replied. "But if what he's saying is going to keep you from being Roy Bean's punching bag, then I can't argue."

"I'm sure you'd like him if you gave him half a chance," Ava Dawn said.

"Right now I just want to go to sleep."

"I'm sorry I woke you up." Ava Dawn fidgeted on the bed. "I just didn't have nowhere else to go."

"I know," Caroline said. Her cousin had been running away ever since Caroline could remember, since even before Ava Dawn's daddy died and her mother ran off. Most of the time she came to stay with Caroline's parents, who were more than happy to have her, but Ava Dawn always ran away from them, too. It wasn't until she married Roy that she stopped taking the nearest Greyhound out of town the minute she got angry about something. "And you know you're welcome here."

"Thanks."

"We'll sort it all out during the daylight." Caroline let go of Ava Dawn's hand. "I have to get up in four hours."

"Can I go with you?" Ava Dawn asked.

Caroline cocked her head to the side. Ava Dawn hated the bait shop. "Why do you want to go to work with me? The last time you were there you said the shop smelled like dirt and that you were never coming back."

"I don't remember that." Ava Dawn batted her eyelashes. "Besides, I heard there was someone new taking over Cranwell Station, and I want to get a good look at him."

"How have you already heard that?" Caroline demanded. Then, thinking better of it said, "You know what, never mind. I don't want to know. You can go with me tomorrow as long as you promise not to cause me any trouble."

"I promise!"

"Great, now leave me alone."

"You care if I take a shower?" Ava Dawn didn't

wait for a response. "I feel sorta bad for wakin' you up and all. I've been workin' the night shift for so long I forget when normal people sleep."

"Knock yourself out," Caroline replied, crawling back underneath the covers. "Just don't turn on the hair dryer or my dad will throw a fit."

Ava Dawn's muffled reply was lost on Caroline. She was already asleep.

Chapter 4

Caroline stopped just before she turned onto the gravel road that took her to the bait shop, at the last gas station for almost fifteen miles—Gary's One Stop. Gary made the best chicken salad sandwiches in three counties, and if she got there early enough, she could nab one before the tourists heading down to the river could get to them. The tourists from the cities acted as if Gary's was their last stop in civilization before they gave themselves to the wild, and Gary made a mint keeping that fear alive. What the tourists didn't know was that Gary also sold the best moonshine in three counties. He kept it hidden underneath the counter behind the register, and only locals knew to ask for a jar of his granny's finest.

"Hey, Gary," Caroline said, pushing through the door. "I think I'm going to need a couple sandwiches today. I've got Ava Dawn in the car with me."

"Caroline, is that you?" Gary stuck his head out from inside the cooler at the back of the store. "You're early this mornin'."

"I am?"

"Or maybe I'm runnin' late," Gary replied. "You got a few minutes to wait on an old man?"

Caroline grinned. Gary was no more an old man than she was an old woman. He couldn't have been more than ten years or so older than she, but he acted like those ten years were a lifetime. "You know I've got plenty of time."

She busied herself staring into the cold cases full of soda and energy drinks, trying to decide which one would go best with chicken salad. Caroline was reaching in to grab a Mr. Pibb when she heard the bell above the door ring, signaling another customer inside the store.

"Hello? Is there anyone here?" called a voice at the front of the store. "I need to pay for my gas."

Caroline peered around an endcap full of candy to find Noah Cranwell standing impatiently at the counter. He had a baseball cap shoved down onto his head, and there were traces of morning stubble jutting about his jawline. Gone were the khakis and white shirt from the day before, and she hardly recognized him in a pair of jeans and work boots. He almost looked like he belonged.

Almost.

"I can't get the card reader to work," he continued. "I need to pay for my gas. Pump number seven . . . Where in the hell is everybody?"

"Gary is in the back." Caroline came out from where she'd been hiding.

Noah swiveled his head around at the sound of Caroline's voice. When he saw her, a small smile crept across his lips. "I thought I recognized that truck parked out there from yesterday." He eyed the empty store. "Does everybody around here move this slowly in the morning?"

"It's not just the morning," Caroline replied. She nodded past Noah over at Gary, who was ambling towards them.

"Okay, Carolina, I've got your sandwiches," Gary said, making his way behind the counter. He stopped when he saw Noah. "What can I do ya for?"

Noah turned his attention away from Caroline, and laid his credit card down next to Gary's hand. "I just need to pay for my gas. The card reader out there isn't working."

"They ain't never worked," Gary replied. He slid the card towards Noah. "Cash only here, son."

"I don't have any cash."

Gary sniffed, and folded his arms across his chest. "Says no cards right there at the pump. You can't read?"

Noah's jaw tightened. "I don't have any cash.

All I have is this card right here." He shoved the card back to Gary.

"And I done told ya we don't take cards," Gary said. He placed his pointer finger in the middle of the card and pushed it over to Noah.

Caroline rolled her eyes. Honestly. "Gary, just put it on my tab."

"You don't need to do that," Noah said. He was fidgeting with his card, rolling it over in his hands.

"How else you gonna pay?" Caroline asked. "Gary here'll take it out of your hide before he lets you leave without paying for gas."

"I'll pay you back."

"Go ahead, Gary," Caroline said.

Gary eyed Noah suspiciously. "You sure?"

"I'm sure."

"You know this stranger?" Gary continued.

"Gary, this is Noah Cranwell. Noah, this is Gary Ray Boyd." Caroline motioned between the two men.

"Cranwell, eh?" Gary rubbed his chin. "You belong to them Cranwells out there in the hollers?"

"You know any other Cranwells, Gary?" Caroline asked.

"Sure don't." Gary continued rubbing his chin. "I reckon that'd make Jep Cranwell your grand-daddy."

Noah nodded. "I reckon it would."

Caroline put her hand over her mouth to stifle

a giggle at the way Noah said "reckon." It only made him seem like even more of an outsider. "Well, I'm glad we've got that all sorted out. No strangers here," she said.

"You don't do business with strangers?" Noah asked.

"Strangers pay cash," Gary replied, finally letting go of his chin. "I'll add this'n' to your tab, Carolina."

"Thanks, Gary." Caroline pushed Noah out the door before he could say anything else.

"That was unbelievable," Noah said to her once they were out of earshot of Gary. "Cash only?"

"You're not in New Jersey," Caroline reminded him. "Nobody around here is gonna trust a man wearing a Yankees hat. You're in Cardinals country down here."

"I reckon you're right," Noah replied. "I better switch hats." He was grinning down at her as if he'd just eaten a whole pie all by himself.

"Don't say that word again," Caroline said, resisting the urge to grin right back. "It doesn't sound right with that East Coast accent you've got goin' on."

"If you say so."

Caroline ignored the excited hand motions her cousin was making from the passenger's seat of the truck. "Think you can make it to where you're headed without my help?"

Noah winked at her before slipping into his car.

"I reckon we'll find out." He roared off down the road, leaving Caroline alone to explain herself to Ava Dawn.

"Was that Noah Cranwell?" Ava Dawn asked before Caroline had a chance to say anything. "It is, isn't it?" She was practically bouncing off the seat.

"It was."

"Lord have mercy, Caroline. He's gorgeous."

"He's not bad lookin'," Caroline agreed. "Puts me to shame first thing in the morning."

"Hell, me, too."

"Oh, shut up." Caroline started the truck and pulled back onto the gravel road. As she drove, she stole a glance over at Ava Dawn and wondered how it was that her cousin could look fresh as a daisy on zero sleep when she herself looked like a Raggedy Ann doll. She'd tried to coax her crow's nest of hair into a ponytail, but she'd given up and let it spring freely from her scalp in frizzy curls. "Listen, if you're going to be here, you're going to have to do more than spend your day staring across the street." Caroline pulled into the bait shop driveway as Yara came running.

"Uh-huh." Ava Dawn was turned around in her seat, staring in the direction of Cranwell Station.

Caroline rolled her eyes. "Please, at least put your tongue back in your mouth." She got out of the truck and reached down to pet the top of Yara's head. When that wasn't enough, Yara jumped up on Caroline, her paws reaching Caroline's shoulders, and licked her square on the face. "Ogooorfph," Caroline said, pushing the dog away and wiping her face. "And feed this beast while you're at it."

"Fine, fine."

Caroline walked around to the back of her truck to grab her tackle box and fishing pole. Maybe she'd have time to do some fishing later, if Ava Dawn was here. She paused for a moment when she heard a screeching of tires just behind her, and the distinct melody of Hank Williams Jr. playing from someone's radio. Caroline didn't have to think about who'd just pulled up in front of the shop. She knew, and she silently cursed at herself because she should have been expecting it.

Smoke from the dual exhausts of Roy Bean's pickup truck billowed out into the dewy morning air. It was so thick, Caroline could taste it.

"Get on out of here, Roy," Ava Dawn hollered, jumping out of the truck. "I ain't got nothin' more to say to you."

"Well, I got plenty to say to you," Roy replied. He spit a wad of tobacco onto the dirt road. It made a disgusting plop that Caroline could hear from where she was standing.

"Don't waste your time," Ava Dawn continued. "I ain't goin' nowhere with you."

"Come home with me, baby," Roy needled. He took a step onto the grass. "I miss you."

"Yeah, well, I need you like I need a hole in my head, Roy Bean," Ava spat back. "Get on out of here with that talk. You're a liar."

Roy took a menacing step forward and grasped one of his thick hands around Ava Dawn's arm. He was done being nice. "You're gonna wish you had a hole in your head by the time I'm done with you."

Ava Dawn pulled out of his grasp and stumbled backwards, falling to the ground with a pop, prompting Yara to circle around in front of her, baring her teeth at Roy.

Caroline found her feet in time to reach her cousin before Roy did. She pulled her up and stepped in front of her cousin and her dog. "Get out of here, Roy," Caroline said. She didn't take her eyes off of him. She knew better than to do that.

Roy split his glare between Caroline and her cousin. "This is between me and *my wife*."

"I thought I told you after the last time not to come back," Caroline said. She took a deep breath in through her nose. She wasn't scared of Roy, not when he was sober, but she didn't like to ruffle his feathers all the same.

"I don't recollect that."

"That's because you were piss drunk," Ava Dawn screamed from behind Caroline.

"Shut up." Roy sneered. "And get your fat ass into the truck."

The ringing that had begun in Caroline's ears was getting louder. She wanted to slap the chew out of Roy's mouth. Behind him, she saw Noah Cranwell watching them. It looked like he was stuck in place, one hand on the wheelbarrow he'd been pushing, and the other shielding his eyes from the sun to see the commotion. "Roy, I'm only going to ask you one more time to get off my property."

Roy's hands balled into fists, and he leaned into where Caroline stood. He was so close that Caroline could smell the Skoal tucked in between his lip and his teeth. He spit again, and this time, it hit the ground just inches from Caroline's feet, some of it splattering up onto her flip-flop and exposed toes.

Before Caroline could react, Noah Cranwell was between them. He placed one of his hands palm down on Roy's chest. "I think I heard this lady ask you to leave," Noah said. His jaw muscle was flexing in and out.

Roy let out a gravelly laugh that sounded more like a cough. "I hate to break it to ya, buddy, but she ain't no lady."

"It's time for you to leave," Noah said. He was taller than Roy by at least six inches, but Roy had puffed himself up so big he looked like a blowfish.

"Who the fuck are you?" Roy demanded.

This time, they were interrupted by yet another

set of screeching tires. When the dust cleared, Court Brannan emerged from his truck. He ambled over to them, one hand on the gun he always wore around his waist. He wasn't wearing his uniform, and Caroline wondered how he even knew to come out here. Somehow, Court always knew.

"I thought I heard you tell Dwayne at the Dollar General that you were headed out this way," Court said. "Now, tell me, Roy, what good can come of this?"

Roy glanced from Noah back over to Court, squaring his shoulders to both of them. "I ain't leavin' until I get my wife."

"I don't think your wife wants to go with you," Court said. "You're outnumbered here, friend."

"He's too dumb to figure that out!" Ava Dawn hollered, still hiding behind Caroline.

"Shut up!" Roy growled.

"Go on home," Court urged. Then he looked over at Noah, as if noticing him for the first time. "You, too," he said. "I can take it from here."

"I'm not going anywhere," Noah replied.

"I don't know who you are," Court said. His voice was calm and even. "But I'm the law around these parts, and I'm not asking ya."

"Come on, Roy," Caroline said. "Go home and think about what you're doing."

"I know what I'm doing," Roy said, his words

firing between Court and Noah. "You better shut up. You all better shut up."

Caroline turned and walked up the steps and inside the shop, dragging Ava Dawn behind her. There wasn't going to be any blood spilled on her property today. At least, not any blood that she didn't spill herself. She could still hear the men arguing outside as she bent down and pulled out the .22 gauge shotgun she kept behind the counter. Gun in hand, she walked back out onto the porch. "Roy Bean!" Caroline hollered. "I'm going to give you fifteen seconds to get off my property before I shoot you."

Noah, Court, and Roy stopped and stared at Caroline.

"One, two, three," Caroline began to count.

"You better do what she says," Court said. He nodded at Roy. "You know good as I do she'll shoot."

"Four, five, six . . ."

"I ain't goin' nowhere."

"Seven, eight, nine . . ."

"I don't know about this urban cowboy." Roy jabbed his thumb in Noah's direction. "But Court 'n' me both carry."

"That may be so," Caroline replied, hoisting the shotgun to her shoulder. "But you both know I'm a better shot. Now you've got six seconds to decide how this is gonna turn out."

Roy sniffed, placing his thumb on the side of his

nose. "A'ight, a'ight." Roy pointed at Ava Dawn. "You best be gettin' home, or you and your bitch cousin will both regret it." He turned and hopped back up into his truck, peeling out in a show of dust and rocks.

Caroline lowered the shotgun to the relief of her aching arms. Both Noah and Court were still standing there. Noah was staring at her intensely. She couldn't tell if he was angry or impressed, and Caroline felt goose bumps begin to prick up on her arms. With his dark hair and even darker eyes, Noah stood in stark contrast to Court, who had sandy blond hair and blue eyes.

"Don't worry, man. She ain't gonna shoot ya," Court said to Noah, clapping him on the back.

Noah tore his eyes away from Caroline and looked at Court. "I keep forgetting everybody around here carries a gun."

"You ain't from around here, I'm guessin'?" Court asked.

"I was born here," Noah replied. "But I grew up in New Jersey."

"Shit, people in New Jersey have guns, right?"

"I did."

"You ought ta get along just fine." Court stuck out his hand. "The name's Court Brannan."

"Noah Cranwell."

Court stopped mid-shake. "Well, I'll be damned. Nice to meet ya."

Caroline turned her back to them and headed back inside the shop to replace the gun.

"Caroline, I'm sorry," Ava Dawn began, still standing where Caroline left her. "I should have known Roy'd come out here half-cocked."

"It's alright." Caroline sighed. "I should have figured it out on my own when you told me you left while he was asleep."

"Looks like I'll be staying with you for a while."

"You know that's okay with me," Caroline said. "Dad and I are always here for you, and if my mom could help, you know she would."

"Seemed like maybe Noah Cranwell wanted to help us," Ava Dawn replied with a wink. "Jeezus, he's cute."

"We didn't need his help."

"I thought it was mighty gentlemanly of him."

"It was pretty stupid," Caroline said. "Roy was pissed."

"Havin' him around might come in pretty handy." Ava Dawn winked at her cousin.

"I don't need his help."

Ava Dawn leaned farther onto the counter and said, "I ain't talkin' about *needin'* to depend on *nobody*. I'm talkin' about wantin' to depend on someone, just because it's nice to have a shoulder that ain't attached to the head of a relative. I'm talkin' about havin' a good man by your side."

Caroline rolled her eyes. "You act like good

men come easy as cow patties out here, Ava Dawn. Besides, I don't think either one of us have any business deciding what constitutes a good man considering the luck we've had."

"It ain't about luck," Ava Dawn continued. "I picked Roy fair and square, and I got exactly what I bargained for."

"Nobody bargains for that." Caroline reached out to hug her cousin. As aggravating as she was, Ava Dawn was the closest thing to a sister Caroline had ever had. "I'm sorry. I didn't mean to hurt your feelings."

"I know you didn't."

By the time Caroline went back out to check on Noah and Court, Noah was gone. He'd disappeared back inside Cranwell Station, and Court was waiting for her, sitting on his tailgate. She walked outside and slid herself up onto the tailgate next to him. "I've been calling you," she said.

"I know," Court replied. "I didn't know what to say."

"Court, I'm just, I'm so sorry."

"Don't be," he said, giving her the brightest smile he could muster. "She made me promise not to be sad, but I won't be able to keep from it if you keep on tellin' me you're sorry."

Caroline rested her head against his shoulder. "Okay, but you know I'm here for you, right? You know that."

"Of course I know that." Court placed his cheek onto the top of Caroline's head.

"Are you on duty today?"

"Not until later," Court replied, straightening himself up. "We can't afford for me to take the time off right now. Not with the funeral."

Caroline swallowed. "When is it?"

"Friday." Court jumped from the tailgate to the gravel beneath them. "I'm glad that you're going to have Noah Cranwell for a neighbor."

"Why?" Caroline narrowed her eyes at him. "So he can protect me in all his manly glory?"

"So *you* can protect *him*," Court replied. "Didn't you hear him say he grew up in New Jersey?"

"Well, he did live here until he was five," Caroline conceded. "I guess he's from here."

"Can you even imagine what it was like growing up with that ogre Jep Cranwell as your grandfather?" Court shuddered. "Awful."

Caroline waved as Court drove off. She couldn't remember a time when he wasn't cracking jokes, and she wished she could be the kind of friend to him, especially right now, that he was to her. He'd been there for her when her mother was diagnosed with Alzheimer's. His whole family—his dad and Pam included—had been there. It didn't seem real that Pam was gone.

When she turned around to head back into the bait shop, she caught sight of Noah Cranwell from inside Cranwell Station. The windows were old and cracked, but he was cleaning them, none-theless. He was so intent upon his work that he didn't notice her staring at him. Caroline had never been to New Jersey, but she couldn't decide if it was good or bad to have an outsider on the inside, bringing attention to a few of the cracks.

Chapter 5

Cold River was settled in 1832 by a man named Jacob Powell, a man with little directional sense who fell headfirst, so the legend goes, into the river. When he finally emerged, soaking wet in the middle of the winter, he commented to his wife that the water sure was cold. He promptly died of pneumonia, leaving his wife and children to settle what would eventually become the town, which ended up sitting right on the Union-Confederate line. Half the Powell kids fought for the North, half fought for the South, and the town was practically burned to the ground during the Civil War.

After the war, to this day referred to by the townspeople as the only war that mattered, both sides came together to rebuild, making Cold River the county seat. A statue of Jacob was erected in his honor. Even as a child, Caroline thought it was ridiculous that her town had chosen to honor a man who stumbled into a river rather than the woman who really settled the town, a woman whose name nobody could even remember.

As for the O'Conners, they could trace their lineage to no one, although Caroline's father grew up in Cold River. His great-grandparents emigrated from Ireland, and they owned and operated a shoe repair store in the middle of town—not far from the Jacob Powell statue. Her father was the first person in his family to go to college, which is where he'd met Maureen—a nice, Irish Catholic girl from New York.

"I thought your father had taken me to the ends of the earth," Caroline's mother would say. The story of her first few years in Cold River had always been one of her favorites to tell. "Imagine me, a girl from Syracuse, here!"

"She sure did stand out," her father would chuckle. "With her bangle bracelets and wild, curly hair."

The only thing her mother couldn't learn to love, the only thing she couldn't understand, was how even after decades in Cold River, people still considered her an outsider. The townsfolk often referred to her, even after she was well into her forties, as "that girl from New York." It wasn't, Caroline learned, that the people in Cold River didn't like her mother. In fact, most people adored her. It was simply that they didn't trust outsiders, and she was an outsider. Caroline assumed her mother opened the Wormhole in an attempt to win over the townspeople, and in some ways it worked. They still thought of her as an outsider —that was never going to change. But they didn't talk about it nearly as much.

If Maureen was an outsider, Caroline's father was the opposite. He returned to Cold River the golden boy—the town's very own doctor, one of the only doctors in the county when he first began. There was a small hospital in town, but the doctors there were mostly volunteers from neighboring counties. As the years passed, more doctors filtered in, and Max O'Conner opened a family practice.

After medicine and his family, Max O'Conner's love was the river. It was his escape, their escape—the one place where Maureen could hide from the watchful eyes of the town, where Max could fish, and where their children could swim. They'd paid practically nothing for a small parcel of land back in the '70s. It was one of the only pieces of land that far down that wasn't owned by a member of the Cranwell family.

It was the O'Conners' campsite until Maureen opened the bait shop when Caroline's brother, Jeremy, started school. The shop was successful for the most part, and even during the years when it wasn't successful, Maureen was still there, every day in the summertime, until she could no longer drive herself. For a while after she moved home, Caroline drove her mother back and forth, staying with her for a few hours at a time. Last year, she'd begun staying with her mother full-time, and it wasn't long before her mother could no longer make the trip at all. They had a nurse who came every single day, even when the shop was closed and even when her father was there on his days off. There were two nurses, rotating days, Monday through Sunday, and sometimes Caroline felt like a visitor in her own home, always tiptoeing around so as not to disturb the nurses. She wondered if maybe that was why she was so insistent upon keeping the shop open because selfishly, the shop was hers, really the only place where she could be herself.

Max O'Conner suggested more than once that they close down the shop, maybe even sell it, but Caroline couldn't bear to see the shop closed, or worse, owned by someone else. The thought made her sick to her stomach. No, Caroline had to keep the store open, at least while her mother was still alive. Even if she was partially motivated by selfish reasons, it would be one thing she could do for her, the only thing, really, and so she drove there every day from April to September. She kept the lights on and bait in the coolers. She smiled at customers most of the time, and she tried to remember that when the doors were open, she represented Maureen O'Conner.

This day, however, the bait shop was closed

because she and her father were sitting in a pew at the Second Coming Baptist Church. Just a stone's throw from the Dairy Queen, the church had once been a bar called The Barn and so the building was subsequently built to resemble a big, red barn. When the owner had a religious epiphany while in county lockup for methamphetamine possession, The Barn was donated to Second Coming and quickly became one of the fastest-growing churches in all of Cold River. That's when Haiden Crow moved to town. He, his wife, and three children were outsiders, but just from the neighboring county, so they weren't considered outsiders in the same way that Caroline's mother was. They were still from the Ozarks, and that's what counted. Pam Brannan had been one of the first to begin attending Second Coming, and it didn't take long before most of the town counted Haiden Crow as one of the best Southern Baptist preachers in the state.

Brother Crow, as he liked to call himself, was outside welcoming guests when Caroline and her father arrived for Pam's funeral. "Thank you for coming, Dr. O'Conner." Haiden Crow reached out and shook Max O'Conner's hand.

"Thank you for having the service here, Father Crow," Max O'Conner replied.

"It was the least we could do. She was a member of our church family," Haiden said "And please, call me Brother Crow. I tell you that every time we meet. We're Baptists, not Catholics."

"Alright then, Brother Crow."

"How is Mrs. O'Conner getting along?"

Caroline's father stiffened. He didn't like to talk about his wife, especially not out in public. She'd been the one to attend services with Max. Now the job had fallen to Caroline while her mother stayed home with the nurse. "She's well."

Ava Dawn shoved herself in between Caroline and Max. "Brother Crow!"

"Sister Bean," Haiden Crow greeted her. "I didn't see you at Bible study last week."

"I've been busy."

"Too busy for Bible study?"

Ava Dawn leaned in to Haiden until she was so close to him that their hair was touching. "I left Roy," she half yelled and half whispered. "I left him, just like you told me to!"

Haiden Crow's pale complexion reddened. "Ava Dawn, I didn't tell you to—Well, that's not what I meant." His eyes scanned the crowd of interested funeral-goers. "We'll talk about this at a more appropriate time."

"We better take our seats now," Max O'Conner said, saving Brother Crow from the clutches of Ava Dawn. "We're holding up the crowd."

"I figured he'd be happier," Ava Dawn said as they walked away.

"I don't think Baptist ministers are supposed

to be happy about divorce," Caroline whispered.

"You're probably right," Ava Dawn replied. "He didn't exactly tell me to leave Roy."

"What did he say, then?"

"He told me I deserve to be happy. That God wants me to be happy."

Caroline shrugged. "I reckon he does."

The whole town packed into the pews like sardines. Despite the uncomfortable hotness of the crowd, Caroline was glad that so many people turned out to tell Pam goodbye. She and her father situated themselves in a back pew, just as Haiden Crow took his place at the pulpit. "Thank you brothers and sisters, servants of the Lord." A hush fell over the crowd, and Caroline snapped her attention to the front of the sanctuary. "Thank you for coming today to celebrate the life of Sister Pamela Brannan." He paused for a moment to rake his hand down the length of his long, black beard. "Sister Brannan was a faithful soldier in the War for Christ, and today she has gone home. Her fight on this broken earth is over."

Caroline's legs were sticking to the cracked vinyl padding on the pews. Every time she moved, her sweaty legs made noise.

"Sit still," her father scolded.

"Pam's life will not be forgotten," Haiden continued. "Let her life, her good, long life, be a lesson to us all."

"A lesson?" Caroline whispered.

"Shhhh."

"Let us remember that we must put the Lord first always. That we must devote our lives to Him and not to the earthly pleasures that we so oft dive into. Sister Brannan came to me several months ago deeply troubled. She was mentoring a woman who was living a lifestyle that commonly leads the young women of our society to struggle. Let us not forget 1 Corinthians, Chapter 6: 'Know ye not that the unrighteous shall not inherit the Kingdom of God? Be not deceived: neither fornicators, nor idolaters, nor adulterers, nor effeminate, nor abusers of themselves with mankind, nor thieves, nor covetous, nor drunkards, nor revilers, nor extortioners, shall inherit the Kingdom of God.' "

Caroline shifted.

"Shhhh!"

"I spent many weeks counseling this woman, whose name I shall not speak. We discussed her ultimate goals as a Christian woman. She wanted to be a wife and mother. She wanted to live for the Lord. Proverbs 31:30–31: 'Charm is deceitful, and beauty is vain, but a woman who fears the LORD is to be praised. Give her of the fruit of her hands, and let her works praise her in the gates.' " Haiden drew a breath. "Sister Brannan lived her life as an example for this woman and many others. She was a mother to Court and husband to Tom. That is what makes us here in this room feel her loss so deeply. It is what makes her death so sorrowful to those of us here on earth. But I beg of you not to mourn the loss of this righteous woman."

Caroline hoped he was about done.

"Remember instead Revelation 12:13," Haiden continued. " 'And I heard a voice from heaven saying, 'Write this: Blessed are the dead who die in the Lord from now on . . . that they may rest from their labors, for their deeds follow them!' "

A chorus of "Amen!" followed. The congregation leaned forward farther with every word Haiden Crow spoke. It didn't seem to matter if he was telling the truth or not. Nobody in that room took a breath without Haiden Crow taking one first. It was easy to see how his church had grown to be one of the largest in the town. Even her father was wrapped up in Brother Crow's delivery.

Caroline stood with everyone else after the service to hug and cry with the family. Her heart ached for Court and his father, and her despair deepened when she saw them standing at the front of the church, Court dressed in the same suit he'd worn when he took her to prom seven years earlier. It had been a last-minute decision, something nice he'd done for her when she'd been stood up by her date, and she smiled at the memory.

"Mr. O'Conner." Court reached out to embrace Caroline's father. "Thank you so much for coming."

"Pam was a lovely woman," Max replied. "We'll all miss her."

"Thank you," Court's father said, shaking Max's hand. "I know you took care of her like she was your own until you couldn't no more. I won't be forgettin' that."

"I'm so sorry" was all Caroline managed to get out before Court embraced her, and she felt his tears dripping down onto her shoulder. "It's okay," she whispered. "It's okay. I'm here."

Court didn't say anything. He released her only when his father put his hand on his back, quietly reminding him that there were other people waiting to see them. Caroline gave him one last squeeze before hurrying out of the sanctuary and into the bathroom. She leaned against the door and tried to collect herself. She could feel tears pricking at the edges of her eyes.

Wandering farther into the bathroom, Caroline noticed there were no mirrors. Caroline wondered if maybe it was because they didn't want women staring at themselves for too long. After all, it might prompt them to start thinking independently. She felt a pang of guilt for thinking that. Maybe she didn't like Haiden Crow much, and maybe she wasn't a dyed-in-the-wool Baptist, but she did have to thank him for saying whatever it was he said to get Ava Dawn away from Roy —this time, she hoped, for good. Besides, it wasn't like she wanted to look at herself, anyway. Caroline looked down at her black dress. It was her mother's, and it hung on her like a tent. She looked like she was dressed to, well, attend a funeral. Despite the heat, she was wearing a cardigan, because it didn't matter how much time Caroline spent at the river or being outside in general, the only thing the sun ever gave her was freckles—lots of them. Her freckles, she knew, were just about the only things she'd gotten from her mother. Well, them and her mop of unruly red hair. The rest of it, her height (too short), her eyes (too wide), and the gap between her teeth, were all genetic gifts from her father. She took a moment to tighten her ponytail, which sat more like a nest of curly red snakes on her head than anything else. She was not suited for anything other than cutoff jean shorts and a tank top, and she was just sure everyone else knew it, too.

"Caroline? Are you in there?" Max O'Conner's voice wafted in through the hallway. "Come on, we're going to be late for the graveside."

"I'm coming."

"Let's head out," her father said when he saw Caroline emerge from the bathroom. "What do you think about going to the graveside? Do you want to go?"

"It's up to you." Caroline really, really didn't want to go, and she knew gravesides were especially hard on her father, even though her brother had been dead longer than she'd been alive. His grave was in an older plot, originally purchased for Caroline's grandmother. Her father, when he would talk about it, said that it wasn't fair for parents to bury their children. It should be the other way around. It was the only time she'd ever heard her father say that anything wasn't fair. His favorite saying to her as a child had been, "Life's not fair, Caroline," but it wasn't life that got her brother buried in her grandmother's plot at the cemetery—it was death.

"I'm okay to go," her father said, at last. Max O'Conner opened the passenger's-side door to his truck for Caroline. He didn't say anything, but Caroline could tell by the way that his brow was furrowed that he was thinking. It wasn't until they were both in the car and turning onto the highway that he spoke. "I know it's not easy talking to me about these things," he began. "I know your mother was better at this."

Caroline reached out and touched her father's shoulder, momentarily forgetting about Court. "You do just fine, Dad."

Max O'Conner mustered a smile for his daughter. "I miss Mom."

"I miss her, too," he whispered. Instead of following the other cars in the funeral procession and driving straight on towards the cemetery, Caroline's father took a sharp left into the Dairy Queen parking lot. "I think Pam

Brannan would understand our need for ice cream at a time like this," he said. "The grave-yard will be there tomorrow. We can pay our respects another day."

Chapter 6

A week later, and the fish still weren't biting.

Caroline reeled in her line slowly and prepared to cast it out again. She didn't know why it mattered to her if she caught anything—she almost always threw the fish back. She'd been in junior high the last time she took anything home to eat. Nobody had time to clean the fish and fry them anymore, but she continued to go fishing a few times a week, just to relieve stress. Yara was a poor guard dog, but she'd scare off anybody who didn't know her and thought they might be able to take their fill from the shop. Most every-body else knew if they couldn't find Caroline at the shop they could walk a few hundred feet down to the water's edge and find her there, lolling her line in and out of the Cold River.

She knew it wasn't the dream of most women her age to run a bait shop for their family and spend their time fishing and caring for their ailing mother. Truthfully, it hadn't been Caroline's dream, either. She'd wanted to become a teacher, a history teacher, and that's what she'd gone to college for. Her dreams included coming back to Cold River, but in her mind she'd had her own house, her own job . . . her own life. She assumed her dreams were like those of the other girls she'd gone to high school with, although most of them got married right after graduation and had kids before they were even old enough to drink. Caroline, on the other hand, never really thought about marriage. She never really thought about children or what it might be like to raise her own family until she looked all around her and nearly everyone was coupled up. Her cousin Ava Dawn was one of the only women she knew who was married and didn't have children.

Childless women scared people.

When Caroline first returned home from college, friends of her parents tried fixing her up with any man they deemed suitable. After a while, the "suitable" part became less of a necessity when Caroline remained single. Once folks around town realized that it might be a choice on her part to stay unmarried and childless, they became all at once fascinated and confused. *What kind of a woman likes being alone?*

Once her mother's condition became town gossip, Cold River's inhabitants began to leave Caroline alone. She had responsibility now. She had a reason to continue living with her parents, and people began to feel sorry for her for a whole new reason.

Caroline stared off into the water, watching it ripple and splash over the rocks on the bank. When she'd been a little girl, her father told her stories about the first people who lived on the river—the first people who made their homes in this part of the Ozarks. She supposed it was the reason she grew up fascinated with history—the reason she wanted to be a teacher. Her favorites to hear were the stories of Prohibition, and she would ask her father to tell them over and over again. Sometimes, her father would amuse her by taking her in a johnboat down the river, retracing the steps of rumrunners who'd used the river to transport alcohol between neighboring counties.

"Of course," her father would say, "it wasn't rum in these hollers. It was moonshine."

The Cranwells were notorious in Cold River for producing generation after generation of moonshine bootleggers. The stills, townsfolk said, could still be found out in Cranwell Corner if you looked hard enough. She didn't know if that was true—she'd never been close enough to Cranwell Corner to look, afraid she might run into the likes of Jep Cranwell. There was no telling what he might do if he found her sniffing around his property. Still, she couldn't help but daydream when the fish weren't biting.

She wondered how much Noah knew about his family's history. If he hadn't been kept up to date by his mother, Caroline was sure that the good people of Cold River would be happy to fill him in. Already traffic to the bait shop had increased, mostly locals hoping to scope out the youngest and newest of the Cranwell brood. Her father would be annoyed with her that she kept on fishing during this busy time, and she had to admit—she had been enjoying the show so far. Although she had to wonder, *Why would someone move back here on purpose?* Surely he had a life and friends and a job back in New Jersey. Why give it all up for Cold River and a run-down gas station?

By the time Caroline got back up to the shop, it was midmorning, and there were customers waiting on her. They were men she knew well— Ed and Fred Johnson. They were twins in their mid-sixties, longtime friends of her father. They reminded her in appearance of Tweedle Dee and Tweedle Dum from *Alice in Wonderland*, a visual that she had to try hard to repress when she was near them.

"Carolina!" Fred chirped when he saw her trudging up the hill from the river. "We thought we was gonna have to call out search and rescue!"

"I'm sorry," Caroline huffed. "I took a little fishing break this morning. You know you can always come down and find me at the river."

"Aw, we didn't want to bother ya none. We woulda gone in and helped ourselves, but we was afraid of wakin' yer Saint Bernard, there."

Yara lifted her head lazily to look at the men and then over at Caroline, giving a false impression that she could hear them discussing her. She wasn't impressed, and soon drifted back into her usual slumber in the grass.

"She's not quite a Saint Bernard." Caroline grinned. "Come on in."

Across the street at Cranwell Station, Noah stood in the middle of the porch, his arms crossed across his chest, nodding along to something another man lounging near the side of a construction truck was saying. Caroline couldn't help but stare at Noah. He stood at least a head taller than any of the men near him. He was so much taller than the man he was talking to that he practically had to squat down to accommodate him. When he looked up over the man's head and caught Caroline staring, he held her gaze until she turned and scurried up the steps of the shop.

"What do you reckon is going on over there?" Fred asked once they were safely inside.

"You know who that is, don't ya?" Ed asked his brother. "That's Alistair Cranwell's boy."

Fred rubbed his chin and stared out the window. The patches on the pockets of his jeans strained each time he leaned forward, and Caroline found herself wondering what would happen if he ever tried to bend all the way over. "You know something, Ed? You're right. He looks damn near identical to his granddaddy."

"'Cept he don't look nearly as mean," Ed retorted.

"Have you met the Cranwell boy, Caroline?" Ed wanted to know.

"I have."

"And what of him?"

Caroline propped her fishing pole against the wall and dropped her tackle box with a thump onto the floor. She didn't want to say something to Ed and Fred that they'd go repeat the second they got back into town. Old women in small towns get bad raps for being gossips, but no women she knew held a candle to Ed and Fred. "He seems nice enough."

"Looks like he's gonna fix the place up," Ed said.

"Well, I don't reckon that'd be a bad thing," Fred replied. "I wouldn't mind havin' another place to get gas 'round here. Gary plumb near gouges my pockets."

"I went in and took a look at that place when it was fer sale," Ed said. "Really didn't need too much work 'cept the plumbin' and the roof."

"I reckon he can find someone in his family to do that work for 'im." Fred continued, straining his pants. "Damn near every one of 'em knows a trade of some kind."

"Well, 'cept the ones up in Jeff City in the pen," Fred said.

"Oh, they knew a trade alright." Ed winked at Caroline. "Just weren't nothin' legal!"

Both men began to laugh, and Caroline walked over to the cooler and opened it up for the men to peer into. There weren't any Cranwells in prison. Well, not that Caroline knew of, and there weren't many Cranwells left in Cold River, either. "Now, take a look at the fresh night crawlers I just got in. The fish are gonna love 'em!" She hoped she'd be able to distract them long enough to stop talking about Noah.

"Girl, where did you get these?" Fred wanted to know. "They look bigger'n last time."

"I ordered out of Arkansas," Caroline admitted. "The local people kept sending me crates full of dead bugs."

"Good," Ed grunted. "Ain't no sense in payin' for dead bait."

"Too bad we're both too old and fat to go diggin' fer worms!" Fred said, bending down to see into the cooler. This time, as he squatted lower and lower to see the night crawlers, his pants really did split down the middle.

It was nearly dark before Caroline was ready to close the shop and head home. Although the sign on the shop door said she closed at 7 p.m., in the summertime Caroline would often stay open until 8 or 8:30—at dusk. Since Ed and Fred, there had been a steady stream of customers all day. Every single one of them wanted to know what was going on across the street. Some of them even marched over to see for themselves what this "Cranwell kid" was all about. Noah took it all in stride, she assumed, as nobody'd called for the law all day.

She scanned the grass for Yara. Normally by this time of night, she was scratching her massive paw against the front door of the shop, ready to be fed. Tonight, however, she made no attempt to show herself.

"Yara," Caroline called, "supper!" She didn't know why she insisted on calling her. But for some reason, Caroline couldn't help it. She too often forgot.

There was no sign of Yara.

"Supper," Caroline repeated, this time more quietly. She felt silly, like someone was watching her.

No Yara.

Caroline sighed. It was going to be dark within the next ten minutes, and she knew she would never find her dog in the dark. Half of her was the color of midnight. "What is wrong with you? It's dinnertime!"

"That dog ever respond to you?"

Caroline closed her eyes. She already knew who was standing behind her, and for a second she wanted to pretend it wasn't Noah Cranwell standing there while she hollered at her damn deaf dog.

"Do you want some help?"

"From you?" Caroline asked. "No, thanks. I've got it."

"Are you sure?" Noah took a step closer to her. "Because I've got somebody's three-legged dog in my building, and if it's not yours . . . well, then I'm starting to worry that Cold River might have a feral dog problem."

"Oh my God, did she try to bite you again?" Caroline brushed past Noah and towards Cranwell Station.

"No, she didn't try to bite me," Noah said. He bounded up the steps and opened the door for Caroline. "She's been in here for the last hour."

"With you?"

Noah knelt down in front of Yara and began to scratch her under her chin. "She's really pretty cute."

Caroline stared at the two of them, shocked. Yara didn't like most people, and she wasn't likely to change her mind about a person once she'd decided. "I can't believe she let you do that," Caroline said at last.

Noah gave her a lopsided grin. "Oh, we're buddies, me and her."

"When did that happen?"

Noah reached into his pocket and pulled out a

handful of what looked to Caroline like beef jerky. "I've been giving her a snack every so often."

"No wonder she didn't want to go home," Caroline replied.

"Well, who would want to leave all this?" Noah swung his arms around the room.

Caroline glanced around the station. It was a mess. There were wires hanging everywhere, rotting pieces of furniture overturned on the floors, and almost everything was covered in a thick layer of dust. "What are you going to do with this place?"

"I want to restore it," Noah said, standing up. "You know, make it what it once was."

"A gas station?"

Noah nodded. "Yeah, with a little deli on one side."

"I don't remember what it looked like before it was closed down," Caroline said, running her finger along a thick layer of dust.

"Me either," Noah said. "I try to remember. I mean, I know it was open when I was a kid, but I just can't remember." He squinted hard, as if at that very moment trying to recall a far-off memory. "Most of my memories of living here are lost to me."

"Sort of like how you lost your Southern accent and gained that slick Northern one?" Caroline joked, trying to lighten the mood. Even in the waning twilight, she could see that not being able to remember bothered him.

"You sound like my grandfather," Noah replied, looking at her and mustering a grin. "He's been calling me a Yankee since I got here."

"Are you?"

"Not at heart."

"That's good to hear."

"How long has your family owned the bait shop?" Noah asked. "You've lived here all your life?"

Caroline nodded. "For a long time." She tilted her head back to think. "My father is from here, and I grew up here. When my parents opened the shop, your grandfather was still running the station."

"And now you take care of it?"

"For the last five years since my mom got sick." Caroline wished she hadn't said that last bit. She could have left it out. Oh well, at least it was true. She just wasn't used to people asking questions . . . about her. Everybody in town already knew everything. "So," she continued, desperate to change the subject, "what about you? What brought you back here?"

"I was ready to get out of the Navy."

"You were in the service?" Caroline hadn't considered that. The Cranwells she knew hated the government just about as much as regular people hated mosquitoes.

"I was," Noah replied. "For a little over a decade, most of it Naval Intelligence."

"Wow." Caroline was impressed. "That sounds exciting."

"It was for a while." Noah shoved his hands down into his pockets. "I got to travel all over the world, meet all kinds of interesting people. It was a good job."

Caroline glanced around the dimly lit room. "And you gave it up to come *here?*"

Noah laughed. "Well, I joined the military when I was eighteen. I shipped out three days after my birthday. I had a great apartment, but I was never home. I lived out of a suitcase. I couldn't even keep a cactus alive."

"And yet here you are, feeding my dog treats from your pockets."

"I'm working on my nurturing skills, as my grandfather isn't in the best health. He's sick a lot of the time, and the family was getting ready to lose this place." He glanced around. "I couldn't stand for that, you know? I've made a little money, not a lot, but enough to help out. I owe him. He's been just about the only stable force in my life."

Caroline shuddered at the thought of Jep Cranwell being anybody's stabilizer. "You're close with him, then?"

Noah nodded. "My mother would never let me come down for a visit after we left, but he called every week and always sent presents for holidays and my birthday." He picked up a leather-bound book and placed it in front of Caroline. "I've been looking at all these old photos I found when I was cleaning, and I've realized that most everything that's in here is original."

"Most everything in here is junk," Caroline replied. She peered down into the album.

"You're just not looking at it the right way," Noah said. His dark eyes were sparkling. "Look here, at this one." He leaned over her and pointed at one of the pictures. "I saw those gas pumps in the shed at my grandfather's house."

Caroline looked over her shoulder at him. He was staring down at her, one of his arms practically wrapped around her as he turned the pages of the album. There was a five-o'clock shadow beginning to appear around his jawline, and Caroline forgot herself for a moment wondering what it might be like to put her skin up next to his. "I, uh," she cleared her throat, "I better get going. It's getting late."

Noah lingered for a moment, his hand resting just above hers on the album. "Sure, of course."

"I'm sorry." Caroline didn't know why she was apologizing. "It's just this night is a late one, anyway, and I don't like to leave my dad at home for long alone with my mom."

"No need for an explanation," Noah replied. "Let me walk you and your attack dog out."

Chapter 7

Caroline was driving down the road in silence, thinking about her conversation with Noah. He seemed so excited to be getting Cranwell Station whipped back into shape, and the excitement was infectious. It might be nice to have a neighbor across the road, especially one as good-looking as he was. What she couldn't understand was the way Noah felt about his grandfather. True, she didn't know Jep Cranwell, but she had a hard time imagining him giving *anybody* a warm, fuzzy feeling.

She almost drove off the road when her phone began to ring, busting up the silence and her thoughts. It was Court.

"Hello?"

"Carolina."

"What's up?"

There was a pause on the other end of the line before Court said, "Have you left the shop yet? Want to come over for a drink before you head home?"

"It's getting late."

"Just one drink."

"Okay," Caroline agreed. "But just one."

"Great, I'll meet you at my house," Court said. "My shift is over."

Court's house was in one of the new sub-divisions of Cold River. It was the kind of subdivision often seen in the suburbs of cities, where all of the houses look the same. However, in Cold River, these subdivisions were created just outside of town, in what had once been farming land. It created the look of a community dropped in the middle of nowhere, and Caroline didn't understand why anyone would choose to live in a house that looked the same as twenty others. Pleasant Valley Sunday homes, her father always called them. But that was just like Court. He bought the house just after finishing the sheriff's academy, and ever since then, people had been expecting him to get married, probably to Caroline, and raise a family. Of course, now, just like Caroline, he had an excuse to stay single. His stepmother was dead, and his father could no longer afford a house of his own, and Caroline heard around town that Court moved his father in just before the funeral.

Court was sitting on the porch in a rocking chair. In his hand was a glass full of whiskey. "I thought you quit drinking during the week," Caroline said.

"It's the Devil's Cut," Court replied, a wry smile on his face. "You can't say no to the Devil's Cut." He offered the glass to Caroline.

She took a swig. "Thanks, I needed that."

"It ain't moonshine, but it'll do."

"Rough day?" Caroline asked.

"Not rough so much as long," Court replied. "It's the first night since Mom died that I haven't been on call."

"Hell, they couldn't give you a night off?"

Court reached for the glass in Caroline's hand. "They woulda given me the time off. I just figured it was best for me to stay busy."

"I understand that," Caroline said. It was one of the reasons she opened up the shop every day. "So how are . . . things?"

"I guess you've heard Dad moved in."

"I heard." Caroline sat down in the chair next to him. "How is that going?"

Court shrugged. "He didn't tell me they were foreclosing on him and Mom. Didn't tell me until we got the papers last week."

"I'm sorry, Court."

"I mean, I should have known. I probably did know, really, but I kept hopin' it wasn't true. A man shouldn't be damn near sixty years old without a roof over his head. Not when he works as many hours a week doin' the work he does." Court took a drink. "Fucking cancer."

Caroline reached over and grabbed his hand. "I wish I could help."

"There's nothin' anybody can do."

They sat in silence for a minute, soaking in the night air. Caroline's face felt hot from the whiskey, and she was grateful for the breeze finally blowing in. "How is he? Your dad?"

"The man just lost his wife, and the day I moved him out of the house he's lived in for twenty years, he lost his goddamn pride, too," Court said. "How would you be?"

Caroline picked up the bottle of whiskey and handed it to her friend. "I reckon I'd need a good, stiff drink."

It was enough to make Court smile. "He's been havin' one or two a night, but he's never been much of a drinker. Not like the rest of us. Hey, speaking of the rest of us, guess who's back in town?"

"Who?"

"Just guess."

"I'm too tired for this," Caroline replied, rolling her eyes. "Who is it?"

Court sighed. "You're no fun."

"Just tell me."

"Reese Graham."

Caroline sat back. It had been a long time since she'd thought about Reese Graham, and it had been even longer since she and Court had talked about him. For a little while after she moved back to Cold River, he'd been Caroline's boyfriend. But once his daddy got him a job working on the railroad, he'd hightailed it out of Cold River as fast as his Ariat boots would carry him. He'd wanted a life bigger than Cold River could offer him, and although Caroline couldn't say she blamed him, she wasn't much interested in that kind of life, which is one of the reasons why they'd called it quits almost four years ago.

"I can't believe you haven't heard."

"How would I have heard?"

"I figured someone in town would tell you," Court said with a shrug. "I figured Reese would come lookin' for ya."

"That was four years ago," Caroline reminded him. "I'm sure he's over it by now."

"You know how Reese is. He's not likely to give up on something."

"I'm not *something*," Caroline replied. "I'm *someone*."

"Same thing to Reese."

Caroline stood up. "I really have to go."

"Oh come on." Court stood up as well, wobbling slightly. "I didn't mean to upset you. Just one more drink."

"I'm not upset," Caroline said. That was only half true. "I told you just one drink. I do have to drive home, *Officer*."

Court sat back down. "I can't argue with that."

"So you've seen him, then?"

"I have," Court replied. "Stopped by the day he got into town. Asked about you."

Caroline could see the jealousy setting in on Court's face, even though he was trying hard to conceal it. He'd hated Reese in high school, but Caroline served as common ground for the two of them, and now they kept up a friendship. She'd always wondered if Court was glad that she and Reese hadn't worked out. "I hope you told him I'm not interested," she said finally.

"I did."

"Good." Caroline bounded back down the steps, hoping that the town was going to be big enough to hold every person she knew and the secrets each one of them carried.

Once Caroline was back in her truck, she tried to take her mind off of everything, but of course, she couldn't. Maybe Court didn't think high school was so long ago, but for Caroline, it had been a lifetime. She'd meant what she said to Reese all those years ago, and she meant it still. She hoped he wasn't back in town trying to dredge up old memories. Because if that was the case, Caroline wasn't interested.

As she drove, her headlights shone upon a familiar figure weaving about the sidewalk, occasionally stumbling off and into the road. It was Smokey, the town drunk. She considered driving on past him. Surely he would make it home safely. It wasn't as if this was the first time he'd wandered down the street, drunk and alone. It happened just about every night that he wasn't working a job. He was the best roofer in three counties, and he was sober so long as he was employed, but his propensity for drinking in between jobs kept him from working for any of the roofing companies in town. Smokey spent most of his time at Mama's bar.

Caroline cranked her window down and stuck her head out. "Hey, Smokey. Headed home?"

Smokey stopped walking and turned to face the truck. "Heeeyyy, Carolina, what are you doin' out so late?" The more he tried to stand still, the more he wobbled back and forth. His long gray beard swayed with him, the only part of his body that seemed to weigh more than five pounds. Every time Caroline saw him, he was a shadow of his former self.

"You need a ride?"

"Nah, darlin'."

"Get in the truck, Smokey."

"Alright, alright." Smokey shuffled over to the truck. After a few unsuccessful attempts at opening the door, Caroline leaned over and opened it for him. "I appreciate it, girly."

Smokey was the only person Caroline would allow to call her things like "darlin' " or "girly." She'd been giving him rides home since she was sixteen, and before that, her mother had done it. Every time she pulled over to let Smokey in her truck, she heard her mother's voice in her head. *Open that door, Caroline, and see if he needs a ride.* Her mother hadn't cared if people thought she ought not to be offering rides to drunken men. She hadn't cared if people would talk about what side of town she was on after dark. And now that it was Caroline's turn, she didn't care, either.

"You got any jobs lined up?" she asked him once he'd managed to pull himself inside the truck.

"It's slow right now, Carolina." Smokey rested his head against the window. "Everything in this town moves so damn slow."

"You better come up with something," Caroline warned him. "You know Court will arrest you if he sees you wandering the streets."

For a moment, Smokey looked scared and almost sober. "I reckoned he had enough to deal with, ya know, with his step-mama 'n' all."

"You reckoned wrong."

"Preacher man says I got to get right with the Lord," Smokey said. He focused his gaze on Caroline. "Says the Devil is in the bottle."

"You been drinking the Devil's Cut?"

"You think he's right?" Smokey continued. "He give me this Bible." He held out a small, green Bible—the kind generally passed out by kindly older gentleman called Gideons.

"Who gave that to you?" Caroline asked, even though she knew the answer.

"Brother Crow," Smokey replied. "He says my soul is in jep . . . jeparody."

"Jeopardy?"

"You think he's right?"

Caroline pulled into Smokey's driveway and threw the truck into park. "I think you need to go inside and sleep it off. You can get right with the Lord in the morning."

Smokey nodded. "Thank you for the ride, Carolina." He pushed open the door and poured himself out onto the lawn. "Get on home now."

Caroline did as she was told. She didn't notice until she was already at the end of the street what Smokey had left behind—the green Gideon Bible on the passenger's side of the truck seat. *Maybe,* she thought when she noticed it lying there, *we'll all get right with the Lord tomorrow morning.*

Chapter 8

The sound of metal scraping against metal woke Caroline out of a dead sleep. At first she thought the noise had been remnants of a far-off dream, but when the clanging continued, she sat straight up, accidentally smacking Ava Dawn in the face in the process.

"Oomph, ow," Ava Dawn mumbled. She rolled back over without waking. The woman could sleep through a freight train crash in the living room, a trait of which Caroline was more than a little envious. A sneeze two towns over was enough to wake her.

Caroline slipped out of bed and wandered into the kitchen, to the source of the noise. It wasn't yet dawn, and there was no reason for anybody in the house to be awake yet, but there was her mother, standing in front of the sink with a pot, filling it with water. There were already pots on every single burner on the stove. Caroline watched as her mother removed one pot from the stove, set it aside, and put the freshly filled pot in its place.

"Mom, what are you doing?" Caroline asked, walking into the kitchen. She touched her mother's arm gently. "What's with all the water?"

"I'm drawing a bath," her mother said simply, as if that should explain everything.

"A bath?"

Her mother stopped what she was doing to look at her. "I don't like to take a bath in cold water." Maureen O'Conner picked up the pot she'd set aside and carried it into the bathroom, pouring the water into the tub.

"Mom, you don't have to heat the water. We have hot water on tap," Caroline replied. She remembered her mother telling her about how when her mother had been a child, she and her family hadn't had hot water for many years. They'd heated water on the stove in order to take a hot bath. Caroline turned off the burners and took her mother by the arm. "Here, let me show you."

"I don't want to take a cold bath," her mother repeated.

"I know," Caroline said. She led her mother into

81

the bathroom. She bent over the bathtub and turned on the hot water. "Put your hand in and feel. Doesn't that feel nice?"

"Yes."

"Do you want me to help you get into the tub?"

Caroline's mother shook her head. "I can do it."

"Okay," Caroline replied. "But I'll be right outside the door if you need me." She walked out of the bathroom feeling relieved that she didn't have to help her mother bathe. It wasn't that she wasn't willing to help her mother—she did it almost every day, but try as she might, she couldn't escape the embarrassment she felt undressing her mother and helping her clean herself. Caroline tried to express this embarrassment to her father and then again to the nurse, but neither one of them understood. She supposed this was because they were both used to seeing naked people. They were used to seeing naked bodies other than their own. Caroline, however, didn't even like to see herself naked. Seeing her mother that way, vulnerable and exposed, reminded her that her mother was not the woman she'd once been—strong and fiery and redheaded. More and more, she was becoming someone Caroline didn't recognize.

Caroline shook those thoughts from her head and padded down the hallway to look for her father. It was unusual that her mother was left to her own devices in the morning, and the nurse was almost always here by now. "Dad?" she called into her parents' bedroom. "Are you in there?"

"Caroline?" her father called.

He sounded far away, and Caroline realized her father was in the shower in the master bathroom. She guessed that was why her mother had been busy filling the tub in the hallway bathroom. "Did you know Mom was awake?" she asked.

Max O'Conner stuck his head out of the bathroom doorway. "What?"

Caroline stepped farther into the bedroom. "Mom is awake, and she's boiling water to take a bath."

"Did you take care of it?"

"Yeah," Caroline replied. "But where is the nurse?"

"She can't come in today. One of her kids is sick."

"And the agency couldn't send anybody else?"

"I told them not to worry about it."

Caroline glanced from the bathroom, where she could hear her mother singing softly to herself, and then back to her father. "Who's staying with her today?"

"I thought maybe Ava Dawn could do it," her father replied.

"She worked a double last night," Caroline reminded him. "She didn't even get home until 4 a.m."

"I can't stay home today," her father lamented, closing the door to the bathroom so that the rest of his response came out muffled. "I work at the Christian Clinic."

It was just like her father to think that someone else could take care of her mother but forget to ask anybody first. "I don't guess I have to open the shop today."

Max O'Conner reemerged from the bathroom. "It's the busy season."

Caroline sighed. She knew what he was getting at. "Do you want me to take her with me?"

"Would you mind?"

"No, I don't mind," Caroline replied. She really didn't mind taking her mother with her, but it had been a long time since they'd been at the shop all day alone together. Usually if Maureen O'Conner went to the bait shop, it was just for a couple of hours, and that was only when she was having a good day.

Today wasn't looking like a good day, and sometimes it galled her that her father wouldn't admit it, that he wouldn't just sit down and talk about her mother, his wife, like he would a normal patient—why he always pretended like this was *normal*. That they were normal.

Her father pulled his shoes onto his feet. "Thank you, kiddo."

An hour later, Caroline rested her head on the seat of her mother's car. She was thankful to be driving the Jeep since it had air-conditioning. She wondered why she didn't drive the Jeep more, especially since her mother hadn't driven it in over a year. Sometimes her father took it to work, but it mostly sat in the garage, gathering dust.

She looked over at her mother who was staring straight ahead at the road in front of them, clutching her knitting bag. "Are you okay, Mom?"

Her mother's gaze didn't deter. "I'm fine. Where are we going?"

"You're going to the shop with me today." Caroline had to make a conscious effort not to add "remember?" to the end of every sentence she repeated. It didn't do any good, and too many of these agitated her mother.

"What shop?"

"Mine," Caroline said. "Ours. The bait shop."

Her mother nodded, clutching the bag tighter.

"We can go home," Caroline added. "If we get there and you feel uncomfortable, we can go home."

Her mother looked at her for the first time since they'd gotten into the car. "I know, honey," she replied. "I'll be fine."

Caroline felt a wave of calm wash over her. For a moment, it was like her mother was back with her, the way she used to be, warm as honey and concerned only with the happiness of her daughter. It was on this drive, only a few years before, that Caroline told her mother about her plans to stay home indefinitely. That was when the good days were more frequent than the bad days and when her mother still remembered Caroline's name. Now, a good day was when Maureen O'Conner was able to get out of bed without asking where she was—without trying to fill the bathtub with hot water from the stove.

As they passed Cranwell Station, Caroline craned her neck to see if Noah was there yet. She was still thinking about the night before, but this morning the station looked all but abandoned. Caroline felt an unwelcome ping of disappointment.

"Do you want some help out of the car, Mom?" Caroline asked once she'd pulled up next to the shop. "I'll carry your knitting for you."

"Are we here?"

"We are."

"I'll carry my bag myself."

Caroline grinned. Maybe her mother was having a good day after all.

It was already *so hot*. Caroline wished she'd left the air-conditioning on in the store over-night, even though she'd hear from her father once he got the bill. In the summertime, she knew they made enough to cover a few overnight air-conditioning bills, especially since their air-conditioning unit was *ancient* and probably needed to be replaced, anyway.

Caroline settled her mother on the little couch in the back room and prayed it would cool off quickly. She pulled out a jug of sweet tea from the mini fridge and poured a glass for both of them.

"Here you go, Mom." Caroline handed the glass of sweet tea to her mother. "I'm sorry it's so hot in here."

"Don't worry about me," her mother replied. "I'm just happy to be here."

"I'm happy you're here, too." Caroline kissed her mother on the top of her head. "I'm going up front to open up."

She had no more than put the money into the cash register when a Subaru with two kayaks strapped to the top pulled up to the shop. Tourist season had officially begun.

A woman and man both wearing Chacos got out of the car, followed by three kids. They stood outside for a few minutes, looking around confusedly, before ambling inside. "I told you we should have stopped at the gas station a few miles back," the woman whispered to the man.

The man's only response was to scratch the balding spot on the back of his head.

"Welcome to the Wormhole bait and tackle shop," Caroline said. "Can I help you find anything?"

"You only sell bait?" the woman wanted to know.

Caroline nodded. "Live and synthetic."

"I'm hungry." The youngest of the children pulled at her mother's peasant top.

"Just a minute," the woman said, pushing the little girl's hands down. "So, you don't have *anything* else but bait?"

Caroline fought the urge to roll her eyes. "I have some tackle boxes and a couple of kid's fishing poles." She pointed to one corner of the store. "But that's about it."

"I can get these night crawlers cheaper back in that town we just passed through," the man finally spoke up. "Cold River."

"I'll match any price."

Another one of the kids let out an audible sigh. "This place is a dump."

Caroline felt herself losing patience. Why did the asshole customers have to come in so early? It set such a bad tone for the rest of her day. Did they really want sandwiches sitting next to the earthworms? Did they really want soda in the cooler with the crickets? She was just about to suggest they head back to Gary's when her mother came wandering out from the back room. She was holding her knitting.

"Can I go to the bathroom?" she asked.

"Of course, Mom." Caroline felt her cheeks redden. "You don't have to ask permission for that."

Her mother didn't move. "I don't . . ." She

leaned in closer to Caroline. "I don't know where it is."

The people in the shop were staring at them now, five sets of eyes asking questions that were too uncomfortable to verbalize. "Come on, Mom," Caroline said. She took her mother's knitting and sat it down on the counter. "Let me show you."

By the time she got back up front, the family had gone. She glanced around the empty room. She couldn't say she was sad they'd left without buying anything. Then she noticed the corner where the children's fishing poles sat. One of them was missing. "Shit," she said, running out the door. The Subaru had already started down the gravel road, and Caroline took off after it, waving her arms and hollering, "Hey, wait!"

It was too late. She was left in a cloud of dust and rocks. She turned and began trudging back up to the shop. She could feel a blister beginning to form between two of her toes, and she wished that she'd known she was going to be chasing after customers. She would have worn something other than flip-flops.

Those people had some nerve. She ought to call the sheriff, but she knew she'd never get them out here for a six-dollar fishing pole. She sat down on a pillow of grass to inspect her feet. Sure enough, there was a blister on each foot right in between her big toe and the toe right beside it.

"Assholes," she muttered. "Damn those no-good, Subaru-driving bunch of assholes . . ." She trailed off when she felt a shadow being cast over her.

"Go ahead and finish," Noah Cranwell said. "Once you're done I'll ask you why you're cursing at your feet in the middle of the road."

Caroline looked around. "I'm not in the middle of the road. I'm on the side of the road."

"Cursing at your feet."

"I wasn't cursing at my feet," Caroline replied. "I was cursing at . . ." She turned around to point at the road. "I was cursing at . . . Well, hell, never mind."

Noah reached down and offered Caroline his hand. "It wouldn't have anything to do with that car you were chasing, would it?"

Caroline eyed Noah's hand skeptically. "So you saw that."

"I did," Noah replied. "You gonna take my hand or what?"

Caroline stared up at him. He was smiling at her, almost laughing, but it didn't seem like he was making fun of her. Although she wouldn't have blamed him for laughing at her. She was sure she looked just about as stupid as she felt. She reached for his hand. "Thanks."

"No problem," Noah replied. He was still holding on to her hand. "Why were you chasing that car?"

"One of them stole a fishing pole," Caroline

said. "I turned my back for five minutes, and one of those little urchins stole a damn fishing pole."

"What are you going to do about it?"

Caroline shrugged. "I'll call Court later on, but it won't make much difference. Even if they sent someone out here to find them, they'd say it was just a misunderstanding," she said. "It's always a misunderstanding with city people."

"Hey, now." Noah cocked his head to one side. "Not all city people are jerks."

"Oh, so you're a city person now?" Caroline asked. "Here I thought you was a Cranwell from the hollers."

Noah let out a laugh that was contagious. "Why do I feel like you're mocking me?"

"I wouldn't know." It felt good to Caroline to laugh.

"Do you want to come over for a few minutes?" Noah asked. "I found some more old photos in the station, but the only people I recognize are my great-grandfather and grandfather. I was hoping maybe you could tell me who the other people are."

Caroline wanted to say yes, but she knew she couldn't leave her mother alone in the shop. "I better get back to work," she said at last. "Maybe another day?"

"Oh, come on. It'll just take a few minutes."

Caroline looked over at the shop, debating. Surely her mother would be okay for a few minutes. How long could it take? "Okay," she said. "But just for a few minutes."

"Great!" Noah clapped his hands together. He led her over to Cranwell Station, holding the door open for her to step inside. "I know it's a mess in here, but I'm working on that."

Caroline didn't care. The only thing she wanted to do was look at the pictures he'd told her about. They were laid carefully out on a table in the middle of the room. Plastic covered the floor and parts of the walls. There were tools littered about everywhere, and the table stood naked, the only static thing in an otherwise chaotic room. That's when she saw a lump in the corner of the room— a large, hairy lump—a snoring lump. "Is that Yara?" Caroline asked. "I couldn't find her earlier. I figured she was just wandering down by the river."

"She's been in here since you closed up yesterday," Noah said, a bit sheepishly. "I hope that's alright."

"Of course it's okay," Caroline replied. "I'd rather she have a nice, cool place to sleep at night, but she won't ever come into the shop."

"Watch this," Noah said, his eyes lighting up. He picked up his right foot and brought it down hard on the wooden floor beneath him. Twice more he did this, before Yara, sensing the vibrations in the floor, lifted her head, cocking it slightly to the side. "Come here," Noah said to her.

"She can't hear you."

"Just wait for it," Noah replied, not taking his eyes off of Yara. "Come here," he said again, taking his hands and making a scooping motion in the air before bringing his palms to his chest.

Without hesitation, Yara was up and trotting towards him.

"Now, sit," Noah said, this time taking his hands off of his chest with a downward motion.

Yara sat.

"Good girl!" Noah pulled a treat from his pocket and gave it to the dog. "Good girl!"

Caroline stared at them both, openmouthed. She'd never seen Yara do anything like that before. "How did you . . . I mean, when did you teach her this?"

"About an hour ago," Noah said. "Well, I taught her to come to me last night. She kept pacing back and forth in front of the door, so I let her in. Caroline, she is so smart. She picks up on everything so quickly."

"I couldn't even get her to come inside."

"Do you mind?" Noah looked panicked. "I wasn't trying to steal your dog or anything."

Caroline grinned down at Yara, giving her a pat on the head. "Of course I don't mind. I just wish I'd thought to teach her sign language before."

"It's a trick I learned in the service. All of the dogs we used knew sign language commands."

"That's amazing."

An awkward silence fell between the two of them, and Caroline wasn't sure what else to say. After what seemed like an eternity, she remembered the reason she'd come over in the first place. "Where are those pictures you wanted to show me?" she asked.

"Here," Noah replied. He pointed to them. "I found them in a box in the old woodstove at the back of the station. I have no idea why someone would put them in there."

"Maybe they meant to burn them and forgot," Caroline offered. She glanced down at the pictures. "Wow. Some of these are old."

"From the '20s and '30s, I think," Noah said.

"They're in surprisingly good shape for being in a woodstove for God knows how long," Caroline said. "Holy hell, this one is amazing." She pointed to one of the earliest photos; it was of two men standing arm in arm in front of Cranwell Station. They were both smiling and squinting into the apparent sun. One of them had a cigar hanging out of his mouth. He looked a lot like Noah.

"That's my great-grandfather," Noah said. He pointed to the man with the cigar. "I'm named after him."

"The other man is Boss Tom Pendergast," Caroline marveled.

"Who?"

"He practically ran Kansas City during Prohibition." Caroline slid the photo off of the table. "He was a politician and probably the only reason Harry Truman was ever elected president."

"Are you serious?"

"This is an amazing find," Caroline said, scarcely able to control her own excitement. "He and his brother had their fingers in every pot, especially organized crime, prostitution, and I reckon bootlegging alcohol. It makes sense he might have had connections with your family."

"What's that supposed to mean?"

Caroline looked over at Noah. She hadn't thought about what she was saying as she said it. She was used to talking to *others* about the Cranwells, not to talking to an actual Cranwell. "I'm sorry," she said quickly. "I didn't mean it like that."

Noah crossed his arms over his chest. "Didn't you?"

Caroline bit at the corner of her bottom lip. Now she'd done it. She was contemplating her next move when from out of the window she saw her mother step out of the shop, teeter down the steps, and start trudging unsteadily towards them. She was wild-eyed, looking lost. "Oh shit, it's my mom." She rushed out of the station.

"Wait," her mother was mumbling. "Wait, please, wait."

"Mom, I'm not going anywhere," Caroline said, calling out to her. "I'm right here."

But her mother rushed past her and over to

Noah, who'd come out of the station, as well. He was standing in the doorway. "Where have you been?" she demanded. "I've been waiting to see you all day."

Noah glanced from Caroline to her mother and back again. "I'm sorry," he said, "but I don't think we've met."

"Of course we've met, don't be silly!"

"Mom." Caroline grasped her mother's arm. "Mom, let's get you back over to the shop."

"No, thank you," her mother replied, wrenching herself from her daughter's grip. "I've been in there long enough."

"Do you want to go home?"

"No, thank you."

Caroline let out an exasperated sigh. There was no way Maureen O'Conner was going to go anywhere she didn't want to go, and Caroline refused to scold her like a child. "I'm sure it's cooled off in there some by now. Let's head back."

"I said no."

Caroline looked helplessly at Noah. He wasn't looking at her. He was instead smiling at her mother. He held out his hand to her, the same way he'd held out his hand to Caroline minutes earlier. "What about if I walked you back over?" Noah asked her.

"Only if you'll come inside and sit a spell," Maureen replied.

"This is my mom, Maureen O'Conner," Caroline said, walking behind them.

"How are you today, Mrs. O'Conner?" Noah asked.

"Lord, child, you don't have to introduce us," her mother replied. Then, turning her attention to Noah, she said, "Since when did you start calling me Mrs. O'Conner? It's Maureen to you, same as always."

"Okay, Maureen." Noah took her hand. "Let's go over to your shop and sit a spell."

Caroline followed behind them and listened to her mother chatting happily with Noah. Caroline didn't know just who her mother thought Noah was, but he didn't seem to mind being mistaken for someone else. She thought about the pictures she'd seen in the station, the ones of Jep Cranwell looking an awful lot the way Noah Cranwell looked now. Was it possible that her mother thought he was Jep? She doubted it, as her mother *never* had anything nice to say about Jep. Just then, Noah turned around to smile at Caroline as he helped her mother up the steps, and she found herself grinning right back. Yep, no way could he be mistaken for Jep.

"I like the name of this place," Noah said as he stepped inside. "Very clever."

"It was my mother's idea." Caroline nodded towards her mother, who without another word had walked into the back room and picked up her knitting. "She had a great sense of humor."

"Is it Alzheimer's?"

"Yes."

Noah stuffed his hands down into the pockets of his jeans. "My grandmother, my mom's mom, had it. She lived with us until I was twelve."

"It's a vicious disease," Caroline replied. "My dad is a doctor, and I think he thought he could slow it down, but it's gotten worse over the last year."

"How long has she had it?"

"About five years, but it's only been bad the last couple." Caroline walked around behind the cash register. She could feel his eyes on her, studying her. "I don't know who my mom thought you were, but thank you for playing along. It makes everything a lot easier when people just play along."

Noah leaned onto the counter in front of Caroline. "My Gram used to think I was a kid she went to school with back in Poland. She would get so angry when I couldn't understand Polish," Noah said. "My mom told me he and his family were arrested during the war and that my Gram never saw him again."

"How sad."

"It was." Noah nodded. "It's strange the things the mind is able to remember when it's forgotten almost everything else."

"So your grandmother emigrated here from

Poland?" Caroline wasn't sure why she was asking Noah questions about his family, except that she didn't want to go back to talking about her mother, and she didn't want the conversation to end.

"Yes," Noah replied. "She came over with my great-grandparents after the war and settled in New Jersey. My mom and I moved back there when . . ." Noah paused, taking a deep breath in through his nose and out through his mouth. "When my father died."

Caroline was searching for something to say when the door opened and Ava Dawn burst through. She was all lipstick and daisy dukes, her blue eyes wide with a story to tell. "Carolina, you are never gonna guess who I just seen!" she exclaimed. "Never!" She stopped when she saw Noah Cranwell watching her, an amused smile on his face.

"I don't think we've officially met. I'm Noah Cranwell." Noah stuck out his hand to her.

"I'm Ava Dawn." Her cheeks turned pink when Noah engulfed her hand with his. "Pleasure meetin' *you*."

Caroline glared over at Ava Dawn. "What are you doing here?"

"Uncle Max called and said to come pick up Aunt Maureen when I got up and around," Ava Dawn replied. "And then I ran into Reese on the way over. Did you know he was back in town?"

Caroline's heart leaped into her throat. She wished Ava Dawn would keep her mouth closed about Reese until they were at least out of earshot of Noah. She just knew Ava Dawn was going to say something else to make sure Noah knew Caroline's history with him. She kicked herself for not telling her cousin the night before, or at least leaving her a note or something. "Court told me last night."

"I figured Court knew about it," Ava Dawn said. "He always seems to keep a tab or two on Reese."

"Yeah, well . . ." She trailed off. Caroline didn't want to talk about Reese *or* Court right now. "Mom is in the back. I don't know if she'll go with you, though."

Ava Dawn ignored Caroline and continued to talk. "Seems like he's here to stay—Burlington Northern finally transferred him back here. Says he's real glad, too. You know he's makin' a ton of money workin' for the railroad."

Caroline glared at her cousin.

"He said he was comin' to the pie auction tomorrow night. Asked me all about you. Wanted to know how you were and what you was doin'. I told him you could tell him yourself since I reckon you'll get to see him then."

"I reckon I will."

"Wait, what's a pie auction?" Noah wanted to know.

"Well, ain't you cute," Ava Dawn replied. "It's

a benefit sort of thing—for Court Brannan and his daddy—to help pay for his step-mama's funeral. Everybody brings a dessert, usually a pie, to auction off. All the money goes to them."

"Court's the deputy, right?" Noah asked. "He was there that day you aimed a gun at me?"

"I wasn't aiming a gun at *you,*" Caroline corrected him. "I was aiming a gun at Ava Dawn's no-good, piece-of-trash husband."

"She'da shot him, too, if you 'n' Court hadn't shown up," Ava Dawn chimed in.

"Oh, I don't doubt that."

"She's a real good shot. Scares most men off."

"Thanks," Caroline replied sarcastically.

"Well, not *all* men," Ava Dawn continued. "Reese sure did get a kick out of your fiery side, that's for sure. Think you two will reconnect? Maybe Wyoming isn't lookin' so bad right about now, huh?"

Caroline wanted Ava Dawn to shut up. She hadn't seen Reese since the day she broke it off with him. He'd been sent to Wyoming with the railroad, and he hadn't been happy when Caroline rebuffed his offer for them to get married and for her to move with him. He'd known she couldn't leave her mother and father, but he'd thought the allure of not having to work for a living would be too good for her to reject. It was just further proof that Reese hadn't known her at all, and they both knew it. Court never liked

Caroline and Reese together, and in the end, he'd been right about Reese running all over the county with any girl who was willing. And here Ava Dawn wanted to open all those old wounds right here in front of Noah Cranwell. It clearly wasn't lost on Ava Dawn that Reese had been the only boyfriend she'd ever had.

"Well, ladies," Noah said, tipping an imaginary hat to them. "I better be getting back across the road."

Caroline shot her cousin a look the second Noah was outside. "What in the hell, Ava Dawn?"

"What?" Ava Dawn asked. She innocently twisted a strand of blond hair between her fingers.

"Don't you think you could've kept a lid on it until *he* wasn't here?"

"Why do you care, Carolina?"

Caroline threw up her arms in exasperation. "Just forget it. You are ridiculous, anyway."

"Don't you want to hear about Reese?" Ava Dawn pressed. "He was drivin' a *brand-new* Toyota Tundra. Extended cab. Offered to take me for a ride, but I said no cuz I had to get out here."

"I'm sorry you had to make that sacrifice," Caroline said dryly, sticking her head into the back room to check on her mother. She was sitting with her knitting. When she noticed Caroline looking at her, she smiled.

Ava Dawn wasn't listening to her. She was

looking out the window and across the street at Cranwell Station. "Hey, come look at this," she said. "Ain't that Jep Cranwell out there?"

Caroline squinted. "Yep. It sure is."

"What do you think they're talking about?" Ava Dawn whispered.

"I don't know." Caroline couldn't tell what they were saying, but neither man seemed particularly happy. "But whatever it is, it isn't good."

Noah was pointing to the bait shop with one hand and waving the other in the air. Jep was shaking his head back and forth in disagreement with whatever Noah was trying to tell him.

"Ooooh, Noah looks mad," Ava Dawn said. "Looks like they're talking about us."

"It's not our business." Caroline backed away from the window. "Go get Mom. Will you fix her some lunch when you get home?"

"Sure thing," Ava Dawn replied. "Come on, Aunt Maureen, let's go home."

Maureen looked up at Ava Dawn. "Your hair is so pretty. I had a little niece with hair like yours."

Ava Dawn took her aunt's hand. "I am that niece. Now let's get on home, and I'll fix you some lunch if you're hungry."

"Mashed potatoes would be nice," Maureen said, taking Ava Dawn's hand.

The two women led Maureen O'Conner out the front door as Jep Cranwell was getting into his truck, lugging his oxygen tank as he went. Jep stopped when he saw them coming out of the shop. He stared at them long and hard for a few seconds, just long enough to make Caroline nervous, and then he got into his truck.

"I know that man," Maureen said, watching the truck pull out onto the gravel road.

"I'm sure you do, Mom," Caroline replied. "That's Jep Cranwell."

"Hop in, Aunt Maureen," Ava Dawn said, opening the door for her aunt.

"I need my knitting," Maureen said, sitting down in the front seat. "Let's get a move on it. Those taters aren't gonna cook themselves."

Ava Dawn looked over the hood of the car at Caroline, who could only shrug and grin. Some days were better than others, and some days there was nothing else a body could do but laugh when things were funny.

Chapter 9

Caroline watched Noah inside his shop. He was pacing back and forth in front of the windows. She knew she ought to go back inside her own shop and mind her own business, but she found herself walking over to him, anyway.

She knocked on the door. "Noah? Can I come in?"

Noah looked up, seemingly startled by the disturbance. "Sure," he mumbled, continuing to pace.

"Hey, uh . . ." Caroline searched for her words. "I'd like to look at the rest of those pictures."

But Noah was already gathering the pictures up and stuffing them down into his jeans pockets. "I've got to get back to work."

"Oh, okay," Caroline replied. It stung a little. He'd been so friendly and eager before. "I'll just see you later." She turned and headed for the door. When she got there, she stopped, turned back around, and said, "Hey, can I ask you something?"

"Uh, sure," Noah said, not looking up.

"I saw your grandfather outside with you a bit ago . . ." Caroline paused. She knew she'd told Ava Dawn it wasn't their business what the two men had been discussing, but she wanted to know. At that moment, she *had* to know. "Were you two talking about me?"

"What?"

"I saw your grandfather point at the shop is all," Caroline said with a shrug, trying to sound nonchalant.

"I forgot that people have eyes in the backs of their heads in these little towns," Noah replied.

"I wasn't spying on you." Caroline was indignant. "You're right across the street from me. I can see you from my window."

"Well, we weren't talking about you," Noah said. His tone was curt. "If you must know, I need a new roof, and my grandfather wants me to hire three of my cousins to do it."

"Okay," Caroline replied. She wasn't sure if she believed him. "What's the problem with that?"

"For one, they're my cousins."

"So?"

"So I don't want to hire relatives," Noah said as if Caroline had asked a ridiculous question. "It's not good business."

"This business is family," Caroline replied. "It's Cranwell Station."

"And family ran it into the ground," Noah spat. "I'm not going to let that happen again."

Caroline took a step back. "So if you're not hiring your cousins, who are you going to hire?"

Noah shrugged. "I don't know, and I don't care as long as I don't share a last name with them."

"Come on." Caroline motioned for Noah to follow her. "I know a guy."

"You know a guy?"

"Yeah," Caroline replied. "I can take you into town to meet him if you want. It won't hurt to close down the shop for a couple of hours."

"You don't mind doing that?" Noah asked. He looked skeptical. "I don't want you to lose out on any business."

Caroline rolled her eyes. "Is business all you think about?"

Noah grinned, his dark eyes dancing. "Not the only thing."

Caroline felt her cheeks redden. "Come on, I'll drive." She turned and headed out of the store. Despite what she had said to Noah about closing down the shop, it wasn't something that she normally did. She probably would miss out on a few sales, but the fishing-pole-stealing yuppies from earlier had been enough for one day. Maybe he had been telling the truth about needing a new roof. It did look pretty patchy now that she thought about it.

"I thought you drove a truck," Noah said when they neared the Jeep. "I mean, I can usually hear it clear in the back of the station, it's so loud."

"I do," Caroline replied. "But it doesn't have air-conditioning, and I didn't want my mom to get hot."

"You drive that thing every day without air-conditioning?"

"The windows do roll down," Caroline replied. "But admittedly, she does need some work."

"Some?"

"The engine is solid."

"You know a lot about cars?" Noah asked. He was smiling at her, as if he was genuinely interested and not skeptical that a woman might know how to fix an oil leak or a blown head gasket.

"A little." Caroline shrugged. "I keep it up

enough to get me from place to place, but that's about it. It was my brother's."

"Why doesn't he help you keep it up now?" Noah asked.

Caroline took a deep breath and let the air rush back out of her before she said, "He's dead."

Noah's eyes widened, and he looked down at the dirt. "Oh, shit, I'm sorry."

"Don't be. It was a long time ago," Caroline replied. "It was before I was even born."

Noah cleared his throat, avoiding eye contact with Caroline. "Okay, so who are we going to meet?" He slid into the passenger's seat.

"His name is Smokey."

"Smokey?" Noah asked. "The roofer's name is Smokey?"

"I think it's more of a nickname than an actual name," Caroline replied.

"What's his actual name?"

"Beats the hell outta me."

"You're telling me you want me to hire someone whose real name you don't even know?"

Caroline took her eyes off the road long enough to catch Noah's eye. "Well, it ain't Cranwell."

The Jeep went silent. Noah was staring out the window, almost as if he was in some far-off thinking spot in the back of his mind. Caroline couldn't tell what he was looking at. All she saw were hills and trees. The same scenery on repeat every day of her life. She wondered if he was bored seeing the same thing every day, especially since he'd spent so much time traveling around. How could somebody like him be happy in a place like this?

"So this is what you do?" Noah asked. "Run the bait shop for your family?"

Caroline couldn't tell if he was just curious or if he felt sorry for her. "My parents are getting older. My mom was forty-five when she had me." Caroline curled her fingers around the steering wheel as they rounded a curve. "They needed my help, because of my mom's, you know, illness."

"I was five when we left," Noah said. He was still looking out the window. "My mother and me."

"And that's when you moved to New Jersey?"

"First we lived in New York State for a while. My mom married a mechanic. Then after they divorced, she moved me and my two younger sisters to New Jersey to live with family."

"You have sisters?"

"I do."

"How old are they?"

"Lenore is twenty-two and Claire is twenty."

"Do they live in New Jersey, too?"

"No," Noah replied. "I haven't seen them in a long time. They went back to New York with their dad a year after we moved to New Jersey."

"Didn't they come visit?" Caroline wanted to know. "Didn't you go visit them?" She couldn't imagine having a sibling and not seeing them.

Even though she'd never gotten to meet her brother, his presence was all over her house. In pictures and in the things of Jeremy's her parents kept.

"No."

"And you didn't get to visit them?"

"No."

Caroline waited for him to continue, but Noah didn't offer any more explanation, and something told Caroline not to push the issue. He wasn't looking at her and he wasn't looking out the window. Instead, he was looking down at his hands, his jaw muscle clenching and releasing with each bump on the road. It was easy to believe he'd been in the military. Everything about his exterior looked hard, from the square jaw to the thick neck muscles bulging beneath his T-shirt, all the way down to the way his hands rested on his jeans, everything was crisp, starched, and at attention. There were no soft lines.

Except, Caroline thought, *for his eyes.* There was softness in his eyes that appeared when he talked about the siblings he never saw, and it had been there the first time he bent down to scratch Yara behind the ears. She doubted he wanted anyone to see it.

"My brother, Jeremy, was eighteen years older than me. I never got to know him," Caroline blurted. She wasn't sure why she was telling him this, but she couldn't stop herself. "I always wished for more family. It's always just been me and my mom and dad and my cousin Ava Dawn. Everybody else has moved away or died, and my mom, well, she's still around, but she's not at the same time, you know?"

Noah was looking at her now.

"I'm sorry, I don't know why I told you that," Caroline added. "It's not usually a conversation I like to have with strangers. 'Hey, my name's Caroline. I have a dead brother; my mom has Alzheimer's. My family is basically broken. Nice to meet you.' "

"Do you just say everything that pops into your head?" Noah asked finally.

"Lord, no. I'd be in prison if I said half the things that cross my mind. Besides," Caroline continued, "most everybody around here knows my family dynamics. I don't have cause to talk about it much."

"Well, if it makes you feel any better, most families are basically broken." Noah gave her a smile, the tiny lines around his eyes crinkling.

It didn't make Caroline feel better, but she smiled anyway.

The town square had once been the heart and soul of Cold River, a place where beauty and commerce came together in a way most people would call charming. Through the years business had grown up and away from the courthouse, but the townspeople worked hard to keep the square thriving. It had been the place where Caroline's grandparents opened the shoe repair shop, and although the family business was replaced with a restaurant called Sissy's in the '80s, the owners had kept the original hardwood floors and every time Caroline went inside she was reminded of her grandparents and the hours they must have spent repairing the shoes people wore all over town.

Just like the shoe store, most of the old businesses had been replaced, but the buildings were there, and once a month, the shops hosted a Stroll Around the Square, staying open later in the evenings so that families could mill around downtown with their children.

Caroline drove around to the back parking lot of the Cold River Bank and Trust, parking as close to the bank's alleyway as she could. "You can just sit here if you want to. I'll be right back."

"The roofer works at the bank?" Noah asked, sliding out of the passenger's seat. He followed Caroline to a steep set of steps on the opposite side of the alley.

"What?" Caroline replied. "Oh, no, not at the bank." She pointed down the steps. "He's at the bar beneath the bank."

"The bank has a bar?"

"The bank doesn't own the whole building."

"So the guy you say can put a roof on my station is at the bar?"

"Yup."

"At 11 a.m.?"

Caroline sighed and placed her hands on her hips. "You got any more questions for me, or can we go get this over with?"

Noah shrugged, shoving his hands down into his jeans pockets. "Okay, let's go."

Caroline bounded down the steps, taking them two at a time. Just above the entryway, a faded sign read, "Mama's." When Caroline opened the door, she and Noah were greeted with a gust of stale air.

It took Caroline a minute for her eyes to adjust to the dim lighting, but it didn't take long for her to zero in on Smokey. He was sitting with a group of three other men at a table full of empty beer cans and cigarette butts. They were the only ones there taking up the biggest table in the middle of the bar. They had the run of the place, and they liked it that way.

When Smokey saw her, he stood up, wobbled slightly, and then crashed back down into his chair. "Carolina!" he rasped, his voice barely audible above the jukebox warble. "Carolina, what are you doin' here, girl?"

"Looking for you," Caroline hollered. "I've got a job for you."

"What needs doin'?"

"A roof."

Smokey nodded, then for a second his eyes

drooped and he appeared to be asleep. When he opened them again a few seconds later, he said, "You need a roof where? The shop or the house? Didn't I just put a new roof on that shop last spring?"

"You sure did." It never ceased to amaze her how well Smokey could carry on a conversation even when he was drunk as a skunk. "It's not for me," she said. "It's for a friend."

"Who?"

Caroline turned around to find that Noah was no longer beside her. He was standing at the bar, talking to the surly woman behind it. To Caroline's surprise, the woman, also known as Big Mama, was smiling. Big Mama never smiled. "Noah!"

Noah turned around and waved.

"Get on up," Caroline ordered Smokey. "Let's get out of here and get you something to eat."

"Aw, come on now, Carolina, just one more drink?"

"Absolutely not." Caroline crossed her arms over her chest. "Do you want this job or not?"

"You know I do," Smokey replied. He stood on wobbly legs. "Let me pay my tab."

"You ain't never paid nothin'!" Big Mama hollered from her position behind the bar. "Don't pretend like yer gonna start today!"

Caroline handed Smokey off to Noah, who looked both terrified and amused by what was taking place. Then she placed a twenty dollar bill into Big Mama's beefy palm. "Will this at least cover today?"

Big Mama snorted, which made her sound so much like Yara that Caroline almost laughed. "I reckon this'll do," the woman replied. "Bring that one back next time," she nodded over at Noah, "and drinks are on the house."

Caroline fought the urge to laugh as she and Noah led Smokey silently up the steps and out to the Jeep. She pulled the tailgate down and ordered Smokey to "get in."

"I ain't fit to start a job today," Smokey protested.

"Don't worry," Caroline replied. "I'm just taking you to the clinic. My dad will get you all fixed up. You don't have to worry about startin' a job until tomorrow."

Smokey mumbled a response, but neither Caroline nor Noah could understand what it was since he was lying down, belly first, his face planted into the backseat of the Jeep.

"*This* is the guy you think I'm going to hire to finish my roof?" Noah asked, his tone incredulous.

"He'll be fine once he sobers up," Caroline said. "He's the best roofer in three counties."

"Somehow I doubt that."

"It's true. I wouldn't be wasting my time dragging his drunk ass out of a bar before noon if it wasn't," Caroline replied. She motioned for Noah to get into the Jeep. "He'll do you right or I'll pay for the next roofer myself."

"Is he going to be okay flopping around in the back like that?" Noah turned around to stare at Smokey who was still facedown. "He looks like a fish that jumped out of his bowl."

"We aren't going far, he'll be fine," Caroline said.

"Where are we going?"

"My dad's working down at the free clinic today. He'll keep an eye on him until he sobers up enough to go home."

"Your dad?"

"Yeah, my dad," Caroline replied. "He's a doctor. Well, he's retired now, but he volunteers down at the clinic a few days a week."

"So I'm going to meet your dad?"

"Yes?" Caroline gave him an odd look. "Is that okay?"

"I guess," Noah replied. "I just hadn't planned on meeting him today, that's all."

"Well, he's not going to bite your head off or anything," Caroline said. "He's a nice guy."

"Is this something you do a lot?" Noah wanted to know.

"Is what something I do a lot?"

"This." Noah waved his arms around the Jeep.

"I don't know what you're talking about."

"Fine, this is totally normal behavior," Noah replied.

"It is when the town drunk is also the best roofer in three counties." Caroline pulled into a small strip mall two blocks away from the bar. She parked in front of a door that read "Cold River Christian Clinic. Walk-ins Welcome."

"This is it?" Noah wanted to know.

"This is it." Caroline flung the Jeep into park, and Smokey hit the back of the seat with a muted thud. "Help me get Smokey out of the back."

Noah obliged, pulling open the side door and helping the man out of the back. "You alright, man?" he asked.

Smokey's eyes rolled to the back of his head and then he attempted to focus on Noah. He staggered into him and half whispered and half yelled, "Sometimes I think that girl is tryin' to kill me."

"Don't think I haven't thought about it once or twice," Caroline replied before Noah could speak. "Now put one arm around me and one arm around Mr. Cranwell, here, and let's try to get inside without causing a scene."

"Not likely," Noah said under his breath. He pulled open the door to the clinic with his free hand. "See? They're all staring at us."

Caroline scanned the waiting room. She knew every person sitting there except for an older man in a pair of camouflage overalls. "They're not staring at us," she said. "They're staring at *you*."

"Why?"

"Because they don't know you," she replied. She sat Smokey down in one of the orange plastic chairs. "Sit down; I'll tell Jolene we're here."

Jolene Simpson was awful pretty, and as her father would say, there wasn't a mean bone in her body. Her perfect petal of a mouth was almost constantly smiling, and absolutely everything about her was perky from her hair down to her feet. Caroline often wondered how she got along with all the rough-and-tumble people who came into the clinic—the roughnecks without insurance, the newly turned out convicts with staph infections, the asthmatic children whose parents smoked with the windows up the whole way there—but she figured that since Jolene had been employed there since the day she graduated from high school, it was working out pretty well. She had a lot of respect for Jolene. "Hey, Caroline," Jolene said when Caroline stepped up to the reception desk. "I already ran back and told your daddy that you're here. He says to bring him on back."

"Thanks, Jolene," Caroline said. "You're the best."

"Hey, Smokey," Jolene said as they pulled Smokey to the double doors beyond the waiting room. "Good to see you again, sugar."

Smokey gurgled a response.

Jolene raised an eyebrow at Caroline as they

passed. "Jolene, this is Noah Cranwell. Noah, this is Jolene Simpson."

"Nice to meet you," Noah said, batting one of Smokey's hands away from his face. "Caroline says this happens a lot. I don't believe her."

Jolene's petal of a mouth twitched into a smile. "Oh, honey, believe it."

Max O'Conner was waiting for them. He did a double take when he saw Caroline at one end of Smokey and Noah on the other. Ever the professional, he addressed his patient first. "Sit down, and let me have a look." Her father flipped on his medical flashlight and pulled up one of Smokey's eyelids. "When was the last time you had anything to eat, son?"

Smokey blinked back the doctor's fingers. "I reckon yesterdee?"

Max sighed. "I'll have someone bring you a bite to eat once you can sit up straight. For now, we'll get you started with some electrolytes and ibuprofen. You're really getting too old for this, you know."

"I know, but I got me a job with that'n over there." He jerked his thumb in Noah's direction. "Gotta be sober for th' mornin'."

"You'll feel like hell," Max replied. "But by tomorrow you'll be on the mend. Stay in this room. You can lie down on the bed if you want. I'll take you home tonight after I finish up here."

Smokey nodded.

Caroline's father ushered them out of the room. "Caroline, I know you mean well," he said, "but you cannot continue to bring Smokey here. I haven't the time or room for him today."

"Noah needed a roofer," Caroline said. She shrugged, forgetting that her father and Noah had not yet been introduced.

Noah stuck out his hand. "I'm Noah Cranwell, sir. I bought the gas station across from the bait shop."

"I knew who you were the second you walked through the door," Max O'Conner replied, shaking his hand. "I'm Dr. Max O'Conner, father to this urchin next to you."

"My father thinks I have a bleeding heart," Caroline said. She grinned at both men. "But I'm not the one volunteering at the free clinic."

"It's a tax write-off," her father replied.

"Sure, that's why you do it."

"Regardless, I'd prefer it if you let Smokey find his own jobs from now on. You're *both* too old for this."

"It's what Mom would have done."

Max O'Conner cleared his throat. "You've got me there." He turned his attention to Noah. "Caroline isn't wrong about Smokey—he'll do you a good job. And he'll stay sober while he's doing it."

"So I've heard," Noah replied. "Where I come

from, we call up someone from the yellow pages, but I suppose this way has its charms."

"I remember you as a small boy, but of course that was when you were from here," Max said. "Where did you grow up?"

"New Jersey, mostly."

"That's a far piece from here."

Noah knitted his eyebrows together. "If by *far piece* you mean whole other country, then yes, it's a far piece from here."

"That is what it means," Max O'Conner said with a laugh. "Now, if you'll excuse me, I do have other patients to see today."

"Thanks, Dad." Caroline reached out to give her father a hug.

Once he released his daughter, he extended his hand once more to Noah. "It was nice to meet you."

"Likewise, Dr. O'Conner."

Caroline's father held Noah's hand for just a little longer than she was comfortable with. He was looking at Noah, really looking at him, and Caroline wondered what in the hell he was searching for. After her father finally released him, Caroline led Noah back out the front door, all eyes, especially Jolene's, on them. "I don't know how you do it," Noah said, once they were back in the truck. "It must be exhausting."

"Do what?" Caroline wanted to know. "It's not like I pick up drunk guys every day. Just Smokey, and only when I know he needs a job."

"Not that," Noah said. "The way everyone pays so much attention. I'm just not used to it."

"Well, get used to it," Caroline replied. "You're new in town, but your family isn't. There were rumors going around about you long before you moved back to town."

"That's insane."

"That's Cold River."

Noah was quiet for a moment. "Your father seems nice."

"He is," Caroline agreed. "A bit stuffy, but he's a good guy. He has a lot on his plate what with taking care of my mother and all. I don't know how he manages to still devote time to his patients at the clinic."

"Well, you help with that."

"I do, some. But I spend my days at the shop. My father spends at least three days a week with my mom by himself, and that's no easy task, no matter how much you love a person."

"How long have they been married?" Noah asked.

Caroline wrinkled her nose in thought. "I'm not sure," she said, embarrassed. "I'd say forty-five years, at least."

"That's a long time."

"I can't even imagine being married," Caroline admitted. "Let alone being married for that long."

"I was married once."

Noah said it so casually that Caroline almost drove off the road. *He was married?* She gripped the steering wheel and tried to focus on the road. "You were married?"

"A long time ago," Noah replied. "I was eighteen. Just enlisted. We thought we were soul mates." He laughed. "It lasted just shy of two years."

"I'm sorry."

"Don't be. Besides, it's not like I knew what a good marriage looked like," Noah replied, just the slightest hint of bitterness rolling off of his tongue. "It was a nightmare, and we both hated each other by the end."

Caroline wasn't sure what to say. It had never occurred to her that Noah might have been married before. *Of course,* she thought to herself, *I hardly know him.* Still, she couldn't imagine him at eighteen. She couldn't imagine him being anything other than the person sitting next to her in the cab of her truck. "Well, I think marriage is probably hard no matter how many good examples you have," she said, finally. "Most of the people I know who got married right out of high school are already divorced. And my mother doesn't even know who my father is half of the time."

"But your father takes care of her anyway," Noah countered. "You've got to admit, that's not something everybody would do."

"True," Caroline said, thinking of the way her father continued to dote on her mother, even after all these years. Even after her brother died. Even after the diagnosis. "You know, I know my father loves her. He is so utterly devoted. But I can't remember hearing him say it to her. Or to me. He doesn't like to talk about his emotions. He doesn't really even like for other people to have emotions. I guess that's why he doesn't like to talk about how sick my mother really is."

"Some people are like that."

Caroline nodded. Something about the way he said *some people* made Caroline think that he knew someone like that, too—someone shut up tight like her father.

"No marriage is perfect," Noah continued. "Everybody has secrets, even married people. There's a reason people act the way they do."

"Not my parents," Caroline replied. "Remember, they live in Cold River. There's simply no place left to put secrets around here."

Chapter 10

"Don't you have anything that isn't an old T-shirt or a ripped-up pair of jeans?" Ava Dawn asked, riffling through her cousin's closet. "Neither one of us is gonna look cute in any of this."

"It's a pie auction, not a fashion show," Caroline reminded her cousin. "Everybody will be wearing jeans and T-shirts."

"Too bad half my clothes are bein' held hostage by Roy."

"What do you mean?"

"I mean, he said he'd call the cops if he caught me there."

"That doesn't seem legal."

"It's his house," Ava Dawn said with a sigh. "Been in the family for years. Ain't a damn thing I can do about it."

"Well, you can wear something of mine."

"Do you have anything that you didn't buy in junior high?"

"Don't be hateful. I'm sure I have something nice in there."

"I doubt it."

"Why do you care?" Caroline crossed her arms and looked over at Ava Dawn. "You got someone special you want to look good for?"

"Oh, so now I gotta have someone special to want to look nice?"

"That's not what I meant."

"It's just that I'm always just gettin' off work or gettin' ready to go to work whenever I go to church for anything," Ava Dawn said. "Brother Crow probably thinks I live at the diner."

"Brother Crow probably shouldn't be thinking about it," Caroline replied.

Ava Dawn giggled. "He's cute, though, ain't he?"

"He's married."

"So am I."

Caroline smirked over at her cousin. "But not for long, right?"

"Lord, I hope not."

Caroline began to laugh, and so did Ava Dawn. It felt good to Caroline to be laughing with her cousin. She couldn't remember the last time they'd had a conversation that wasn't centered on something serious. She was eventually able to find her cousin a denim skirt and pink lace tank top tucked in the back of her closet, and she settled on a pair of jeans approved by Ava Dawn and a similar tank top in black.

Caroline's father was sitting in the living room when the girls emerged. He looked up from his book and gave them a grin. "You girls look lovely."

"Thanks, Dad," Caroline replied. "Where's Mom?"

"She said she had a headache. I helped her to bed early."

"Do you need me to stay home?"

"Absolutely not," Max O'Conner replied. "Go and bring home one of Widow Johnson's cherry pies."

"But I don't want to leave you if Mom is sick."

"It's a headache," her father replied. "And I'm a

doctor. I think I can handle it alone for a few hours."

"Come on," Ava Dawn said, pulling at Caroline's arm. "We'll be late if we don't scoot."

Outside, Caroline peered into the bed of her truck. "What are all these trash bags doing in here?" she asked.

"I picked up some clothes from the hospital thrift shop." Ava Dawn replied. "Uncle Max called and got them to part with some of their overstock from the back room. I don't know who donated this stuff, but you're right, it smells like an old, wet dog."

"Why do you have it?"

"For the church clothing drive," Ava Dawn replied. "I told Brother Crow I'd help out with it."

"Do you ever tell Brother Crow no?"

Ava Dawn shrugged. "I figure it's a little bit like telling Jesus no, you know? I figure he's got a direct line to Jesus, and tellin' him no is like punchin' Jesus in the face."

Caroline burst out laughing. She couldn't help herself. "I don't think it's quite that dramatic, Ava Dawn," she said. "Brother Crow ain't Billy Graham."

"I'm late." Ava Dawn squinted into the fading daylight. "I said I'd help set up."

"I'm sorry," Caroline replied. "You could have gone on without me."

"Nah, it's fine." Ava Dawn smiled over at her

cousin. "You needed to get out just as bad as I did."

When they turned into the church parking lot, it looked like everybody in the whole town had turned out. Caroline was glad to see so many people turning out to support the Brannans. Court's father worked full-time at the sawmill just outside of town and had been there for as long as Caroline could remember. Pam had been a CNA before she got sick, and even with both of his parents working money had always been tight. Most of the other families in Cold River lived paycheck to paycheck just like the Brannans, but it didn't matter; everybody gave what they could.

Ava Dawn broke off from Caroline once they entered the building. "I'm gonna go find Brother Crow and see what he needs me to do."

Caroline felt a pang of panic. She knew all of the faces she saw, but she was alone. Ava Dawn was almost always her buffer at social functions. She scanned the crowd for Court, who she knew would be equally uncomfortable, but he was nowhere to be found. As she searched, she began to wonder if she really would see Reese. She knew that Court kept up with him, even though he pretended not to like him much. They'd kept up a friendship long after Caroline and Reese were through. And through was something they'd been for a while. It wasn't the rumors of him cheating on her that had bothered her as much as it was that Reese thought she'd be stupid enough to believe that he *wasn't* cheating on her. She'd known who he was when they'd gotten together, and the only thing she'd been stupid about was thinking that he was going to change—that with her he'd be different.

Luckily, she didn't see Reese anywhere, but out of the corner of her eye, she did see Court. He was leaning up against a wall in the back, a can of Coca-Cola in one of his hands. She made her way over to him.

"I've been looking for you," Court said. "You'll never guess who's here tonight."

"Who?" Caroline asked. "Is it Reese?"

"No," Court replied. "You know Reese. He said he'd rather write me a check than show up at one of these things."

"I figured he could at least come here for you," Caroline said, trying to hide her relief.

Court slung an arm around Caroline's shoulder. "That's your job."

"Caroline?" There was someone waving to her through the crowd. "Hey, Caroline!"

Caroline looked towards the sound of the voice and spotted two of her high school friends, Kasey and Tyler. Kasey was waving at her frantically, jumping up and down.

Tyler and Kasey moved two towns over after high school graduation to work for Kasey's parents at their farm supply store. At first, they'd come back often to see everyone, but Caroline couldn't remember the last time she'd seen them. "How are you guys?" Caroline asked, reaching out to embrace both of them.

"Good, good," Kasey replied. She held Caroline out at arm's length. "You look good, girl."

"Thanks," Caroline replied.

"You seein' anybody special?" Kasey winked at her.

"No," Caroline replied.

"I was just telling Court over here that it's about time for him to get hitched." Tyler clapped Court on the back.

Caroline rolled her eyes over at Court. "And what did he say about that?"

"The same thing he always says," Kasey replied. "Not everybody is as lucky in love as the two of us." She linked her arm through Tyler's.

"Well, he's right there."

"Twenty-five might as well be fifty in Cold River," Tyler continued. "You and Caroline both better figure somethin' out."

"If Caroline and I aren't married by the time we're fifty, don't you worry, we'll partner up," Court said, a sly smile cropping up on his face.

"Speaking of partnering up," Kasey gave the room a once-over, "where is Reese? I heard he was gonna be here tonight."

They were all staring at Caroline. She shrugged

her shoulders. "Why are you all looking at me?"

"You haven't heard from him?" Tyler wanted to know.

"No."

Kasey and Tyler exchanged glances.

"You never shoulda turned him down," Kasey said, shaking her head. "You coulda been married to a railroad man!"

Caroline shifted on her feet uncomfortably. As if the only important thing in life was to be married. She searched for an escape, and instead saw Roy Bean walk through the double doors. He was holding the hand of a woman she'd never seen before, and he was making a beeline for the pie table where Ava Dawn was sitting. She hadn't seen him yet, too busy arranging pies and handing out auction numbers.

"Oh, this is going to be bad," Caroline muttered.

"What's wrong?" Kasey wanted to know. "You see Reese?"

"It's Roy."

"So?"

"So he and Ava Dawn are separated, and he's just showed up with some other woman."

"That ain't nothin' new," Tyler replied. "Them two are always goin' back and forth."

"It's different this time," Caroline replied. "I better get over there before something happens."

Roy beat Caroline to the table by a split second, but it was enough for Ava Dawn to look up and get an eyeful of him and his companion. Caroline could practically see the smoke coming out of Ava Dawn's ears.

"What are you doing here?" Ava Dawn demanded.

Roy grinned. It was the same shit-eating grin he always wore just before he got mean. "You better be Christian-like, Ava Dawn. We're in a *church*."

"I *know that,* Roy," Ava Dawn replied through gritted teeth. *"What are you doing here?"*

"Just tryin' to show my support for Court and his daddy."

"You hate Court."

"Aw, come on now. You know that ain't true." Roy was still grinning.

Ava Dawn sighed, gathering her composure. "You want a number?"

Roy looked surprised, clearly expecting more of a fight from his wife. "Well, I reckon so," he said, eyeing her.

"Here." Ava Dawn handed him a paper fan with a number written in Sharpie. She didn't even look up at him as he took it.

Roy stood there for a few seconds, waiting for Ava Dawn to say or do something. When she didn't, he said, "Don't you wanna know who I'm with?"

"Sure don't."

"She's younger'n you. Prettier'n you, too."

Finally, Ava Dawn looked up. "Roy, I wouldn't care if you brought the damn Queen of England into this church. You ain't my problem no more."

Roy leaned over the metal table, palms squishing into two fresh pies when Haiden Crow stepped up next to him. His long, black beard gleamed in the fluorescent lighting of the fellowship hall.

"Howdy there," Haiden said, placing a hand on Roy's shoulder. "Do you need a number for the auction?"

"I got me a number."

"What about the lovely blonde?" Haiden gestured to the woman standing uneasily beside Roy. "You want a number?"

"I want to get outta here," she replied. "I didn't know your ex-girlfriend was going to be here."

Ava Dawn let out a snort. "Honey, I'm his wife, but as soon as them papers are signed, he's all yours."

"You're married?" The woman stepped back from Roy, frantically glancing between him and Ava Dawn. "You said you'd never been married. Never!"

Roy ignored her. "Ain't nobody signing papers."

"I'm sorry, Mr. Bean." Haiden Crow returned his hand to Roy's shoulder, more forcefully than before. "But we're getting ready to start the auction. If you'd please take your seat."

"I ain't going nowhere."

Haiden Crow was shorter than Roy by a couple of inches and was roughly half his weight, but it didn't matter. When Haiden Crow spoke, people listened. "Please have a seat, *sir*."

Roy looked from Haiden over to Court, who nodded at him. Caroline could tell Roy was hedging his bet, but the odds were stacked against him, and he was at least smart enough to realize it. With a grunt, he took a step back, turning on his heel. "Let's go," he said, jerking the woman along with him. "Let's get out of here."

Ava Dawn put her head in her hands and muttered, "Jesus Christ."

"Yes, he does need Jesus Christ," Haiden said, just a hint of a smile crossing his face. He patted Ava Dawn on the hand. "I'll pray for him tonight. You should do the same."

"Thank you," Ava Dawn said. "I'm beginning to think he'll never leave me alone."

"He's angry right now," Haiden said. "But with time, he will subdue."

"Roy doesn't know the meaning of that word," Caroline said. She noticed Haiden Crow's hand was still resting on her cousin's. *Where was his wife?*

"We should all pray for him," Haiden replied.

Caroline rolled her eyes up to the church's ceiling. She wondered how much *Brother Crow* really knew about Roy. She wondered how much Ava Dawn told him. All he had to do was look at the police reports and hospital records to know that it was going to take a whole lot more than praying to make Roy stay away from Ava Dawn. She was scared for Ava Dawn, because she knew that if Roy set his mind to it, he could make sure the only thing Ava Dawn ever saw again was the inside of a pine box.

"I'll try prayin' for Roy," Ava Dawn said at last. "But I won't like it none." She was looking up at Brother Crow, adoration in her blue eyes.

"Good," he replied, finally letting go of her hand. "If you'll excuse me, I better get up to the front of the room and get this shindig started."

"Well, that was intense," Kasey said once Haiden Crow was gone. She sat down next to Ava Dawn. "I didn't know you and Roy were getting divorced."

"Didn't know it myself until a couple of weeks ago," Ava Dawn replied.

"I think I speak for everyone when I say that it's about time," Court said.

"I'm sorry about Roy showin' up here. I swear I didn't tell him." Ava Dawn twirled a piece of curly hair around her finger.

"I know you didn't." Court grinned at her. "I begged my dad not to do this, anyway. I mean I reckon it'll help, but I've had my fill."

"He's just such an asshole," Caroline muttered.

"Hey, I have an idea," Court said. "Let's get out of here."

"What do you mean?" Caroline asked. "Leave the pie auction?"

"Yeah, why not?"

"But the church is doing all of this for you," Kasey reminded him.

"I'd never stepped foot inside this church before Pam's funeral," Court said. "They're doing this for her. And my dad."

Tyler's eyes lit up. "We could go out to my dad's new fishin' cabin. It's down by your shop, Caroline."

"As long as we're drinkin', I'm in," Ava Dawn replied.

Caroline shifted from one foot to the other. She wanted to go with them. She couldn't remember the last time she'd gone out and done anything fun. "I hate to leave my dad at home alone for that long with my mom."

"Come on, Carolina." Ava Dawn rolled her eyes. "Uncle Max is a *doctor*. Surely he can do without you for a few more hours."

"If I know any of you, it'll be longer than a few hours."

"I'm sure it will be fine," Court agreed. "You can call him on the way."

"Fine," Caroline relented. "But when I say it's time to go, it's time to go. You got it?" She pointed at Ava Dawn.

"I got it."

"Great," Tyler replied, pulling his phone out

of his pocket. "I'm gonna call a few people."

"You sure you can handle all of us, Officer?" Caroline asked Court. "It might get wild and crazy."

"Since when is anything *not* wild and crazy with you, Carolina?" Court asked. "Besides," he pointed to his hip, where his gun usually rested, "you're on your own tonight, because I'm off duty."

Chapter 11

Their first stop was Gary's. Despite being a gas station, he had one of the best selections of alcohol in town, and it was on the way. He eyed them warily when they entered, laughing and too full of energy for his liking. "What are you kids up to tonight?"

"Not much," Court said. He pulled a case of Bud Light from the cooler in the back. "Just headed out to have a few drinks."

"Oh yeah?"

Caroline and Ava Dawn exchanged glances from the front of the store. "He wants us to invite him," Ava Dawn whispered.

"No way," Caroline said, turning her back so Gary couldn't see her talking. "He'll invite the whole damn town."

"I bet we can make it worth our while," Ava

Dawn replied. "I ain't had a snuff of his granny's moonshine in ages."

"Don't you think you've made enough moonshine memories for one lifetime?" Caroline wanted to know, but she was smiling. Just the thought of that moonshine made her feel warm and happy on the inside. Sure, it didn't taste great those first couple of swigs, but then that Ozark Mountain Lightning did what the regular stuff just couldn't do.

Ava Dawn gave her cousin a wink. "Come with me. I'll bring my boobs, and you do the talking."

"Fine." Caroline sighed, pretending to be annoyed. "But if this doesn't work, you're payin'."

The two women ambled up to Gary, who was standing behind the cash register. "How's it goin' tonight, Gary?" Ava Dawn asked. She leaned over the counter in front of him.

Gary didn't even bother looking Ava Dawn in the eye. "Alright, I reckon."

Caroline leaned in next to her cousin. "We're mighty thirsty tonight, Gary."

"I got a good selection there in the back." Gary nodded towards where Court stood. "Just came in today."

"We're lookin' for something stronger."

"What do y'uns mean, exactly?"

"Come on, Gary," Ava Dawn purred. "You know what we mean."

Gary eyed Court at the back of the store, and then looked back down at Ava Dawn's breasts. There was clearly a debate going on in his head.

"Don't worry," Caroline said, sensing his hesitation. "Court's off duty tonight."

"Ain't him I'm worried about, Carolina." He gave Caroline a look and nodded towards the back of the store.

Caroline turned around to see what Gary was talking about. If Court was on duty, neither she nor her cousin would have tried to swindle Gary out of his shine. Although most deputies looked the other way, especially now that so few of the original moonshining families were still in business, Court might not have been so willing to ignore it had he not been engaged in conversation. In the back of the store, Court was chatting happily with someone.

It was Noah Cranwell.

Caroline swallowed when Noah looked up from Court and grinned at her. Even from where she was standing she could see how his eyes darkened when he looked at her. She couldn't tell if that was good or bad, and it made her all the more desperate to get at what Gary was hiding. "He's alright," she assured the man behind the counter. "He's my neighbor." She leaned in closer. "He's a Cranwell."

"You give us a couple of jars of what you've got behind the counter, and we'll give you directions to where we're headed," Ava Dawn said.

Gary reached down beneath the counter and pulled out two mason jars filled with a clear liquid. "One of the reg'lar and one of the apple."

"Your granny fill these up today?"

"Night 'fore last."

Ava Dawn grinned. "Give me a pen."

Caroline was busy stuffing the moonshine into her purse when she noticed Court and Noah walking towards the front.

"I told Noah here he ought to come down to the cabin with us," Court said. He eyed Caroline's purse. " 'Course I didn't know we were gonna be hittin' the hard stuff."

"Can't handle it since you became a lawman?" Ava Dawn asked. Her eyes were dancing all over the two men. "Caroline and me always could drink ya under the table."

"Not all of us were raised on the stump whiskey," Court shot back.

"You comin' with us, or what?" Ava Dawn asked Noah, turning her attention back to him.

"If that's alright with everyone," Noah replied.

He said everyone, but he was looking down at Caroline. She felt her face flush. "It's alright with everyone."

"Can I just follow you there?"

"You can follow Court." Caroline grabbed Ava Dawn's arm. "We're gonna head on out."

"I can't believe Noah is coming with us," Ava

Dawn said excitedly, shoving her cousin towards the door. "He's so freakin' cute."

"He's trouble," Caroline replied. But Ava Dawn was right, he was cute. Well, cute was an understatement. He was flat-out gorgeous, and she figured every single woman between the ages of eighteen and ninety-nine knew it. Her stomach did a little flip-flop. What if he knew it, too?

"Let's be sure and show him a good time," Ava Dawn said, as if she were reading Caroline's mind. She slammed her door closed as Caroline took off down the dirt roads. "Slow down, would ya?"

"I bet he's never been to a backwoods party before," Caroline replied.

Ava Dawn reached over and into Caroline's bag and pulled out a jar of the moonshine. "I think I'm gonna start early tonight."

"We aren't even on the back roads yet, Ava Dawn."

"Honey, this whole town is the back roads."

Ava Dawn had taken her first swig before they were out of the parking lot, while Caroline glared over at her from the driver's seat. For a moment it was just like they were back in high school. Except, of course, they would have been headed to one of Reese's famous get-togethers. Court joked about her and Ava Dawn being able to drink him under the table, but that was only because Court rarely drank. Nobody could outdrink Reese

Graham. Nobody could outsmoke him or outparty him or outtalk him. They'd had some good times, she and Reese, but the truth was she was happy she hadn't yet seen him. Reese had a way of always getting what he wanted, and for a long time, what he'd wanted had been her. She'd only ever been able to say no to him once, and she wasn't damn sure she could do it again. Maybe she'd take a cue from her cousin tonight and let loose. Lord only knew when she'd have another opportunity. "You better not drink too much of that just yet," Caroline said as they bounced along the now gravel road. "You ain't had none of Granny Dye's shine in a while, I reckon."

"I'll be fine." Ava Dawn tipped back the jar and winced as the liquid burned all the way down her throat. "It's stronger than I remember."

"It ain't any stronger," Caroline replied. "You've just gotten older." She pulled into the driveway beside Tyler and Kasey's truck, throwing the truck into park seconds before pulling the jar away from her cousin and taking a swig of her own, letting the grain alcohol burn all the way down her throat and into her belly. Ava Dawn's father, Caroline's uncle, used to stay drunk on the stuff for days at a time, and he'd once told the girls that the reason the clear, strong liquid was called "moonshine" was because after drinking the stuff a man began to see the world as though he were seeing it through the light of the moon.

Caroline went home and asked her father, and after being angry at his brother for drinking in the middle of the day while Caroline and Ava Dawn watched, he told her that, no, that's not actually why it was called moonshine.

"The reason is far less glamorous," her father had said. "When the government imposed a high-distilled spirits tax on the sale of the whiskey that US citizens made, in part to fund the Civil War, moonshiners started making their alcohol illegally. They weren't making whiskey as a fun hobby; they were making it to feed their families."

"What do you mean?" Caroline had asked. "How did moonshine feed a family?"

"Well, the moonshine itself didn't feed them," her father laughed, "but I reckon it kept many a hungry man warm on a cold night. What I meant was that times were tough back then and any extra cash helped. If people agreed to pay those high taxes, they might not have enough money left over to put food on the table and take care of their families, and lots of farmers turned to moonshining to keep their kids fed, and so they kept producing their liquor in secret, by the light of the moon, so they wouldn't have to pay those taxes."

"So they just kept on breaking the law like that?" Caroline was in awe. "There wasn't an honest way to make a living?"

"Some might argue that it was the federal

government committing the crime by imposing such high taxes."

Caroline had thought about this, and she was thinking about it still as she drank from the jar containing Gary's granny's shine. She stared at the fishing cabin in front of her, already beginning to swell with people. The "fishing cabin" wasn't much more than an old trailer thrown on a piece of land facing the river. It was past the bait shop, but not quite as far down as Cranwell Corner. Everybody in town knew that Tyler's daddy used the cabin to escape from Tyler's mama with one of his lady friends. It was actually the second cabin to sit on the lot. The first one burned down mysteriously a few years back, and nobody was quite sure if Tyler's daddy did it for the insurance money or if Tyler's mama did it to get back at Tyler's daddy.

But there was a private dock, and that was enough for most anybody in Cold River.

Caroline replaced the lid on the moonshine. Tyler and Kasey were already sitting on the front porch. "Look what I brought!" She held up the mason jars from out of the driver's side window.

"We had some saved back!" Kasey hollered, holding up her own jar. "Tyler called damn near everybody in town. It's a good thing y'uns brought extra."

Caroline and Ava Dawn were already up on the

porch by the time the two men started towards the trailer. "So you traded Gary an invite for that shine?" Court wanted to know. "That's kinda ornery, even for you, Ava Dawn."

"It was her idea." Ava Dawn jammed her thumb towards Caroline. "You've been to parties with Gary. I shoulda charged him more."

Court took the jar from Ava Dawn and gave it a sniff. "I think I'll pass on this tonight. Work comes mighty early tomorrow." He handed it off to Noah.

Noah held the jar back at arm's length.

"What's the matter?" Court asked playfully. "You ain't never had a snout full of Ozarks Mountain Lightning?"

"Oh, I've had some," Noah replied. "But it's been a long time."

"How long?"

"Let's see," Noah said. "I guess it's been about twenty-six years."

"How old were you?" Court replied, scratching the back of his head. "Five?"

"I was four," Noah corrected him. "I stole a mason jar out from under my grandfather's sink. All the adults were drinking it. I wanted to give it a go."

"And how did that turn out?" Caroline asked. She felt warm from the moonshine, despite the fact that it had cooled off outside. There was a thunderstorm headed their way according to the news, and everything at that moment felt just right.

"I was sick for a week." Court laughed. "Then of course I couldn't sit down for a week once my grandfather got ahold of me."

"Your granddad is Jep Cranwell, right?" Kasey asked.

"He is." Court nodded.

"You look just like him."

"I've heard that once or twice." Noah took a swig from the jar and winced.

"Don't hog it all," Ava Dawn said. "Hand it over, big boy."

"Oh, guess what?" Kasey said, her eyes lighting up.

"This isn't really a *fishing cabin?*" Court replied, a lopsided grin beginning to form on his face. "We already knew that."

"Hush." Kasey smacked Court on the arm. "Tyler bought himself a stock car! Gonna be racing it at the Cold River track in a couple weeks." She turned to Tyler. "Tell 'em about it, Ty!"

"It ain't much to look at," Tyler said. "But Kasey's mom and dad are gonna sponsor me." He held up his hands. "We just got 'Burgess Bail Bonds' painted on the side."

"You just gotta come see him race!" Kasey broke in, unable to contain her excitement.

"Of course we'll come," Caroline said. For as

146

long as she'd known Tyler, the only thing he'd ever wanted to do was race cars. As kids, he'd idolized Mark Martin, even going as him for Halloween years and years in a row. Now he was a bail bondsman for Kasey's parents, and they all knew the closest he'd ever come to the Indy 500 was the Cold River dirt track just outside of town. Still, it would be fun to watch him race. "When is it?"

"Two weeks from Saturday," Tyler said. "I'll make sure Kasey reminds everybody. Let's get ourselves inside before the rain starts." He ushered everyone inside. "At least get some music goin'."

Noah followed in behind Caroline, placing his hand on the small of her back. "It's good to see you tonight, Caroline."

"It's good to see you, too, Noah."

"I'd been hoping to run into you after dark."

Caroline felt her pulse quicken. What did *that* mean?

She was about to respond when Ava Dawn grabbed ahold of Noah's arm to introduce him to someone else. Caroline wrapped her fingers around the jar of moonshine in her purse and found the couch and sat herself down as a steady stream of people began to enter the cabin. She knew most of them. They were people she went to high school with, people who came into the bait shop, and people whose faces she knew even if she didn't know their names. That's what it was like living in a small town—everyone at least knew your face.

"Well, Caroline O'Conner," said a man in a sweat-stained T-shirt with the sleeves cut off. "I ain't seen you in forever."

"Hey, Daryl," Caroline said. She smiled over at him. "How's it going?"

"Oh, same old, same old." He took a swig of his beer.

"Daryl!" Caroline looked up to see Daryl's wife, Bobbie, coming towards them, full speed ahead. "Don't you tell Caroline our news! I want to tell her myself!"

"What news?" Caroline asked.

"We're havin' a baby!" Bobbie squealed, squeezing herself in between Daryl and Caroline. "Finally! After all these years!"

"That's wonderful!" Caroline replied. "Really, that's great."

"It is, ain't it?" Bobbie rubbed her belly. "Due in January."

"Guess the docs were wrong," Daryl said. He was beaming. "Ain't nothin' wrong with my baby maker."

Bobbie punched Daryl in the arm. "Hush. Nobody wants to hear about your baby maker."

"Well, I'm thrilled for both of you," Caroline said. "I know you've been trying for a long time."

"I'm sure you'll be next." Bobbie winked at her.

"Lord, I hope not."

Bobbie cocked her head to the side. "You don't want kids?"

"Maybe someday," Caroline said. She looked around the room for a place to escape or another person to latch on to. "But not right now."

Bobbie leaned in so close that Caroline could see down the gap in her tank top. "Those eggs of yours ain't gettin' any younger, you know. My baby doctor up in Springfield says girl babies are born with all the eggs they'll ever have. Did you know that?"

"Aw, let her alone," Daryl scolded his wife. "Who's she gonna marry? Court?"

"I don't see why not."

Daryl made a snorting sound and nearly choked on his beer. "That ain't gonna happen. That boy is fruitier than a fruitcake, if you know what I mean."

"Daryl!"

Caroline stood up, trying to keep a smile on her face. "I'm going to get another drink."

She grabbed a discarded jar of moonshine and headed outside to the dock. To her delight, there was no one outside, and no one sitting on the dock. Caroline sat down and pulled off her shoes, dangling her feet in the river. She took a swig from the jar, wishing she could jump right into the water. It felt so cool and soothing.

Caroline craned her neck to see the cabin behind her. She doubted anyone even knew she was out there. There wasn't even anybody left on the porch. They'd all gone inside to escape the rain.

The moonshine no longer burned going down, and for a moment, everything was quiet and perfect. It wasn't often she was alone on the water. Most of her alone time consisted of being holed up in her room, reading books about gangsters—about the men and women who ran jars like the one she was holding from one county to the next. *They were risk takers,* she thought. *I can't remember the last time I took a risk.*

She dipped one of her legs farther into the water. Damn, she wanted to go swimming. But it was dark. And the river could carry her off if she wasn't careful. *Maybe if I just hold on to the dock,* she thought. Looking around once more to make sure no one was watching, she unbuttoned her jeans and slid them off. Then she pulled her tank top over her head, leaving her standing on the dock in her bra and panties.

Caroline let out a contented sigh when she lowered herself down into the water. It was just cold enough so that she wouldn't want to stay in forever, but not so cold that her teeth were chattering. Sometimes she and Ava Dawn had gone swimming at night when they were in high school. They'd often gone to the riverbank with Court and Reese, but Caroline had to be careful that her parents couldn't tell where she'd been. She was sure most parents were protective over their children, but her parents went beyond protective. They'd made her wear a life jacket until she was in college. They rarely let her go anywhere without them until she was well into high school, and a car at sixteen? Forget about it.

She knew that it came from the pain of losing her brother. She knew they probably thought about losing her more than any parent should have to, but the older she got, the more she chaffed against their watchful eyes. It wasn't until she moved home and her mother was sick that her father was distracted enough not to ask too many questions, and she was granted the freedom she'd always yearned for. In fact, sometimes her father seemed annoyed that she didn't want to stay out with friends. It was a freedom she'd gladly trade to have her mother back.

"Caroline, are you down there?" Noah Cranwell's voice floated down from the top of the dock.

Caroline popped up out of the water so fast that she didn't realize she'd been under the dock. She bit down hard on her tongue when her head hit the wooden planks of the dock, and the last thing she remembered before everything turned dark was the metallic taste of blood.

Chapter 12

The next time Caroline opened her eyes there was a figure above her, his mouth hovering over hers. She tried to speak, but it came out as a cough full of river water.

"Caroline! Fuck! Caroline!"

Caroline blinked, trying to make the figure in front of her come into focus. "What happened?"

"You almost fucking drowned, that's what happened." Noah Cranwell sat back, pulling her up with him. "What were you doing in the water?"

"Swimming," Caroline replied. Her head felt fuzzy. "Floating, really."

"Are you okay?" Noah reached up and touched her face, pushing wet strands of hair away from her eyes.

"I hit my head on the dock."

"I heard it."

"Did you jump in after me?" She squinted in the darkness. His clothes were sopping wet. "Oh my God. I'm so sorry."

"It's okay," he said. He moved his hand down from her face to her shoulder, his fingers stopping momentarily at her bra strap.

That was when Caroline realized she was sitting in front of him half naked. "Oh, shit." Her hand flew up to his. "My clothes."

"Your clothes?" Noah asked. "At least your clothes are dry."

"At least you're wearing your clothes!"

Noah stood up, his hand still intertwined with hers. "Well, if I'd known I was going to be jumping into rivers after dark, I'd have worn my glow-in-the-dark swimming trunks."

Caroline knew she should probably be embarrassed about standing in front of him in what could now only be described as see-through underwear, but she wasn't. "I hadn't planned on almost drowning," she replied. "You startled me."

"What were you doing in the river, anyway?" Noah wanted to know.

Caroline shrugged. "It seemed like a good idea at the time." Her head was pounding. She broke away from Noah and trudged up the bank to the dock.

"You could have gotten yourself killed."

"I would have been fine if you hadn't walked up and startled me." Who did he think he was? She bent down and picked up her pants, sliding them up over her damp calves.

"You make a habit out of this?"

"Out of what?"

"Drinking moonshine and taking off your clothes."

Caroline narrowed her eyes at him. "I reckon my habits are my own business."

"Not even gonna say thank you, huh?" Noah

bent down and picked up her shirt. "Like I said, at least your clothes are dry."

Caroline grabbed at her tank top, and when she did, Noah grabbed ahold of the waistline of her jeans and pulled her all the way up to him, so close that her bare stomach was touching his. She put her hands up to push him away, but she didn't. Instead, she placed them, palms down, onto his chest. She could feel the heat from his skin penetrating through his soggy shirt.

Caroline looked up at him. Everyone was right. He sure did look like a Cranwell, and he sure did look the most like Jep Cranwell. She figured moonshine ran through his veins, and all she could think about was pulling him down to her level and tasting him. "I don't even know you," she said, her voice hoarse.

"We could change that."

Behind her, Caroline heard voices, loud voices calling her name and coming from the direction of the cabin. She snatched her shirt out of Noah's hands and pulled it on as quickly as she could.

"Caroline!" Ava Dawn was charging towards her, full speed ahead. "Car-o-line!"

"What?" Caroline hollered, sliding her flip-flops onto her feet.

"What in the hell are you doing all the way out here?" Ava Dawn stopped short when she saw Noah. "Ohhhh . . ."

"What do you want, Ava Dawn?"

"Why is your tank top on inside out?" Ava Dawn asked. She looked past Caroline and at Noah. "Why is he all wet?"

"I'll tell you about it in a minute," Caroline replied, turning her cousin around.

"Why are *you* all wet?"

"Just shut up and walk."

"Caroline, wait!"

Caroline ignored her, continuing to push her forward.

"I need to tell you something," Ava Dawn persisted.

"It can wait," Caroline replied. She looked back at Noah still standing on the dock. She pushed Ava Dawn all the way back to the cabin where quite a crowd had amassed. "Jeezus, is there anybody who's not here?"

"Nope." Ava Dawn managed to jerk herself away from Caroline. "*Everybody* is here."

"Oh yeah?" Caroline absently scanned the room. She wasn't thinking about *everybody*. She was thinking about Noah. She was thinking about his damp shirt. She was thinking about the way he looked at her at Gary's, and the way he looked at her when he'd pulled her close to him.

"Caroline?"

Caroline was standing face to face with Reese Graham. She looked desperately at Ava Dawn who only mouthed the words, "I tried to tell you," before shrugging her shoulders.

"Caroline?"

Caroline focused on the man standing in front of her. Damn, it had been a long time. "Reese!"

"How are you, Carolina?" He reached out to embrace her.

"I'm good, I'm good," she mumbled into his shoulder. She hadn't expected such a warm greeting. He'd been good and pissed the last time she saw him. In fact, he'd said he never wanted to see her again. *Ever.*

"Why is your hair wet?" Reese pulled away from her, holding her back at arm's length. "Don't tell me you went skinny dippin' in the river without me!" He was grinning, little lines forming in the corners of his pale, blue eyes.

"You know I don't go skinny dippin'."

"Well, not without me."

He sounded like Reese, and Caroline guessed he looked like him, too. The last time she'd seen him, he'd had long hair and a stupid little earring in one ear. Now his long, reddish hair had been replaced with a buzz cut, and the earring was gone. She wondered what else about him had changed—back then he'd been the guy always up for a good time, the guy who always had an angle *and* always had a girlfriend. Caroline was just one girl in a long string of girls, and she wondered if people at the party were looking at the two of them and thinking, *Oh no. Here we go again.* "When did you get back into town?" she asked, even though she already knew the answer.

"A few days ago," he replied. "Looks like I'm back to stay for a while at least. I can't believe Court didn't tell you."

"Hey now," Court, who'd clearly been listening in on their conversation, said. "I don't tell her everything."

Reese rolled his eyes. "Yes you do. You knew she was gonna dump me before I did."

Caroline and Court shared an uncomfortable look.

"It doesn't matter now; it's all water under the bridge. Water under the bridge." Reese said, that familiar gleam in his eye. "Let's get together, you and me, sometime soon."

"Sounds good," Caroline said, nodding, but her eyes were narrowed. What did he want? Her head was still fuzzy from hitting it on the dock . . . and everything that happened after. She could feel Court staring at her. She knew he wouldn't be happy. She'd just have to talk to him about it later.

"We've got a lot of catching up to do."

"Do we?"

Reese looked down at his shoes. "Come on, Carolina, don't make me say it."

"Say what?" Caroline was confused. And she was cold. She wished her hair wasn't wet.

"I've missed you."

Now she had to fight to roll her eyes. She hadn't

missed him. Well, not really. She hadn't missed uncomfortable conversations like this one. That was for sure. "Well, I've missed you, too." Again, it was the only thing she *could* say.

Before Reese could respond, an already drunk Daryl tackled him. "REEEESE!" Daryl slung an arm around Reese's neck, spilling his Budweiser all over Reese's shirt. "I been lookin' for ya all night, man!"

Reese wiped in vain at his shirt as he was dragged away. He looked back and grinned at Caroline. "I'll call ya, Carolina!"

Caroline watched him go. She knew he'd call her. Reese always did what he said he was going to do. Unfortunately, that got him into a lot of trouble. She scanned the room for Noah. She'd forgotten about him when she saw Reese, and her heart sank when she realized he wasn't anywhere inside. Wading through the crowd, she went outside onto the porch and sure enough, Noah's car was gone. She didn't want to go back inside and deal with Court and Reese again. She was tired. Flagging down Ava Dawn, she said, "I'm exhausted. Can we go home now?"

Ava Dawn nodded. "Are you alright?"

"Of course," Caroline said. "Why wouldn't I be?"

"Oh, I don't know." Ava Dawn shrugged. "Maybe because I found you half naked rubbing up against Noah Cranwell and then Reese Graham comes in lookin' all hot. It's bound to confuse and confound a girl, wouldn't you say?"

"I am neither confused nor confounded."

Her cousin wasn't convinced. "Well, we'll have plenty of time for you to pick your own adjectives on the way home." Ava Dawn linked her arm through her cousin's. "But I think I hit the nail right on its confused and confounded little head."

Chapter 13

Caroline often wondered if her father wished she had been born a boy. It wasn't because she thought Max O'Conner believed, as many did in her small Ozarks town, that boys were still preferable to girls. No, her father had never been that kind of man. He'd raised her to ignore that kind of logic; he'd been an advocate for women's rights during the '60s and '70s. He'd even proudly advertised birth control and the Gardasil shot for his female patients, much to the chagrin of the town's many social conservatives. Women in the O'Conner family were very often heard long before they were seen.

No, Caroline wondered if her father wished she had been a boy because it might have been easier for him to deal with the death of his son. Maybe if she'd been a boy, she could have eased his pain instead of being born to him as he was on the cusp of middle age, a screaming, freckled girl-child. Sometimes her father looked at her as if he didn't quite understand her, didn't quite know how to relate, even after she'd become an adult. In fact, Caroline thought, he looked at her this way more now that she was an adult.

Her father hadn't been the only one to give Caroline odd looks. She'd been getting them her whole life. It started in the second grade. Rather, it was the first time she truly began to realize she was different from the other kids. It was during circle time, two days before her eighth birthday, in Mrs. David's classroom. The subject of circle time had been "family."

"What's your family like?" Mrs. David had asked. She clasped her hands together expectantly. She was a pudgy woman with a ruddy complexion, and Caroline thought she was very smart-looking in her large, round glasses. "What are your traditions?" Mrs. David continued, using the plural form of the word *tradition* that they'd learned about the day before. "Who makes up your family?"

At first, it had been just fine. Caroline jabbered about Christmas stockings and fishing trips. But when it got to the part about siblings, Caroline hadn't been entirely sure what to say. Most of the other kids were the oldest or only children, like her cousin Ava Dawn. Some had sisters or brothers, and one unfortunate student, Lilly

Barker, was the younger sister of Milly and Tilly Barker. Caroline supposed she was an only child, and she figured that's what she'd say when it got to be her turn, but before she could make a sound she heard the words *dead brother* escape past the lips of Bobby Boyd.

There were eighteen sets of eyes staring at her, nineteen if you counted Mrs. David, who was new that year and didn't know any better.

"She ain't neither," Bobby said, his shaved head dipping up and down like a fuzzy potato. "My mama told me she's got a dead brother buried in the cemetery across from our house."

As Mrs. David sputtered an inaudible response, Caroline glowered over at Bobby. She'd hated him right then. She didn't care that his mama was probably drunk when she said it or that his daddy dug those graves for the house they lived in with no running water and a damn dirt floor, or that the whole reason Bobby was practically bald was because the Boyd kids kept lice, even after his drunk mama shaved their heads—even the girls. All of this she knew because her daddy, her doctor daddy with the dead son, still made house calls.

Caroline stood up, clenching and unclenching her fists. "I'm going to send my brother to haunt you, Bobby Boyd!" she'd screamed. "I'm going to send him to kill you in your sleep!"

She'd spent the next hour in the bathroom,

hot tears streaming down her face, trying to figure out if there really was a way to make her brother rise up, a bony white skeleton, and seek revenge on Bobby. By the time Mrs. David found her, Caroline had already made a mental note to check out that book about voodoo she'd seen at the library the week before.

During recess, the teachers whispered and stared over at Caroline, too busy to notice Ava Dawn corner Bobby behind the tornado slide and sock him right in the nose. He bled all the way to the nurse's office.

"He won't never say another word about Jeremy," Ava Dawn assured her. "Ever." She draped an arm around Caroline's shoulder.

Caroline always had something to say, something that would make the other kids bite their tongues and run off, but Ava Dawn was the muscle, the enforcer. If there was a scrape Caroline couldn't talk herself out of, or more likely, had talked herself into, Ava Dawn would appear tan and strong to fix whatever problem her cousin and best friend had created. It made sense to Caroline why Ava Dawn would later pick Roy from all the other men she could have had to marry, even though by the time they were eighteen she'd outgrown her penchant for fighting. Roy solved things in a way Ava Dawn could understand, and that was a bond difficult to break.

Most of the townspeople of Cold River, even

Roy, were just a little bit more forgiving of Caroline because of her brother's death. Jeremy O'Conner, who would have been eighteen years older than Caroline, died in a car accident five years before she was born. It wasn't a remarkable story. Her brother's life had been cut short on a dark night in February when he hit a patch of black ice coming home from the movies and wrapped his little Ford Ranger around a tree. He was dead before morning, dead before anybody found him, crushed between the steering wheel and the seat. If he'd been driving his bigger truck, the one Caroline now owned, he probably would have lived. That was why, even though the old truck sounded like an angry banshee when started, Caroline continued driving it. She somehow felt safe in it; it felt like Jeremy was watching over her.

Her parents didn't like to talk about it, and gave her very little information about her brother. When Caroline asked, her mother went to baking, and her father became not her father, but the doctor he was at the clinic, explaining everything in a sterile voice with words she couldn't comprehend. It hadn't been until after that awful day during circle time that Caroline had sought to find out more than her parents were willing to tell. It was all there, inside that room in the white house that her parents kept locked. Everything about Jeremy she could have wanted to know.

He'd played baseball and won awards for mathematics. He'd had lots of friends and girlfriends, Caroline knew, from his affable smile and from the way his eyes crinkled, blue like their mother's. Jeremy had been tall, with no visible freckles that she could see, and with a mop of thick, dark hair, a magical gift passed down through the genes of family members Caroline had never met. In the pictures, everyone looked happy, and her parents looked like younger versions of themselves, a blinding sort of youth that died the day Jeremy died, she assumed, because they'd been old since she could remember.

Caroline had lost all track of time, and when her mother found her, she'd expected to be in trouble. Instead, her mother sat down beside her on the floor. She took Caroline's hand in one of her own and Jeremy's baseball mitt in the other.

"Mrs. David called me," her mother said. "She told me what happened."

Caroline didn't say anything. She just looked down at her legs, silently counting the freckles.

"Do you want to talk about it?"

"Bobby Boyd is stupid," she'd responded finally. "He can't come to my birthday party."

"Not even if he apologized?"

"No," Caroline said. "He'd probably give us all head lice anyway."

Maureen O'Conner set the glove back on the floor and lifted Caroline's chin so that their eyes met. "Bobby Boyd wasn't trying to be mean, Caroline. He just doesn't know any better. He hasn't had anyone to teach him the difference." Her voice was soft, but firm. "But you have, and you know how badly words can hurt. Don't you think it would hurt his feelings if you said that to him?"

"I guess," Caroline mumbled. "It's not fair."

"What's not fair?"

"Bobby's mama and daddy are awful. Everybody knows." Caroline felt the tears welling up in her eyes again. "But they get to keep their children, all of them, and they don't even like them!"

"All the more reason for you to be nice to him."

"They get to keep Bobby, and his brothers and sisters," Caroline continued. "They don't even have to make sure they're clean and they get to keep them. Mama, I don't understand why you couldn't keep Jeremy. He was so good and tall and loved. Why couldn't you keep him?"

Her mother pulled her close, and Caroline buried her face into her mother's hair, smothering the tears that were begging to spill out. It was the first time she'd seen her mother cry for Jeremy, the first time Caroline cried for her mother. She cried for the great gaping hole inside of her mother, for the fact that she knew she could never fill it. She cried for the birthdays and Christmases her mother would never have with him, for the phone calls and cards she'd never get. She cried for the parts of Jeremy her mother couldn't bring herself to pack away, and the sheets on the bed she couldn't wash because they still smelled like him, even after all this time, even after a decade locked away in this room, and she cried hardest of all for the mother in the pictures smiling brilliantly into the sun, the young mother, the happy mother, the mother who, so much like her brother, Caroline would never know.

Chapter 14

Caroline sat sweating inside the bait shop, a fan blowing directly on her face. The air conditioner stopped working the day before, and nobody could come out to look at it until the next week. She'd tried fixing it herself, and her father had come out and tried his hand at it, but it was no use. It was miserable outside, and it was worse than miserable inside.

Caroline felt sweat trickle down her neck and begin to pool in her clavicle. "This is ridiculous," she said to her empty shop. She looked down at herself, wishing she could just strip down naked —she'd discarded her flip-flops and bra long ago, but her jean shorts and tank top still felt cumbersome. She stepped out onto the porch. Smokey was hard at work across the road. When he saw her standing there, he waved from the roof.

It had been a week since the party and her mishap on the dock. Noah hadn't spoken to her since. She hadn't even been able to make eye contact with him. He was already there when Caroline arrived in the morning, and he was still working at night when she left. He was making progress, that much was true, but she wondered why he didn't seem to want to see her. Had he really been that mad at her for swimming alone? Had he overheard her conversation with Reese and thought it was more than it was? Surely he understood how complicated relationships, even old ones, could be. After all, he'd been *married* before.

It wasn't like she and Reese were ever going to get back together. She'd promised Court, and even if she hadn't, they never would have lasted. Reese Graham wanted a woman to stay home and iron his clothes while he had a woman somewhere else to iron, well, other things. Caroline would sooner die. But it was making her crazy thinking about Noah every time she looked at the station, which was pretty much any time she walked by a window or went in and out of the bait shop.

"Yoo-hoo, Carolina!" Smokey stood up on the roof and waved to her.

"Hey, Smokey!" Caroline waved back.

"It's hot out, ain't it?"

"Sure is!"

Smokey reached into his pocket and pulled out a handkerchief. As he began to mop his face, one of his feet slid out from under him, and he tumbled headfirst down the roof. He landed with a sickening splat onto the dirt.

"Oh, shit!" Caroline rushed down the steps and across the road over to the station. "Smokey, Smokey!"

Noah beat her to him by a split second. "What in the hell happened?"

"He fell off the damn roof!" Caroline knelt down in front of Smokey. He was out cold, but he didn't appear to be bleeding.

"How?"

"I don't know, he just slipped."

"He's breathing, at least," Noah said, leaning down to inspect Smokey's face. "Should we call 911? Do they come all the way out here?"

"We could put him in the ground faster than they could get out here," Caroline replied. "Get me a glass of water."

"What for?"

"Just get me one, will ya?"

Noah returned a minute later with a glass and handed it to her. Caroline took it and without warning splashed the water onto Smokey's face.

Smokey bolted upright. "What? Who? Where am I?"

"Works every time," Caroline said. She handed

the glass back to Noah. "Smokey, are you okay? You fell off the roof."

Smokey looked around dazedly. "I did?"

"You did."

"Am I alright?"

"Well, I don't know." Caroline laughed. "You tell us. Do you hurt anywhere?"

Smokey tried to stand up. He shook his hands and his shoulders. "I'm alright, but my noggin feels like mush."

"You should probably take the rest of the day off," Noah said. "Do you want me to drive you to the doctor just to make sure nothing is broken?"

"Nah, ain't no need." Smokey rubbed his head. "Ain't the first time I've tumbled off a roof, and I don't reckon it'll be the last."

Caroline looked up at Noah. He looked like he was trying to hold on to his laughter. "Well, let's not make a habit of falling off of my roof, okay?"

"I'll do my best, but I can't make no promises."

"Why don't you come inside where it's cool?" Noah offered. "I've got a window unit upstairs where I'm not renovating."

"Nah, I'm fine. I'm just gonna go have a smoke."

Smokey wandered off towards his rusty truck, mumbling to himself, leaving Caroline and Noah alone. Noah was looking down at her, his hands shoved down into his pockets. He didn't say anything, and Caroline felt she might melt between his stare and the sun. "Well," she said, "I guess I'm going to head back over to the shop."

"You look hot."

"What?"

"Hot," Noah repeated. "You look like you've been out in this heat all day."

"The air conditioner is broken, so . . ."

"Do you want to come inside?"

Yes! Caroline screamed inside of her head. Yes, she wanted to go inside where there was air-conditioning. "That's alright," she said instead.

"Oh, come on," Noah said. He opened the door for her. "You really want to go back over to that sauna?"

"No." She ducked underneath Noah's arm and into the station. She saw Yara snoring in the corner, just as she'd seen her the day Noah asked her over to show her the pictures he'd found. In fact, Yara'd been spending all of her time over at Cranwell Station. It was like she lived there now, and Caroline fought a jealousy that she hadn't expected.

"Come on back this way," Noah said. He stepped in front of her and motioned for her to follow him. "There's just one part of this place that's tolerable right now."

She followed him all the way to the end of a long hallway and up a flight of stairs. "I always wondered what was up here," she said. "The windows used to be covered with old newspapers, which seemed odd to me."

"It's a little apartment," Noah replied. He opened the door at the top of the stairs. "It's not much, but it's mine, and surprisingly, it's in better shape than the downstairs."

Caroline stepped into a one-room studio that had been lost in time. There was a tiny kitchenette with an old refrigerator in one corner. There was a brass bed in another corner, and in the middle there was a box television set on the floor and a couch with clawed feet. She wasn't sure what era she was in, but it thrilled her. "Look at all this old stuff!"

"My grandfather told me that whoever was running the station lived up here," Noah said, sitting down on the couch. "So it became kind of a catchall for the things everybody brought in."

"You live up here?"

"I was staying with my grandfather and aunt," Noah replied. "But last week I got the electricity turned on, and I moved out here."

"That explains why you *always* seem to be here."

"Where else am I gonna go?"

Caroline shrugged. At least she wasn't sweating anymore. For the first time it occurred to her how she must look. No wonder Noah invited her up. He probably thought she was suffering from heatstroke or something.

"Caroline, your foot is bleeding." Noah pointed to her big toe on her left foot. "What happened?"

Caroline looked down at her bare feet. Maybe

she did have heatstroke, because she hadn't felt a thing. "I must've stubbed it running over to check on Smokey."

Noah stood up and walked over to the sink. "Where are your shoes?" he asked, wetting a paper towel underneath the sink.

"I took them off," Caroline replied. She followed him to the sink. "It's nine hundred degrees in the bait shop. They'd practically melted onto my feet."

"You're a mess."

For a moment, Caroline thought he was going to laugh at her, but instead he reached out and pushed a piece of hair out of her eyes. Before she could stop herself, her hands were around his neck, pulling him down to her, pulling him as close as she could get him to her until he thrust his mouth onto hers.

Noah pushed her back against the refrigerator, pinning her to it with his hips. He let his hands wander past the boundaries of her shirt until there was nothing between his fingertips and her breasts. He let out a moan as he rolled one of her nipples in between his thumb and forefinger.

"Noah!" There were footsteps on the stairs. "Boy, are you up there?"

"Shit," Noah said, breaking away from her. "It's my grandfather."

Jep Cranwell burst into the apartment without knocking. He stopped at the doorway when he

172

realized that Noah wasn't alone. He hooked his thumbs through the straps in his overalls and said, "I didn't realize ya had comp'ny."

Caroline wrapped her arms across her chest, suddenly very aware of the fact that she wasn't wearing a bra. "The air conditioner is out over at the shop," she offered when Noah didn't say anything.

Jep squinted over at her. "You Maureen's girl?"

"I am." Caroline nodded. She was surprised to hear him call her *Maureen's girl*. Most people would ask if she belonged to her dad.

"It's all them freckles."

Caroline smiled.

Jep ventured farther into the room. "I just thought my fool-headed grandson might like to know his drunk roofer is takin' a smoke break instead a doin' his job."

"Oh, he's not drunk," Caroline replied. "He never drinks when he's doing a job."

"Is that right?"

"That's right," Noah spoke up. "And he's doing a great job."

"Your cousins woulda done a good job, all the same."

Noah nodded. "We talked about that," he said.

"Still, it'd be nice if you listened to me," Jep replied. Then he looked back over at Caroline and said, "About everything."

Caroline didn't know what *that* was supposed

to mean. "Well, I guess I better get back over to the shop."

"I came to tell ya that yer Aunt Hazel is fryin' up the last of the deer meat tonight, and she wants ya to come for dinner," Jep said, not even bothering to look at Caroline as she brushed past him and towards the stairs.

"Sounds great," Noah replied. "Hey, Caroline, do you want to come?"

"I, uh . . ." Caroline trailed off. She wasn't sure what to say. From the look on Jep Cranwell's face, he wasn't exactly thrilled that she'd been invited.

"It'll be fun," Noah urged. He grinned over at his grandfather.

Caroline looked from Noah to Jep and back again. It was almost comedic how much they looked alike. She was sure that if she pointed it out right then, however, Jep wouldn't find it funny. Why didn't he like her? All she wanted to do was disappear, but Jep was still standing too close to the door for her to make a clean escape.

"Fine," Jep said at last, as if he'd been defeated in a silent battle. "The girl is welcome to come. Unless," he sniffed, "she don't like deer meat."

"I love deer meat."

"Great!" Noah clapped his hands together. "We'll see you later this evening, Gramps."

Jep was out the door as fast as he came in, and

left Noah and Caroline with nothing but an awkward silence hanging over them. "I'm sorry that I put you on the spot right there."

"It's okay."

"You don't have to go if you don't want to."

"Does your grandfather not like me or something?" Caroline asked, narrowing her eyes at Noah. "It seems like the only reason you asked me was to annoy him."

"What?" Noah feigned surprise. "He doesn't even know you."

"Which is why it would be weird for him not to like me."

"Meet me here about 6:45?" Noah asked, changing the subject. "It'll take about fifteen minutes to get out there from here."

"I'll have to check with my dad," Caroline said with a sigh. She wanted to go. In fact, she was *dying* to go. She'd been aching to see Cranwell Corner since she'd been a kid. "He's at the clinic today, and he usually comes home pretty tired."

"Do you think he'll mind?"

"I think it'll be fine."

"Great. See you tonight."

Caroline walked back down the stairs, wondering what in the hell she'd just gotten herself into. She wasn't sure which part made her more nervous—the thought of going to Cranwell Corner or the thought of what might've happened if Jep Cranwell hadn't walked in on them. Would she be under the covers in Noah's big, brass bed? Her face reddened at the thought. For now, Caroline decided, she would concentrate on going to dinner, and dinner would require shoes, and at the very least, a bra.

Chapter 15

Caroline stood in the middle of the living room, shifting nervously from one foot to the other. "So I went and got KFC for you tonight," she said to her father as soon as he walked through the door. "Mom seems to be having a pretty good day."

It wasn't the first time Caroline had stood in the living room, nervously waiting for her father to arrive; in fact, it seemed to be a constant in her life. This house, the one she'd grown up in, knew all of her secrets—it had borne the brunt of some of them, too. They'd moved when she was ten from the house her parents had bought before her brother, Jeremy, was born. Although neither one of her parents ever said it, she'd always supposed that the memories of the old house had been too much. Jeremy's bedroom was strictly off limits, and Caroline had been happy to move to a new house where none of the doors were locked.

Their first order of business after they'd purchased

the house on Polk Avenue was to add on to it a bit—an extra bedroom for Ava Dawn since she was there so often, an extra bathroom, and larger closets for her parents. The foreman on the job let Caroline help knock through one of the walls on the first day with a sledgehammer. After he and the rest of the workers left for the day, Caroline sought out her father's hammer in the tool shed and knocked through her own wall in her bedroom, just to help. When her mother found out, she'd made Caroline wait for her father in the living room, long past her bedtime, to explain to Dr. O'Conner why her room was now a demolition site, as well.

Caroline wondered how many more times she'd stand here like this.

"What's the occasion?" her father asked, eyeing the spread. "I could have cooked if you weren't feeling up to it."

"I know you're tired after being at the clinic all day."

"Honestly, Caroline, I can take care of myself."

"I know, Dad." Caroline reached up and pecked him on the cheek. "But if you don't care, I'm going to go out tonight."

"You know I don't care," her father replied. He picked up a chicken leg.

"I'm going to supper."

"Oh, that's nice."

"At Cranwell Corner."

Max O'Conner pulled the chicken leg out of his mouth and stared at Caroline. After a few seconds of noisy chewing, he said, "Noah invited you down there for supper? Does Jep know?"

"Yes." Caroline fidgeted with the bracelet she was wearing. "Jep Cranwell was there when Noah invited me."

"Jep was at the station?"

"Yes," Caroline said again. "He came to invite Noah to supper, and then Noah invited me." She wasn't about to tell her father that Jep Cranwell didn't seem the least bit happy about it, either.

"Caroline." Max O'Conner set the chicken leg down on the edge of the table. "There are some things you don't know about Jep Cranwell."

"You always told me the rumors weren't true."

"They aren't," her father said. "They're mostly embellishments of bored townsfolk."

Caroline put her hands on her hips. "So why are you acting like I'm gonna go out there and get sacrificed or something?" She'd known her father would be surprised, but she hadn't anticipated this reaction. He looked worried.

"I just wish I'd known earlier," was all her father said.

"Well, I only found out a couple of hours ago. I don't have to go if you don't want me to."

Her father looked down at the chicken leg on the table. "Don't be silly. You go on and have a good time."

"Dad, if there's some reason you don't want me to go, you can tell me," Caroline said. "I won't go. I'll stay here if you want me to."

"Of course not," Max O'Conner replied. "But be careful on your way back. You know how the deer are out that way after dark."

Caroline watched as her father walked over to her mother, kissed her on the top of her head, and sat down next to her. She wondered if her father ever got tired of coming home to her mother every night—of talking to someone who didn't know his name most of the time. When she'd been younger, Caroline would sneak into the hallway long after she was supposed to be asleep and listen to her parents talking. They had the most fascinating conversations. They talked about everything from the pyramids in Egypt to the crawfish crawling the Cold River. Sometimes they caught her listening, and once in a while they wouldn't make her go back to bed. They'd just continue on as if she wasn't there, even though she knew they'd seen her.

Maybe her father, just like Caroline, held on to these moments as the good days became fewer and farther between. She didn't know how either one of them could go on, otherwise. She took one last look at them before she headed out to meet Noah.

Noah was waiting for her outside the station. He'd shaved since she'd seen him last. There was no more of the day-old stubble. He flashed her a nervous smile. "You look nice."

"Thanks." Caroline looked down at herself. She'd borrowed a denim skirt from Ava Dawn and layered a couple of tank tops. "I wasn't sure what to wear."

"We'll probably both be overdressed." Noah motioned for her to get into his car. "I don't know that my grandfather owns anything other than overalls."

"Where are your overalls?" Caroline teased.

"I haven't worn overalls since I was a kid."

"I went through a phase when I was twelve," Caroline admitted. "It was a regrettable experience."

Noah's eyes were all over her. Before Caroline had time to react, Noah leaned over and brushed his lips against hers, soft at first, and then with more force. "I'm sorry," he said, "I just felt like we had some unfinished business."

"Is it finished now?" Caroline asked, a wry smile on her stinging lips.

"I hope not," Noah replied. "But after an evening with my family, who knows when you'll want to see me again."

"I'll see you every day." Caroline shifted in her seat in an unsuccessful attempt to keep the heat she felt at her core from spreading. "We're neighbors, remember?"

Noah looked over at her as they bumped along

the gravel road. "You look genuinely excited to be going to a deer dinner in the middle of nowhere."

Caroline shrugged. "I am."

"Why?"

"You'll think it's stupid."

"Try me."

"You didn't grow up here, so you don't understand it, but there's a bit of mystery surrounding your family," Caroline said. "I've spent my whole life looking across the street at Cranwell Station. It hasn't been much since we've been alive, but before that, it was one of the busiest places in the county."

Noah nodded. "I remember my dad talking about the good old days."

"Well, I don't know what he or your grandfather told you," Caroline continued, "but Cranwell Station was a huge deal during Prohibition. People used to say that the store was really a front for a speakeasy somewhere on the property . . . they say that your family had stills hidden away where the law could never find them."

"My dad used to tell me stories about his grandfather," Noah said. "But anytime my grandfather heard that kind of talk, he shut it down."

"Because they weren't true?"

"Because it's Cranwell business." Noah pulled up to a locked cattle gate. He threw the car into park and got out. "Sit here." He let out a long, piercing whistle before he unlocked the gate.

"What was that all about?" Caroline asked when he got back into the car.

"Just letting them know we're here."

Caroline looked out the window and into the fading daylight. They were surrounded by forest on both sides, and she could see nothing through the thicket except for the winding gravel road that stretched out in front of them. Eventually, the forest gave way to a few small houses, an abandoned car or two, and farther down, where the road abruptly ended, there was one house.

The house began where the road ended, as if the purpose of this road, maybe even all roads, was to lead to this house. It was an old farmhouse, nothing special as far as Caroline could tell. The white clapboard needed a coat of paint, and a couple of the windows appeared to be cracked. There were two middle-aged men sitting on the porch in rocking chairs. One of them was smoking a pipe.

"Here we are," Noah said.

Caroline got out of the car just as Jep Cranwell stepped outside. He stood just as he had in Noah's apartment—with his thumbs looped through the straps of his overalls. Standing in front of his house, he looked to Caroline like a painting she'd once seen at a heritage festival, the quintessential Ozarks hillbilly.

The two men on the porch stood up when they saw Jep.

"You're late," Jep said. He pointed to the men next to him. "These here are my nephews Silas 'n' Thomas."

"Hi." Caroline waved to the men.

The man smoking the pipe nodded at her. The other man spit a wad of tobacco onto the porch.

"Come on in." Jep beckoned to Noah and Caroline. "No sense in standin' outside with these two imbeciles."

Caroline followed Noah and his grandfather inside. It was a cozy little house, a bit warm with no air-conditioning, but with the windows open it was tolerable. There was a well-worn couch in the living room and two recliners. An older television set sat on the floor. There was a large dining room with a wooden table and mismatched chairs. About the house there were hints of a woman's touch—some tattered floral curtains and a few knick-knacks—but it seemed to Caroline that it had been a long time since a woman lived there. "Does he live here alone?" Caroline whispered to Noah.

Noah nodded. "My grandmother died when my dad was just a kid."

"If you're wonderin' who takes care a me, ya don't have to look far," Jep said, sensing Caroline's concern. "My sister lives down the road. You passed her place comin' in."

"I'm sure you can take care of yourself just fine," Caroline replied.

"Not very well," said a female voice from the kitchen.

"This is my sister, Hazel."

"Holler at them boys outside. Supper's 'bout ready," Hazel said. "You checked on that meat out there in the smoker?"

"It's ready when we're ready."

Hazel nodded. She was a stout woman, as round as she was tall. Her gray hair was pulled into a bun so tight that it pulled at the edges of her eyes. She wiped her hands on a faded apron. "You look familiar to me, child."

"She's Maureen's girl," Jep said before Caroline could reply.

Hazel's eyes widened ever so slightly, and only for an instant. "It's all them freckles."

Caroline grinned. "That's what Mr. Cranwell said, too."

"It's Jep, girl."

Silas and Thomas wandered inside, shuffling past them and to the dining room table. "Smells good, Ma," one of them said.

"Let's go sit down," Noah said. "If those two get ahold of the food first, nobody will get anything."

Caroline sat herself down beside Noah, directly across from the two men. Jep sat down at one end, and once the table was full of food, Hazel sat herself down, too.

"Jep, go on and say the blessin'."

Jep launched into a prayer. Caroline was pleasantly surprised that Jep was being so nice to her. Of course, it wasn't like he'd ever been rude. It was just a *feeling* she got when she was around him. The memory of the way he acted at the clinic was also there, lingering in the back of her mind.

"Your mama still run that bait shop?" Hazel wanted to know once the prayer was done. She passed one of her boys the mashed potatoes. "Lord, I ain't seen her in ages."

"Not since she got sick a few years ago," Caroline replied. "I've been taking care of things for a while now."

"I didn't know," Hazel said. She gave Jep a look. "Did you know?"

Jep cleared his throat. "I did know. Didn't think it was nobody's business."

"It ain't," Hazel agreed.

"Mama, where are the brown sugar peaches?" Silas asked. He was scowling at the table.

"Hang on." Hazel pushed her chair back. "I forgot 'em."

Thomas stared Noah down from across the table. "How is that roof comin' along, cuz? Gramps says that fool drunk you hired smokes more'n he works."

Noah clenched his jaw. "It's fine. Everything is coming along just fine."

"We coulda been done by now."

"Really?" Noah leaned forward across the table. "You could have been done in a week? Last time I checked, it took a week for the two of you to get off the damn porch."

Hazel hurried back into the dining room, in her hands a Pyrex dish full of peaches. "Here you go." She squinted down at Silas. "You got chew in yer mouth?"

"No ma'am."

"Spit it out."

"I said I don't have none."

In one swift movement, Hazel slapped the side of her son's head so hard that a wad of tobacco came flying out of his mouth and landed in the middle of the bowl of peaches with a sickening plop. "Don't lie to yer mama, child."

"Sorry, Mama."

"Now yer gonna eat them peaches."

Caroline had to bite down on her lip to keep from laughing. Noah was sitting next to her looking horrified. She couldn't imagine something like this ever happening at her house. It had been a long time since anything much happened at their dinner table—well, anything she wanted to laugh about. "This meat is really good," she said, smiling over at Hazel.

"That was all Jep," Hazel replied. "He's been savin' it for a special occasion."

From across the table, Thomas rolled his eyes. "I don't see what's so special about tonight."

"The whole family is together tonight," Hazel said. "Don't happen too regular these days."

"What's left of the family," Thomas mumbled.

"Well, and whose fault is that?" Hazel shot back. "Neither one a you two did nothin' about it."

Caroline glanced around the table at the faces in front of her. "Are you all that's left of the family?"

"There are a few cousins down in the boot heel," Jep replied. "But they're distant cousins. Ain't nobody we claim."

"That means this'n here better get to makin' some babies." Thomas pointed his fork at Noah.

"How old are you, Caroline?" Silas wanted to know.

Caroline shifted in her seat. "I'm twenty-five."

"And you ain't married?"

"No."

"And you ain't got no kids?"

"No."

Silas sniffed. "Used ta be that the women stayed home. Took care of the kids and their man. Left the work up to them. Now it's different. Women runnin' around like they think they's men."

"Tell me now, Silas," Caroline said. She stabbed at a piece of meat with her fork. "What is it that you do? For a job?"

Silas knitted his eyebrows together, taken aback by her question. "I used ta work the farm when we had it."

"You don't have it anymore?"

187

"Got some cattle, but we ain't got what we used ta."

"So now you don't have any job?"

Silas scratched at his head. "I take care a my mama."

"Boy, you don't take care of me," Hazel cut in. "You live in my house."

"We help," Silas protested, the color in his cheeks starting to rise. "We do our share."

"I know ya do, baby." Hazel reached out to pat her son's hand as she stood up to collect the plates. "Yuns go on into the living room. I'll bring out the pie."

Caroline waited until Jep, Thomas, and the glaring Silas had retreated to the living room before she stood up. Noah was waiting for her. "Silas may never forgive you," Noah whispered. "My grandfather says he's never worked a day in his life."

"But he wanted you to hire them to roof the station?"

Noah shrugged. "I guess fifty isn't too old to suddenly acquire a work ethic."

Caroline giggled. "I reckon not." She felt Noah's hand on the small of her back, guiding her into the living room. The moments in his apartment earlier that afternoon came rushing back. Neither of them had mentioned what happened, and she wondered if he was thinking about it, too. It had been a long time since she'd navigated feelings like this, too long, and she wasn't sure she remembered how she was supposed to act. She sat down on the floral sofa in between Noah and Thomas.

"Honey, do you want some coffee with your pie?" Hazel smiled down at her.

"Yes, please."

"How do you take it?"

"Black is just fine."

"I knew I was gonna like you," Hazel said. She scuttled off into the kitchen.

Jep lowered himself down into one of the recliners. He rested his hands on his expansive belly and said, "Noah, when do ya think you'll be open for business?"

"I'm hoping by early fall."

"Just in time for the slow season."

"I don't mind to start slow."

"You been that way since you was a kid," Jep said. He was smiling at Noah. "It's nice to have you back here again, son."

Hazel brought the pie and coffee, and there was nothing but the scraping of forks against plates and slow sipping. Caroline finished her pie and looked about the room. "I'm excited about seeing the station open again," she said. "It's been mostly closed since I can remember."

"I closed it up not long after you was born," Jep said. "I tried rentin' it out, but it never made nobody a profit."

"I know my mom was sad about it being closed," Caroline offered. "She said it wasn't the same after the station was gone. She said it was too quiet."

Jep smiled. "Yer mama didn't like things too quiet."

"You're right about that." Like Jep said, it was ancient history by the time Caroline was born, but she'd been thinking about Jep Cranwell in connection with her mother more and more lately. The only thing Maureen O'Conner ever said about Cranwell Station was that it had gone quiet—too quiet—after it shut down. "Were you friends with my parents?" Caroline asked.

Jep and Hazel shared a look with one another. Hazel stood up and busied herself with clearing the plates and coffee cups. She didn't say anything, and she didn't look at Caroline.

"We was neighbors," Jep said at last. "Your daddy wasn't around much then—he was busy bein' a doctor. I helped yer mama out from time to time. We was friendly, but I don't know that we was friends."

Caroline wanted to ask Jep what that look between him and his sister meant, but something told her that she wouldn't get an answer. There were people in town who thought her mother was stuck-up, that she thought she was too good for everybody with her East Coast accent and strange habits. Maybe that's what Jep and Hazel thought, too. "My mother wasn't full of herself, if that's what you're thinking," Caroline blurted out. She couldn't stop herself. "She was just different. She grew up in New York."

Jep sat up straight in the recliner, his hands gripping the sides. "Is that what she told you? What I thought of her?"

Caroline shook her head. "No, not at all. She never talked about you. She never talked about any of you, except to talk about the station."

"Good," he said. He leaned back again. "There never was no reason to talk about none of us."

Caroline didn't know what that meant. She looked over to Noah, who just shrugged his shoulders and stood up. "Well, we should head out. Caroline still has to drive all the way back into Cold River."

Jep nodded. "Make sure one of the boys follows ya to the gate."

"I won't forget to lock it behind me," Noah replied.

"Have 'em follow ya, just the same."

Noah sighed. "Come on, Thomas."

"Ask Si. I don't feel like it."

"Fine."

Caroline stepped out onto the porch with Noah on her heels. Silas was sitting on the porch, smoking what was left of the pipe. He glowered over at the two of them, obviously still stung by the conversation at the table.

"Si, I need you to follow me to the gate," Noah said.

"Fine." Silas puffed on his cigar. "I'll be along."

"You can ride to the gate with us."

"I'll just walk."

Noah didn't say anything as they started driving back towards the gate. He was staring out into the darkness in front of them. "Did you have fun?" he asked once they were back onto the gravel road.

"I did," Caroline said. "Everyone was really nice, well, except for Silas."

"He can't help himself," Noah replied.

"I know."

"My grandfather thought it was funny that you pushed his buttons."

"He was nicer than I expected him to be."

Noah turned his head towards her, momentarily taking his eyes off the road. "He doesn't dislike you, not at all."

"He doesn't like me much, though."

"It's complicated with him," Noah said. "His health isn't what it used to be, and that doesn't help."

"I noticed he didn't have his oxygen tank," Caroline said. "At dinner."

"Today was a good day, I think."

"You sound like me," Caroline replied. "When I'm talking about my mother."

"He doesn't like to use his tank in front of people," Noah said. "It embarrasses him. I think that's why he doesn't go out into Cold River as much anymore. He thinks it makes him look weak."

"It doesn't."

"Try telling him that."

"Do you think he and my mother were better friends than he's letting on?" Caroline asked. She was thankful for the darkness of the car. It would have embarrassed her to ask otherwise.

"What do you mean?"

"I mean, do you think that they were friends, you know, like the way you and I are friends?"

"We're friends?"

When they pulled up in front of the station, Caroline realized that she didn't want the night to end. She wasn't ready to go home. She turned to Noah and said, "Do you want to see something amazing?"

Noah raised an eyebrow.

"I'm serious," Caroline said. She opened the door to the car. "Come on, we'll take my truck."

"Where are we going?"

"You'll see."

Chapter 16

Caroline drove back past the turnoff for Cranwell Corner, driving farther down the gravel road than she had in years. They drove until she took a left at a folded-over "Dead End" sign.

"Where are we?" Noah asked, uneasy next to her.

"We're here," Caroline replied.

"Should I be hearing banjo music or something?"

"Just get out." Caroline reached past him and pounded her fist against the front of the glove compartment. She pulled out a flask. "I about forgot this was in here."

Caroline slid out of the driver's seat and pulled down the tailgate. In a second, Noah was next to her. "So what are we doing?"

"Look up."

He did as he was told. "I see stars," he said. And then, after a minute, he said, "Whoa, I see stars."

"Pretty cool, huh?" Caroline handed him the flask. "I didn't figure you saw too many of them in New Jersey."

"You figured right."

"I used to come here all the time when I first got my license," Caroline said. "I've about decided that it's the best place in the whole world to look at the stars."

"I've been to a lot of places." Noah handed Caroline back the flask. "And most of those places have been beautiful, but I don't think I've ever seen quite so many stars."

"I haven't been out here in years."

"How come?"

"I don't know. Got busy, I guess. This place

may be small, but something always needs doing."

"I suppose every place is a little like that."

"Don't get me wrong, this is my home and I love it," she continued, "but what they say about small towns is totally true—if you don't know what you're doing, someone else is bound to know and can tell you all about it. I guess you're experiencing a bit of that right now."

"You've got that right," Noah replied.

"I think they mean well."

"Just because they're my family doesn't mean that they mean well."

"I know."

"It's not that I don't think they mean well. It's just that it's been a long time since I've had a family," Noah added.

"What do you mean?"

Noah lay back into the bed of the truck. "We left when I was five. My mother hated them. She used to tell me that after my father died they didn't want us anymore. She told me that's why we had to move."

"Those are awful things to say." Caroline lay back next to him.

"My mother says a lot of awful things."

"Surely you know that's not true," Caroline replied. "What your mother said."

"I do now," Noah said. "But no matter how nice my grandfather was or how much he tried to do for me, my mother always made sure I thought that he didn't really mean it."

"I'm so sorry, Noah."

"It's okay," Noah replied. "I mean, it's not, but I got away from her a long time ago."

"Is that why you joined the Navy, to get away from your mom?"

Noah shook his head. "I got away from my mother when I was fourteen."

"Where did you go?"

"I lived with friends, mostly."

"Why didn't you come back here?"

"I know my mother wasn't the best mother, but she was still my mother, you know?" Noah turned his head to look at Caroline. "I figured if she didn't want me, she was probably right about how my family here didn't want me. It was wrong, I know that now, but at the time, it's what I thought."

Caroline felt her heart break into a million little pieces. She wanted to reach out and take his hand. She wanted to tell him that everything was going to be okay. She turned and looked at Noah. His hands were clasped behind his head, and his eyes were closed. His chest moved up and down in a slow, rhythmic kind of way that made her sleepy. She wondered what his heartbeat sounded like.

"I don't know your mother." Caroline stared back up at the sky. "But I do know that since you've been here nothing has been as awful as it could have been without you here, and I can't imagine anybody not wanting you."

Noah didn't say anything, but after a few moments, she felt his hand, warm and smooth, on top of hers. He curled his fingers up under her palm. Caroline couldn't remember the last time she'd had a conversation with a man, or anyone for that matter, that made her feel the way it felt when she talked to Noah. She felt as if she could stay right here, lying in the back of her rusty truck, staring up at the sky with him for the rest of her life.

Chapter 17

Ava Dawn stood in the dressing room at JCPenney in Cold River, her hands on her hips, waiting for Caroline to say something encouraging. It was one of the only stores in town with the exception of the Walmart that sold clothes. All of the newer shops were located up and away from the downtown, across town really, in little clusters. "Well?" she asked. "What do you think of this one?"

"It looks nice," Caroline replied, trying not to roll her eyes. "It looks just like the other four you've tried on."

"You're not bein' very helpful."

"They all look great!" Caroline threw up her arms, exasperated. "Why do you care so much about a dress you're just going to wear to church?"

"I want to look nice," Ava Dawn replied, looking hurt. "All my good clothes are still at Roy's. I'm tired of borrowing Aunt Maureen's dresses for Sundays."

Caroline eyed her cousin. "Are you sure you just don't want to look good for *Brother Crow?*"

"Would that be so bad?"

"You know it would be."

"I know, I know." Ava Dawn smoothed the tangerine-colored dress. "I just like to look proper on Sunday mornin' is all."

"That better be all," Caroline replied. "Now go get changed. I'm tired of standing in an ocean of polyester."

"You're my least favorite person to go shoppin' with." Ava Dawn pouted. "Uncle Max would even be better than you!"

Caroline knew that Ava Dawn was right. At least her father would have paid. Caroline hated going shopping, especially with her cousin. Ava Dawn spent *hours* trying on clothes and prancing around in front of mirrors. She sighed and waded back out of the dress department. Maybe she could find a new pair of boots or something.

As she made her way to the other end of the store, she saw a familiar face picking through the clearance lingerie. It was the girl Roy'd been with the night of the pie auction. She was concentrating so hard on a tiny pink thong that she didn't notice Caroline standing in front of her. Caroline backed up and hurried over towards the dressing rooms, but Ava Dawn was already in line with three dresses.

"I narrowed it down to three," Ava Dawn said. "Ain't they cute?"

"Can we come back and get them later?" Caroline asked. "I don't feel so good."

"I'm next," Ava Dawn replied. "Won't be but a minute."

"But I really don't feel good."

"You were fine five minutes ago."

The girl was coming towards them now, pink thong in hand. There was nothing Caroline could do to keep her cousin from seeing her. "I'm sorry," she whispered to Ava Dawn when the girl placed herself behind them in line.

Ava Dawn stiffened, but she said nothing. It wasn't until the girl got on the phone and began giggling and talking about her underwear that Ava Dawn turned around. "Honey, are you talking to my husband on that phone?"

"Let me call you back," the girl said. She slid her phone into her purse and looked Ava Dawn in the eye. "So what if I was?"

"He ain't a big fan of those things." She nodded her head towards the lingerie in the girl's hand.

The girl put the underwear behind her back and said, "Maybe he just ain't a fan of *you*."

Caroline braced herself for the inevitable. She

was sure that it was going to take herself and several sales associates to pry Ava Dawn off of the girl. If she hadn't been standing there so smug in front of them, Caroline might have felt sorry for her.

"What did Roy tell you about me?" Ava Dawn asked.

The girl looked from Ava Dawn to Caroline uncomfortably. "Umm . . ."

"Go on."

"He said you left him all alone," she said. She bit at her bottom lip, thinking. "He said you didn't love him, didn't take care of him. He said you didn't appreciate him none, either."

"How old are you?"

"Twenty-two."

Ava Dawn sighed. "I'm gonna tell you the truth now, and it'll be up to you what to do with it, you understand?"

The girl nodded.

"I'm sure Roy's bein' real nice to ya right now, ain't he? Takin' you out on the town, buyin' you stuff. I bet he's been real sweet so far," Ava Dawn said. She handed Caroline the dresses she'd been holding. "Look at my arms." She held out her arms for the girl to see. "You see those? Those tiny round scars?"

The girl nodded.

"Those are cigarette burns from two months after Roy'n me got married. I forgot to pack his favorite chips in his lunch." Ava Dawn pulled up her T-shirt to just above her navel. "You see those scars? The ones that go across my belly? Those are from when I came home from work one morning too exhausted to do the laundry."

The girl took a step back from Ava Dawn.

"He broke my nose last summer. He broke my wrist summer before that," Ava Dawn said. "I stayed with him after all of it. I loved him, you know?" She shrugged. "I reckon I love him still. But I don't deserve that, and honey, neither do you."

"Ma'am?" The salesgirl drummed her fingers against the countertop. "Are you ready to pay for those?"

Ava Dawn took the dresses out of Caroline's hands and placed them on the counter. "Sure am." She didn't say anything else to the girl behind them, and Caroline watched as the girl hurried back over towards the lingerie section, threw the panties back into the clearance bin, and ran out of the store as fast as her legs would carry her.

Chapter 18

"Are you sure you want me to cancel your mom's nurse?" Max O'Conner asked his daughter. "You know I won't be home until late."

"It's fine," Caroline replied. She'd woken up the

next morning feeling like she and her mother ought to have a day together—something the two of them rarely did. "You're always telling me I need to get out more and that you can handle Mom alone. So can I."

"Alright, alright." Her father held his hands up in the air.

"Besides," Caroline continued, "nobody can be out at the shop to look at the air for two more days. I can't spend another blistering day inside. It was 115 degrees in there yesterday by noon!"

"Did you call Boyd's?"

"They're the only ones in town."

"Alright, well, you two have fun today, and try to stay out of trouble."

"I make no promises!" Caroline hollered as he walked out the front door.

After her father left, Caroline led her mother outside, and they both sat down in the rocking chairs on the porch. It was a beautiful morning. Caroline wanted to savor every minute of it before the sun got too high above their heads.

"It feels nice out here," her mother said, stretching her legs out lazily.

"Yes, it does."

"I love to sit out here."

"We should do it more often," Caroline replied. Her mother used to spend every morning out on the porch. She'd sit in one of the rocking chairs and drink her coffee, waving and chatting with people as they passed by. One of the neighbors had a pig named Clementine, and he would walk his pig down the road every morning. The neighbor stopped to chat with Maureen O'Conner, and the pig would enjoy special treats Caroline's mother kept in a little jar on the front porch.

One morning the neighbor stopped by, and Caroline's mother didn't know who he was. She was afraid of the pig and got so flustered she couldn't get back inside of the house. It was the last time their neighbor walked Clementine down their street, and it was the last time Maureen sat outside on the porch without someone else to sit next to her.

Caroline remembered feeling embarrassment swell up inside of her when she opened the front door to find her mother huddled down behind one of the rocking chairs, screaming at the man to get away from her and to take his rabid animal with him. The embarrassment sat like an inflated balloon inside her throat and kept her from doing anything except staring at her mother helplessly until her father rushed outside and calmed her mother down enough to get her back to bed, where she stayed for the rest of the day.

"Do you want to go inside and have some breakfast?" Caroline asked, feeling a small surge of panic at the memory. "I'll make us some coffee."

"I'd like that."

Caroline helped her mother back inside and got

her settled on the couch with her knitting. "I'm going up to the attic for just a minute," she said once the coffee was ready. "I'll be right back."

"Okay," her mother replied.

Caroline pulled down the staircase to the attic and began climbing up. There was something that had been bothering her since the first time Caroline saw Noah, and she thought he looked familiar to her, but she couldn't figure out why. Then when she had dinner at the Cranwells, Jep said that her mother hadn't exactly been a friend, but there was something about the way he said it . . . something about the looks he shared with his sister. There had to be more going on than everyone was telling her.

She pulled at the string to turn on the light and glanced around the room. There were boxes everywhere, but she was looking for a specific one. She knew where she'd seen Noah before, only it wasn't Noah Cranwell she'd seen; it was Jep Cranwell, and it was in a picture in one of her mother's photo albums in the attic. She looked down at the dusty boxes. She couldn't remember the last time she'd been up here, but it took her exactly two minutes to find the picture. It was in her mother's album with pictures from the bait shop. Caroline flipped through the album. There were pictures of the shop being built, there were pictures of her mom, dad, and brother standing in front of the shop at the grand opening, and there, at the end, was the picture she'd come for. It was faded and blurry, taken with an old Polaroid camera, but she knew the two people smiling in the photo—it was her mother and Jep.

Jep was smiling.

Her mother and Jep were sitting on the steps of the shop, her mother's wild hair was everywhere and she had about sixty bangle bracelets on her wrists, and Jep was in overalls and with bare feet. They looked happy.

Caroline carried the album back down the ladder with her and into the living room. Her mother and Yara were in the same positions in which she'd left them. She sat down next to her mother. "Hey, Mom, can I show you something?"

"Sure." Her mother continued to knit.

"Can you put down your knitting?"

Maureen O'Conner set the knitting into her lap, and Caroline placed the album between them. "Mom, do you know the man in the picture?" She pointed to Jep Cranwell.

Her mother squinted down at the picture. After a few seconds, she peeled back the plastic page and took the picture out. "That's me there, you know," she said. "I was so young then."

"You were beautiful, Mom."

"Wasn't I?" Her mother held the picture up closer to her face.

"What about the man you're sitting next to?" Caroline asked. "Do you know him?"

"His wife died," her mother said. "Cancer. He was very sad."

"I didn't know that."

Maureen O'Conner nodded. "It was a long time ago. When his son was small. He raised him alone, all alone, and he was so sad. But look here." She pointed to the picture. "Look how he's smiling."

Caroline watched her mother stroke the picture with her thumb. She was lost in her thoughts, and Caroline wished she knew just the right words to say to unlock what was inside. "I'm glad you were his friend."

"Yes," her mother murmured. "I was his friend, and he was mine . . . my friend."

"How come you never told me about any of this before?"

Caroline's mother turned the page in the album. "That's my son," she said, pointing to a picture of Jeremy and Max O'Conner fishing. "He died, too, didn't he?"

Caroline swallowed. "Yes, a long time ago."

Both women looked up when the doorbell rang. Caroline hadn't been expecting anyone, and it was odd for someone to be there in the middle of the morning without calling first. She handed her mother the album and answered the door.

"Hello, Carolina." Reese Graham stood in front of her, smiling like it was Christmas. "I saw your truck parked outside when I was driving by."

"What were you doing driving by?"

"To see if your truck was parked outside."

Caroline couldn't help but grin. "Come on in."

"Hello, Mrs. O'Conner," Reese said when he stepped inside. "How are you today?"

"Fine, thanks."

"I've called you a few times," Reese said, walking farther into the house. "God, it hasn't changed a bit in here."

"I know you have," Caroline replied, following him. "It's the busy season at the shop. You know I don't have a lot of time."

"You have time to go out drinkin' with Tyler and Kasey, but you don't have time to call me back? That hardly seems fair."

"Well, life's not fair."

"You sound like your father."

Caroline looked over at Reese. He was standing in the entryway of the dining room. He'd shaved, probably just before coming over, and smelled like some kind of expensive aftershave. His reddish hair had been cut back since she'd seen him at the river. His ruddy complexion, however, hadn't changed. It told her that he was still drinking far more than he should. "What are you doing here, Reese?"

"I came to take you to lunch."

"I can't go to lunch with you today."

"Why not?"

Caroline sighed. "I'm staying with my mom today."

"She can come."

"No," Caroline replied. "She can't."

"Look, I don't know why you're acting like I'm some sort of scab," Reese said. "I'm the one who should be sore at you still."

"I don't think you're a scab."

"Then why won't you go to lunch with me?" Reese was grinning, and Caroline realized he was teasing her.

"You know why."

"I told you that was all water under the bridge, didn't I?"

"You did." Caroline sat down at the dining room table. "But I don't believe you."

"Pretty full of yourself aren't you?"

"You're one to talk."

Reese sat down across from her. "This is why I liked you so much, Carolina," he said. "Talking to you is always so much fun."

"But you didn't love me, did you?" She didn't know why she said it.

"You cut right to the chase, huh?"

"You didn't," Caroline said. "And you don't now."

"You're right." Reese straightened up. "But it didn't keep me from being angry all those years ago."

"I'm sorry about that," Caroline replied. "I didn't mean to hurt you."

"I know you didn't," Reese said. "I never

should've put you in that position to begin with."

"Well." Caroline straightened herself up. "What was it you said? It's all water under the bridge."

Reese gave her one of his signature lopsided grins. "Does this mean we can go to lunch now?"

"I told you I can't," Caroline said, gesturing to her mother.

"How about I go pick something up? Maybe Chinese?"

"I can't," Caroline said. "But maybe you can catch Court before his shift starts."

For a moment, Reese looked hurt. "Good plan," he said, clapping her on the back. "Old Court always pays!"

Once he was gone, Caroline made her way back over to her mother. She was still sitting on the couch with the album out on her lap, the picture of Jeremy still face up.

Maureen O'Conner closed the album. "I think I'd like to go lie down now."

"Okay," Caroline replied, helping her mother off the couch. "Let me help you back to your bedroom."

"You're nice," her mother said, patting Caroline's arm. "My regular nurse can be gruff sometimes, but I like her, too."

"I'm glad."

"You're nice," her mother said again. "What's your name? I want to tell my nurse to send you again."

Caroline sat down on the bed, willing herself not to cry. "Caroline," she said at last. "My name is Caroline, and I'll come and stay with you anytime you'd like."

"That's a pretty name," Maureen O'Conner replied, sitting down next to her daughter. "That's a very pretty name."

Chapter 19

"You're gonna need a new motor," the repairman said. He was sweating through his Boyd's Heating and Air uniform. "This unit is from 1979. I don't even know if I can find a motor."

"It took you a week to get out here, and now you want to tell me you can't even do your job?" Caroline asked.

"Look, lady, I've been outside for over an hour trying to fix your ancient unit," the repairman replied. "Do you want me to try to order the part or not?"

Caroline sighed. "Yeah, I guess."

"I'll give you a call once I get back to the shop," he said. "Try to stay cool."

"Oh, you're a comedian, too?" Caroline said to his back as he walked out of the shop. "Hilarious!" She was about to say more, but stopped when she saw Noah coming up the steps.

"Good luck," the repairman said to Noah.

"What's his problem?" Noah asked once he got into the shop. "Holy shit, it's awful in here."

"I don't know what his problem is," Caroline replied. "I'm a delight, and yes, it is awful in here, and it is going to keep being awful because the air conditioner is apparently older than I am."

"Is that why the shop has been closed for the last three days?"

"Yep."

"Good," Noah said. "Because I was beginning to think that you were avoiding me."

Caroline grinned. She'd thought about calling him, but then she'd realized she didn't have his number. Then she thought about coming out just to see him, but she was afraid he would think that was weird. So she'd stayed home with her mother and given the nurse a break. "I wasn't avoiding you; I was avoiding dying from heatstroke."

"I think that's still a real possibility."

"I know." Caroline blew a piece of damp hair out of her eyes. "I can't keep this place closed down. I'm losing too much business."

Noah looked around the shop. "Unless people can crawl into those coolers with the bait, I don't think anybody is going to want to come in here."

"I'm going to go into town and buy a couple of window units," Caroline said. "That will keep me from dying at least until tomorrow."

"Do you want some company?"

"You want to go buy air conditioners with me?"

"Sure."

Caroline looked up at him. He was looking down at her with those dark eyes of his. Part of her wanted to see if he would take her back upstairs to his place, where the air-conditioning worked, and finish what they'd started days before. But neither of them had mentioned it since, and she was starting to believe that perhaps it had been a mirage from the heat. "Okay," she said. "But you're driving."

The Cold River Walmart was located right in the big fat middle of town. It was like the Mecca of the county, a super Walmart, and all roads led there.

Noah stood out in front of the store and stared up at it. "I don't think I've ever seen a Walmart so big."

"Are you sure you've ever even seen one at all?" Caroline replied. "Come on, it'll save time if we go through lawn and garden."

"Look at all these cars," Noah marveled. "I didn't even know there were this many people in town!"

Caroline rolled her eyes. "Just come on."

They walked through the doors and into an ocean of plastic lawn ornaments, plastic lawn furniture, and charcoal and gasoline grills. "Do they sell everything here?" Noah wanted to know.

"Have you seriously never been inside a Walmart?"

"It's been a long time," Noah admitted. "Most of

the places I've lived didn't have them. They're not very popular in more urban areas."

"Lucky you," Caroline grumbled. "I hate this place."

"Why?"

"Because it's crowded, I always see someone I know when I'm looking particularly awful, and even when I go in for just one thing, I end up coming out with 200 dollars' worth of crap."

"Hey, I need this." Noah picked up a double pack of Old Spice deodorant. He threw it into the cart Caroline was pushing. "I need toothpaste, too."

"No," Caroline said. "No, we are not here to shop for you. We're here to get air conditioners and get out."

"Aw, come on," Noah replied. "I haven't done any shopping since I got here. I'm out of everything."

His eyes were dancing around excitedly, and Caroline couldn't help but laugh. She'd never in her life seen someone so excited to be inside a Walmart. "Fine," she relented. "But when we get back to the shop, you've got to help me install the air conditioners."

"Like I wasn't going to have to help you do that anyway," Noah said. He slid one of his hands onto the cart and said, "I'll push."

Caroline followed beside the cart, watching him throw random things inside of it. "Is there anything you don't need?"

"Nope." Noah handed her a can of shaving cream. "I've been living out of a suitcase for a decade. Everything I own is travel sized."

"You've been all over the world," Caroline said, crossing her arms over her chest.

"Yep."

"And the inside of a Walmart in Cold River, Missouri, excites you?"

"Yep."

"You are a ridiculous person."

"Oh, I'm a ridiculous person?" Noah put the razors he had in his hands back on the shelf. "The first time I met you, your three-legged *Tibetan mastiff* tried to eat my shirt."

"Yara would never have eaten your shirt," Caroline said, pretending to be offended. "She's a lady."

Noah began to laugh. "I'm pretty sure that my shirt would disagree."

"I guess I owe your shirt an apology."

"You do." Noah pulled her into the aisle with him.

Caroline allowed him to pull her up close to him. She wasn't sure if he was playing or if he was serious by the way he was looking at her. "People are staring at us."

"I thought it was me they were all staring at."

"This time it's both of us."

"Let them stare." Noah pulled her closer still, so close that his lips brushed against hers.

Caroline felt every muscle in her body tighten, and she wished like hell they weren't standing in an aisle at Walmart, but instead somewhere private. From over Noah's shoulder she saw a familiar face. It was Reese, and he was walking right towards them.

"Carolina?"

"Oh, hey, Reese." Caroline pulled herself away from Noah. "What's going on?"

"Just gettin' the necessities." He was grinning like a Cheshire cat at the two of them. "What are you two doin' here?"

"We're just here looking for air conditioners."

"Hey, man, I'm Reese." He stuck out his hand to Noah. "I don't think we've actually met."

"Noah."

"Oh, sorry," Caroline said, her cheeks flushing. "I should have introduced you."

"Hey, it's alright," Reese said, turning his attention away from Noah. "So that air's still not fixed, huh?"

"Nope." Caroline looked down at her feet. She didn't know why she felt so awkward, but she did. "I don't even know if it can be fixed."

"Did you call those morons at Boyd's?"

"They're the only morons in town."

Reese sighed. "Why didn't you just call me? You know I would have come over and taken a look at it. I told you that the other day when I stopped by your house."

Caroline had known. She'd even considered calling him in a moment of 100 degree weakness. "I'm just not used to you being around."

Reese put his hand on her shoulder. "Well, get used to it." He looked back over at Noah and said, "It was nice to meet you, man."

"Yeah, you, too."

As Caroline watched Reese walk away, she could feel Noah's eyes on her. When she turned back around, he was busy surveying the razors again. He threw a package in the cart and pushed forward. "Let's go find the air conditioners" was all he said.

They walked in silence for a few minutes. Finally, she said, "I've known Reese since elementary school." She wasn't sure what to say, but the silence was grating on her.

"I remember your cousin mentioning him."

Caroline ran her hand down a line of box fans. "He was more than my friend for a little while," she said. "He was my boyfriend."

"I remember her mentioning that, too."

"He works for Burlington Northern, you know, the railroad?"

"Good job."

"It is," Caroline replied. "Really good. More than most people around here can hope for."

Noah stopped the cart. "Is that why he was your boyfriend?"

"No."

"Does he want to be your boyfriend again?"

"No," Caroline said. "And I don't want him to be my boyfriend."

"Good."

A little thrill ran through Caroline's body as she stared at him. She wanted to ask him what he meant, but she didn't want to push it, to push *him* away from her. *Not all men are like Roy and Reese,* she thought. *Some men are calm and even. Some men are like my father.* The more Caroline thought about it, though, the more she realized she didn't want either one of those kinds of men. She wanted, well, she wasn't sure what she wanted, but she hoped more than anything that he was standing right there next to her in the Cold River Walmart.

Chapter 20

Reese Graham had been the most popular boy at Cold River High School. His parents had money, family money, and nothing was ever too big or too much for Reese. He threw parties every night of the week in the summertime, and although Caroline was never allowed to go, Ava Dawn always came back with stories of moonshine and skinny dipping and so much fun that nobody ever left before sunrise.

While Caroline wanted to go and pined for the

freedom her parents would not give her, Court flat out refused any part of that world. "He's trouble. Pure and simple" is all he would say, acting much more like Caroline's father than her friend. They were all seniors in high school before Caroline got up the courage to lie to her parents about where she was going. And after that, despite feeling guilty about this lie, there was no turning back.

Although Reese never paid much attention to her when they were in high school, things were altogether different once she came home to take care of her mother. Court told her that it was because he'd already been through all the women in Cold River, but Caroline ignored him. She'd seen him give Reese long looks during high school when he thought no one was watching, and even though she knew it might hurt Court just a little, Caroline was flattered when Reese asked her out for the first time. After a while, it was the three of them—Court, Reese, and Caroline, hanging out every spare second they got, and if it bothered Court, well, he never let on that it did.

That first year hadn't felt like she'd come home to care for her sick mother. Caroline still went out with Reese all the time, and her mother's health was still good enough that most days were good days. It was when Maureen O'Conner's Alzheimer's began to worsen that Caroline realized Reese was coming around less and less.

He called her less and less. He said it was because he was preparing to leave for his new job, but Caroline knew better—hell, everyone knew better.

"I don't like him much," her father admitted after Caroline told him she'd broken up with Reese. "I can't say I'm sorry to hear it."

Caroline knew her father wasn't trying to make her feel worse, but he was. Her mother wouldn't have said those things. She longed for her mother to pat the cushion next to her on the couch and ask her daughter to tell her all about it—to listen to her mother talk about the boys she'd dated long ago, to feel safe knowing that her mother always said the right thing, always made her feel better. It was the first time since her mother had been diagnosed that Caroline realized what the diagnosis really meant—that she was losing her mother.

Caroline stayed in bed for days after that, not talking to anyone—not her father, not Court, and most especially not her mother. Talking to her only made her sad, and Caroline allowed everyone to think that she was heartbroken about Reese—about the cheating and the parties and the lying, because it was easier than admitting the truth. It was easier than admitting that she felt angry and selfish and sad all at the same time. All she wanted was her mother, and no matter what she said or did, her mother was never coming back to her.

And she hadn't even been allowed to say goodbye.

Chapter 21

Caroline gripped the window, willing it to open up, but it wouldn't budge. "I don't understand why this damn window won't open."

"Do you want some help?" Noah leaned against the countertop, a Coke in one hand.

"I can do it," Caroline replied. "It's just being stubborn."

"It's not just the window being stubborn," Noah replied, taking a drink. "I doubt those windows have been opened since the air conditioner was installed."

Caroline ignored him. All she needed to do was get a couple of window units put in and turned on, and then she could leave. Tomorrow, she could stay inside the shop all day with the doors closed and not suffocate and not have to deal with Noah or Reese or anyone else who wasn't interested in buying a Styrofoam cup full of earthworms. "I've almost got it."

"If you say so."

She gave the window one more push with the bottom of her palms and the wood splintered off in her hands. Caroline fell back onto the floor, still holding the wood. She lay back and stared up at the ceiling, resisting the urge to stomp her feet like a petulant child.

"Do you want my help now?" Noah stood over her, grinning.

"No." Caroline sat up. "I'm done for the day. I'm going home, and I'm going to seriously consider burning this place to the ground."

Noah stuck out his hand. "Get up. I want to show you something."

Caroline waved his hand away from her. "I already know you can open the window."

"Not that," Noah replied. "Come on." He led her across the street and over to the station. "Stay right here. I'll be back."

"What are you doing?"

"Getting a flashlight."

"What for?" Caroline hollered. "It's still daylight."

Noah emerged a few minutes later with a flashlight tucked under one arm. "I'm going to show you something, but you have to promise that you won't say anything to anybody about it."

Caroline crossed her arms across her chest. "You're freaking me out a little."

"Do you promise?"

"I promise."

Noah led her around the station and back into the thick brush behind the building. It had been a long time since anybody kept up with the land, and Caroline found herself wishing she'd worn jeans and boots instead of cutoff shorts and flip-flops. "I'm going to be covered in seed ticks and chiggers by the time we're done out here," she said.

Noah batted at the brush with his flashlight. "You won't care in a few minutes."

The farther back they walked, the more curious Caroline became. They'd moved so far back that she could no longer see the station or her shop. She couldn't see the road or the river. All she could see was Noah in front of her and sunscorched land behind her. "This is all Cranwell land, isn't it?"

"Yep," Noah said. "This goes all the way back to my grandfather's house."

"Do you own it all?"

"I do."

"Even his house? And your aunt's house?"

"Uh-huh." Noah stopped at a rocky ledge. He peered over the top. "It's about a three foot drop from here. Think you can make that?"

"In flip-flops?"

Noah jumped down into the gorge. "Here, give me your hand."

Caroline sat down, scooting to the lip of the ledge on her bottom. She reached for his hand and propelled herself down. She landed with a thud next to Noah, gravel digging into the foam soles of her flip-flops. "I'm never going to get back up there without a forklift."

"We're almost there," Noah said. He grabbed Caroline's hand. "It's just right around the corner."

When they rounded the rocky ravine, Caroline saw something she never expected to see. But there it was, right in front of her, partially hidden by foliage. "Whoa, it's a . . ."

"Cave," Noah finished for her. "Cranwell Cave, to be exact."

"I didn't know there was a cave within miles of here," she said. "The closest caves I know of are at Grand Gulf, but that's over in Oregon County."

"Most of the people who knew about this cave are long gone," Noah replied. "Do you want to go inside?"

"Are you kidding me?" Caroline could hardly contain her excitement. "Of course I want to go inside!"

"Follow me." Noah switched on his flashlight. "It can get tight through the entryway, but it'll widen out."

Caroline stuck close to Noah as they entered the cave. After a few seconds, the opening gave way to a huge room, and a blast of cold air hit her in the face. It took a second for Caroline's eyes to adjust. "It feels great in here," she said, her voice echoing off of the cave's walls.

"I know," Noah replied. "It's not a huge cave. This is the main room, but there are three or four passageways that give way to other rooms. The rest of the passageways are too small for people to get through, so I know there are caverns farther down that haven't ever been seen."

"How long have you known about this place?"

"A long time," Noah said. He handed Caroline the flashlight. "My father showed it to me just before he . . . before he died. He made me swear I wouldn't tell my grandfather."

Caroline shone the flashlight around the cave and stopped at a dripping stalactite. "Why would you want to keep this a secret?"

"Jep Cranwell keeps everything a secret," Noah replied. "But at least with the cave he had a good reason. Here, let me see the flashlight."

Caroline handed it over.

Noah shone the light high on the walls. "Do you see what's up there?"

Caroline squinted. "It looks like lamps on a string?"

"Gas lamps," Noah said. "The whole cave is full of them."

"Why?"

"Because my great-grandfather needed the light." Noah led her back farther into the room. "It would have been hard to have a speakeasy without some light."

"You're kidding me." Caroline couldn't believe it. "Your family had a speakeasy *in a cave?*"

"Sounds crazy, I know," Noah said. "But look." He shone his light onto the remnants of something wooden. "There was a bar back here, and even a little stage for music."

"I read about this," Caroline said. She placed

her hands on one of the wooden planks. "There are others like this one, here in Missouri. But I never imagined there would be one across the road from me."

"Now that I own the land, I've thought about making it public," Noah said. He sat down on what was left of the damp stage. "But my grandfather would never forgive me."

"I don't understand why it matters," Caroline replied. "If he'd done it himself, he could have saved the station with the money."

"My grandfather hates money." Noah laid the flashlight down next to him. "He hates it almost as much as he hates people in his business. He would never tolerate people he doesn't know crawling all over his land."

"But it's your land now."

"I own it, that's true, but I respect my grandfather too much to do something like that," Noah said. "Maybe someday, but for now, this has got to stay our secret."

"Of course. I just can't believe it's all true."

"This is the only evidence left that my family was involved in making moonshine."

"Everybody knows that the Cranwells still have stills out here in these hollers."

"But can you prove it?"

"I guess not."

"It's all just become Ozark folklore, and that's how my grandfather likes it."

"I used to try to sneak out to Cranwell Corner when I was a kid. I'd tell my mom I was going fishing and then walk all the way down to that cattle gate. Once I even got brave enough to climb over it, but my mom caught me and about blistered my hide."

"What did you think you were going to find?"

"I don't know." Caroline shrugged into the darkness. "Sometimes I think my mother knew, and that's why she wanted to keep me away."

Noah scooted closer to her, filling up the space that was between them. "Ever since this afternoon, all I've been able to think about is getting you alone and undressing you."

Caroline could hear her heart pounding in her chest. It was so loud she was certain that it was echoing off the walls of the cave. "So this was all a ploy to get me alone in the dark?"

"Something like that." One of his hands wandered between her thighs.

Caroline wanted, more than she could ever imagine wanting anything, to let Noah undress her. Even in this damp, dark cave . . . especially in this damp, dark cave. She pulled him hungrily towards her; she felt like she was starving, as if she'd been starved, and she needed him closer to her, right up against her, inside of her.

Noah eased her down onto the wooden stage, hooking his thumbs through her belt loops and pulling down, kissing her belly, his mouth wet and hot against her skin.

Caroline watched his shadow in the dark as he raised himself up from on top of her, pulling at his clothes. She wished for the flashlight so she could see him, all of him, but instead she pulled him back down to where she was. Her fingertips grazed his body and she felt a jagged, puckered line of skin amidst the smooth skin of his back. It felt like a scar, but she couldn't tell, couldn't think about it.

Noah grabbed her hand where she was touching him, and laced his fingers through hers. "I've never met anyone like you."

When his free hand brushed against her panties, Caroline felt her whole body quiver. "I don't think I can wait any longer," she said.

Noah hovered over her, his teeth grazing her bottom lip. "Are you sure this is what you want?"

She'd been waiting forever for him, for this moment, as strange and silly as it sounded inside of her head. She knew that he was what she'd been searching for out here all these years. He was everything she wanted, but the only word she could muster was, "Yes."

This time Noah's hand did more than brush against her panties—it pushed aside the delicate fabric, his fingers lingering for just long enough to make Caroline even wetter with anticipation.

And then suddenly, without warning, he was inside of her.

Caroline gasped, breathing in for the first time in what felt like forever. Her lungs were on fire. Her face was on fire. Every piece of her was on fire, and there was nothing she could do to make it stop except meet Noah's rhythm with her own, lifting her hips to meet each thrust, to meet his lips on hers.

When they finally collapsed, intertwined together amongst scattered boards and dripping stalactites, Caroline could feel Noah's heart beating against her own chest, she could feel his sweat against her skin, and despite the cavern's blanket of darkness, Caroline could see, really and truly see, for the first time in a long time.

Chapter 22

On December 19, 1931, two members of the Ma Barker Gang shot and killed Sheriff C. Roy Kelly in West Plains, Missouri. The gang had been hiding out in Thayer, Missouri, for weeks when the sheriff was murdered in front of Davidson Motor Company. The night before, C. C. McCallon's clothing store was robbed of 2,000 dollars' worth of merchandise. Alvin "Creepy" Karpis and Fred Barker entered the store through a back window. The two men were only interested in the latest fashions. The most expensive socks, ties, gloves, sweaters, and shirts were stolen, as well as an expensive, diamond-encrusted lady's watch.

Barker, Karpis, and a young hitchhiker pulled into the garage needing two tires replaced. The garage owner, Carac Davidson, recognized the clothing two of the men were wearing as clothing that had been reported stolen. Additionally, the tread on the tires matched tire marks left at the scene of the crime. Quietly, Davidson slipped away to call Mr. McCallon to see if he could come down and identify the clothing.

As McCallon headed down to investigate, Sheriff Kelly came out of the post office. Davidson walked across the street to let the sheriff know what was going on at his garage. Sheriff Kelly proceeded to slip his gun under his coat and followed Carac Davidson over to the garage to question the men in the blue DeSoto.

Just as the sheriff got to the garage and opened the car door, Barker and Karpis began shooting. One of the men ran outside, reloading his pistol as he fled. Turning down an alley, he made his escape from the sheriff, McCallon, and Davidson. The blue DeSoto roared out onto the street, hitting the curb, and disappeared down East Main Street.

The Barker Gang escaped, and Sheriff Kelly was dead. The sheriff was shot twice in the chest and two more times in the left arm. His right hand was still inside his overcoat.

The people of West Plains began looking for the outlaws, but the only thing they found was a red scarf. A group of men went in search of the sheriff's killers, and crowds of people gathered in front of the police station, waiting to hear whether or not the gang had been caught. Even state lawmen came to West Plains to help with the manhunt, and they soon discovered that the gang had been hiding out in Thayer, a twenty-two-mile drive from West Plains.

Eventually, the abandoned DeSoto was found by a group of hunters. When they realized there were bullet holes in the back of the car, they knew something was wrong and called the law. After checking the registration, the lawmen discovered that the car belonged to Alvin Karpis.

When the lawmen arrived in Thayer, Missouri, they found an abandoned farm that had been rented by a Mr. and Mrs. Arthur Dunlop of Oklahoma. However, "Mrs. Arthur Dunlop" was *really* Ma Barker. The gang had been using the farm as a hideout, and it was rigged to make a bell ring inside the house if the front gate was opened. This allowed the gang to escape. Half of the clothes stolen from C. C. McCallon's store were found in the farmhouse, and more had been burned in a barrel outside. On the kitchen table, the lawmen found a map of the First National

Bank of West Plains. The gang clearly planned to rob the bank, but the incident at Davidson's spoiled their plans.

The Barker Gang left a trail of blood behind them when they went, killing a night watchman in Pocahontas, Arkansas, and a policeman in Monett, Missouri.

Three years after the murder of Sheriff Kelly, Ma Barker and her son, Fred, were killed in a bloody shootout in Florida, and a year and a half after their deaths Alvin Karpis was arrested in New Orleans by the head of the FBI, J. Edgar Hoover. Like so many of the gangs of the Midwest, the members of the Barker Gang died by gunfire or were remanded to prison. Decades later, it was still one of the most exciting things to have happened in the Ozarks.

Caroline learned about it in elementary school when her sixth grade class did a unit on local history. The story of the Barker Gang was by far her favorite. She went to the Cold River library the next day and tried to check out books about Ma Barker and other 1930s gangsters like John Dillinger and Baby Face Nelson, but the librarian told her she wasn't old enough to read about such violence and sent her home empty-handed. She was eventually able to convince her father to get the books for her with the promise that she wouldn't ask for a tommy gun for her next birthday.

In one summer, she devoured every book the library had to offer about the gangsters, and she was crestfallen when her father came home one evening empty-handed. "Alright," he'd said. "I can tell you some local lore, but don't you dare tell your mother or she will have my head. She doesn't like to talk about this kind of thing."

At once, Caroline was interested. It wasn't often that Max O'Conner did anything against the wishes of his wife. Her mother, for reasons unknown to Caroline, never liked to discuss local rumors, *especially* if the rumors had to do with the Cranwells. "Tell me!" she'd practically screamed with excitement.

That was the night that her father told her about their neighbors across the road from the bait shop, the owners of the old Cranwell Station. Caroline couldn't remember a time when the station had been occupied. Once in a while a man came to check on it—unlocking the door and staying inside for a few hours—but that was it. She'd tried asking her mother about it, but all she would say was, "It's been closed down almost as long as you've been alive."

Max O'Conner wasn't one for gossip, but what he told his daughter that night went beyond the stories old women tell each other over the phone on Sundays after church. It was the story of the Cranwells and their secret bootlegging operation. Caroline couldn't believe that the decrepit store across the road from the bait shop could hold such mysteries. "Did they still sell grain alcohol?" she wanted to know. Did any of the gangsters she read about ever frequent the joint?

Her father couldn't say for sure. After all, he hadn't been born until 1945, nearly twelve years after Prohibition ended. All he knew was what his father told him and what he heard about from the other boys at school whose fathers spent time out at Cranwell Station. As for him, Max O'Conner was never out that far without a sibling with him, just in case the eldest son got any wise ideas about sampling the wares, as the younger kids would surely tell their father.

Caroline remembered wishing after that her father hadn't been such a square. She wished that her grandfather had at least been out there one time so that there would be another story to tell. At school, none of her friends were interested in Cranwell Station. None of them were interested in long-dead gangsters. Even Ava Dawn, who tried so hard to placate her cousin, said that Caroline should find a better hobby, something cool like boys or music, and her father eventually tired of discussing the Cranwell clan, leaving Caroline to her books—the books she'd read time and time again.

Max O'Conner, while sympathetic to the poverty-stricken folks of Cold River, believed that everyone could dig themselves out of hard times if they simply worked hard enough; after all, that's what his parents had done. He didn't believe that there was ever a reason to turn to illegal activity like bootlegging moonshine like the Cranwells or running methamphetamine across state lines like Reese's family. Caroline's father saw those activities as lazy, driven by the need for instant gratification rather than a solid work ethic like the one he had. Although he never let it show while he owned his family practice, Caroline spent enough time with him throughout the years to know when he was silently judging someone. His stories about Cranwell Corner were tinged with an all too familiar disdain for his neighbors.

Maureen O'Conner, on the other hand, lived in a world of gray rather than black and white, having been the oldest of eight children in a strict blue-collar Roman Catholic family in New York. She'd seen struggle, a never-ending struggle that she'd fled the city and her family to escape. She argued for hours on end about the difference between generational poverty—the kind of poverty in which most of the townspeople lived, and situational poverty—the kind of poverty in which she and her husband had lived while Max was putting himself through medical school. "For us, there was always a light at the end of the tunnel," she'd said. "What kind of means might you resort to if there was no light for you? For your family?"

Her husband waved her off. "I wouldn't resort

to *that* kind of morally bankrupt activity, if that's what you're suggesting."

Maureen O'Conner only shrugged, winking over at her daughter. Her mother always let her father win in front of her, but Caroline knew that the conversation would continue long after her mother put her to bed that night. It had been one of Caroline's favorite things to do, to sneak into the hallway and listen to them argue. Their discussions were rarely angry, and they almost always ended with laughter and with her father saying, "I love you so much, Maureen."

Now Caroline longed for those kinds of conversations between her parents. She wished she could quietly watch them debate, and she wished more than anything that she could ask her mother more questions about the Cranwells. She wished she could ask about her friendship with Jep. Caroline wished she could confide in her mother about Noah.

She wished she could confide in her mother about anything.

Instead, she muddled through the last five years of her life hoping she didn't make a mess of things. *At least,* she thought, watching the air-conditioning repairman walking up the steps and inside the shop, *I haven't let this place fall down around me.* And for that, she knew her mother would be proud.

Jackie Dale, the repairman Boyd's sent out to

install the new motor, eyed Caroline cautiously. "Give her a whirl and see if she starts up."

Caroline did as she was instructed, and slid the switch over to "Cool." She let out a sigh of relief when the familiar whirr of the air kicked on seconds later.

"I got yer bill right here." Jackie Dale produced a smudged piece of paper.

Caroline glanced down at the bill—380 dollars was only a few more than she'd expected. "Hang on a second. I have a check for you." She emerged from the back room a few minutes later with a leather binder full of business checks. She hadn't written one in ages. Almost all of the monthly bills were paid online, even the local vendors. "Do you have a pen?"

Jackie Dale reached into his shirt pocket and handed her a black ballpoint pen. "I gotta say, Carolina, I wasn't expectin' you to be so agreeable."

Caroline knitted her eyebrows together. "What are you talking about?"

"Lloyd told me how you wasn't happy about the motor takin' so long to get here," he replied. "I figured you'd have somethin' to say about it, that's all."

Caroline scribbled her name down at the bottom of the check and replied, "Lloyd doesn't have the good sense God gave him to come in out of the rain. You've known me since high school, Jackie Dale. I've never been anything but nice to you."

"True enough," he agreed. "I reckon I was expectin' hell, more on account of I was friends with Roy."

"Oh." Caroline ripped the check from the binder. She'd forgotten about Jackie Dale and Roy being friends. She'd almost forgotten about Roy. She hadn't seen hide or hair of him since that night at the church. "Well, who you choose to be buddies with is your business."

"Will you tell Ava Dawn I said hello?"

"You can tell her yourself," Caroline replied, handing him the check. "Her number's still the same."

Jackie Dale managed a smile. "You never was one to mince words, was ya?"

"Nope."

"Well," he replied, waving the check in the air, "it was good seein' ya. You'll be cool as a cucumber in here in no time."

"I sure hope so," Caroline called after him. Jackie Dale had always been a nice guy. They'd never really been friends in high school—he was older than she was, in Roy's class, but he'd married one of the girls in her class, and they had a couple of cute kids. She didn't understand how he could still be a friend to someone like Roy. Surely he knew, just like everyone else knew, that Roy was a mean drunk and almost always drunk. It was the worst-kept secret in Cold River that he'd beat Ava Dawn senseless on more than one occasion. Maybe none of Roy's buddies said anything because they figured that he and Ava Dawn would get back together again, just like always. Or maybe they were just as scared of him as Ava Dawn was. Caroline didn't know, but she did know it was about damn near time that Roy Bean's reign of terror ended.

For good.

Caroline closed the shop to let it cool off. She decided the best way to clear her head was to go for a swim in the river, this time in the daylight when she wasn't drinking. Maybe the reason she'd been so nice to Jackie Dale was because really, the only thing she could think about was Noah and the cave and what she and Noah had done in the cave. She wasn't sure what she'd expected after they came back out into the sunlight, but Caroline, for one, felt completely changed, and it wasn't just because they'd made love. Noah had shown her something that, until now, nobody else except his family knew about. She hoped he understood just how much that meant to her.

Today, the heat was an added bonus for Caroline, because she had the river to herself, and that was just how she liked it. Most locals came fishing or swimming in the morning and evening to avoid the heat, and most of the tourists stayed indoors during the hot part of the day, as well.

Once she got herself situated and stripped down to her bathing suit, she was grateful for the heat on her bare skin. She couldn't remember the last time she'd worn her bathing suit. It didn't seem right that a girl could live so close to a body of water and not jump in every once in a while. She dipped her toe into the river. It was chilly, but it felt good.

Before Caroline knew it she was up to her waist in the water, wading through the current. She looked down at her threadbare bikini top and couldn't remember how long she'd had it, but it had been years and years. There were summers when she'd needed three or four bathing suits in three months, but that was when she spent more time swimming and fishing than she did helping her mother at the shop. Her first bikini had been given to her by Ava Dawn the summer they were thirteen. Ava Dawn had outgrown just about everything by then, and the still-waiting-to-develop Caroline became the proud owner of a wardrobe her mother would never let her wear out in public. The bikini was okay so long as she wore a shirt over it, something Caroline did only when her mother was present.

At twenty-five, Caroline figured she could probably still wear most of those clothes if she had them. As a kid, she'd hated being smaller than everyone. She'd hated when boys called her scrawny. She'd wanted to be tough like everyone said her brother had been. She wanted Ava Dawn's voluptuous curves, but despite her insecurities, summers in the Missouri heat kept her from being modest. Eventually, she learned to appreciate her small stature. Small didn't necessarily mean weak, and by the time she was eighteen, scrawny gave way to proportion.

Caroline dipped her head underneath the current. The river was pulling and pushing her, lulling her into acquiescence. She felt at ease in the water; she felt calm. Sometimes, the only way she could think clearly was to get into the water. She was so enjoying herself that she hadn't even noticed that someone was watching her, that someone had been watching her since she first stepped into the river. When she opened her eyes she saw Noah standing next to her fishing tackle, his arms crossed over his chest. He was wearing sunglasses that covered most of his face, but she could have seen the smirk set on his lips from a mile away.

She put one hand above her eyes to shield herself from the sun and hollered, "What are you doing here?"

"I live here," he called back. Noah stepped closer to the water's edge.

"You wanna go for a swim?"

Noah seemed surprised at the offer, taken aback for a few seconds before replying, "I don't like to swim."

"Oh yeah?" Caroline splashed towards him,

cupped her hands underneath the flowing stream of water, and splashed it up onto the bank, soaking Noah's shoes and pants in the process. "I seem to remember you jumping in the river after me at least once."

He moved back, emitting a noise from his throat that sounded more like something that would come out of Yara than a person. "That's because I thought you were drowning."

Caroline began to laugh, losing her footing and toppling into the water, her head submerging. By the time she came back up for air, Noah was stripped down to his boxer shorts, making his way out to where she was standing.

"You better start swimming!" he exclaimed, his hands just barely failing to catch her around her waist. "Shit! This water is freezing!"

Caroline swam her way to a shallow sandbar in the middle of the river. She continued to laugh while Noah continued to curse about the temperature of the water. He splashed his way over to the sandbar and plopped down beside Caroline. She tried not to stare at the way his boxer shorts clung to his skin, but she couldn't help it. She knew she was blushing thinking about what happened the last time he'd been this close to her. They hadn't really spoken since that afternoon in the cave, other than to wave hello or to have a brief conversation under the watchful eye of Ava Dawn or one of Caroline's customers.

She had hoped that he would come over and say something, *anything* that would let her know he didn't regret what they'd done.

"What are you thinking about?" Noah asked, scooting closer to her. He propped his elbows up on his knees.

"Nothing," Caroline lied.

"Your face is red."

"I'm probably getting a sunburn." Caroline tried to stand up. "I should head in."

"Wait." Noah reached out and pulled her back down to the gravel. "Seriously, what are you thinking about?"

Caroline's first impulse was to ask him why he cared. She didn't want to be skeptical of him, but she was skeptical of everyone. "I guess I'm just wondering why we haven't . . ." She paused. She didn't even want to hear herself say what she was about to say. "I'm wondering why we haven't talked about what happened in the cave."

"Shhhh . . ." he said. "The cave is a secret, remember?"

"What, you think the water might steal your secret?"

Noah laughed. "No, I'm not worried about that."

"Then what *are* you worried about?"

"You want the truth?"

Caroline felt her heart sink. She knew what was coming. "Yes."

Noah pressed his hands into the sandbar, little

pieces of rocks sticking to his palms. "The truth is that you're all I've been able to think about since then," he said. "I've been trying to get you alone for days, but I didn't want you to think I was too eager."

Caroline looked over at him. He was staring at her so intently that she felt like his eyes were cutting right through her chest. Before she could say anything, Noah reached over and pulled her closer to him, his lips gently brushing hers. "Give me a chance," he said, before standing up and splashing back across the river.

She pushed her fingers up against her still-tingling lips and watched him go. She waited until he was gone to wade back into the water. She knew she should probably go back up to the shop. It had probably more than cooled off by now. But the water just felt so good. Caroline knew wandering too far into the river would put her in way over her head, but something told her that maybe being in over her head was exactly what she needed.

Chapter 23

Caroline sat idly on Court's front porch, drinking a cool glass of his father's famous lemonade. Court was next to her, dozing off in the other rocking chair. It felt good to sit and do nothing. It reminded her of their lazy teenage summers. There was always a porch, and there was always lemonade.

"Think we'll still be here doing this when we're ninety?" Caroline asked, the ice in her glass tinkling as she brought it to her lips.

"I reckon rocking chairs will hover in the air by then," Court joked. "Hey, get me another glass of that, will ya?"

"You get it yourself."

"Please?"

"I think Tyler's right," Caroline said. "You need a wife."

Court opened his eyes and looked over at her. "I need a wife like I need a goddamned hole in my head."

"I bet a wife would get you lemonade."

"That's awful sexist of ya, ain't it?"

"Shut up." Caroline couldn't help but laugh. Court knew just how to pull her strings. It made sense that so many people thought they should get married. It made even more sense that so many people wondered why they hadn't. After she and Reese broke up, folks around town speculated that it was because of Court. They were sorely disappointed when the two of them hadn't run off together. If they knew the truth, that Court did love someone, but that it wasn't Caroline, well, it would have caused for more rumors than the town could have handled, she supposed. He was never going to have a wife. Begrudgingly she stood up and held out her hand. "Give me your damn glass."

"You're the best."

Caroline rolled her eyes and walked inside to the kitchen. Court's father was sitting at the kitchen table, reading the newspaper. A stack of at least twenty papers sat beside him. "Catching up?" Caroline asked him.

Joseph Brannan nodded. "I got a bit behind recently."

"Understandable." Caroline liked Joe. He was a nice man and didn't deserve most of what life handed him. Her father used to say if it wasn't for bad luck, Joe Brannan wouldn't have any luck at all, but Caroline thought that it was more opportunity than anything else. In another life, Court's father might have been a doctor. She filled the glass full and headed back outside.

Out on the porch, Court was staring down at his phone looking worried. "Well, shit," he said.

"What's wrong?" Caroline asked. "I thought you weren't on call today."

"I'm not."

"What's the problem?"

"Oh, Reese wants to come over and barbecue."

"Oh." Caroline nodded. "You want me to go on home?"

"What?" Court asked. "No, hell no, it's fine. It's just I don't think my dad is up to a barbecue just yet. Not the way Reese likes to barbecue."

"Tell him he can't invite anybody," Caroline said. "Surely he'll understand that your dad isn't up to a party."

"I told him." Court stuck his phone back into his pocket. "He says he won't bring nobody but himself."

Caroline sunk back down into the rocking chair. Leave it to Reese to spoil a perfectly lazy day.

Reese stayed true to his word and didn't bring anybody with him out to Court's house. Instead, he brought a cooler full of beer and four thick, Kansas City strips. "My dad butchered beef last week," he said, heaving the steaks onto the kitchen table in front of Court's dad. "These were the best-lookin' steaks."

Caroline rolled her eyes. It was always about showing off. "They do look good."

"You bet your sweet ass." He winked at Caroline. "And if I'm cookin' 'em, ain't nobody gonna have 'em cooked clean through."

"I prefer not to have my food bleeding," Caroline replied. "If it's all the same to you."

"I'll go get the charcoal started," Court said.

Joe Brannan folded his paper and laid it neatly on top of the others. "I reckon I better go get washed up."

Caroline and Reese were left alone in the kitchen. She took a beer out of his cooler and cracked it open. Now it really felt like high school. "You really have to bring KC strips out here?" she asked him. "Just to show off?"

"Huh?"

"Don't play dumb with me, Reese Graham. I know you too well."

Reese shrugged, pulling a beer of his own from the cooler. "I was just tryin' to be nice. I thought Mr. Brannan could use him a nice steak."

"The man just lost his wife and his house," Caroline replied. "No steak is gonna make him forget that."

"I'm not a complete asshole, you know," Reese said, setting down his beer and looking at her. "I don't know why you have such a low opinion of me. I was good to you when we were together."

"It's not about that," Caroline said. "Just be gentle with Court and his daddy right now, okay?"

"You like that Cranwell?" Reese asked. "What's his name? Noah?"

"It's not about that, either."

"You like him, though, don't you?"

"So what if I do?"

"I ain't gonna give you any shit for it, if that's what you're thinkin'."

"Can we just go back to how it used to be?" Caroline asked. "You know, back before . . . everything?"

"Only if you can handle seein' me out on the town with the ladies," Reese replied, wiggling his eyebrows at her.

"I'll try to control myself," Caroline replied dryly. *Besides,* she thought, *it won't be me you'll have to worry about.*

"So what does Court think about this Cranwell?"

Caroline shrugged. "I don't know. I haven't really asked him."

"Why not?"

"I doubt he cares too much."

"You know, I figured that you and him'd be shacked up by now."

Caroline glared over at Reese. *Like hell you did.* "Really? Is that what you thought?"

"Why not?"

"You know why not."

"I don't reckon I do," Reese replied easily. He looked away from her and down at his beer.

Neither one of them said anything until Court emerged from the back deck, carrying a pair of tongs. "Come on, you two. I sure as hell hope you don't expect me to do all of this cooking alone."

Chapter 24

Missouri's cash crop was rocks.

While some states had soil that grew cotton or tobacco or corn, Missouri had soil that grew rocks. A person didn't have to dig too deep to find them—hell, there were even state parks named after them like Elephant Rocks in Belleview and Johnson's Shut-Ins in Middle Brook.

Everywhere a person went, they'd find piles and piles of rocks in Missouri.

That was why working the land in Missouri meant owning a farm full of animals. Much of the time, especially in the Ozarks, the farm consisted of cattle—either beef or dairy. There were goat farms and pig farms and even a chicken farm or two. Some people had a mishmash of all of them, and the farmland stretched out for miles and miles as far as the eye could see throughout the hills of Cold River, Missouri.

Caroline stared at the rocks littering the yard at Roy and Ava Dawn's house. She couldn't count how many childhood summers she'd been tricked by an older cousin into picking up rocks to sell only to find out nobody wants to buy rocks when any yard comes with hundreds of them for free.

"So you're tellin' me," Ava Dawn said, rummaging through her purse for her keys, "that you went to Cranwell Corner for dinner and nothing interesting happened?"

Caroline pushed herself up from the porch steps. "No, what I'm telling you is that nobody offered me moonshine fresh from the stills or stabbed anybody in a knife fight."

"Sounds pretty boring."

"It was nice," Caroline said. "Weird, but kind of nice." She wanted to tell her cousin about what happened the day before—about the cave and about Noah—but she couldn't. She'd promised Noah she wouldn't tell anyone about the cave, and she figured that included everything that happened inside of it, at least until she could work through her own feelings about it.

"I still can't believe you got invited over there," Ava Dawn replied. She pushed her key into the lock. "My daddy used to tell me stories about how him and Uncle Max would go fishin' and Jep and his brothers would be there, but none of 'em ever talked. Didn't even look at each other. Kept to their own, ya know? Jep's daddy made them all quit school after the eighth grade."

"I remember those stories," Caroline said. "The thing is, I don't think Jep likes me very well."

"Why would you say that?"

"I don't know." Caroline shrugged. "Just a feeling I get. Although he was really nice at supper."

"He's just a crotchety old man," Ava Dawn replied.

"Maybe," Caroline said. That could be it, of course. Noah didn't seem to think it was anything to worry about. Still, she couldn't shake the feeling that all of this was tied up with her mother somehow.

"You should have told me about this before. It happened a damn week ago," Ava Dawn said, struggling with her keys in the lock. "This damn lock is so stubborn."

"I would have told you sooner, but you haven't even been home. If I didn't know any better, I would've thought you moved back in here with Roy."

"I told you it's over with me and him." She pushed on the door with her shoulder. "I've been pullin' doubles at the diner, and then Brother Crow has me at three Bible studies a week, and divorced women's counseling on Tuesdays."

"Why?"

"I need the money to save up for my own place."

"Not about the diner." Caroline rolled her eyes. "About all those Bible studies and the counseling."

"He says I need to *immerse myself* in the word of God." Ava Dawn shrugged. "I don't even know what that means."

"I didn't realize there were enough divorced women at church that you'd need a whole night of counseling."

"So far, it's just me, but Brother Crow says that will change soon."

"I think that's pretty weird, Ava Dawn," Caroline said.

"Shit!" Ava Dawn threw her key ring onto the porch. "Shit, shit, shit."

"What's wrong?"

"My key doesn't work!"

"Are you sure it's the right one?"

"Yes!"

Caroline peered down at the key, trying to push it into the lock. It didn't work. "He must've changed the locks."

Ava Dawn kicked at the front door. "That bastard."

"He knew you'd eventually try to get your stuff," Caroline said. "And he knew you'd do it while he was at work."

"I paid for everything in that dang house," Ava Dawn fumed.

"I can pick a lock. I've done it before." Caroline squinted into the lock.

"It was your parents' door, Caroline," Ava Dawn replied. "It ain't breakin' and enterin' if it's your own damn house."

"Well, this is your own damn house," Caroline said, except she knew that it wasn't. It was now and always had been Roy's house.

The Bean house was located in the oldest part of Cold River, close to the downtown. The little one-bedroom shotgun house was just a block from Caroline's father's office, but she had been there less than a dozen times in the seven years Ava Dawn and Roy had lived there. It was no secret that Roy didn't like Caroline, and Caroline liked Roy even less than he liked her.

"It's because you tried to run him over on our wedding day," Ava Dawn said as if she was reading her cousin's mind. "It's hard to forgive a thing like that."

"I didn't try to run him over!" Caroline protested, rolling her eyes. "He was three sheets to the wind and wandering all over town in his tuxedo. *You're* the one who asked me to go find him, remember?"

"I remember," Ava Dawn moaned. "He and his fool-headed groomsmen insisted on those camouflage tuxedos."

"They were pretty awful," Caroline admitted. Generally speaking, she didn't mind camouflage. Folks in Cold River wore it year-round. However, there was just something tacky about using it in a wedding. It was like people forgot that camo was supposed to be for hunting. If you were getting married, well, the hunt was over.

Caroline walked around to the side of the house. She knew that Court had been to this house more times than she could count for disturbances of the peace, which reminded her about something he'd told her once. He'd been called out because one of the neighbors heard yelling. Court told her that he couldn't get inside—Roy had barricaded the door so that Ava Dawn couldn't get out. Ava Dawn was hollering and crying so loud he thought she was dying or something, so he ran around to the washroom window. It was missing the screen, and he was able to crawl inside.

"Some things never change," Caroline muttered to herself.

"You need me to lift you up?" Ava Dawn appeared behind her.

Caroline jumped, knocking into her cousin. "Shit. You scared me."

"Sorry."

"Give me a boost."

Ava Dawn squatted down and hooked her hands underneath one of Caroline's feet. With a grunt, she hoisted her up until Caroline could pry the window open. "You okay?"

"Yeah," Caroline panted. "I think I've got it. You can let go." She wiggled through the window and landed on the floor with a *thunk*. She picked herself up and leaned out the window to pull Ava Dawn inside.

Ava Dawn looked around the house. "This place is filthy."

Caroline nodded in agreement. "Looks like he hasn't done a load of laundry in a month."

"Or the dishes." Ava Dawn gestured towards the sink. "I didn't even know we had this many plates."

The dishes and laundry weren't the only things overflowing. So was the trash can. There were discarded cigarette cartons and empty bags of potato chips scattered everywhere, along with the clothes that hadn't quite made it to the clothes hamper.

"Roy was always messy, but I ain't never seen him this messy," Ava Dawn marveled. "I don't even want to know what the bedroom looks like."

Caroline wandered around the house while Ava Dawn collected her clothes, makeup, and knick-knacks. Occasionally she looked out the front window for Roy. She knew that they needed to hurry. Roy had eyes everywhere, and she was sure one of the neighbors would call him. She walked back to the bedroom where Ava Dawn was hurriedly shoving clothes into her suitcase. "I can't remember the last time I was inside this house," she said. "Court's been here more times than me."

"Well, if it makes ya feel any better, Roy doesn't like Court no better than you."

"Roy doesn't like anybody," Caroline said.

"He really doesn't like Court," Ava Dawn replied.

"Because he's the law?"

"Well, that doesn't help." Ava Dawn sat down on the bed. "But Roy always, you know, well, he said stuff about Court."

Caroline knew what *stuff* Roy said. He wasn't the only one to say it. "How would Roy even know?"

"Said he could just tell." Ava Dawn looked down at the clothes in her hands. "He said that Court used to look at the boys in the locker room in high school."

"How would Roy know unless he was lookin', too?"

Ava Dawn giggled. "Roy always did need to make sure his was the biggest."

"Gross!"

"I just feel bad," Ava Dawn continued. "I never took up for Court when Roy was sayin' those things."

"It wouldn't have mattered if you had." Caroline sat down next to her. "Roy never listens to anyone."

"You know, one time when Court was here after one of the neighbors called the cops, he practically had to bust down the door before he figured out he could get in through the window," Ava Dawn said. "Roy caught him climbin' in, and tried to shove him back out. They was both screamin' and hollerin' at each other. Roy said . . ." She paused, taking a breath. "He said he wasn't gonna let no faggot into his house."

Caroline felt her chest tighten. She'd felt the same way that night at the cabin when Daryl said Court was "fruitier than a fruitcake." But *that* word, the word Roy used, made her want to punch something, and it made her wonder how many times Court had heard it come out of people's mouths in his presence. "He never told me that."

"He pretended not to hear it," Ava Dawn said. "But I know he did. I saw it on his face." She stood up and resumed throwing clothes into her suitcase.

"You need me to help you with something?" Caroline asked finally. She knew there was nothing she could say that could make Ava Dawn feel better . . . or worse. "I think we've about finished with the bedroom."

"Thanks for helping me today," Ava Dawn said.

"Are you kidding?" Caroline asked.

Ava Dawn looked up at Caroline and said, "I bought that TV, ya know." She pointed to the dresser where a sixty-inch television sat. "Not even a year old."

"Let's take it then."

"Just a sec. Let me throw these suitcases in the back and run and get a blanket to put over the TV."

Caroline pulled back the dresser to unplug the television. As she pulled it back, she heard a rustling from within the dresser. It sounded like glass clinking together. She opened one of the drawers. There were dozens of beer and bourbon bottles amongst Roy's socks and underwear, all of them empty. Caroline frowned into the drawer. She considered telling Ava Dawn but decided against it. Her cousin left and got back together with Roy as often as some women bought new pairs of shoes. Something told her that this time was different. She didn't want to do anything that might jeopardize that.

"I found a sheet," Ava Dawn said jubilantly as she reentered the room with a blanket.

Caroline shoved the drawer shut. "Let me unplug the cords."

"I thought you already did that."

"I'm working on it." She bent down and pulled the cord, sliding herself behind the dresser.

Ava Dawn plopped back down on the bed. "I wish it hadn't come to this, you know?" she said, glancing around the ramshackle room. "This wasn't how I thought it would turn out."

"I know."

"It wasn't all bad."

"I know it wasn't."

"I really did love him."

"I know you did." Caroline did know. Ava Dawn had loved Roy since they were freshman in high school and he was a senior. She'd married him the summer that she graduated. While Caroline was going to college orientation and meeting her dorm roommate, Ava Dawn was picking out china patterns and buying a wedding dress. Caroline always said that the only thing they had in common was that they were related, and even though Ava Dawn's daddy and Caroline's daddy were brothers, that's where the similarities ended.

Rory O'Conner was Max's baby brother, nearly twelve years his junior. Maureen O'Conner liked to say that Rory was spoiled rotten, born after the O'Conners had built their successful business and made smart investments—he never wanted for anything. He never did marry Ava Dawn's mother, and she left town before Ava Dawn's first birthday. When Rory married a woman from Arkansas when Ava Dawn was in high school, he'd lit out of town without so much as a second glance at his only child.

It made sense to Caroline that she picked Roy. He was older. He had a job at his family's tire shop. He had a house that had been given to him by his grandparents. In short, he had everything Ava Dawn had ever wanted. Yes, Ava Dawn loved Roy, but more than anything, Ava Dawn just wanted to belong to someone—to anyone, even if that meant belonging to Roy Bean.

Ava Dawn stood up and took one last look around the room. "This place always was a dump." She threw the sheet over the top of the TV. "You get that side, and I'll get the other."

The two women carried the TV through the front door and out onto the porch. "Is this the only TV you two had?" Caroline wanted to know.

"Yep." Ava Dawn grunted. "We had one in the living room, but Roy threw a beer bottle at it when the Cards lost to the Cubs last summer." She set her side down on the porch.

In the distance, there was a rumble from an exhaust pipe.

"Shit!" Ava Dawn was panicked. "It's Roy!"

"Shhhhh!" Caroline hissed, moving backwards as fast as she could to the back of the truck. She yanked the tailgate down and lifted her end of the television into the back, climbing in and positioning herself behind it. "Help me get this thing up here."

"What are we going to do?" Ava Dawn shoved her end of the TV into the truck so hard that Caroline lost her footing and tumbled down on top of Ava Dawn's suitcases.

"Get in the truck," Caroline replied. "The keys are in it."

"Are you sure?"

Roy neared the house. He was so close Caroline could see his outline behind the wheel. "Do you want to be here when Roy figures out we looted his house?"

Ava Dawn slammed the tailgate shut and jumped into the cab of the pickup. "Hold on!" she screeched.

Caroline grabbed on to the TV and squeezed her eyes shut tight. Gravel flew over her head, and she looked up just in time to make eye contact with Roy as he pulled into the driveway. She couldn't help but grin and use her free hand to wave at him as he watched his wife and his television speed away from him, down the road, and off towards the Missouri skyline.

Chapter 25

Caroline stared out the window of the shop at Smokey up on the roof of Cranwell Station. He was a little over halfway done, and it looked great. It wasn't the tin roof that so many of the older buildings had, and that Caroline loved, but the shingles still looked nice. She wondered what Noah's plans were for the rest of the outside. He'd already replaced the windows and the front door, but with the new roof, the rest of the station didn't look half bad. In fact, it looked good.

There had been a constant stream of customers since she'd opened the bait shop back up, and most of them wanted to know what was going on across the street. People were asking her father, as well, during the days he spent at the clinic. Tonight, he was working extra late—they were giving free physicals for all school-age children.

Caroline grinned and waved when she saw Noah watching her from across the street. He motioned for her to come over, and she noticed Yara already waddling her way over to him. Smokey was climbing down the ladder from the roof by the time she made it over there. "Hey, Smokey. How is it coming along?"

"Just fine, Carolina." Smokey dabbed at his forehead with a handkerchief. "I reckon I'll be finished in a couple weeks."

Caroline frowned. That was great for Noah, but it was bad for Smokey. He could stay sober only long enough to finish a job. She'd be back to pulling him out of the bar in no time. "Well, take your time. I'm sure there's no hurry."

"You're doing a great job," Noah replied, Yara

at his heel. "But I would like to open this place before Christmas."

Caroline squinted over at Noah. He was smiling at her, his white teeth a sharp contrast to his deeply tanned skin. She envied his skin color. She never got anything but freckles, but he'd been outside in the Missouri sun for a mere few weeks and he looked like he should be surfing on a beach somewhere. "Not many people spend their Christmases swimming in the Cold River."

"My point exactly."

Smokey stuffed the handkerchief down into his pocket and said, "I better git. I'll see ya tomorrow mornin' bright and early."

Caroline and Noah waved him off.

"You ought to let him work a bit longer," Caroline said, once Smokey was gone. "It's not like you're paying him by the hour."

"He's going slow enough," Noah replied, crossing his arms across his chest. "Don't get me wrong, he's doing a great job, but I'd hoped to have this hammered out by now."

"I know," Caroline replied. "It's just that he'll go drink up every penny you've paid him the minute he's done."

"I can't help that. It'll be his money."

"I know."

"Hey, you can't help it any more than I can." Noah softened. "It's his choice."

"He wasn't always like this, you know,"

Caroline said. "When I was a kid, he had his own business. He had a family and everything. I don't know what happened. It was like one day he was a decent guy and the next he was falling down drunk."

"I'm sure it looked that way," Noah replied. "But that's not how it happens, overnight, you know. My mom and dad were drunks—and they always looked good on the outside until they couldn't keep it straight anymore."

Caroline looked at Noah. What a rotten childhood he must have had. "I'm sorry."

Noah shrugged. "Don't be."

Caroline was about to say something else when she saw a truck coming from the direction of the river. As it neared them, she realized that the person behind the wheel was Jep Cranwell. He threw the truck into park and sat there for a few minutes, readying his oxygen tank to get out of the truck. Eventually, he opened the door of the truck and stepped out. He was every bit as tan as his grandson, and despite their stark contrast in dress and the deep, craggy lines jutting across Jep Cranwell's face, it occurred to Caroline that the two men were exact mirrors of each other.

"I need to talk to you, boy," Jep said. He didn't look at Caroline. "Best we go inside to do it."

"I've already closed up for the night." Noah dangled the keys in front of Jep. "I'd rather not open it back up."

"It's family business."

"I should be heading out anyway," Caroline said, finding her voice.

"I reckon that's as good'n idea as any," Jep said to her.

"She doesn't have to leave," Noah said.

Caroline wasn't sure if she should leave or stay, and an uneasy feeling crept up the back of her neck. *What am I supposed to do?* she thought.

Jep took a step towards Noah. "You think it's okay, now that you own this land, to share the family secrets with someone who ain't blood?"

"What secrets?" Noah wanted to know.

"You know what I'm talking about."

"Have you been sending Silas to spy on me?" Noah asked. "What did he tell you? Did he tell you I took Caroline to the cave?"

"He told me more'n that."

Caroline felt a wave of nausea wash over her. Did he know about *everything?*

"You tell Si he better not let me catch him snooping around here again," Noah warned. "I need you to trust me, and I need you to trust my judgment."

"It ain't you I don't trust."

Noah rolled his eyes. "Come on, Gramps. Things are different now."

"They don't look so different to me." Jep glanced over at Caroline. "In fact, they look an awful lot alike."

"It's time for you to go now, Gramps," Noah said. His jaw was clenched.

"I pulled you out of trouble once," Jep replied, turning back towards his truck. "This will be a scrape I won't be able to fix."

"That was fifteen years ago," Noah replied. "I'm a grown man. I don't need your help anymore."

A fleeting look of hurt flashed across Jep's face, and then without another word, he turned on his heel and got back into his truck. He sped away from the station, bits of rocks and dust flying up and stinging Caroline's arms and legs. By the time she got the courage to look back over at Noah, his back was turned to her, his muscles tightening beneath the white T-shirt he was wearing. When he turned around, his eyes were as dark and menacing as the clouds above them, threatening rain at any moment.

Caroline had a million questions running through her head. What had Silas reported back to Jep? What kind of trouble had Noah been in fifteen years ago? What kind of mistakes and secrets was Jep talking about? What did they have to do with her?

Noah must've realized she was staring at him, because his expression softened. "Look, I'm sorry about that."

"No, no, it's okay," Caroline replied. "I guess I really should get out of here. Ava Dawn's alone with my mom, and my dad's out late."

"Okay," Noah replied. He gave her a tight-lipped smile.

Caroline wanted to go to him and put her arms around him. She wanted to tell him she was sorry for whatever it was that was hurting him and keeping him from seeing eye to eye with his grandfather, but she didn't know how to say it. Instead, she said, "I'll see you tomorrow."

"Yeah."

She was walking away when she heard Noah calling after her.

"Caroline," he hollered. "Hey, Caroline, wait." He jogged up to her. "I didn't, um, I didn't know that Silas was tailing us that day at the cave."

Caroline felt a shudder run through her. "Surely he didn't follow us inside."

"I think we would have heard him."

"I just hope he didn't hear us."

For a moment Noah looked mortified, and then he broke into a broad grin. "The bastard was probably traumatized."

Caroline started to laugh. "I know. I almost feel sorry for him."

"Don't," Noah replied.

"Okay, I won't," Caroline said. She didn't want to leave things this way. She wanted some answers. "Hey, do you want to get out of here for a while?"

"What did you have in mind?"

"Well, like I said, my dad is going to be working

late. Ava Dawn has the night off, and she's pillaged Court's garden."

Noah raised his eyebrow.

"His vegetable garden," Caroline continued. "He grows the best tomatoes in three counties, and Ava Dawn promised to make fried green tomatoes tonight."

"Like the movie?" Noah asked.

Caroline rolled her eyes. "Like the food."

"I've never had them before."

"Well, then, Mr. Cranwell," Caroline said, taking Noah by the arm, "you've not lived."

Chapter 26

Ava Dawn stood in front of the stove wearing one of her aunt Maureen's old aprons. She had her iPod tucked down into one of the pockets, and she was singing so loudly that Caroline and Noah could hear her before they even opened the door. Her voice was only slightly louder than Caroline's mother's, who stood beside her singing and dipping the tomatoes into a bowl full of egg yolk. *Oh, so hang on to the ones who really care, Cuz in the end, they'll be the only ones there . . .* Noah looked from Caroline to Ava Dawn and back again. "Are they singing . . ."

"Hanson?" Caroline finished for him. "Yes. Yes they are."

"Why?"

"Why not?" Caroline replied, grinning from ear to ear. "Ava Dawn and I were about seven when 'MMMBop' came out. It was our favorite song. We must have listened to it fifty times a day that summer. My poor mom had to hear it all the time."

"They look happy."

"They are." It was as if everything was completely normal—her mother and Ava Dawn side by side singing and cooking dinner. It was a scene she'd come home to plenty of times over the years. Five years ago, Caroline would have burst through the front door with Noah and feigned embarrassment over the song while her mother wiped her hands on her apron and serenaded Noah with a cornmeal-covered spatula. But now, Caroline knew, when the song was over the spell would be broken. Maureen O'Conner would turn around, and it was very likely that she wouldn't know either of the people standing in her doorway. She wouldn't even know it was her doorway. She could remember all of the words to a pop song that came out in 1997, but she couldn't remember her own daughter.

It wasn't fair.

Caroline felt tears pricking at her eyes, and she wiped at them furiously. "Let's just stand here until the song is over," she said to Noah. "Just give me another minute."

Noah didn't say anything, but he reached down and grabbed her hand, giving it a squeeze just before Ava Dawn turned around and noticed them.

"Well, hey, you two," she said, fumbling for the iPod inside of her apron pocket. "Caroline, I didn't expect you to bring company."

"It was kind of spur of the moment," Caroline replied. She was dying to tell Ava Dawn everything.

"She took pity on me, is what she means," Noah cut in. "I wasn't having the best night."

Ava Dawn eyed Noah up and down and then turning to her aunt said, "Look who's here, Aunt Maureen."

Maureen O'Conner turned around from the stove. "Hello," she said. For a moment, she let her hands wander up to her hair, smoothing it down. It wasn't as red as it used to be, but it was every bit as curly. Then she turned back around to the tomatoes, humming "MmmBop."

Ava Dawn shrugged. "She's had a good day."

"Do you want a beer or something?" Caroline asked Noah, desperate to take the focus off of her mother. "I'm sure we've got one or two in the fridge."

"I'm fine," Noah said, walking over to the stove. "This smells delicious."

"Oh, it is," Ava Dawn assured him. "Fried green tomatoes are Caroline's favorite."

"I've never had them."

"Well, your life is about to change."

Noah laughed. "I haven't had a home-cooked meal since Caroline and I went to my grandfather's for dinner."

Ava Dawn raised her eyebrow over at Caroline. "Yeah, I heard about that."

"I can't say that I'm a huge fan of deer meat," Noah admitted. "But my aunt has always been a good cook."

"I met your aunt a few times," Ava Dawn said. "She used to bring her old truck into the shop where Roy works. It's been years, though."

Noah nodded. "I don't think she drives much anymore. Her eyesight isn't what it used to be."

Caroline's mother turned to them. She was holding a slice of tomato between her thumb and index finger. "I really don't like Roy much."

"To be fair," Ava Dawn said after a moment of silence, "nobody does."

"And you." Maureen walked up to Noah and stood directly in front of him. "I thought I told you that I don't like this scruff," she said, reaching her free hand up to his face. "Clean shaven, that's what a man should be."

Caroline, Noah, and Ava Dawn all looked at each other. To Caroline's relief, Noah smiled. "I'm sorry, Mrs. O'Conner," he said. "I didn't have time to shave this morning."

Caroline's mother backed away from Noah. "Call me Maureen."

"Okay, Maureen."

"We better get back to cookin'," Ava Dawn said to her aunt. "I've still got to fry up the chicken."

"Do you need some help?" Noah wanted to know.

"Sure. You two can set the table."

Caroline busied herself taking down the dishes from the cabinets. She noticed Noah looking around as if he'd never been inside her house before. That was when she realized that he hadn't. It was so strange—him being here felt natural, normal, even after the awkward conversation with her mother. He probably thought she'd lost all of her manners. "I'm sorry," she said to Noah, setting down a pile of plates onto the table. "I forgot you've never been here before. Let me show you around."

"I was beginning to wonder," Noah said. "I thought about just wandering around on my own."

Caroline grinned. "Well, there isn't much to see. It's a pretty small house." She led him into the hallway and to her parents' room. "This is my mom and dad's room. Back there is the other bathroom. There's another porch off the back, as well. We added on to it when we bought the place. It's bigger than it once was, but it still feels pretty small sometimes."

"Where's your room?" Noah asked.

"At the other end of the hallway," she said. "Come on, I'll show you."

Noah stood in the doorway of Caroline's room. "How long has this been your room?"

"Oh, since forever," Caroline replied. "My parents moved here when I was a kid. They'd had a larger house outside of town, close to the river, but I think it was just too hard for them to live there."

"That makes sense," Noah said. He walked inside the room, his arms crossed over his chest while he looked around.

Caroline felt her cheeks burn as he gazed around her room. *What is he thinking?* she wondered. *My whole life exists in here.*

Noah ran his fingers along one of the many bookcases. "You've got some interesting titles in here."

Caroline walked over next to him and picked up a book titled *Gangsters and Grifters: Classic Crime Photos from the* Chicago Tribune. "I got this one for Christmas a couple of years ago. It's one of my favorites."

"Interesting."

"Hey," Caroline said. "Not all of us are born into a family people write books about."

"Nobody has written any books about my family," Noah replied. "Trust me, if they had, my grandfather would have had them drawn and quartered."

"I bet half of the people in this book came through Cranwell Station," Caroline said. She sat down on the bed. "Those pictures you showed me were so cool."

"There are a lot more where those came from." Noah sat down next to her. "You may be right."

"I still can't believe your family had a speak-easy in a *cave*," she whispered.

"I'd really like to go back there again some-time," Noah replied.

For the first time in a long time, Caroline wished she had her own house like most people her age. If she had her own house, the two of them would be alone together. She wouldn't have to deal with Ava Dawn setting the smoke detectors off with her tomatoes. She wouldn't have to worry about her mother thinking Noah was someone else, maybe even Jep. Surely her mother had never worried about Jep Cranwell's beard. *Had she?* Caroline felt a pang of guilt at those thoughts. In an attempt to shove them aside, she said, "I'd like that, too."

Noah scooted closer to her on the bed. He laced his fingers in with hers. He was leaning in to kiss her when they both heard the front door slam. "Did someone just leave?" Noah asked.

"I better go check on my mom," Caroline replied. "Sometimes Ava Dawn forgets she has to keep an eye out." She stood up to leave the room, and that was when she saw her father standing in the hallway.

"Hey, kiddo," he said.

"Dad? What are you doing home so early?"

"One of the schools' buses broke down," her father replied. "They had to reschedule. And it's pouring down rain outside, in case you hadn't noticed."

"I hadn't," Caroline admitted sheepishly.

"Hello, Dr. O'Conner." Noah appeared behind Caroline.

"Oh, Noah, hello." Max O'Conner glanced from Caroline to Noah. "I didn't know we were having company tonight."

"Dinner's ready," Ava Dawn called from the dining room. She narrowed her eyes at Noah and Caroline when they came in behind Caroline's father. "I thought you two were going to set the table."

"I found them in Caroline's bedroom," her father said, raising an eyebrow. "Can you not keep your eyes on everyone at the same time, Ava Dawn?"

"Not while I'm slaving away in the kitchen," Ava Dawn replied, grinning at Caroline's obvious embarrassment. "Sit down, I'll get you a place set. Everything else is ready."

Maureen O'Conner was already at the table. She was looking at Noah, her mouth set in a hard line. Caroline sat down beside her. "Is everything okay, Mom?"

"Who invited him?" She nodded over at Noah, who had taken a seat across from them. He was chatting with Caroline's father.

"I did, Mom."

"They shouldn't be sitting by each other," her mother whispered, leaning over closer to Caroline.

"Why not?"

Her mother rolled her eyes. "Isn't it obvious?"

In fact, it *wasn't* obvious, but she thought it best not to agitate her mother further. Nobody else seemed to notice something was wrong, and she didn't want to ruin the dinner. It was a relief that, at least, her mother hadn't mentioned Jeremy. "Well, the tomatoes look great."

"Don't they?" Ava Dawn asked, sitting down at the end of the table. "I should have invited Court and his daddy. I bet they ain't had a home-cooked meal in a while, either."

"Court cooks pretty well," Caroline said. "Not as well as Pam did, but he'll be able to keep them alive."

"I saw the house for sale," Max O'Conner cut in. "Did Court get his father all moved into his place?"

"He did." Caroline nodded. "Just after the funeral."

"What funeral?" Maureen wanted to know. She stuffed a piece of tomato into her mouth.

Caroline looked helplessly at her father. She knew telling her mother that Pam was dead would upset her. She didn't know why she'd said funeral, except that she hadn't been thinking. All she could think about was Noah. She couldn't stop thinking about him in her bedroom, and she couldn't help but wonder why her mother was so annoyed at his presence in their house. Even though she knew there was often no rhyme or reason for the things her mother said, Caroline felt like she was missing a step. She made a mental note to ask her father about it later.

"Maureen, did you cook these?" her father asked. He held up a piece of fried green tomato on his fork.

"I did," she replied. She looked down at her plate and began to eat again, while everyone else at the table let out a collective sigh of relief.

"They came from Court's garden," Caroline said, careful not to mention Pam or the funeral. "He always has the best tomatoes."

Her father nodded. "He does. Remember when he had that pumpkin patch that fall you all were about twelve? I'm sure he made a mint!"

Caroline smiled at the memory. "Oh, I remember. I had to help him, and I didn't even get paid!" Court could grow just about anything, and he could make money off of just about anything. It was this talent that kept his family afloat during some of the leaner times. She admired that about him.

"I really should have invited him and his daddy," Ava Dawn said again. "Now I feel awful."

"I just can't figure out," Caroline's mother began, pointing her fork at Noah, "what on earth you're doing here."

Noah glanced around the table. His cheeks were tinged with pink. "Your daughter invited me, Maureen."

Caroline placed her hand on her mother's arm, lovingly but firmly. "Mom," she began. Before she could finish her sentence, the lights in the house went out and the air conditioner quit whirring. The only sound left in the house was that of the rainstorm outside.

"I better check the breaker box," Max O'Conner said. He pushed back his chair and gave Noah an encouraging pat on the back as he left the room.

Caroline stood up and looked out the window. "I don't think you'll have to do that, Dad. It looks like the power is out all over the neighborhood."

"I'm just going to check it anyway," he said.

The house was dark, but not so dark that Caroline couldn't see. She wondered if maybe the storm was responsible for the power outage. Sometimes the older parts of Cold River lost power during storms, especially if there were high winds. She looked out the window again. Half of the trees in her yard were bowing so far down that their limbs practically dragged against the ground.

"You think it's the storm?" Noah appeared behind her.

"Probably," Caroline replied. She felt his hand on the small of her back.

"Well, it's not the storm," Max O'Conner said, stepping back inside the house. "The hospital just called. Bill Joyce ran into a damn light pole with his tractor down on Grace Avenue."

"He did what?" Caroline asked. "What was he doing on his tractor in the middle of town?"

"Who knows," her father replied. "And now of course he's refusing to go to the hospital. I'm going down there to see if I can convince him otherwise."

"In this weather?"

"He's almost ninety years old." Her father gave Caroline a kiss on her forehead. "Stay inside, and if the sirens go off, get down to the cellar, okay?"

"We will."

"Don't wait up," he replied, heading back out the door.

"Do you think the sirens are going to go off?" Ava Dawn asked worriedly. "You know that cellar freaks me out."

"I don't think they are going to go off," Caroline replied. "But I bet it's going to be a while before the power comes back on. Maybe we should go find the candles and the lighter."

"Okay, Noah and I will clear the plates, won't we?" Ava Dawn winked at Noah.

Caroline looked over at her mother who was still sitting at the dinner table. She was alone, still eating her fried green tomatoes. She wondered if her mother had even noticed what happened—

the lights, the storm, Caroline's father leaving the house. She seemed to be continuing to focus upon Noah, watching him with Ava Dawn as she ate. "I'm heading up to the attic for a few minutes."

Caroline found a flashlight in the hallway closet and pulled the stairway down. She never had understood why her parents kept the candles upstairs. It was pitch-dark in the attic when the sun was shining. She shone the flashlight around the room. The candles were in the box on the top shelf of the dresser at the opposite end of the attic. She sighed, stumbling through the boxes and knickknacks littering the attic floor. She was loading up on candles when her flashlight shone upon the picture of her mother and Jep Cranwell. She'd left the photo album lying open the last time she was up there. She kept the beam of the flashlight on the photo. Caroline reached down, grabbed the picture, and stuffed it into her back pocket before heading downstairs.

"It's about time," Ava Dawn said when she saw Caroline.

"Where's Mom?" Caroline asked.

"She said she had a headache." Ava Dawn shrugged. "She went to lie down in the bedroom."

"Okay," Caroline replied. She handed her cousin a few candles. "Let's get some better light in here." She set to work lighting the candles.

By the time they were finished, it was completely dark outside, eerily dark without the streetlights. The storm had settled some, but the rain was still coming down in sheets, and inside the O'Conner house was filled with flickering candles. "Well, what are we gonna do now?" Ava Dawn wanted to know. "The Wi-Fi is out, too."

Caroline shrugged. She was sitting on the couch next to Noah, watching shadows dance across the walls. She was okay with sitting there and doing nothing, but her cousin looked like she was about to explode from boredom. "We could play cards or something."

"Perfect!" Ava Dawn clapped her hands together. "I think there's a deck in the spare bedroom." She stood up.

A knock on the front door made all three of them jump. It swung open without prompting, and there stood Court Brannan. His face was barely visible through the yellow rain poncho he was wearing. "Everybody okay in here?"

"Well, we were," Ava Dawn said, shaking rain off of her arms. "Until you brought in the damn monsoon."

Court closed the door. "Sorry."

"What are you doing here?" Caroline asked, standing up to help him out of his raincoat. "I figured you'd be out taking care of catastrophes tonight."

"I was," Court replied. He held out his hand to Noah who, realizing he was the only one left sitting down, stood up. "I'm on call the rest of the night. Thought I'd come by and check on ya, seein' as how Doc is out workin' the tractor crash."

Noah let out a snort. "I'm sorry," he said, biting down on his lip. "I just can't believe the entire town's lost power because of a tractor."

"Believe it," Court replied. "Last winter one of Old Man McGuiness's cows slipped on a patch of ice, slid through the fence, and out into the road. Poor cow couldn't get herself turned right aways. Held up traffic for two hours."

Noah looked to Caroline for an explanation, but all she said was, "That really happened."

"You gonna stay?" Ava Dawn asked. "We were about to play some Spades."

"Beats goin' back out into the rain," Court said.

Ava Dawn disappeared into one of the dimly lit bedrooms and appeared a few minutes later with a pack of cards in one hand and a glass bottle in the other. She sat them both down on the dining room table. "Look what I found." She pointed to the bottle. "It ain't shine, but it'll do in a pinch."

"It's rye whiskey," Caroline said. "Dad keeps it hidden in the spare bedroom. I'm not even sure why anymore. Used to be because Mom hated the stuff."

"I can't drink tonight," Court said. "But you three can have at it."

"None for me, thanks," Noah said.

"Fine, more for us," Ava Dawn replied. She

placed two glasses on the table and then slid one across to Caroline.

"You boys know how to play Spades?" Caroline asked. She nodded to Ava Dawn, silently telling her to continue filling her glass.

Court shot her a look across the table. "Really? You don't remember the last time I kicked your ass at Spades?"

"That never happened."

"Sure did," Court replied. "Senior year at Reese's graduation party."

"You didn't go to Reese's graduation party." Caroline began shuffling the deck.

"I was there just long enough to beat you at Spades."

Caroline rolled her eyes. She hadn't remembered ever playing Court in a game of Spades. Of course, the night of Reese's graduation party was a hazy memory at best. She remembered drinking too much and being afraid to call her father to come and get her from a party he had expressly forbidden her to attend. She remembered fighting with Reese when she'd told him she wanted to go home. "We playin' in pairs or single?"

"Single," Court said. "I'm gonna beat you on my own."

"Oh, big man," Caroline replied. She took a sip of the whiskey and winced. "This is going to be a rough night."

Chapter 27

Caroline squinted into the darkness at her mother's sleeping form. She hovered above her just long enough to make sure she was still breathing. She wasn't sure why, but lately she'd taken to checking on her mother while she slept, especially in the middle of the night. Caroline's father was almost always snoring away next to his wife, but some nights Caroline woke up in a sheer panic, and the only way to make herself feel better was to wander into her parents' room and check on her mother.

It was almost midnight, and her father still wasn't home. Caroline knew better than to be worried, but she also knew enough to know he probably wouldn't be home for hours. The hospital would need all hands on deck. "Mom's fine," she said as she sat back down at the table. She looked at Court, who was pulling on his rain poncho. "Where are you going?"

"You mean where am I going after I kicked your ass *four times* in Spades?"

Caroline sighed. "That's what I mean."

"Headed out to the county. Got a call that there may be a low water bridge out and a car washed off the road," Court replied. "I'm bettin' all the low water bridges are out, 'specially the one out by the bait shop."

"That's alright," Ava Dawn chirped, twirling her half-empty glass. "Tall, dark, and handsome can stay in my room."

"Well, on that note," Court said, reaching out to give Caroline a playful punch on the arm, "I'm out of here."

"He's a nice guy," Noah said once Court was out of the house. "You've been friends for a long time?"

Caroline nodded. "The three of us have been friends since we were kids."

"I think he went into the sheriff's academy to make sure me 'n' Caroline stayed outta trouble," Ava Dawn said.

"But neither of you ever . . ." Noah trailed off.

"Dated him?" Caroline finished.

Noah nodded.

"Lord no!" Ava Dawn exclaimed.

"Why not?"

Caroline and Ava Dawn shared a look.

"Well, Caroline over here ain't ever had more than one boyfriend," Ava Dawn said. She winked at her cousin.

"Reese?" Noah asked.

"Reese," Caroline and Ava Dawn said at the same time.

"Right."

"Well," Ava Dawn said, standing up and

stretching her arms out as far as they would go, "I'm headed to bed."

"I guess we all better do that," Noah said. He was staring a hole through Caroline.

"Carolina, I'll stay with Aunt Maureen tonight. I know you ain't gonna let her stay all night in there alone," Ava Dawn continued.

"You don't have to do that," Caroline said.

"I don't mind," Ava Dawn replied. "The sheets in the spare room are clean. I just changed 'em yesterday. It'll be more comfortable than the couch."

Caroline followed Ava Dawn into the hallway bathroom. "You don't have to stay in the bedroom with Mom," she said. "My dad will be home soon."

"You gonna let her stay in there alone 'till he gets here?"

"No."

"That's what I thought," Ava Dawn replied. "Look, clearly Noah likes you. He's endured a whole night of crazy with our family, and I don't care what Court says, you and I both know that bridge ain't full of water."

"Well, then maybe I should just take him home," Caroline said, crossing her arms across her chest.

"Suit yourself." Ava Dawn grinned at her cousin. "But I'm going to bed."

Caroline waited a few minutes before she went back out into the living room. Noah was still sitting at the table, shuffling the cards. "I can probably get you back to the station if you want to go home," she said.

"Sit down," Noah replied. "Let's play a few rounds of blackjack."

"Aren't you tired?" Caroline asked. She sat down across from him.

"Not really," he replied. "Are you?"

Caroline poured what was left of the whiskey into the two glasses on the table, pushing one of them over to Noah. "Deal."

Noah laid two cards in front of her.

Caroline looked at her cards—a ten of spades and a two of hearts. "Hit me."

He gave her another card.

The queen of hearts. "Bust," Caroline said.

"Is Court gay?" Noah asked. He collected the cards.

Caroline narrowed her eyes at him. "Does it matter?"

"Not to me," Noah replied. "But I know it might to a lot of people around here."

"It would matter a lot to a lot of people."

"Then why does he stay here?"

"Where else is he going to go?" Caroline asked. "He's lived here his whole life. Everyone he knows is here. His job is here."

"He could make a life somewhere else."

"I suppose he could," Caroline agreed. "But he'll never leave his dad."

Noah dealt two cards.

An eight of hearts and an ace of spades. "I'll stay," Caroline said. She laid out her cards. "I have nineteen."

"Let's see what I get," Noah replied. "A three of hearts and a king. I think I'll take another." He dealt another card. "King of hearts. I bust."

Caroline pulled the picture out of her back pocket and laid it on the table. "I found this when I was up in the attic the other day," she said. "It's my mother and your grandfather."

"I see that," Noah said. He squinted down at it. The candles on the table flickered as he leaned in to get a better look.

"I think they were better friends than they let on, maybe even more than that," Caroline said. "What do you think?"

"I think it doesn't matter," Noah replied.

"It matters to me."

"Why?"

Caroline shifted in her seat. She wasn't sure why it mattered to her so much, but at that moment, it was all she could think about. "Because I'm pretty sure my mom thinks you're him. I think when she looks at you, she sees Jep."

"I think you're borrowing trouble." Noah dealt her two cards.

"Would you tell me if you knew?"

Noah looked back down at his deck. "Sure I would."

Caroline nodded. "Hit me."

Noah slid a card over to her.

"Bust."

"Was that Reese guy really the only boyfriend you've ever had?"

Caroline sat back in her chair. Damn Ava Dawn and her big mouth. "He's the only *serious* boyfriend I've ever had."

"So you've had others?"

"Other what?"

"Boyfriends."

"No."

Noah collected the cards. "Did you love him?"

"Deal," Caroline replied.

Noah handed her two cards.

"Blackjack." Caroline turned the cards over.

"Well done."

Caroline smiled over at him. Two could play at his little game. "What kind of trouble did you have fifteen years ago?" she asked.

Noah wrapped one of his hands around the glass of whiskey and brought it to his lips. After draining the glass he said, "My friends and I robbed a house."

Caroline sat back. She hadn't expected that.

"I had a gun," Noah continued. "Aggravated burglary is what the state of New Jersey called it. If they tried us as adults, I was looking at five to ten years. It wasn't my first offense."

"Oh," Caroline replied, her voice scarcely above a whisper.

"I was a dumb kid," Noah replied. "Look, I'm not making excuses, but the fact is that I was living on the streets. My mom didn't want me. So I took off." He wasn't looking at her anymore. "I was just trying to survive."

"I'm sorry." Caroline knew that was a lame response, but she didn't know what else to say. She *was* sorry.

"My grandfather paid for my lawyer. Helped me cut a deal." Noah twirled the glass around with his fingers. "He paid the restitution," he said. "I never would have gotten into the Navy if it hadn't been for him."

"So you moved back here to try to make it up to him."

Noah nodded. "In part. But I was tired of traveling. I've never had a place that I could really call home, you know?"

Caroline didn't know. She'd always had a home. She reached out and placed her hand on top of his. "Well, now you do."

"I'm not used to it yet," Noah confessed. "I don't think I'm doing a very good job at being a part of a family."

"Why not?"

Noah shrugged. "I'm used to being on my own . . . to doing things on my own."

"You'll get better at it."

"Easy for you to say," Noah replied. "You've always had a family."

"So have you," Caroline said. "It's just that you haven't always lived near them."

"I guess." Noah stood up. "I'm tired. I think I'll head on to bed."

Caroline felt her heart sink. "Okay. I lit a couple of candles in the spare room."

"Thanks." Noah was already heading towards the room. Without looking back at her, he said, "Good night, Caroline."

Caroline waited until the door to the spare room had closed and then she put the glasses in the sink and made her way back to her bedroom. She wasn't sure what to do with the information she'd been given. She hadn't meant to upset him, and now she wished she could take her question back. If he'd wanted her to know, he would have offered up the information instead of waiting to be asked. *At least he told me the truth when I asked,* she thought. Surely that meant he was telling the truth about everything. Maybe she was making too much out of her mother's relationship with Jep. Nobody but her seemed to be concerned with it, anyway.

She rummaged around in her laundry basket for a clean nightgown. When she didn't find one, she pulled on a camisole and threw herself down on top of her bed. She was just drifting off when she heard someone knocking at her bedroom door.

Caroline sat up and squinted into the darkness, willing her eyes to adjust. "Is someone there?" she

290

whispered. Maybe her mother had wandered out of her bedroom.

"Did I wake you up?" It was Noah.

"No, it's okay," Caroline replied. "Come in."

"I can't sleep."

Caroline sat up in bed. "Is there something wrong with the bed? Ava Dawn said she put clean sheets on it. Sometimes she eats crackers in bed. I hope she didn't leave crumbs."

"No." Noah laughed. "No, the sheets are fine." He sat down in the chair by her bookshelf.

"Okay, then," Caroline said. She drew her knees up to her chest underneath the covers when she realized the only thing she was wearing was a camisole and panties.

"The wind has picked back up again."

"I heard."

Noah shifted in the chair, his elbow catching on a stack of books, sending them crashing to the floor. "Shit, I'm sorry."

"It's okay," Caroline replied.

"I came in here to apologize." Noah said.

"Apologize for what?"

"For acting like an asshole earlier," he replied. "I'm not . . . I'm not used to talking about my past."

"You don't have to apologize," Caroline said. "I shouldn't have asked you about it. It's not my business."

"I asked you about yours."

"True."

"And I could tell it made you uncomfortable."

Caroline nodded, even though she knew Noah couldn't see her. "I guess I'm not used to talking about it, either," she said.

"I've spent most of my life alone," Noah continued. "I just assumed when I moved here that it would be the same way."

"You can't be alone in Cold River," Caroline replied. "It's impossible."

"I'm beginning to figure that out."

"It's taken you this long?"

"I'm a slow learner."

Caroline grinned into the darkness.

"It's just that I don't want to live that way anymore." Noah straightened up in the chair. "I don't want to go from place to place. I don't want to pretend that my past doesn't exist. I don't want to shut down when someone asks questions that they have every right to know the answers to."

"You gave me answers," Caroline said. "You told me the truth, and that counts for something."

When Noah didn't say anything, Caroline pushed the covers off of her legs and stood up. She didn't care that she was standing half naked in front of him. She just wanted to be near him. She just wanted him to feel better. Without saying a word, she reached down and laced her fingers through his and lowered herself down onto his lap. "I don't want to talk anymore," she whispered.

Noah let go of her hands and hooked his thumbs around the fabric of her camisole, lifting it up and over her head. "There are no words for what you are," Noah said.

Caroline could feel his breath on her bare skin, and it was almost more than she could handle. She wanted to be patient, but she was finding it more and more difficult to control herself when she was this close to Noah. She leaned until their lips met, drawing her into him more and more with every kiss.

Finally, just when she thought she was going to have to beg him, Noah stood up, lifting her up with him. She wrapped her legs around him and allowed him to carry her to the bed as he continued kissing her. He sat her down on the bed, and Caroline watched as he undressed in front of her.

Noah was so confident. *Of course,* she thought as he peeled off each layer in front of her, *why shouldn't he be?* Even in the dark, Caroline could see the outline of his body. She could see the way his muscles rippled and that little trail of dark hair that traveled from his navel down past his boxer shorts—the boxer shorts that were now discarded on the floor. More than his confidence, there was something honest in his nakedness.

Noah slid in next to her. His skin was warm next to hers, and he lingered there for a moment, anticipation building so that Caroline couldn't breathe. "I need to take these off now," he said, kissing his way down her stomach to the band of her panties. "It's only fair."

"Well, by all means, let's be fair." She guided his hand down and allowed him to pull at the fabric until her panties were discarded at the foot of the bed.

Noah settled himself between her legs and thrust inside of her. Caroline had to bite down on his shoulder in order to keep from crying out, which only made him quicken his pace. He didn't stop until they were both exhausted and he was collapsed on top of her.

She let him lay there, the scent of him mingling with her own. Caroline wasn't sure if it was the whiskey or Noah, but she felt herself drifting off into one of the most delicious sleeps she'd ever known.

Chapter 28

The rain was still coming down in a slow drizzle the next morning when Caroline opened her eyes. Through the crack in the doorway, she could see that the hallway light was on, which meant power had finally been restored. She tried to roll out of bed, and heard a muffled yelp from the opposite end of the bed.

"Hey, ow!" Noah sat up. "You kicked me in the face!"

"What are you doing down there?"

"Well," Noah began, looking sheepish. "You were snoring."

"Oh my God." Caroline felt her face grow warm. "I was?"

"I thought if I moved to the bottom of the bed that it wouldn't be so loud."

Caroline drew her knees up to her chest and buried her head in them. "Why didn't you just leave?"

"Because," Noah said, pulling her legs out from under her, "you're so cute when you're asleep."

"Did being at the end help?" Caroline wanted to know. She couldn't help but grin at him, despite her embarrassment.

"Not really."

Caroline kicked at him playfully. "Now you're just being mean."

Before Noah could respond, Ava Dawn rushed into the room without knocking. She took just a second to look from Caroline to Noah before saying, "Caroline, you've got to get up. Aunt Maureen is gone!"

"What do you mean she's gone?"

Ava Dawn took another step into the room. "I mean I woke up and she's gone."

"Where is my dad?" Caroline asked. She swung

her legs off the bed and pulled on a pair of crumpled yoga pants from the floor.

"I don't know," Ava Dawn replied. She handed Caroline the camisole hanging from the chair by the bookcase. "He hasn't come home yet."

Caroline felt panic rising in her throat. She ushered Ava Dawn out of the room so that Noah could get dressed. "You didn't hear her get up out of bed?"

"No. I didn't even realize she was gone until a few minutes ago."

"Did you check outside?"

Ava Dawn nodded, her face pale. "I checked all around the house and even in the cellar before I woke you up."

"Call Court," Caroline said. She stuffed her feet into a pair of flip-flops. "I'm going to walk around the block and see if I can find her."

"Do you want me to call Uncle Max?" Ava Dawn called after her.

"No," Caroline replied, reaching for the door. "Not until I know we have to." She walked outside and into the already sweltering day. It was the kind of muggy Ozarks morning they got just after a rainstorm, but the rain had done nothing to keep the summer heat at bay.

She walked around the house just in case, hoping maybe her mother was there and Ava Dawn had just missed her. It wasn't the first time Maureen O'Conner had wandered out of the house, but most of the time she stayed in the yard. The fear of her disappearing was real, as her father warned her over and over could be typical of people with Alzheimer's. It was why last night Ava Dawn slept in the bedroom with her aunt. Caroline knew it wasn't Ava Dawn's fault, but she couldn't help but feel angry with her that it had happened.

"I just got off the phone with Court," Ava Dawn said. "He's heading out to look for her right now."

"What can I do?" Noah asked, appearing from Caroline's room.

"I'm going to take the truck out," Caroline said. "Why don't you stay here in case she comes back?"

"Okay," Noah replied. "Are you sure you don't want me to go with you?"

"You go on with her," Ava Dawn spoke up. "I'll stay here."

"I don't care which one of you goes," Caroline said, already halfway out the door. "Give it half an hour, and if we're not back, call my dad, okay?"

"Okay," Ava Dawn replied miserably. "Caroline . . . I'm so sorry."

"It's not your fault."

"I'll go with you," Noah said, scurrying to catch up with Caroline. "Here, give me the keys. I'll drive; you look."

Caroline handed them over. "I can't believe this is happening."

"It's never happened before?"

"She's wandered off once or twice grocery shopping or wandered into the yard, but she's never taken off before and gone so far that we couldn't find her."

"I'm sure she's fine."

Caroline pulled herself up into the passenger's seat of the truck. "My dad is never going to forgive me for letting her leave."

"It's hardly your fault," Noah said. He started the truck.

"I don't know how he does it," Caroline continued. "I don't know how he goes to sleep next to her every night not knowing what she's going to be like in the morning or if she'll . . . if she'll take off in the middle of the night."

"Where do you want to go first?"

"Just drive down the street here towards downtown," Caroline said. "I can't imagine that she's gotten very far."

"How long do you think she's been gone?" Noah asked. He looked at his watch. "It's just 6:30 a.m."

Caroline hadn't realized it was so early. "I don't know."

Cold River was practically a ghost town this early, especially downtown. None of the shops opened until eight o'clock, and except for the occasional car or jogger, the streets were empty. She knew it wouldn't do any good to try and rationalize her mother's actions, but she couldn't help it. *Why would she just get up and leave in the middle of the night?*

"Hey," Noah said, swerving into a parking space on the left-hand side of the road. "Is that your mom right down there?"

Caroline squinted. "Yes!" She was elated. Her mother was sitting on the front steps of a little pizza shop. She was still in her nightgown.

Noah put the truck into park. "Want me to walk down there with you?"

"No," Caroline replied. "Just sit here. I'll be right back." She handed Noah her phone. "Call Ava Dawn and tell her we found her."

Caroline hopped out of the truck, the sense of relief so overwhelming she thought she might cry. She knew why her mother was sitting there. Until last year, the pizza place had been the hair salon where her mother got her hair trimmed every few months. Before the place moved, her mother had gone every week for a blowout. In fact, she'd gone every Friday.

Today was Friday.

"Hey, Mom," Caroline said, approaching her mother. "The salon isn't open yet."

"I'm early," her mother replied. "But my hair is a mess."

"Why don't you come on home, and I can bring you back later."

"I'll just wait here."

Caroline sat down next to her mother. It was then that she noticed that she wasn't wearing any shoes. There were spots of blood on the pavement from the soles of her feet. "Mom, I really need you to come home with me."

Her mother pursed her lips together. "I am not leaving. I can't let *him* see me with my hair looking like this."

"Who?"

Maureen O'Conner didn't answer.

Caroline didn't know what to do. She knew she couldn't just drag her mother from the stoop. She'd seen her mother put up a fight before, many times before, when her father tried to get her to do something she'd set her mind against doing. It rarely ended well for anyone.

"Hello, Maureen."

Caroline looked up to see Noah standing in front of them.

"What are you doing here?" Maureen demanded, her hands flying up to her hair.

"I've been looking for you." Noah extended his hand out to her. "We were worried when we couldn't find you at home this morning."

"You were at my house?" Caroline's mother looked panicked. "Did he see you?"

"Did who see him?" Caroline wanted to know.

Maureen O'Conner took Noah's hand and stood up. "My husband," she whispered, ignoring her daughter. "Did he see you?"

"He's not home, Maureen," he said. "He was working at the hospital all night."

"Oh, thank God." Caroline's mother hooked her arm in with Noah's. "Let's go home, then."

Caroline stared at Noah, but he avoided looking at her. Somehow he knew that her mother would come with him. He knew it, and now she knew it, too.

Caroline's father was waiting for them when they got home. She prepared herself for her mother to be upset, but all her mother did was wave when she saw Max O'Conner standing on the front porch. Caroline knew she should leave it alone, everything her mother said in front of the pizza shop. There was no point in asking questions or trying to find out the truth right now—her mother, even if she was having a good day, wouldn't tell her anything. But when she saw her father standing expectantly on the porch, worry written all over his face, she couldn't help herself.

"Mom," Caroline said, grabbing hold of Maureen O'Conner's arm just as she was about to exit the truck. "Mom, I need to ask you something."

Her mother glanced down at Caroline's hand around her arm and said, "You're hurting me."

Caroline didn't let go. "Mom, I need you to tell me the truth, can you do that?"

"Let go!"

"Caroline," Noah interrupted. "Let go of your mom."

Caroline ignored him. "Look at me, Mom."

"What is it?" Her mother looked up from her arm and at her daughter.

"I need you to tell me if you know who this man is." She pointed at Noah. "What's his name?"

Maureen's eyes flitted over to where Noah was sitting, in the driver's seat of the truck. She smiled at him, blushing slightly. "You know who he is."

"I need you to tell me."

"I can't understand why," her mother replied. "Alright, alright, it's Jep Cranwell. Can't you see who he is? Don't tell your father. I promised not to see him anymore."

Caroline let go of her mother's arm.

"Can I get out of the car now?"

Caroline didn't answer her. She simply turned herself back around to face the front of the truck while Noah hopped out and helped her mother. She watched him help guide her mother to the front porch where he and Doctor O'Conner sat her down in one of the rocking chairs so her father could inspect her mother's feet. Noah watched her carefully from the porch, but Caroline couldn't look at him.

After a few minutes, Ava Dawn came out to the truck and climbed inside. "Are you mad at me?"

Caroline blinked back tears, willing herself to

302

keep from crying in front of her cousin. "Of course not."

"Then why are you still sitting out here? Uncle Max isn't mad, either."

"I'll be in, in a minute."

"Okay," Ava Dawn said. "He's taking her to the hospital, just to be sure. He thinks she might need a stitch or two on one of her feet."

"Ava Dawn?" Caroline asked.

"What?"

"Did you sleep in that outfit?"

Ava Dawn looked down at herself. "No, I put it on this morning."

"Before you even looked for Mom?"

"Yes."

"And you put on makeup, too?"

Ava Dawn wrinkled her nose. "This is from last night."

"It looks fresh."

"Well, it's not," Ava Dawn said.

Caroline sighed. "I'm sorry. I'm just overwhelmed, I guess. I was so worried something bad had happened."

"Well, don't worry." Ava Dawn reached out to pat Caroline's thigh. "Everything is fine."

"You're right." Caroline forced herself to smile. "Everything is fine," she repeated. "Everything is just fine."

Chapter 29

The Cold River hospital waiting room was one of Caroline's least favorite places. She was sure that it probably felt that way for everyone, but she'd spent more time there than anyone in the whole county, she was certain. As a child, it had been a source of entertainment when her father was working long hours. She would sit in the reading corner and look through the books. She would play in the activity center with the toys, and during those rare occasions when she was alone, Caroline flipped through the channels on one of the high mounted television sets. She liked to pretend that the waiting room belonged to her, and that it was really her apartment; the rest of the hospital a tall high-rise nestled in the heart of some far-off Eastern city like the ones her mother told her about.

It went on that way until the summer she was ten years old. Caroline had been reading in the corner when she saw her father walk into the waiting room and sit down next to a man sitting alone. He looked young to her, and she thought maybe he had been waiting for his mother or another elderly relative. Most of the time she didn't pay much attention to the people coming in and out of the waiting room, but Caroline liked this man. He'd been nice to her and let her watch whatever she wanted on the television. He'd even chatted for a few minutes with her about the book she was reading. So when her father came in and sat down next to him, Caroline listened.

"I'm sorry," she heard her father say. "We did everything we could."

"I know you did, Doc," the man said. His voice wavered, and he began to cry quietly into his hands.

"I'm sorry, Joe," her father said.

The man looked up at her father. "Can I see them?"

"Are you sure that's what you want?"

"Please."

Max O'Conner stood up and led the man away. Caroline knew something awful must've happened. She'd never in her life seen her father look as sad as he had that day. On the way home that night, Caroline asked him what happened.

"He lost his family," her father said. He was gripping the steering wheel so hard his knuckles were turning white.

"His whole family?"

"Yes."

"How?"

Caroline's father sighed. "His wife was pregnant, and the baby had something wrong with his heart."

"Did the baby die?" Caroline wanted to know.

Her father nodded. "We tried to save him and his mom."

Caroline swallowed. "The mom died, too?"

"Yes. She lost too much blood."

"Does he have any other family?" Caroline asked. She could feel her heart breaking for the man in the waiting room.

"Nobody that can help him," Max O'Conner replied.

They rode the rest of the way home in silence.

Caroline tried to go back to the waiting room the next week, but all she could do was wonder who in the waiting room was going to lose someone they loved. After that, she didn't go back until the winter they found out that her mother had Alzheimer's. She'd been sitting in the same spot that young man had been sitting in, and at the time she remembered thinking how lucky she was that the doctors weren't telling her that her mother was dead. Five years later, she sometimes wondered if her mother being dead would have been better . . . easier.

Today Caroline was back in the waiting room. The reading corner was gone and the chairs weren't nearly as comfortable, but other than that, it looked exactly the same. "How is she?" Caroline asked when she saw her father.

"She's fine," he replied. He was wearing his white doctor's coat. "The lacerations on her feet aren't bad. Just two of them needed a stitch."

"Then where is she?" Ava Dawn wanted to know.

Caroline's father sat down, yawning. He looked like he'd aged twenty years. "They're keeping her overnight for observation. She's dehydrated, although it's unlikely her little stroll this morning caused it. It's a combination of her medicine and simply not drinking enough fluids."

"I'm sorry," Caroline murmured. "I haven't been paying as much attention as I should."

"It's not your fault, kiddo," her father replied. "I think we're just going to have to hire someone to be with her all the time, even when we're home."

Caroline nodded. She looked over at Noah who was sitting on the other side of Ava Dawn. They hadn't spoken since they were in the truck with her mother. She didn't know what to say to him, and he didn't seem to be in a hurry to talk about it. Caroline looked away from him and back to her father. "Are you staying here?"

"Just for a while. You three should go on home."

"I'll stay with you," Caroline said, quickly. "Ava Dawn can take the truck and take Noah home."

"I don't mind staying here and waiting with Uncle Max," Ava Dawn replied.

"Go ahead," Caroline said.

"You don't have to stay," Caroline's father told her, standing up to give his daughter a hug. "But I know you're going to, anyway."

Behind them, Noah stood up. He had his arms crossed over his chest, and when Caroline turned and saw him standing there, she thought that he looked like he was about to bolt. Instead, he said, "Can I talk to you for a minute, Caroline?"

Caroline shrugged. She didn't really want to talk to him, but that wasn't something she could say. Not in front of her father and her cousin. "Sure."

Noah led her outside the waiting room and down one of the never-ending white halls. "Do you want to talk about this?" he asked once they were out of earshot of everyone.

"About what?" Caroline crossed her arms over her chest, mirroring him. She absolutely *did not* want to talk about it.

Noah sighed. "About this morning."

"Not really."

"I'm sorry." Noah ran his fingers along the stubble on his chin. "I wish you hadn't found out like this."

Caroline narrowed her eyes at him. "What do you mean?"

"Look, I begged my grandfather to tell you," he began. "I told him you deserved to know the truth."

"You acted like I was making a big deal out of nothing." Caroline took a step back from him. "You acted like it was all in my goddamn head."

"You have to understand, it was years ago." Noah sighed. It was a heavy, defeated sigh. "It was before you were even born."

"How long have you known?"

"It was a family rumor since I was little," Noah

replied. "Then when I got to Cold River, my grandfather told me to stay away from you, and that's when I knew for sure."

"Oh my God," Caroline said under her breath.

"I found pictures, more pictures of your mom and my grandfather, that I didn't show you." Noah was reaching out to her. "I'm sorry, I should have told you myself, but I didn't know how."

Caroline felt the anger bubbling up from her core. He'd known. He'd known for practically his whole life. "How could you lie to me?"

"I didn't want to upset you," Noah replied. "And my grandfather didn't want you to know. He doesn't want anybody to know."

"It's a little too late for that now."

"I don't want it to change things between us," Noah said. "Caroline, this has nothing to do with me . . . nothing to do with you."

"This has *everything* to do with us!"

"It doesn't," Noah replied. He reached out to her. "We aren't them. I'm not my grandfather."

"Don't touch me!" Caroline tried to contain herself, but she couldn't. Her emotions came flowing out of her, and before she could stop herself, she shoved Noah back as hard as she could with both of her hands. She shoved him so hard that he went tumbling backwards, landing with a thud onto the cold tile.

Caroline hurried past him, ignoring the people staring at her, coming out of rooms and offices to watch the scene unfold. She didn't care. The only thing she cared about was getting away from Noah.

Away from her mother.

Away from the sterile hospital walls and that awful, awful waiting room.

Away.

She just had to get away.

Chapter 30

Caroline left for the bait shop the next morning before her father or Ava Dawn were up. She'd pretended to be asleep the night before when Ava Dawn finally returned from taking Noah home, and although she felt slightly guilty, Caroline let her think that she was mad at her for letting her mother escape rather than telling her the truth. She'd heard Ava Dawn crying in the spare room into the wee hours of the morning, but Caroline knew if she went in there to check on her, she wouldn't be able to keep from telling her everything.

It was cruel to let her cousin beat herself up like that, but Caroline just didn't want to talk about it. She didn't want to say it out loud, because she knew the moment that she finally did, it would become real.

Truthfully, she didn't want to open the shop, either. She knew she'd have to see Noah, and he was, aside from her mother, the absolute last person she wanted to see. She hoped he'd at least be smart enough to stay on his side of the road.

She pulled up in front of the shop and hopped out of her truck. Relief flooded through her when she realized it was far too early for Noah, or anybody else, to be up and at 'em. She headed down to the river, squinting into the early morning sun. It had been dark when she left the house. It felt good outside—it was too early for the heat to be miserable, and when she sat down in front of her tree, the mist coming off of the river made it all the more enjoyable.

She baited her hook and cast a line out into the water. Caroline usually came to this spot to think. It was, and had always been, her safe place. But today, she didn't want to think. She just wanted to sit and watch the water ripple without worrying about that awful, empty feeling that had begun to grow in the pit of her stomach. She didn't understand how things could be perfect one minute—sharing a bed with Noah—and spectacularly not so perfect the next.

Of course, she thought, *deep down I knew my mother was cheating on my father.* Caroline cringed as the word *cheat* ran through her head. But that's what it was, wasn't it? Cheating. There was no sugarcoating it. Her mother was a cheater, and oh God, did her father know? Surely he didn't know. How could he still be married to her if he knew?

Their marriage was a lie. She remembered what Noah told her about perfect marriages—about how they didn't exist. He'd known then about her mother and his grandfather, and still . . . *still* he'd said nothing.

Caroline tried to shake those thoughts from her head as she felt a familiar tug at the end of her line. Slowly, she began reeling in from the water. She continued to tug and reel, coaxing the line and whatever was hanging from it out of the water. It was a dance she knew well, and it was thrilling when for the first time all summer, a shiny small-mouth bass popped up out of the water, dangling from the hook jutting out of its mouth.

Before she could revel in her catch, she heard footsteps behind her. She knew who it was, who it had to be. "Go away," she said, without turning around.

"Caroline, can't we talk?" Noah asked.

"No."

"Why not?"

"Because you lied to me." Caroline wanted to turn around and yell at him, but then he might see the tears streaming down her face. She reeled the line in enough so that the fish was dangling just out of the water. "Please just go away."

"Caroline."

"Please."

Noah didn't say another word, but she heard

him walking away from her. She listened until she could no longer hear his footsteps and then she brought the fish in closer to her and out of the water. Caroline considered keeping it and fishing for her dinner like she and her father used to do when she was a kid. They'd gone out every weekend when her father wasn't on call to the Cold River. Sometimes they went out on her father's old, rickety johnboat, but most of the time they sat right where she was sitting now—at the old, rickety tree. The first time her father taught her to clean a fish, that's where they'd been.

They'd caught almost a dozen smallmouth bass that day. Their cooler was full, and their bait was gone. Max O'Conner placed a fish on an old stump and told Caroline to watch as he ran his knife along the belly of the fish. "Now you try it," he said when he was done. He put another fish on the stump and handed her his knife.

"I don't think I want to," Caroline said, crossing her arms across her chest.

"You've gotta learn sometime."

Caroline took the knife and squatted down next to the fish. "What do I do?"

"Just like I showed you," her father replied. "Hold his head and cut as close as you can to the backbone."

Caroline did as she was told.

"Careful, careful," he said. "Don't cut through his backbone."

After she made the cut, she grabbed at the insides of the fish with one of her hands, something she'd actually done once or twice when her father made the initial cut. But this time, something was different. Something else came out with the fish's guts—hundreds of tiny, white balls. It took her a minute to realize that they were eggs, fish eggs. The bass had been a female, and she was pregnant, or had been pregnant until Caroline gutted her with a filet knife. "Dad," she whispered, falling back onto her behind into the grass, "Dad, she was *going to have babies*."

Her father took the knife out of her hand. "It looks that way. Happens sometimes, kiddo. Don't worry about it."

Caroline hadn't wanted to worry about it, but she had for the rest of the day. Still, years later, she thought about it. She was thinking about it right now as she held the fish up to eye level. Was this fish a girl? Was it pregnant? Of course there was no way to tell without killing it, and it just stared at her, open-mouthed, until Caroline wasn't sure which one of them was on the hook. She wasn't sure which one of them was out of her element, which one of them was gasping for air until she pulled the hook out of the fish's mouth and threw it back into the river, watching it swim away from her as fast as it could, making the tiniest of ripples beneath the water's surface.

Chapter 31

"I cannot believe this is happening to me!" Ava Dawn wailed, throwing herself down onto the bed.

Caroline rolled her eyes. Lord have mercy, did her cousin have a flair for the dramatic. "It's not the end of the world, Ava Dawn."

"Why did Darlene have to go and have her damn baby on the night of the races?" Ava Dawn picked up one of Caroline's pillows and screamed into it. "Whyyyyyyy?"

"I don't think she planned on having her water break all over the diner's kitchen floor," Caroline replied.

"Darlene ruins everything," Ava Dawn said. "I cannot believe I have to work tonight. Now I'm going to miss *everything*."

"You've been to the races before," Caroline replied, losing patience. "It's not anything new."

"Except Tyler's racin'," Ava Dawn reminded her. "That's new."

Her cousin was right. Tyler racing a stock car at the Cold River Speedway was new, and it was honestly pretty exciting. "I don't have to go, either."

"Of course you do. You promised Kasey. We all did."

Ava Dawn was right again. "I'll tell them you had to work and you couldn't help it," Caroline offered. She didn't really want to go, but she didn't want to stay at home, either. She'd spent the last few days avoiding conversation with both of her parents. She was afraid her father, at least, was starting to notice.

"Thanks," Ava Dawn sniffed. "I guess I better go wash my uniform."

Caroline couldn't remember the last time she went to the race track. It had been years ago with Court and his family before Pam got sick. Pam loved the races, and so did Court. Caroline enjoyed them, too, but the loud noises and exhaust fumes almost always gave her a headache.

She was waiting on the porch when Court and Reese drove up.

"Hey, whose Corolla is that in the driveway?" Reese wanted to know. "Surely that ain't your new rig."

"It's the new nurse's," Caroline replied. She hoisted herself up into Court's truck. "Dad hired someone to be here full-time, even at night."

"So you've got a stranger in your house all the time?" Court asked.

"Is she hot?" Reese wanted to know.

"There are two of them," Caroline replied. "They take shifts. They stay in the spare room when they're here at night. Ava Dawn and I are sharing my room. And no, neither one of them is *hot*. They're both about fifty."

"Don't be rude, Caroline," Reese said. "Fifty-year-old women can still be hot."

"They're married."

"Details, sweetheart." Reese waved his hand in the air. "Mere details."

Caroline rolled her eyes. Reese wasn't the only person she knew who seemed to think that. She bit down on her lip, determined not to think about *that*. She was going to have a good time tonight.

The Cold River Speedway was located just outside of town on the outskirts of the county. It sat on eighty acres with a dirt track and wooden bleachers surrounding it. In the summertime, people from all over brought their RVs and camped during the racing weekends. Sometimes, on particularly quiet summer evenings, the sounds of the racing cars could be heard all the way in the center of Cold River.

Tyler was busy unloading his hobby stock car from the trailer when Caroline, Court, and Reese arrived.

"Isn't she a beauty?" Tyler beamed. "She's gonna win tonight. I just know it."

Beauty wasn't exactly the word Caroline would use to describe the dented Monte Carlo that Tyler was caressing like a newborn. "I'm sure you'll do great," she said.

Just then, Gary sauntered past them, holding the keys to his own stock car. "Hey, kiddos. Hope you're ready for a real race tonight."

"I'm ready for just about anything you got," Tyler replied, crossing his arms over his chest. "But don't you be fillin' that tank with none of your granny's grain alcohol. You know that's against the rules."

"Wouldn't dream of it." Gary gave them a grin that said he'd been doing more than dreaming about it. "Besides, your thirsty friend over there at Cranwell Station's been drinkin' me outta house and home."

"Noah?" Caroline cut in. "You've been selling your shine to Noah?"

"Shhh . . ." Gary put his finger to his lips, glancing nervously around at the crowd. "Don't say it so damn loud."

"Oh, come on," Kasey said. "Your granny's shine is the worst-kept secret in Ozark County."

"Let's just keep our heads in the race," Gary replied, reaching down to jerk up his pants. "Good luck out there, Ty."

"You're gonna beat the shit out of 'em with that beast!" Reese cut in, clapping Tyler on the back. "We're gonna find our seats and grab a beer. See ya in the winner's circle, brother."

Once they were out of earshot, Court said, "That POS won't even make it a lap. Why did you have to get his hopes up, Reese?"

"That's what friends are for," Reese replied, stepping into line at the refreshment stand. "Man, we shoulda brought a cooler. Beer is gonna cost us a fortune."

"I don't want any," Court replied. "Get me some nachos. I'll go find us somewhere to sit."

"What bug crawled up his butt?" Reese asked Caroline, jamming his elbow into her rib cage. "He's been like this all night."

Caroline shrugged. "Maybe he's just having a bad night."

"Seems like I'm the only one he's sore at."

"I don't know," Caroline replied.

"Well, you know him better than anybody else."

Caroline turned around from her place in line to look at him. "What do you want me to say, Reese?"

Reese stared at her for a long time before hunching his shoulders over and replying, "Nothing, I guess."

"It's not your fault." Caroline gave him a pat on the back. "It's nobody's fault, really."

"If it ain't my fault, how come I feel so dang guilty?"

Caroline felt sorry for Reese. She'd been pretty insensitive to him in all of this between him and Court, but he had feelings, too. He just didn't show them very well. Reese loved Court, he really did, but he was never going to love Court in the way that Court wanted, and deep down, she knew that it broke Reese's heart just as much as it did Court's. "I'm sorry," she said.

"Aw, it's alright." Reese sniffed into the dusty air. "Here, take this money." He shoved two twenty dollar bills into her palm. "I see me a fine-lookin' brunette over there that I gotta talk to."

Reese swaggered off, and Caroline just shook her head. That was just his way. Reese needed to remind her that he was, after all, a man. A man who liked women. As if she didn't know that already. She was so lost in her thoughts that she didn't realize it was her turn at the concession stand until the person behind her cleared his throat. "I'm going," she said, turning around.

"Well, hello, Caroline." It was Haiden Crow, smiling at her.

"Hello, Haiden," she said. She noted the tick in his face when she called him Haiden and not *Brother Crow* as he preferred. "How are you?"

"I'm fine 'n' dandy. How about yourself?"

"Oh, mostly the same." Caroline turned around to the woman behind the concession stand and said, "I need two Bud Lights, a water, and some nachos. Extra jalapeños."

"I've never seen you at the races before," Haiden continued on behind her. "You here to watch someone?"

"It's been a while since I've been out here," Caroline replied. "One of my friends is in his first race tonight. Tyler Jenkins."

"Oh, good, good." Haiden Crow fidgeted with his money. He rolled it up into a ball in his hand and then shoved it back into his pocket only to remove it again a few seconds later. Despite the cool evening, there was a line of sweat above his brow.

"Everything okay?" Caroline asked.

"Oh, yes. Yes," he replied. "Everything is fine. But I was wondering . . ." He trailed off.

"About?"

He shoved his money back down into his pocket. "Well, the thing is, I haven't seen your cousin much lately. I was worried about her is all."

"You haven't seen her at church, you mean?"

"Yes, yes. Of course."

"She's been busy," Caroline said. "Picking up extra shifts at the diner and helping Dad and me out with Mom."

"She, uh, she told me about your mama wandering off."

"Did she, now?"

Haiden nodded, in earnest. "We've been prayin' for her."

Caroline wanted to roll her eyes, but instead she said, "Thank you."

"Will you tell Ava Dawn I asked after her?" Haiden looked at her, a glint of hopefulness in his eyes. It made Caroline nervous.

"Sure will," she said. "I'll let her know you've been missin' her . . . at church."

"Thanks."

Caroline stepped away from the concession stand to allow him to order, starting off towards the bleachers where she saw Court sitting by himself on one end. "Here," she said, handing the nachos up to him. "Take these so I can get up there."

"Where have you been?" Court wanted to know.

"Reese ran off and left me with everything," Caroline huffed, making her way up the crowded bleachers. "And then Haiden Crow cornered me in the concession line wantin' to know why Ava Dawn hadn't been to church."

"He sure seems to pay a lot of attention to her."

Caroline sat down. "You're tellin' me."

"You think there's something going on between them?" Court asked.

Caroline shrugged. "I don't know."

"I can't believe that the pastor of the largest church in town would risk his career for Ava Dawn," Court said.

"Hey now." Caroline elbowed him. "Ava Dawn is gorgeous and not nearly as stupid as she lets people believe."

Court piled a tortilla chip with three jalapeños and said, "But you've got to admit, it would be pretty stupid of both of them."

"You're right." It would be stupid of them, and a few weeks ago, Caroline would have said there was no way that two people could possibly be so stupid. But now, she wasn't so sure. It seemed to her that the people who had the most to lose were also the most willing to take a risk.

"Speaking of Ava Dawn," Court continued, "did you see that Roy's here?"

"I didn't see him," Caroline replied. "But he never misses a race. His dad's shop sponsors a couple of cars."

"I didn't see that little blonde with him this time."

"Good."

On the track below them, the race was beginning to start. Caroline could see Kasey leaning in to kiss Tyler before he suited up and jumped into the car. Roy wasn't far away, giving a pep talk to one of the Bean family's drivers. It was exciting, especially when the drivers started their engines and the noise could not only be heard but also felt, vibrating off of the bodies of the cheering people sitting in the stands. Caroline found herself wishing she could share it with Noah. So far, he was the only thing she'd ever experienced to make her heart beat as fast as it did during those first few seconds before a race.

But that was over now, the two of them, and when Tyler skidded off the track in the second lap and into the patch of grass into the middle, Caroline figured she probably understood just how he felt.

"Well, that was underwhelming," Court said

once the race was over. "And what in the hell happened to Reese?"

Caroline shrugged. "He ran off after some girl with brown hair."

Court's jaw tightened. "I'll go find him. Wait for us up by the front gate, alright?"

"Okay." Caroline stood up, feeling a little dizzy. She'd managed to drink both her beer and Reese's since he'd never come back. She shakily made her way back down from the bleachers and followed the crowd out towards the parking lot.

It was dark out in the parking lot, but the bright lights from the track illuminated everything else. She waved and spoke to a few people before leaning up against the chain link fence attached to the gate. She didn't even see Roy until he was standing in front of her.

"Evenin', Carolina."

"Hello, Roy."

"What're you doin' out here all by your lonesome?" Roy put his hand up on the chain-link fence and leaned in closer to her.

Caroline took an uncomfortable step back. "Just waiting for Court and Reese. I'm sure they'll be along shortly."

"I seen ya over there talking to the preacher man earlier," Roy said. He tried to smile, but it came out as more of a sneer. "I hear he and my wife's been seein' each other pretty regular."

"I wouldn't know anything about that."

"You sure?" Roy leaned even closer to her.

"It's not your business, anyway," Caroline replied, unable to contain her irritation.

"You've always been more'n half of Ava Dawn's problem."

"*You're* more than half of her problem," Caroline replied. "A problem I hope she's rid of soon."

"I guess it's just as well," Roy sneered. "I'd sure hate to be like yer daddy, takin' care of some bat shit crazy woman who don't even know her own name."

That was the thing about Roy. He always knew where to twist the knife. "That would be better than being married to a drunk," Caroline replied. "From what I hear, that's what runs in your family."

"That what your cousin been tellin' you?"

"That's what everybody's been tellin' me."

"She better not be cheatin' on me with that preacher man." Roy grabbed her arm, his dirty fingernails digging into her flesh. "Because I swear to God if she is, Carolina, I'll kill her."

"You're disgusting."

Roy laughed, letting go of her arm and disappearing into the crowd of people. Maybe Caroline was going crazy, but she could have sworn she heard him laughing all the way home.

Chapter 32

The first time Caroline realized something might be wrong with her mother was when Maureen O'Conner came to visit her in college. Caroline was nineteen, a sophomore, and living in one of the dorms on the Missouri State University campus in Springfield.

It was October, and it was just beginning to get dark. Caroline and her roommate, Amber, had been studying all afternoon for midterms. When they heard a knock at the door, they assumed it was the pizza they'd ordered. Instead, it was Caroline's mother.

"Mom, what are you doing here?" Caroline asked.

"I came to take you to lunch," her mother replied. "Did you forget?"

"We did that last week, remember?" Caroline asked. "And it's almost six o'clock at night."

"No we didn't," her mother said. She stepped inside the dorm room. "I think I'd remember driving two hours to go to lunch with my own daughter."

"Okay," Caroline replied. She was confused, but her mother had always been forgetful, and lately it was getting worse. No big deal. "Let me go get my sweater. Can Amber come, too?"

"Of course."

A few minutes later, Caroline returned to see her mother sitting on the couch in the common area. She was staring blankly into the room, and Amber was sitting next to her and patting Maureen O'Conner's hand. "Mom, is something wrong?"

She looked over at Caroline, and that's when Caroline saw the abject fear in her mother's eyes. "I can't remember why I'm here," her mother said. "I can't remember who this girl is next to me, either. I know I should know. But I don't."

Caroline called her father, and he came right up. Two weeks later, they heard "Alzheimer's" for the first time, and Caroline left school at the end of the fall semester. The first year of her mother's diagnosis was spent seeing every specialist in the country. None of them were able to curb the beastly disease, and Maureen O'Conner began to refuse to travel. She once became so obstinate in the Kansas City airport that she had to be detained and hospitalized. It was the last time they traveled anywhere that required a plane ride.

Caroline had spent the last five years taking care of her mother. She'd kept the bait shop open, the only real thing she felt like she could do to help. She didn't go out much, with the exception of the last few weeks, and everything she'd done throughout the whole of her twenties now felt like a huge, ugly lie.

And she had to keep it up for her father's sake.

She turned from the stove when she heard her father coming in through the front door with her mother and Ava Dawn. "Hey, everybody," she said, trying to muster a smile. "Dinner's almost ready."

"Are you making mashed potatoes?" her mother asked, her voice hopeful. "The hospital food was simply terrible."

"Of course."

Her mother sat down at the table, and her father sat his wife's overnight case on the couch. "Do you need any help in there?" he asked.

"No," Caroline replied, turning back around. "I think I'm good."

Ava Dawn wandered into the kitchen and aimlessly began stirring the potatoes. "You don't have to set a place for me tonight," she said.

"How come?" Caroline wanted to know.

"I'm helping Brother Crow with the teen Bible study," Ava Dawn explained. "His wife has gone to Atlanta to visit her family for a couple of weeks, and she usually helps him with it."

"You've been helping him a lot lately."

Ava Dawn turned to face Caroline. "What's that supposed to mean?"

"Nothing!"

"Look, I know you're still sore at me over what happened," Ava Dawn said.

"I'm not, I swear," Caroline replied.

"But I figured you'd be happy about how much time I'm spendin' helpin' out with the church," Ava Dawn continued. "I've got my own life now, and Brother Crow helped me with that."

Caroline sighed. "I know."

"He's a good man."

"He's a married man."

"I know," Ava Dawn said. "Don't you think I know that?"

"Do you?" Caroline just didn't trust Haiden Crow any farther than either of them could throw him. "I saw him at the races the other night. He seemed awful anxious to talk to you. What do you suppose that was all about?"

"I gotta go," Ava Dawn replied, wiping her hands on the back of her jeans. "I'll see you later."

"I just wish people around here would start telling me the goddamn truth!" she called after her. What Caroline really wanted to do was explain to her cousin why she was really upset—she wanted to take her into her confidence and cry on her shoulder about all that she knew. She wanted to tell her about Noah and the cave and everything else, but she couldn't. She just couldn't. She could barely admit it to herself, and so instead she turned back to the stove and continued to cook her mother's mashed potatoes.

Maureen O'Conner was in good spirits. She was feeling better since her hospital stay. The color was back in her cheeks, and her feet were mending. She was all smiles at the dinner table. "The food looks great."

"Your mother is right," her father replied, smiling at Caroline. "It does look good."

Caroline forced a smile. She watched them eat as she picked at her plate. She wished she could go back to the night she invited Noah over for dinner. She would have left him there at the station. If she'd kept her big mouth closed, none of this would have happened. She watched as her mother shoveled in a mouthful of potatoes. It must have been exhausting for Maureen O'Conner to keep that secret all these years—having to look at the station every single day and pretending that it didn't mean anything to her, sort of the way Caroline was having to do now. *My real mother,* Caroline thought, *my mother before Alzheimer's, would have gone to her grave with that secret.* Now secrets were oozing out like the inside of an overfilled jelly doughnut, and there was nothing her mother could do to stop them.

"Caroline?" Her father looked at her expectantly. "Caroline, honey, are you alright?"

Caroline tore her eyes away from her mother. "Yeah, I'm fine," she said. She stood up and picked up her plate. "I think I'm going to sit out on the porch and eat if that's alright."

"Are you sure?" he asked. "It's still a hundred degrees out there."

"It'll be fine," Caroline replied. *Better than sitting in here,* she thought. *With her.*

She wandered outside and sat on the front steps, leaving her plate to Yara who'd refused to come inside, somehow basking in the million-degree heat. She stared out into the street, watching the evening traffic crawl by. Caroline had lived in this house most of her life, ever since she could remember, and sometimes she forgot that her parents had had a whole other life before she was born, a whole other child. Had that not been enough for her mother? Had she been so unhappy that she needed to seek solace in someone else— in the likes of *Jep Cranwell?*

After a few minutes, Caroline's father came outside. He sat down beside her on the steps. "Want to talk about what's eatin' ya?"

"No."

"I can see you're upset about something."

"I'm not upset about anything," Caroline lied. "It's just been a long couple of days is all."

"A couple of the orderlies overheard you arguing with Noah Cranwell that day at the hospital," Max O'Conner said.

Oh no, Caroline thought. "They did?"

"Yes." Her father nodded. "How long have you known?"

"What?" Caroline turned to look at him. "What do you mean?"

"You know what I mean."

Caroline took a deep breath. So her father knew. He had known. Had everybody known but her? "I found out at the hospital the day we were there with Mom. You know, after she got out of the house," she said. "I guess I knew on some level before then, but I didn't want to believe it."

"I didn't want to believe it at first, either," her father replied.

"When did you find out?"

"Oh," her father said, leaning back on his hands, "probably about thirty years ago."

"You knew the whole time?"

Her father nodded. "Not the whole time, but at the end I knew."

"And you were okay with that?" Caroline was incredulous. "You just forgave her?"

"I wouldn't say I was okay with it," he replied. "I wasn't okay with it then, and I'm not okay with it now. But yes, I did forgive her . . . and Jep."

"Why?"

"Because I love your mother." Her father shrugged, sitting back up.

"But she cheated on you!" Caroline practically screamed. "Not once, for a whole year! Noah told me. It lasted a whole year!" Caroline was furious. How could he be so calm? How could he just . . . sit there as if someone had stolen his lunch instead of his *wife?*

"I don't need you to tell me how long it lasted,"

her father replied, his face reddening. "I lived through it, remember?"

"Do you remember?" Caroline asked. "Do you remember? Because what kind of person stays with their wife after she cheats on him for a whole year?"

"I really thought you'd have a more mature response," Max O'Conner said. His tone was even, but his eyes were flashing. "You can't possibly understand until you've lived through it, and I pray to God that you never have to live through it."

"You're right," Caroline replied, standing up. "I'll never understand it, because I don't understand *you*. I don't understand how you can care so little about everything."

"What are you talking about?" her father asked. "I care about you and your mother more than anything."

"I don't believe you," Caroline replied. "You never act like anything bothers you. You won't talk about *anything*. I'll tell you one thing, I never want to end up like you, married to some old woman who can't even remember who you are, but she can sure as hell remember to go get her hair done for the man she's cheating on you with!"

Caroline felt the slap sting her face before she even saw her father lift his hand. She stood there in stunned silence for what felt like forever until finally her father spoke. "I . . . I'm sorry. I didn't mean to . . . I didn't mean to do that. You pushed me too far . . . I'm sorry."

Caroline pulled her truck keys from her pocket and walked numbly down the stairs. She didn't know where she was going, but she wasn't going to stay there another second longer. Not another second longer.

Chapter 33

Caroline sat in front of Court's house for a long time before knocking on the front door. She would have gone inside sooner if it hadn't been for Reese's truck sitting in the driveway. She kept hoping he would come out to leave; she just wasn't in the mood to deal with him tonight, but she didn't have anywhere else to go. Ugh, why did he and Court have to be friends?

She got out of the truck and trudged up to the front door. Court swung open the door before she even had a chance to knock. "We were wondering when you were going to come insi . . ." He trailed off. "What in the hell happened to you?"

"I'm fine," Caroline said, stepping inside the house. She could see Reese sitting on the couch and Court's father perched on the recliner reading the newspaper. "But can I stay here tonight?"

"Of course." Court pulled her further inside

and beckoned her to sit down. "I gotta tell ya, Carolina, you sure as shit don't look fine."

Caroline didn't even want to know how she looked. She'd been crying since she left her house, and her right cheek still burned. She sat down and the entire story tumbled out—everything, all the way up to the part where her father slapped her across the face. "To tell you the truth, I probably deserved it," she said at last. "But, I mean, how did he think I was going to react?"

Reese handed her what was left of his whiskey. "Here. I think you need this more than me."

"Thanks." Caroline took the glass. "I can't go home right now."

"I'll make up the spare room," Court said, standing up. "You know you can stay as long as you want."

"So you're with Noah now?" Reese wanted to know as soon as Court left the room. He took the glass back from her and drained it. "Like, together?"

"No." Caroline narrowed her eyes at him. He was so nosey. She'd left out the bits about her and Noah in the cave and in her bedroom, but she had a feeling Reese got the picture, anyway. "We're nothing," she said.

"His loss," Court's father said, looking up from his newspaper for the first time. He folded the paper up into a square and placed his reading glasses on the end table beside the recliner. "Now, if you'll all excuse me, this old man needs to get some shut-eye."

" 'Night, Dad," Court called from the hallway bedroom.

"Don't worry," Joe Brannan said, placing his hand heavily on Caroline's shoulder. "I've known your family my whole life. It'll work itself out." He shuffled out of the living room, leaving Caroline and Reese alone together.

"I'm sorry, Carolina," Reese said, after a moment of uncomfortable silence. "Really, I am."

Caroline knew he was. He always said just exactly what he thought. "I know."

"You know," Reese said, scooting closer to her on the couch. "You look exactly the same as you did in high school."

"Oh yeah?"

"Yep. And you act the same, too."

"How so?"

"You know, always running to Court when you've got a problem."

"You're one to talk," Caroline retorted.

"What do you mean?" Reese stood up to fill his glass.

"Oh, come on," Caroline said. "Don't think I don't know about how you almost lost your truck when you first started with the railroad. You didn't know a bank account from a hole in the ground. I know Court made those payments for you until you could get back on your feet."

"He told you about all that?"

"Of course not," Caroline said. "I noticed the bill was coming to him. I put two and two together."

"I guess we both lean on him a little hard," Reese replied.

Caroline guessed he was right. Except the only difference was that Court did things for her because they were buddies and not because Court was in love with her. Court had been in love with Reese since they were in junior high, and she reckoned that Reese knew it just as well as she did. "We should probably work on that."

"Work on what?" Court emerged from the bedroom.

"Nothin'." Reese set his glass on the coffee table. "I better git. Early day tomorrow."

"You sure?" Court looked deflated. "It's just eight o'clock."

"And I've been here since three o'clock this afternoon," Reese replied, giving Court his best lopsided grin. "I'll holler at ya tomorrow."

"Alright," Court said with a sigh. "See ya later, man."

"Later."

Caroline followed Court out onto the front porch and watched Reese drive away. It looked like it was going to rain again with lightning illuminating the sky. She sat down in one of the rocking chairs. "I'm sorry I interrupted your night," she said.

"Oh, it's fine," Court replied, still staring off after Reese's truck. "He's been over here damn near every day since he got back."

"Would you rather he went somewhere else?"

"What do you mean?"

"Court, it's just me," Caroline said. "You don't have to pretend with me."

"I don't know what you mean," Court replied. He sat down next to her. "He's welcome here same as you are."

Caroline sighed. She knew better than to push it. "And I appreciate always being welcome."

"Do I need to go over and have a talk with your dad?" Court asked. He was only half joking.

"No," Caroline replied, grinning for the first time all evening. "My mom is his world, and I insulted her. I insulted him. But I couldn't stop myself even though I knew the words were wrong as they were coming out of my mouth."

"I did that once."

"You did?"

Court nodded. "It was just after my dad and Pam got married."

"What happened?" Caroline wanted to know.

"Pam was trying to boss me around, as usual," Court said, a sad smile crossing over his face. "I got all mad and told her she wasn't my mama. When my dad got home, of course she told him, and he gave me hell. We argued, and I told him that it was all his fault that my mom died. I told him . . ." Court paused. "I told him that if we had more money she'd still be alive."

"Oh Court."

"Wasn't that an awful thing to say?" Court asked. "Cancer doesn't care how much money you have. And he's still paying off those medical bills."

"I'm sure he knows you didn't mean it," Caroline offered, patting his hand. "You were just a kid."

"It seems so unfair that he had to have *two* wives die of cancer," Court continued. "I wonder if maybe he tried too hard to save Pam because of what I said about Mom. Maybe he wouldn't have lost his house."

"You can't try too hard to save someone," Caroline replied, although she knew from experience that you probably could. Memories of her mother's meltdown at the airport flooded back.

"Anyway, I just wanted to tell you that you're not alone," Court finished. "It's going to be alright." It was his turn to pat her hand.

"Thanks."

"So," he said. "Are you going to open the shop tomorrow?"

Caroline shook her head. "No, I don't think so."

"Why don't you sleep in and hang out here?" Court asked. "It'll do you some good."

"You're the best." Caroline threw her arms around him, leaving Court to flounder awkwardly for a few seconds before relenting and hugging her back.

"You're gonna be just fine, Caroline," he said into her ear. "Just fine."

Chapter 34

It was almost August. The days were still sweltering, but there was a glimmer of hope for fall, and that was all it took to get the people of Cold River out of their summer funk. Caroline found herself dividing her time between the bait shop and Court's house. She'd gone home briefly one morning while she knew both her father and Ava Dawn would be gone to gather more clothes. Her mother's nurse looked at her curiously, especially when Caroline hadn't acknowledged her mother. However, she must've known something was going on, probably apprised by Ava Dawn, and the woman didn't say anything.

It wasn't like she planned to ignore her mother and be mad at her father forever. She knew that she would eventually have to go home, especially after the season at the shop ended. Her father usually cut the nurses' hours in the fall, and it saved them money. Still, she couldn't help but think that maybe it was time for her to strike out on her own. Maybe it was time for her to find her own place and make her own mark.

She was thinking about all of this as she watched Smokey from the window of her shop, as he laid new shingles on the roof. He was almost finished. Another day or two, she figured. The day before, two dump trucks came and laid fresh gravel out front, and a concrete mixer came the day before that to lay a fresh new sidewalk leading up to the station. Noah glanced up and over at the bait shop when he placed his hands in the fresh cement, and Caroline could have sworn they locked eyes. It had taken her until just a few minutes ago to get the courage up to look outside again. Caroline had to admit she was impressed with how much had been done over there. Noah was going to make his September opening date. He hadn't tried to talk to her again since that day at the river, although she often wondered about what she would say to him if he tried. Yara, it seemed, was his dog now. Some mornings she'd be up on the porch when Caroline got to the shop, but more often, Caroline saw the two of them, Noah and her, together. The food Caroline left out for her went untouched.

For the first time in a very long time, Caroline felt alone.

As she continued to watch out the window, she saw her mother's Jeep pull up, and out jumped Ava Dawn. She eyed the shop skeptically, shielding her eyes from the sun. It was as if she was deciding if she wanted to come inside. After a few seconds, she bounded up the steps and inside the shop. "Hey, Caroline," she said.

"Hey," Caroline replied, trying to sound casual. "You stop by to pick up some bait?"

Ava Dawn crossed her arms across her chest. "Do I look dressed for fishin'?"

"Not particularly."

The two women stared at each other. After what felt like forever, Ava Dawn said, "I actually came by to apologize."

Caroline was taken aback. "For what?"

"For the way I acted about Brother Crow. I shouldn't have taken it so personally."

"Me either."

Ava Dawn stepped around the counter and gave her cousin a hug. "Uncle Max is worried about you," she said.

"I'm sorry I took off," Caroline said, relieved to have it out in the open.

"I understand," Ava Dawn replied. "And Uncle Max understands. He misses you, though."

"I miss him, too," Caroline admitted. She also missed her mother. "I know he's going to be needing me by summer's end."

"Well, about that," Ava Dawn began. "I was thinkin', and I've already talked to Uncle Max about this, that I might quit at the diner and take care of Aunt Maureen full-time. You know I have my CNA license. I've had it since high school, and I love takin' care of people. Roy would never let me work anything more than part-time, you know? I was thinkin' I might even go back for my LPN someday. What do you think?" She looked at Caroline expectantly. "Lettin' her leave without me knowin' was just a onetime thing, I swear."

"I know it was," Caroline replied. "You could make more money at the diner, though."

"But I'd save more livin' with you and Uncle Max."

"That's true."

"If you don't think it's a good idea, I understand," Ava Dawn replied. She looked down at her feet.

"No!" Caroline exclaimed, reaching out for her cousin's hand. "No, I think it is a wonderful idea!"

"Thank you," Ava Dawn said, sounding relieved. "So does Uncle Max."

"I knew he would."

"What are you doin' tonight?" Ava Dawn wanted to know. "I heard there's a new band playin' down at Mama's."

"Reese mentioned that," Caroline replied. "I just don't think I'm up for that."

"Oh, come on. Please?"

"I knew you had another reason for coming down here," Caroline teased.

"I don't want to go alone," Ava Dawn needled.

Caroline sighed. "Make Reese and Court go with you."

"I don't want to go with them. I want to go with you."

"Will you leave me alone if I say yes?"

"Pick me up at eight!" Ava Dawn said, already halfway out the door. "Wear something cute!"

Caroline stood in front of the hallway mirror at Court's house. She'd spent the last few hours at one of the new boutiques in town, trying to find something suitable to wear to Mama's. Most of the time, Mama's was a hole in the wall bar where Smokey and his buddies went to drink, but on the weekends, it turned into just about the only place in town you could see a live band play. People from all over Ozark County came to hear the music, and a few of the big-name country stars had even gotten their start there. Caroline wanted to look cute.

She was glad she'd had the foresight to grab her pink cowboy boots from her closet when she'd been at her house. It was a cool enough evening to wear them, and they looked great with her blue jeans and tight-fitting peasant top. The top was black with little pink rose embellishments. The salesgirl told Caroline she looked sexy, but Caroline wasn't so sure.

"You look sexy," Reese said with his hands on his hips, appearing in the mirror behind her. "Damn sexy."

"Thanks," Caroline said, giggling. "When did you get here?"

"I've been here twenty minutes already," Reese replied. "You were just too busy starin' at yourself in the mirror to notice."

Caroline felt her face redden. She turned to face him. "Well, you're awful spiffed up yourself."

"Got me a date." He raised his eyebrows at her.

"Oh yeah?"

"Yeah, and you're never gonna guess who with."

"Tell me!" Caroline urged. "Who is it?"

"Jolene."

"Jolene from the clinic?" Caroline asked. "The same Jolene we went to high school with?"

"One and the same."

"What about Jolene?" Court came out of his room, freshly showered and ready to go. "Didn't she just get divorced?"

"Last year," Reese said. "She's coming with us to the bar."

"She is?"

"Yep, and I hope she's coming home with me afterwards." Reese winked at his friends. "We've got time to pick her up, right?"

"I guess," Court replied, shrugging. He was trying to sound nonchalant, but Caroline could tell that he was upset. Reese hadn't dated anyone since returning to Cold River, and this news came as quite a shock.

"Well, we better get going," Caroline spoke up. "We have to get Ava Dawn, too."

"I'll drive!" Reese proclaimed, ushering them out the door. "Don't want to keep the ladies waiting, do we?"

"Hey, I'm a lady, too," Caroline protested.

Court and Reese shared a look. "Of course you are," Court replied, shoving into her with his shoulder. "A total and complete lady."

Chapter 35

Mama's was packed by the time the five of them arrived, but Ava Dawn led them straight over to the table closest to the little stage, which was, miraculously, not being used. "What are we drinkin' tonight?" she wanted to know.

"Whiskey," Court and Caroline said at the same time.

"White wine?" Jolene sounded hopeful. She was dressed to the nines and looked mostly uncomfortable to be at Mama's. It was quite a switch from the relaxed personality she presented at the clinic.

"I'll check on that," Ava Dawn replied.

"I'm coming with you!" Reese hollered over the noise.

"I'll pay!" Caroline called after her, but Ava Dawn wasn't listening. She was engulfed in a bear hug with a 400-pound man in a ten-gallon cowboy hat.

"Do you come here a lot?" Jolene asked her.

"No, not lately."

"How come?"

Caroline shrugged. "Lots of reasons, mainly because Ava Dawn is married to a lunatic, and he never let her go anywhere."

"Roy is a loose cannon, that's for sure," Jolene said, scooting her chair closer to Caroline. "He comes into the clinic sometimes."

"Really?" Caroline asked. "That surprises me since my father is there so much."

"Oh, he's real careful not to come in on days when your daddy is there," Jolene said. "I reckon I shouldn't be tellin' ya this, but his daddy is losin' the auto body shop, and Roy was the first to be let go."

"His own son?"

"Roger Bean don't care for nobody but himself," Jolene replied. "Where do you think Roy learned it?"

Caroline felt a wave of nervousness come over her. She hoped Roy wasn't there tonight. Losing Ava Dawn and his job in the same summer would probably be enough to make him do something stupid—even more stupid than usual. "So he's been coming to the clinic?" Caroline asked.

Jolene nodded. "One of the doctors put him on some antidepressants." She covered her mouth as soon as she said it. "I really shouldn't be telling you that."

"Drinks!" Ava Dawn appeared in front of them. "I ordered you both whiskey neat, and I got a couple of pitchers of Bud for good measure."

"No white wine," Reese said apologetically to Jolene. "But Mama fixed you up somethin' special. Said you'd like it."

Jolene looked at Caroline.

"It'll be good," Caroline assured her. "My mom was never much of a drinker, and Mama always made her somethin' special when she came down here with my dad."

"Okay," Jolene replied. "Thanks."

"The Rattlesnakes should be out in a few," Ava Dawn said. She poured herself a beer. "The lead singer just got out of prison last week. Should be a good show."

Caroline took a drink of her whiskey. It was good. Not as good as the whiskey of her father's that she and Noah had the night her mother wandered off, but good nonetheless. As she put the glass to her lips for a second time, someone at the front of the bar caught her eye. She squinted into the smoky air. The person who'd just walked through the door looked an awful lot like Noah. *No way,* she thought. *It just looks like him because I was thinking about him.*

"Caroline!" Ava Dawn jabbed her in the ribs. "CAROLINE!"

"What?"

"Is that Noah Cranwell?"

There was no denying it. Noah Cranwell was walking towards them, his gaze set intently on Caroline. To her relief, the lights dimmed and four men took the stage. Everyone stood up, and Caroline was able to lose him in the throng of people.

What was Noah doing there? She surveyed the scene from between the shoulders of two men standing behind her. She saw Noah approach Court, and she saw Court extend his hand to him. They were leaning close, talking about something, but of course it was too loud for her to hear anything they were saying. After a few minutes of chatting, Court began to lead Noah over to their table.

No. No. No. This wasn't happening.

When the band took a break, Noah and Court were in front of her. Court gave her one of his looks like he couldn't help but bring Noah over. "Hey, Caroline. Look who I found."

Caroline finished what was left of the whiskey in her glass. She could play nice. *She could.* "Hi."

"Hi," Noah said. He looked just as uncomfortable as Caroline felt. "Smokey said the music was good. I didn't know you'd be here."

"We were just about to get up and dance, boys," Ava Dawn cut in before Caroline could respond. She pointed to the beer on the table. "Help yourself."

Caroline didn't want to dance. She wanted to go

back to Court's house and crawl under the covers for the next year. She opened her mouth to protest, but Ava Dawn gave her a look that told her to shut up. "Okay," Caroline said. "Let's go dance."

"You line dance?" Ava Dawn asked Noah.

"What?" Noah leaned closer as the music started back up.

"Do. You. Line. Dance?"

Noah still looked confused. "No?"

"Oh, son, you gotta get out here!" Ava Dawn squealed.

Noah allowed himself to be pulled up by Ava Dawn. She led him out onto the dance floor and said, "Are you ready?"

"What do I do?"

"First you hook your thumbs through your belt loops, like so," Ava Dawn began. She gave Caroline a wink. "Then you put your right foot out."

"And your right foot back," Caroline finished, wanting to get the lesson over with. "Then out. To the side. Then back." She demonstrated. "Just follow our lead."

Ava Dawn and Caroline fell into step with the rest of the group. To Caroline's surprise, Noah caught on quickly and was even keeping up with them like a pro by the end of the song. "Am I doing it right?" Noah yelled, jumping beside her to kick up his heels.

Caroline nodded. She was laughing too hard to

answer him. Watching Noah dance was the funniest thing she'd seen all day, hell, in months. She almost forgot she was angry with him. She wished that things could go back to the way they were before . . . everything. She wished they could go back to her bedroom when she'd been mortified about the way she snored.

The music stopped and the lead singer of the Rattlesnakes announced they were taking a break. Caroline caught Noah's eye as they exited the dance floor. He gave her a slow smile, and Caroline felt herself smiling back.

When they returned to the table, they saw Reese and Jolene cozied up at one end and Court sulking at the other. He was stabbing the ice in his drink with his straw, occasionally stopping to glare over at the lovebirds.

"Are you okay?" Caroline asked him.

"I'm fine."

"You don't look fine."

Court took a deep breath. "I'm tired, and I have an early day tomorrow."

"We can go whenever you want," Caroline offered. She hated seeing Court upset, and she hated it even more that Reese was the source. She didn't begrudge Reese his love life—she'd once been part of it—especially when Reese possibly had no idea why Court might be so moody.

"Reese drove," Court said miserably.

"I'm sure he'll leave if you want to."

"You sure about that?"

Caroline glanced over at Reese and Jolene. She wasn't sure. "I'll go ask."

Court caught Caroline by the arm. "Don't worry about it. I'm fine."

"You sure?"

"Stop asking me that. I'm not a child, Caroline. Shit."

Caroline was taken aback. He'd never talked like that before. "I'm sorry. I was just trying to help."

"Well, stop." Court picked up his glass and took the last swig. There was a giggle from the other side of the table, and they all looked down to see Reese whispering seductively into Jolene's ear. With that, Court slammed the glass down onto the table, the force shattering it in his hands. "Shit!"

There was blood everywhere. Noah sprang into action, rushing to the bar and grabbing a towel from the bartender and wrapping it around Court's oozing hand. "Are you okay, man?" he asked.

"Goddamnit," Court muttered under his breath. "I didn't think I slammed the glass down that hard."

"It was pretty hard."

By now, Reese and Jolene were paying attention. Shards of glass had been flung all the way down to the other end of the table, and they were both gazing worriedly in Court's direction. "What happened?" Jolene wanted to know.

"What does it look like?" Court snapped.

"Hey, don't talk to her that way," Reese cut in. "We didn't see what happened."

"Well, if you'd been payin' a lick of attention to anybody but each other, you would have seen what happened," Court replied bitterly.

"I think we need to get you home," Caroline said, signaling Reese not to respond. "Reese, why don't you and Jolene stay here with Ava Dawn? I'm sure Noah will give us a ride home."

"Of course I will," Noah replied. He was already pulling his keys out of his pocket.

"Where is Ava Dawn?" Reese wanted to know.

Caroline watched as Noah and Court waded through the ocean of people and to the front door. Then she turned her attention back to Reese. "Last time I saw her, she was heading outside to smoke with one of the Rattlesnakes."

"Great, now I've got to be responsible for her?" Reese replied.

"She can handle herself," Caroline replied, annoyed. "Listen, don't even think about stumbling into Court's house drunk with Jolene. You take her back to your place, you hear me?"

"Caroline!" Jolene exclaimed, her cheeks reddening, even in the dim light.

"You got me, Reese?" Caroline asked, ignoring Jolene.

"I hear ya, I hear ya." Reese held up his hands.

"Good," Caroline replied over her shoulder.

She hurried out the door to catch up with Noah and Court. She knew it wasn't fair to be annoyed with Reese and Jolene, but she was anyway.

Noah was waiting in front of the bar with Court lying down in the backseat. "Do you want me to take him home first?" he asked.

"Um, we're going to the same place," Caroline replied. "You can take us both to his house."

"Okay."

"Just go on straight out of town. He lives in that first subdivision." Caroline could feel Noah giving her a questioning look, but she ignored it. "Court, are you okay back there? Do you need stitches?"

"No," Court groaned. "No stitches. Sheriff Montgomery will kill me if he finds out I was at Mama's."

"Why?" Caroline asked. "It's not like you were in a bar fight."

"I know, but he'll never believe it was an accident. Just take me home."

By the time they got back to Court's house, all the lights were off. "Let's be quiet when we go in," Caroline said. "We don't want to wake your dad. He'll be worse than the sheriff when he sees what happened."

Court nodded. "I'll grab the first aid kit from my squad car."

Noah caught Caroline's arm as she was getting out of the car. "Can we talk for a minute?"

Caroline didn't want to talk. She already knew what he was going to say. But he'd been so friendly at the bar and had kept things from being awkward, and he'd been nice enough to bring them home. It was the least she could do. "Sure."

"I'll go on in," Court said. "If you need me, I'll be right inside."

"I'll be fine," Caroline assured him.

"He sure looks out for you," Noah said once Court was safely out of the car.

"We look out for each other."

"I know you do," Noah replied.

"He's family," Caroline said matter-of-factly. "Family doesn't always mean blood, you know."

"Speaking of family," Noah began, fumbling with the keys in the ignition. "I just want to tell you how sorry I am . . . for everything. You were right to react the way you did."

"I could have handled it better," Caroline admitted. There was so much more she wanted to say, but for some reason she couldn't get the words to come out of her mouth. "I better get inside."

"What are you doing staying here?" Noah wanted to know.

"My dad and I had a fight. He knew about the affair all along."

"Shit, I'm sorry."

"It is what it is, you know?" Caroline shrugged. "My life is a mess right now, and I'm just trying to put all the pieces back together so that they make sense."

"Can't we just, I don't know . . ." Noah ran his hands through his hair. "Start over?"

Caroline sighed. "I wish we could."

"But?"

"But even if I could get past the fact that your grandfather and my mother had an affair, you lied to me about it. You didn't tell me about it when you found out, and you should have," Caroline said, the words coming out in a rush of air. "I asked you about it more than once. I even showed you that picture. You acted like I was making too much out of it."

"I knew how bad it was going to hurt you," Noah replied. "I was just trying to protect you."

"You were just trying to protect yourself," Caroline said. "You were afraid if I found out that I wouldn't want to see you anymore."

"Of course I was afraid of that!" Noah exclaimed. "I don't want to lose you, Caroline."

Caroline shook her head. "It's too late," she said, trying not to cry so hard she almost choked.

"That's not fair," Noah said.

"No, it's not," Caroline replied. "I can't look at you without seeing your grandfather. I can't look at myself without seeing my mother."

"I'm not my grandfather!"

Caroline pushed open the car door. "I can't trust you, Noah."

Before Caroline could even get the door shut, Noah peeled out of the driveway, leaving her in a cloud of dust. He didn't even break at the end of the driveway, and she could hear the screeching of tires as another car squealed to a stop to avoid hitting Noah. He was angry, and Caroline didn't blame him.

She was angry, too.

Chapter 36

Court was standing over the sink when Caroline got inside the house. The first aid kit from his car was on the counter beside him. He was cursing under his breath as the cool water ran over his hand and he began to pick out the shards of glass.

"Is it going to be okay?" Caroline asked, peering into the sink. "It looks pretty gross."

"I'm fine," Court replied. "I'll just put some butterfly strips on it."

"Here," Caroline said, reaching for the kit. "Let me do that."

"I sure hope I don't have to use my gun for a few days," Court quipped. "It'll sting like hell."

"Why were you so angry at the bar?" Caroline asked, even though she knew the answer.

"You know why."

"I just want to hear you say it."

"Why?" Court asked, wincing as she applied

antibiotic ointment. "What good does it do to say it?"

"I guess none," Caroline replied. "Especially if you're not saying it to the right person."

Court flinched, causing Caroline to smear ointment all over his hand. "I could never tell him," he said. "He'd probably never speak to me again."

"You don't give him enough credit."

"Even if he did still want to be friends," Court continued, "he'll never love me. Not the way that I want him to."

"I know." Caroline's heart ached for Court. "I just wish you didn't have to lie about it."

"My whole life has been a lie," Court muttered. "I don't know why I should stop lying about it now."

"I'm tired of people lying," Caroline said. She pulled a couple of butterfly strips from the package. "It seems like everybody in this whole damn town is a liar."

"It's self-preservation, mostly," Court replied. "I'd probably lose my job. Half the people in this town would stop speaking to me."

"The stupid half."

Court laughed. "You always know how to make me feel better, you know?"

Caroline finished with the butterfly strips and looked up at him. "I love you, and you know that. I just want you to be happy."

"I know," Court said. He rested his chin on the top of her head. "I know."

Cranwell Station was silent the next morning when Caroline pulled up to the bait shop. Noah's car was absent from the front, and Caroline didn't see it parked around back, either. *Maybe he spent the night with his grandfather,* Caroline thought, although she knew that probably wasn't true. She didn't think either one of them had spoken to each other since that day Jep came roaring into the station madder than a horny toad.

She'd never been so ready to have a season over at the shop. She was glad that she'd be closing for the year just about the time Noah would be opening the station to the public. He could pick up the slack until the following spring.

It had entered Caroline's mind more than once to shut the shop down for good, especially in light of recent events. After all, keeping it open for her mother seemed unsatisfying now after what Maureen O'Conner had done. Caroline always told people, just like she told herself, that she kept the place open for her mother. It was her way of honoring her. In time, maybe after her mother died, she'd close it down. Maybe she'd return to school and finish her teaching degree. Maybe she'd do something else with her life.

But the truth was that Caroline loved the bait shop, flawed history and all. She didn't know if she could ever give it up. It was yet another thing that she needed to discuss with her father. Eventually, she knew she was going to have to go home. As she was contemplating what that meant, her phone began vibrating in the pocket of her jean shorts. It was Court. "Hello?"

"I've been trying to call you for the last hour."

Caroline pulled her phone away from her ear and stared at it. "It never rang until just now."

"I got a call from one of the deputies out and about last night. Said they picked up a guy joyriding out on AB Highway. The guy ran his car clean through Farmer Tilson's fence. Nearly killed a cow," Court said. "I guess he wandered out into the pasture somewhere with a jug of Gary's granny's shine and passed out near the pond."

"Hilarious," Caroline said, dryly. "Why are you telling me this?"

There was a pause on the other end of the phone. "Because it was Noah Cranwell passed out in Farmer Tilson's pasture, that's why."

Caroline sucked in the air. It had seemingly gone dry all around her. "What?"

"He's been in county lockup," Court replied. "The only reason I know is because when they asked him who to call, he gave them your name."

"Why would he do that?"

"You think Jep Cranwell's gonna bail him out?"

"Wouldn't be the first time," Caroline muttered.

"What?"

"Nothing, nothing," Caroline said hastily. Her head was swimming. What in the hell was he thinking? What was *Gary* thinking, selling Noah a pint of moonshine like he was a goddamn local? He should have known better.

"They'll release him to you," Court continued. "But only you."

"What if I don't go get him?"

"I guess he stays in lockup."

"I'll call you back," Caroline said, hanging up. No wonder Noah's car hadn't been parked in front of the station. It was crashed somewhere out in the middle of a field full of traumatized cows. She shoved her phone back into her pocket and grabbed the keys to her truck.

Caroline had been to the county jail only one other time, and that was with Court. She'd waited in his truck while he ran in some paperwork. She'd never actually been inside. Caroline couldn't help but wonder if anyone had seen her go inside the building—word traveled fast, and surely someone would call her father.

She did her best to smile at the woman sitting behind the Plexiglas at the entrance. "I'm here for Noah Cranwell," she said.

The woman looked her up and down. "Gimme a sec."

Caroline sat down in one of the orange plastic chairs lined up against the wall and waited. After what felt like forever, two uniformed deputies came through the door with a disheveled Noah in between them.

"Court told us you'd take custody of him and see he stays out of trouble," one of the deputies said. He smiled at her. "Think you're up to the task?"

"I'll do my best."

"I'm not a child," Noah muttered. He looked awful. There were cuts and bruises on his face and arms. He was walking with a limp.

"If you wasn't a friend of Court's, you'd be in lockup waitin' on bail," the first deputy said. "Take what you can get, buddy."

Noah shook himself out from between them and followed Caroline out the door and into the parking lot. He groaned into the sunlight. "Is it always this fucking hot in Missouri?"

Caroline pointed to the truck and said, "Get in."

"Fine."

The two rode in silence for a while, Caroline's anger building and building inside of her until she said, "What in the hell were you thinking, Noah? You could have killed yourself."

"What do you care?" he shot back. "I laid it all out on the line last night, and you shook me off like I was some kind of rock in your shoes."

"Oh, so it's my fault now?" Caroline demanded. "It's my fault you downed a jug of moonshine and crashed through a fence?"

"So they told you about that, huh?"

"Of course they told me."

"Then if I'm so stupid, why are you here?" Noah asked. "Why did you come to pick me up?"

Caroline sighed, tightening her grip on the steering wheel. "Because there's somewhere I have to go, and I need you to go with me."

"And where is that?"

"We're going to Cranwell Corner," she replied. "I have some business there I need to finish."

Chapter 37

Despite Noah's pleas for her to change her mind and threats to jump out of the truck at every stop, Caroline managed to get both of them there in one piece. She knew Noah didn't want to explain to his grandfather why he looked a mess, but she didn't care. She needed to talk to Jep Cranwell.

As they drove past the station and the bait shop, Yara began to chase after them, barking and biting at the tires. Caroline slowed the truck down to a stop. "You better get out and talk to your dog," she said.

Noah got out of the truck, and when he did, Yara jumped up, putting her paws against his chest. After a few seconds, he led her around to the back of the truck, pulled down the tailgate, and patted the metal bed. Yara jumped right in.

Caroline was still shaking her head when Noah

slid back in beside her. "I don't know how you do that," she said.

"We have an understanding, me and her," he replied.

"When I found her, she was in awful shape," Caroline said. She stared straight ahead, pretending to concentrate on the road, as if she hadn't been driving the gravel for her whole life. For some reason, she was afraid she might cry. "The vet thought she might die. I nursed her back to health. I even stayed with her overnight at the bait shop after the surgery to remove her leg. She was scared at my house. Out here was . . . is the only place she's ever been comfortable."

"I'm sure if she could talk she would tell you thank you," Noah replied.

"I don't know," Caroline continued. "I was just the person who fed her, but honestly, she never belonged to me. Not in the way most dogs belong to people."

"I don't know why she trusts me," Noah admitted. "I think she just sees something in me that's like her." He looked away from Caroline and out the window. "Something broken, probably."

Caroline wanted to tell him that Yara probably saw in Noah what she saw—someone who was good and kind and worthy of her trust. *Well,* she thought, *until he wasn't anymore.* Everything would be so much easier if they could all just go back to the day Yara ripped his shirt by the door of the station. Maybe Caroline could figure out a way to stay ignorant of everything awhile longer, just long enough so that she could look at Noah, *love* Noah, the way Yara did.

But they couldn't go back, Caroline knew that. So instead of saying anything, she drove until they got to Cranwell Corner. As if by magic, Silas was standing behind the cattle gate when they pulled up.

Caroline opened the door to the truck and got out, walking up to the gate that separated her from Silas. "Open it up, please."

"You ain't got no business here," Silas said, placing a pinch of snuff between his lip and his gums.

"I've got plenty of business here," Caroline replied. She looked to Noah in the truck, but he just shrugged. He wasn't going to be any help.

"No." Silas crossed his arms over his chest.

"I'll hop over this gate if I have to," Caroline threatened. She noticed Silas wasn't carrying a gun, and she figured she could probably beat him in a footrace if she had to. "It'll be a whole lot easier if you just let us in."

"You stupid or deaf, girl?" Silas wanted to know.

Caroline put one foot up on the metal grate of the gate and hoisted herself up. In no time flat, Silas was in front of her, daring her to make good on her threat. "Let me inside, Silas Cranwell," she said, leaning as close to his face as she could without tumbling over the gate. "I need to talk to Jep about the affair he had with my mother."

Silas's eyes widened.

"I know you know about it," she finished. "Now let me in."

"Just calm down now." Silas licked his lips. "I reckon you better come on in."

"I appreciate it." Caroline hopped off the gate and got back into the truck as Silas opened it up for her to drive through.

"What did you say to him?" Noah wanted to know. "I figured I was going to have to get out and wrestle you back into the truck."

"You'd have lost that battle," Caroline said with a slight smirk on her face. "I'm small, but I'm scrappy."

"What are we doing here?" Noah asked. "Now that we're here, you might as well tell me."

"I'm going to talk to your grandfather," Caroline said simply, as if it was as easy as that. "I need to know about him and my mom, and it's not like I can ask her."

"You've lost your mind if you think he's going to tell you anything," Noah replied. "I could hardly get him to admit it." He shifted in the seat as they bumped down the gravel path. "I'm so fucking sore. Every time you hit a bump, it feels like every bone in my body is going to crack."

"You're lucky you're not dead."

Noah gave her a wry smile. "Yeah, you mentioned that once already."

Caroline parked the truck in front of Hazel's. She and Jep were sitting on the front porch, and Jep stood up when he saw them. Silas lagged behind, half running, half walking, hollering that he couldn't stop them. "Afternoon," Jep said, sticking his thumbs into the straps of his overalls. He was trying to be polite, but there was a fire flashing behind his eyes. It was the same fire Caroline had seen behind Noah's eyes a time or two. She wasn't going to let it intimidate her.

"Mr. Cranwell, I was wondering if maybe we could have a talk, just you and me," Caroline said. "I've got some questions, and as far as I know, you're the only one who can give me answers."

Jep and Hazel shared a look. Hazel stood up and brushed off her dingy apron, curls of potato skins falling onto the wooden porch floor. "Lord, child, what happened to you?" she asked.

Noah tried to shrug, but could only wince. "It's kind of a long story."

"Well, come on inside, and you can tell me all about it." Hazel pointed to Silas and said, "You, too, and grab them potatoes."

"Good luck," Noah said under his breath to Caroline.

Caroline followed Noah up the porch steps. "Can I sit down?"

Jep shrugged. "I don't reckon it matters to me."

"You probably know why I'm here," Caroline said, sitting down in Hazel's rocking chair.

"I do."

"I can't ask my mother."

Jep looked over at her from where he was standing on the porch. "She that bad-off?"

"She has good days and bad days," Caroline replied. "But even the good days aren't what they used to be."

"I ain't spoke to her in years," Jep said. "Not since I closed the station down for good."

"She thinks Noah is you."

"We look a lot alike, him and me."

Caroline studied Jep's face. He was right, of course. They were practically carbon copies of each other, except Jep had more wrinkles. It was easy for Caroline to see how her mother could have been attracted to Jep. He'd once been, and still was, a good-looking man despite the fact that the years had worn him down and he often needed an oxygen tank just to walk. "I need to know what happened," she said, finally. "I need to know why you two . . . Why it happened."

Jep walked over to his rocking chair and sat down, placing his elbows on his knees, staring down at the potato peelings, rubbing one of them into the floor with his boot. "I ain't never told no one about it," he said. "Not in that way."

"I need to know," Caroline pleaded.

"It ain't nobody's business but hers and mine."

"I'm her daughter."

"If Maureen wanted you to know, she'd a told ya."

"That's hardly fair," Caroline argued. "Especially now that you know damn well I can't ask her."

"You look so much like her," Jep said. "So much like her."

"Was it because it was convenient?" Caroline asked. "Because you were across the street from each other?"

"She used ta come over for coffee," Jep said. "The year the cancer took my Dottie, I lost near thirty pounds. Yer mama, she would bring me cookies. Tell me ta fatten up. We were just friends then. Nothin' more."

"When did it change?" Caroline was on the edge of the rocking chair. She didn't want to push him too hard, afraid he'd clam up.

"Musta been three years on," Jep said. He scratched at his whiskers.

"Did you start it?"

Jep looked over at her. It was as if he'd never stopped to ask himself that question. "She came over one afternoon for coffee. She was wearing these dangly earrings." He made a motion with his fingers below one of his ears. "It got caught in her hair, and I helped her untangle it. Then she kissed me. God help us both, she kissed me."

Caroline drew in her breath. She'd hoped it had been the other way around. She'd wanted so badly for Jep to tell her that he'd seduced her mother, that he was in some way more to blame than she was. "And then you started secretly seeing each other?"

"Not at first."

"Why not?"

Jep eased himself back into the rocking chair, and took a corncob pipe out of the front pocket of his overalls. He chewed on it a minute before answering. "Yer mama loved yer daddy, and yer daddy was my doctor. Neither one of us wanted to break ties with him over a little kiss. And of course, our sons went to school together."

Oh, Jeremy. In all of this, Caroline hadn't thought of him. She wondered if he'd known. Caroline felt an unfamiliar pain in her chest. Was it longing? Was it sorrow? She didn't know, but she wished her older brother were here to help her through this, to give her someone to talk to.

"But it couldn't be helped, in the end," Jep continued, unphased by Caroline's silence. "We was like magnets, her and me."

"Did you . . ." Caroline cleared her throat. "Did you love each other?"

"I ain't loved but two women in my life," Jep replied. "I married Dottie when we was fifteen. I loved her 'till the day she died, and I love her still."

"And my mother?"

"I loved her, too." Jep nodded, pausing for a

moment to light his pipe. "It was different with Maureen. It was . . . it was *passion*. I loved her so much I thought my heart would break when I had to leave her each day."

That wasn't what Caroline had expected. Jep Cranwell didn't seem like the kind of man who used words like *passion* and *love*. But as she looked at him, as she watched the way his face lit up every time he said her mother's name, she believed him, and, she realized, she didn't hate him.

She didn't hate him at all.

"Why did it end?" Caroline wanted to know. "If you loved her so much?"

Jep took the pipe out of his mouth and perched it precariously on the arm of the rocking chair. "Your brother died."

The pain in Caroline's chest was back. "My dad told me once that Jeremy's death almost killed my mother, too."

"It did," Jep replied. "I had to watch her suffer, and there wasn't nothin' I could do to help. I shook her hand at the goddamn funeral. Like a stranger would."

"You weren't her husband."

"Yer daddy found out a couple months later," Jep said. "He confronted me at the station. I woulda let him take a punch or two, but he said all he wanted was ta look me in the eye."

Caroline smiled, despite herself. "That sounds like my dad."

"Maureen ended things the next day, but I already knew." Jep picked up his pipe once again. "I ain't no match for a doctor, no match for a good man like yer daddy."

Caroline wanted to agree with him. She knew he was right. Her father never would have cheated on her mother, and he never would have cheated with another man's wife. Despite knowing that, though, she couldn't help but feel sorry for Jep. He looked so broken about what happened all those years ago. "So you let her go, just like that?"

"I did," Jep said. "I tried ta keep the station open after that, but it was too damn hard. I couldn't stand to look at her every day, and I knew it hurt her plenty to look at me."

"That's why you closed the store?" Caroline marveled at the revelation. "Because of my mom?"

"I closed it *for* her," Jep replied.

"I heard Cranwell Station closed because you were broke."

Jep snorted into his pipe. "We made more money that last year than we'd ever made," he said. "I reckon we'd a kept on makin' money, too."

Caroline looked around Cranwell Corner as if she was seeing it for the first time, at its dingy appearance and dingy tenants. Everything could have been different for them. Caroline always assumed the rumors were true and that the

Cranwells were just lazy rumrunners living in the past, living in the good old days, and refusing to be seen within society at every turn. No wonder he seemed so agitated with Noah every time he came to see him. No wonder he hated going into Cold River—he had to drive by his old life every single time he went into town.

"I never needed no more than what I got. I used the last of the savings gettin' Noah outta trouble, and been livin' off the land ever since," Jep said when Caroline didn't reply. "It ain't a bad life. It's lonely, but it ain't bad."

Caroline sighed. She could feel the tears pricking at her eyes. She didn't want to cry here, in front of Jep Cranwell. "I'm so angry at her," she admitted.

"That's natural, I reckon," Jep said, placing a big hand on her shoulder. "But you go on and be mad at me, and you go on and be mad at yer mama if ya have to, but don't blame my grandson."

"He should have told me."

"He did it for me," Jep said. "I didn't want ya to know. I didn't want you to judge him 'cause a me."

"I thought you hated me or something," Caroline said, almost laughing, wiping a tear away from her cheek.

"Naw, but I didn't want no one else gettin' hurt," Jep replied. "And you look so much like yer mama it hurts me to see ya."

"Thank you for talking to me."

"Uh-huh," Jep grunted. "You go on now, go on home. I reckon I got another conversation yet to have today." He pointed inside to where Noah sat at the kitchen table, peeling potatoes. "I'll see he gets back to the station."

Caroline thought about telling Jep about the wreck and about Noah's night in jail, but she thought better of it. It wasn't her story to tell. "I'll see myself out" was all she said.

Jep watched Caroline drive away from the front porch. He got smaller and smaller in her rearview mirror until finally she couldn't see him at all, disappearing with the rest of Cranwell Corner, its secrets but a tiny hill among the rolling Ozark Mountains.

Chapter 38

Caroline was asleep on the couch when Court came home from his shift, tired and dirty and still in pain from the fresh wound on his hand. He was sitting in his father's recliner when she woke up. She opened one eye and surveyed him quietly.

"I know you're awake," he said. "I can see your eye open."

"What are you, a cop or something?" Caroline joked. "How was work?"

"Long," Court replied. "Hot."

"Arrest anybody we know?"

"Always."

"Tell me about it," Caroline said, sitting up. She yawned. "Oh, that nap felt good. I haven't slept like that in ages."

"You get things all worked out with Mr. Fast and Furious?"

"No." Caroline stuck her tongue out at her friend. "I told you. That's over."

"I don't understand why," Court needled. "Just because he wasn't honest about one tiny thing?"

"It's hardly a *tiny thing*," Caroline reminded him. "Besides, I don't want to talk about Noah right now. Tell me who you arrested!"

"You remember Jemima Crocker?" Court asked. "She was maybe three or four years younger'n us."

Caroline wrinkled her nose up in thought. "I think so. Did she go by 'Jem' or something?"

"That's her," Court replied. "She's been cookin' outside of town in an abandoned trailer on her daddy's land for, oh, months, but we could never catch her there."

Caroline nodded. She knew that when Court said "cookin' " he meant Jemima had been cooking meth. It happened all the time in Ozark County; it happened all over Missouri, really. But out in the boondocks where there were places to hide out, it happened more often. Court raided a meth house at least a couple of times a month. "So you caught her this time?"

"Her and her daddy," Court replied, looking

pleased with himself. "I've been staking it out for *months*."

"What happened?"

"Her daddy ran out the back door," Court said. "Of course we were waitin' for him. Then Jem tried to wiggle out the damn kitchen window."

"Did she make it out?"

"Well, I was inside, me and Jimmy Parsons," Court continued. "Those damn masks we gotta wear don't make apprehending a suspect easy, but I managed to catch her by the hips as she was wigglin' out." Court stood up and placed his hands into the air, pretending to pull someone from an imaginary window. "She was kickin' and hollerin'. You'd a thought I was tryin' to kill her."

"Did you get her?"

"I'm gettin' to that," Court said. "So I get out from the window and try to calm her down, but it's no use. I had to hog-tie that woman in the backseat of my car!"

"You did *what?*"

"Hog-tied!"

"You hog-tied Jemima Crocker?"

"I had to!" Court replied, sitting back down. "Besides, it was just a matter of time before somebody else did it, so it might as well've been me."

Caroline bit her lip to keep from laughing. Honestly, it wasn't funny. Jemima's life hadn't been easy. Her mother had been dead for years, and her father was well known around the community for peddling the drugs he cooked at various locations out in the woods. Jemima was the youngest of eight, the only girl, and was tough as nails. She and Caroline hadn't exactly been friends, but Caroline had had enough respect for her to clear a path when she walked by, even if Jemima *had* been a freshman when Caroline was a senior.

By now, Jemima had two kids of her own and several family members in jail. If their lives were switched, Caroline couldn't guarantee she wouldn't have tried to escape through a kitchen window, either. Sometimes, the Ozarks could be a bit more like Daniel Woodrell's *Winter's Bone* than people around here wanted to admit. "What will happen to her kids?"

Court shrugged. "They weren't there. I'm sure family services will step in."

"Did she calm down enough so that you could untie her?"

"She tried to bite me when I took her out of the car," Court replied. "If that tells you anything."

"That would just be all you needed."

"Tell me about it." Court rolled his eyes. He began to pull at the gauze wrapped around his hand. "This hurts like a bitch. I think I might need to clean it again."

Caroline got up and went over to inspect his hand. She cringed when she saw it. It was red all the way around the cut, and his whole hand was swollen. "I think you need to go to the doctor."

"No way." Court shook his head. "I told you, I can't do that."

"But it looks infected," she said. "And deep."

"I'll be fine."

"Seriously," Caroline urged. "You might need antibiotics or something."

"No."

Caroline sat back down on the couch, knowing what she had to do. "Give me a few minutes to get changed," she said. "Then we'll go see my dad. He's at home today."

"Are you sure?" Court asked. "And he won't say anything?"

"Honestly," Caroline replied, "you're acting like you cut your hand in a bank heist. He won't tell anyone. It'll be off the record."

"Fine," Court relented. "And thanks."

Caroline sat in the cab of Court's truck, staring at her parents' house. She knew it was her house, too, but it just didn't feel that way. Not anymore.

"You ready?" Court asked. "Or do you want me to go inside by myself?"

"Don't be silly," Caroline replied, although that had been *exactly* what she was thinking. "Let's get this over with."

Yara was lying on the front porch and snorted with glee when she saw Caroline. She got up and shot towards Caroline, nipping at her legs disapprovingly for having been gone so long. Caroline reached down to scratch her behind the ears. When she looked back up, her father was standing in the doorway. She couldn't tell if he was happy or angry to see them standing there.

"Hey, Doc," Court said, breaking the tension. "I have something I need for you to take a look at. Caroline said it would be okay."

"Come in, then" was all he said. He stepped back from the doorway.

Caroline followed Court inside with Yara on their heels. Maureen O'Conner was sitting on the couch, knitting. She looked up when they came inside. "Well, where have you been?" she demanded, her gaze setting on Caroline.

"At Court's house," Caroline replied guiltily. Honestly, she hadn't thought her mother would notice. "For the last few weeks."

"I want mashed potatoes tonight," her mother said, turning once again to her knitting.

Caroline thought she saw the hint of a smile on her father's face. "Court's hurt himself," she offered, motioning for Court to sit down at the dining room table.

"Let's have a look-see." Max O'Connner sat down beside Court and unwrapped the bandage. "When did this happen?"

"Last night," Court said. "Cut it on a glass at Mama's."

"Well, at least the alcohol in the glass killed

whatever flesh-eating bacteria is undoubtedly living at Mama's," Caroline's father said. "But you really should have gone to the ER last night. You could have used a stitch or two."

"He wouldn't go," Caroline said. "He was afraid the sheriff would think he'd been involved in a bar fight."

"Were you?" Max O'Conner asked, as his eyebrow rose ever so slightly.

"Of course not," Court scoffed. "It was an accident. I set the glass down a little too hard." He shot Caroline a look that told her not to say anything more about why the glass had been broken.

"It's really too late to stitch," Caroline's father lamented. "But we'll get it good and cleaned out and put some fresh butterfly bandages on it. I'll write you a prescription for an antibiotic."

"Thanks, Doc," Court replied. "I appreciate it."

"Be more careful from now on, son."

Caroline glanced around the house, realizing for the first time that her cousin wasn't there. "Where's Ava Dawn?"

"Hmm?" Her father looked up from Court's hand. "Oh, she had some Bible study or something to go to. She's sure spending a lot of time with that Brother Crow."

"I guess that's better than spending a lot of time with Roy."

"I reckon so," her father replied. "I don't trust him much, though."

"Me neither."

Caroline's father gave her a smile and then turned his attention back to Court's wound, and Caroline wandered into the living room and sat down next to her mother. She knew it was silly to still be angry with her, especially for something her mother couldn't explain, couldn't talk to her about. She wondered if her mother, her real mother lost somewhere inside this woman's brain, would have told her once Noah came into town and she saw her daughter falling in love with him.

Her breath hitched in her throat. *Love,* she thought. *What a scary word. Love gets everybody into trouble.* Like it or not, that's exactly what she'd been doing—falling in love with Noah Cranwell. And more than anything, more than the anger she felt towards her mother, she just wanted to tell her she was in love with someone. She wanted to tell her mother how she felt. She wanted her mother to hug her and comfort her and be the one to cook the mashed potatoes. Caroline blinked back a tear, but she couldn't stop a few of them from falling to her cheeks. She wiped at them furiously when she noticed her mother staring at her.

"Why are you crying?" Maureen O'Conner asked.

"Nothing," Caroline said. "It's nothing."

"Well," her mother replied, "it certainly seems like something."

Caroline sighed. What could it hurt to tell her?

"I'm just sort of sad right now. I got into a big fight with my dad and there's this guy I like, and I think I've screwed it up with him."

Her mother nodded. "These things happen sometimes."

"I wish they didn't."

Her mother looked down at her knitting and continued on with what she'd been doing. After a few minutes she looked back over at Caroline and said, "Would you like it if I knitted you an afghan?"

Caroline smiled. "Yes. I'd like that very much."

"This one can be yours," Maureen O'Conner replied, beckoning down to the pink yard in front of her. "I think pink is your color."

"It is, Mom. Thank you."

After a few more minutes of Court wincing and her father apologizing, Court was all fixed up and ready to go. Caroline lagged behind, desperate to talk to her father. She wasn't even sure what she wanted to say, but she knew she didn't want to get back into Court's truck without having said *something*.

"I'm going on out to the truck," Court said, reaching out to Max O'Conner with his one good hand. "I'm in no hurry, Carolina." He walked out the door leaving Caroline and her father alone together.

Caroline's father cleared his throat. "How have you been?"

"I'm okay."

"Did Court really cut his hand on a glass?"

Caroline nodded. "Reese asked Jolene to go out to Mama's with us. You can imagine about how well that went over with Court."

"How is he coping?"

"You saw the result of how well he's coping," Caroline replied. "It's not fair." She sat down at the table. "I know you hate it when I say that, but it isn't. So much about love isn't fair."

Her father sat down across from her and began to clean up the mess he'd made bandaging up Court's wound. "You and Court are young yet," he said. "Wait until you're old like me. Love will be the least of your worries."

"Do you ever wish that Jeremy had lived and I'd never been born?" Caroline gasped as soon as the words were out of her mouth. She hadn't expected to say that. She hadn't even been *thinking* about that.

"Is that what you think?" her father asked. "That I wish you'd never been born?"

"No!" Caroline said. She didn't think that. "Sometimes I just wonder what our life would be like if Jeremy hadn't been killed."

"I wonder about that, too," Max O'Conner replied. "But I never wonder what my life would be like without you in it."

Caroline felt tears prick at the corners of her eyes. "Thank you, Dad."

"I love you, Caroline. Just like I love your

mother and just like I love Jeremy." He paused, fidgeting with a piece of loose gauze. "You have been the happiest surprise of my life."

"I love you, too, Dad," Caroline said. "And I'm sorry for the things I said to you earlier. I was angry, and I wasn't thinking."

"I've had almost thirty years to understand why your mother did what she did. She's not the only one to blame. Our marriage wasn't perfect then, just like it isn't perfect now. Your mother was lonely here; she was an outsider. I spent more hours with my patients than I did with my family, and I didn't make time for her or your brother."

"It wasn't your fault, Dad."

"It wasn't all my fault," her father corrected. "I may not have cheated on your mother with another woman, but I know she felt about that hospital like I felt about Jep Cranwell, and that counts for something."

Caroline guessed it did. She forgot sometimes that her parents were more than just her parents—they were people. They'd once been her age. It was an odd thing to think about. "I never thought about it like that."

"We all miss you, especially Yara," her father said.

Caroline looked down at Yara snoring beneath her feet. "Can I come home?"

Her father grinned, reaching out to take Caroline's hand across the table. "I was beginning to think you'd never ask."

Chapter 39

It was the last week of the bait shop being open, and with that came the first week in September. Caroline watched Noah prepare across the street for his grand opening. There had already been a piece in the paper about Cranwell Station being passed on to a younger generation, complete with an interview with Noah and Jep. She'd considered more than once going over to talk to him, especially since it seemed from the article in the paper that he and his grandfather had patched things up. She wanted to hear about it. She wanted to see the inside of the station. More than anything, she just wanted to see him, but she didn't even know where to begin. She hadn't exactly been nice to him. There were so many things she was still working through in her head, and she couldn't think of anybody else she'd rather talk to about it.

She was a bit taken aback when she saw Smokey pull up to the station in his rusty truck. The roof had been done the week before, and Caroline figured Smokey was back to his old tricks, drinking away his roofing money at Mama's. When he saw her staring at him through the window he waved and trotted over.

"How are ya, Carolina?" Smokey wanted to know. "Gettin' pretty late in the season for ya to be out here, ain't it?"

Caroline grinned. For a drunk, he sure had a good memory. "It's the last week," she said. "I probably could have closed a week or two ago. It's been slower than usual."

"I'm hopin' that this cooler weather don't hurt Noah's chances none," he replied. "He's s'posed to open tomorrow. Gonna have a grand opening tomorrow night. Even asked the Rattlesnakes to come out and play out back."

"Really?" Caroline was impressed. "I bet he'll have a good turnout."

"That's what we're hopin'."

"Didn't you finish the roof last week?" Caroline asked. "I'm awful glad to see ya, but what are you doing out here?"

"Didn't Noah tell ya?"

"Tell me what?"

"I work for them Cranwells now."

"You what?" Caroline wasn't sure she'd heard him right. "You work for him?"

"Well, for him and his granddaddy. I'm the hired hand, keepin' this place up to snuff." Smokey beamed at her. "Paid by the week."

"Smokey, that's wonderful!" Caroline meant it. She could tell he was stone cold sober. She'd never known him to do any work other than roofing, but she was sure he could do just about

386

anything he set his mind to . . . as long as he laid off the grain alcohol.

"I ain't had a drink since I started workin' here," he continued. "And I don't reckon I plan on it. Old Jep said he'd throw me out into the river and let me drown if he caught me drunk on the job." Smokey leaned in close to Caroline and whispered, "And you know what? I believe him."

"I believe him, too." Caroline grinned. "You better get to work before one of them sees you slacking off."

"Too late." Noah Cranwell stood with his fists dug into his hips, a look of mock anger spread across his face.

"Don't mind him," Smokey replied, still whispering. "He's been out of sorts for the last couple of weeks. Some girl broke his heart."

Caroline's breath hitched in her throat. Noah was walking towards them, but he didn't look heartbroken. He actually looked good . . . great, even. Maybe Smokey was wrong. "Everything is looking great," she said, smiling up at him.

"Grand opening is tomorrow night."

"I know."

Noah turned his attention to Smokey and said, "Would you mind to get a head start on those windows in the back? I'll be over in just a few minutes to help."

"No problem, boss." Smokey tipped his hat,

and Caroline couldn't help but giggle. "I'll be seein' ya, Carolina."

"Bye!"

"I've never seen a man so happy about manual labor," Noah said, shaking his head as Smokey ambled off.

"It was nice of you to hire him," Caroline replied. "He probably would have drank up all that roofing money by now."

"It's got nothing to do with being nice," Noah said. "He's a hard worker, and I needed someone around full-time to help me out. He's as good as anybody I've met in this town."

Caroline smiled. "Either way, thanks."

Behind Noah, Yara appeared. If a dog could be smiling, Caroline was sure that was just exactly what Yara was doing. "I had Yara groomed this morning," Noah said. "For the grand opening."

Caroline bit back a laugh. He looked so proud. "She looks like a completely different dog!"

"The groomers had one hell of a time with her coat, but she just sat there and let them fix her up, good as gold."

"It used to take three tranquilizers and a whole chicken just to trim her nails," Caroline marveled. She gave Yara's head a pat, and to Caroline's surprise, Yara nuzzled right up to her. "She doesn't look like a different dog, I think she *is* a different dog."

Noah looked down at her, his dark eyes searching

hers. For a moment Caroline was certain he was going to lean down and kiss her. Instead, he jammed his hands down into his pockets and said, "Look, I want you to know that I'm sorry for trying to make this thing between us something it isn't."

Caroline knitted her eyebrows together. "What do you mean?"

"You made it pretty clear on more than one occasion that you didn't want the same thing I did, and I'm sorry that I pushed you. I'm sorry about cornering you that night at Court's house, and I'm sorry about what I did afterwards. I was acting like an idiot."

Caroline felt her heart beginning to pound in her chest. She did want the same thing he did. *She did.* She wanted to tell him she was sorry, too. She wanted to tell him that *she* had been the idiot. But instead she heard herself saying, "It's okay."

"My grandfather told me you two had a good talk. He wouldn't tell me what you talked about, but he said he hopes that one day you'll be able to forgive your mother."

Caroline looked down at her bare feet. She studied an errant freckle on one of her big toes. "I guess that means the two of you patched things up?"

"More or less." Noah shrugged. "We'll never see eye to eye on everything, but I *reckon* that's the way it works. A wise woman once said to me that he's family. I'm just now beginning to realize what that word really means."

"Sounds like a smart woman to me."

"One of the smartest." Noah grinned down at her. "So what do you say, can we still be friends?"

Friends. Caroline mulled it over. He seemed to have his mind made up. And who could blame him after the way she'd treated him? Being friends with him was better than nothing, she supposed. "Okay," she said finally. "Friends it is."

Court was sitting on her front porch when Caroline arrived home. He was in his deputy uniform, and judging from the fact that it was still clean, she guessed his shift hadn't even started. "Did you miss me already?" she called from the truck window.

Court looked up and waved. The cut on his hand was almost completely healed. "I've been sitting here for almost an hour."

"Why didn't you go inside?" Caroline padded up the drive and sat down next to him.

"It's a nice night," he said. "Besides, I have something I need to tell you. I wanted you to be the first one I told. Well, except for my dad."

"What is it?"

"You know how I've always wanted to be in the highway patrol, right?"

"Of course," Caroline replied. "You've been talking about that since middle school."

"Well, I applied last year and didn't tell anybody."

Caroline punched him on the shoulder. "You did what?"

"I applied, and for the last few months I've been going through the interview process, you know, taking the tests and stuff. I found out last week that I've been accepted. I'm going to be in the Missouri Highway Patrol Academy."

"SHUT UP!" Caroline squealed, reaching out to hug her friend. "That's wonderful. I mean, that's really amazing, Court. Congratulations!"

"Thanks." He blushed. "My dad was beyond excited. I figured he might be upset, you know, because now I'll have to move."

"Oh." Caroline hadn't thought of that.

"It won't be for another couple of months," Court hurried on. "But I'll be in Jefferson City for training, and then who knows where after that. It could be anywhere in the state of Missouri."

"What will your dad do?"

"I'm keeping the house," Court said. "He can live there, and I'll keep paying the note. Besides, I'll need a place to come back to, won't I?"

Caroline grinned. "I'm going to miss you. I don't know what I'll do without you."

"I reckon you'll survive."

"I reckon I'll have to."

"Besides," Court continued. "There's always Reese."

"He's nothin' but a poor man's Court," Caroline replied, resting her head against Court's shoulder.

"I have to leave," Court said, suddenly very serious. "You understand that don't you? There's nothing for me here. I'll never . . ." He swallowed. "I'll never be able to be myself here."

"I know."

"I've spent most of my life wishing for someone to love me, someone who will never, ever love me the way I want him to love me, and it's . . ." Court trailed off. "Well, it's just time that I start living instead of wishing."

Caroline reached over and took his hand in hers. "I understand completely. There is nothing I want more in this whole, wide world than for you to be happy." She understood how he felt more than she wanted to let on. Being friends and only friends with Noah sounded excruciating at best. She didn't know how Court lived with something like that for as long as he had.

"Thanks, Carolina. You know I feel exactly the same way about you."

Chapter 40

It was five o'clock, and that meant the Wormhole was officially closed for business for the season. Caroline shut the door and locked it, turning over the sign that read, "Closed for business— See you in April!"

Most of the time Caroline went fishing on the

last evening, fishing well into the dark and heading home only when she knew her father would begin to worry. Tonight, however, was the grand opening of Cranwell Station, and there were people crawling all over the place, especially down at the river. There were children splashing around, people having picnics, all there to get a load of the new and improved station.

Caroline had already decided not to stay. She wasn't going to go fishing, and she wasn't going to wait around for the grand opening, either. Instead she was going to go home, sink into a bubble bath, drink an entire bottle of cheap wine, and read the book her father had given her over a month ago about Pretty Boy Floyd. It seemed like a perfectly uneventful evening, and Caroline was thrilled. She doubted Noah would even miss her.

She was climbing into her truck when Ava Dawn's car came barreling down the dirt road and squealed to a stop beside her. Ava Dawn got out, looking wild-eyed, her makeup smeared and the collar of her T-shirt ripped.

"What in the hell happened to you?" Caroline asked when she saw her.

"Roy happened."

"What did he do to you?"

Ava Dawn wiped at her eyes. "He was waitin' for me when I came out of Second Coming. He pulled me into his truck in the parking lot, and we had a big fight."

"Did he hurt you?"

"I got out before he . . ." Ava Dawn choked back a sob. "Before he could do much besides rip my shirt, but Caroline, I'm scared. He looked at me like he wanted to kill me."

"Come on," Caroline said, grabbing her cousin's hand. "Let's get out of here and back to town. We're going straight to the police station."

Ava Dawn recoiled from her. "There's somethin' I should tell you first."

"Tell me on the way." Caroline motioned for her cousin to get into the truck. "Just leave your car here for the night. It'll be fine."

Ava Dawn did as she was told and jumped into the passenger's side of the truck. "I've seen him mad, but this time it was different."

"I saw him at the races," Caroline said. "He saw me talking to Brother Crow. He thinks there's something going on between you two. I didn't tell you because I didn't want to scare you, but he told me he'd kill you if he found out it was true."

"Oh my God," Ava Dawn whispered.

"What were you doing at the church at this time, anyway?" Caroline continued. "You don't have a Bible study on Fridays, do you?"

"Caroline, listen to me for a second," Ava Dawn said. "I haven't been going to Bible study."

"What do you mean?" Caroline shifted her gaze from the road to her cousin. "You haven't been going to Bible study on Friday?"

"I haven't been going to Bible study *at all*."

Caroline brought the truck to a stop on the gravel road. "Ava Dawn, what have you been doing at the church?"

"It's more like *who*."

"Ava Dawn!"

"I'm sorry!" Ava Dawn squeaked. "I wanted to tell you. I swear, I wanted to tell you. But Haiden made me promise. He made me promise not to tell *anybody*."

"I knew it!" Caroline closed her eyes, counting to ten inside her head. "I knew you two were up to something."

"It's not what you think!" Ava Dawn protested. "We love each other!"

"He's married!" Caroline exclaimed, throwing her hands up into the air. "YOU'RE MARRIED!"

"I know that!"

"How long has it been going on?"

"Not long."

"How long?"

"The night of the storm, you know the one where your mom wandered off?"

"Ava Dawn, you didn't."

"I was only gone for a couple of hours! By the time I got back, she was gone."

Caroline gripped the steering wheel, fighting the urge to shove her cousin out of the truck and carry on home. "You left her alone while you went off with Haiden Crow?"

"I thought she'd be okay," Ava Dawn pleaded. "I swear, I thought she'd be okay."

"Well, she wasn't okay," Caroline muttered.

"I'm so sorry."

"What if this doesn't end the way you want it to, Ava Dawn?" Caroline wanted to know. "What if this ends, and he stays with his wife?"

"He's not gonna stay with her," Ava Dawn replied stubbornly. "He loves *me*."

"That doesn't mean he's going to leave his wife for you." Caroline thought about what Jep told her that day at his house. She thought about the look in his eyes when he talked about her mother. "Loving someone isn't any guarantee."

"It's all the guarantee I need."

"And what about his kids?" Caroline continued. "What will they think when they find out?"

Ava Dawn looked down at her hands. Clearly she hadn't thought about it. "They're sweet, but they're youngins. They'll understand. He'll make them understand."

"They might not."

"What's gotten into you?" Ava Dawn asked. "I knew you'd be pissed when you found out, but I didn't think you'd be givin' me the damn third degree about his damn kids." She sat back against the seat of the truck and sighed.

Caroline gripped the steering wheel. "You just need to think about how it might feel . . . for everyone else involved. What if those kids find out years from now, and it tears their world apart?"

"I don't understand what you're gettin' at."

"That's because you don't understand how it feels."

Ava Dawn twisted herself around so that she was staring at Caroline. "Oh, and you do?"

This was it. Caroline was going to have to tell her. If she wanted her cousin to understand the consequences of what she was doing with Haiden Crow, she was going to have to tell her the truth. "I know exactly how it feels," she said at last. "My mom and Jep Cranwell had an affair thirty years ago. I found out the day you snuck off and left her alone to see *Brother Crow*."

"Oh my God," Ava Dawn whispered. "Does Uncle Max know?"

Caroline nodded. "We got into a fight about it. That's why I left." She was about to say something else when she saw a truck heading in their direction. It was speeding down the road at a much faster pace than anyone should be driving, especially on gravel.

"Shit, it's Roy!" Ava Dawn was panicked. "I shoulda known. I shoulda known he'd find me! He knows I always go runnin' to you!"

Roy was driving smack down the middle of the road. Caroline knew there was no way he'd let them pass, and there was no way she could get the truck turned around on the narrow road before he reached them. "Ava Dawn, get out of the truck," she said. "We're going to have to run for it."

"What do you mean?"

"I have an idea," Caroline said, her heart racing. "I know where we can hide."

Ava Dawn nodded. "Just tell me where to go."

Caroline opened up her door and said, "Follow me."

Both women slid out of the truck and ran across the road and into the pasture beside it. They hadn't gotten far from the river, and the pastureland still belonged to the Cranwells. If they could just get back about half a mile, they would run smack dab into the entrance of the cave. Roy would never be able to find them. They could wait it out until he'd given up, and sneak back to Cranwell Station and call for help.

What Caroline hadn't anticipated was that when Roy saw Caroline's truck abandoned in the middle of the road, he, too, would abandon his truck and take off after them on foot, his shotgun slung over his back.

"Run!" Caroline hissed, grabbing her cousin's hand.

"He's going to catch us!" Ava Dawn screamed, gasping for air. "He's going to kill us both!"

Caroline heard Roy fire two shots in their direction, hollering at them to stop. She kept running, pulling Ava Dawn along with her. By the time they reached the entrance of the cave, she'd lost both of her flip-flops. "Get inside," Caroline whispered. "Hurry."

"What is this?"

"It's a cave. Now shut up and take my hand. It's going to be dark."

"Do you think he knows where we are?" Ava Dawn asked, no longer able to keep from sobbing.

"I don't know," Caroline replied.

Caroline was afraid to pull out her cell phone. She didn't want Roy to see a light from the cave, just in case he'd seen them go inside. She led her cousin blindly through the entrance and tried to feel her way through the darkness. She held out one hand in front of her as she walked. When her hand grasped a forming stalactite, she realized where she was. They could hide inside a little opening just beyond the stalactite. They could crawl inside it, she knew they could, if they could just find it.

From the front of the cave, they heard a voice. It was Roy, and he was still yelling. "Get out here, Ava Dawn! Come on now, I ain't gonna hurt ya none!" He laughed, and it echoed menacingly, bouncing off of the walls of the cave and filling their ears.

"Come on," Caroline whispered, pulling her cousin down with her. She winced as the bottom of the cave scraped her bare knees. She felt for the small opening as she crawled, and when she felt one on either side of the cave wall, she pushed Ava Dawn in first and crawled in behind her, making herself as small as possible, breathing as little as possible. She was just sure that Roy could hear their hearts beating in their chests.

"Come out, come out, wherever you are," Roy said, his voice dripping with saccharine sweetness.

Caroline closed her eyes. He wasn't going to find them. He wasn't going to find them. *He wasn't going to find them.*

"I'm going to find you," Roy continued, as if reading Caroline's thoughts. "Ain't no preacher man here to save you now. Ain't no lawman here to save you now. It's just you two an' me. Well," he laughed again, "me and my gun."

Caroline could hear Roy's boots crunching closer and closer. Just when she thought he was for sure going to discover them, a light shone in from the front of the cave. "Roy Bean!" a voice hollered. "You get out here and leave them girls alone!"

Roy's boots stopped. He was silent.

"We know yer in there!" came another voice. Caroline recognized that voice. It was Jep Cranwell. "I know that cave like the back of my hand. I'll find ya before you find them."

Roy began to move again, this time quietly, and closer to where Caroline and Ava Dawn were huddled. Caroline could feel Ava Dawn bury her face into her back. He knew where they were. He had to know. There was no way Jep and the others at the front of the cave could get there before Roy could get to the two of them.

The voices and the lights from the front of the cave neared them, as the men cleared the cave's entrance. They were calling Caroline's and Ava Dawn's names, beckoning them to scurry to safety.

The quiet crunching of Roy's boots stopped right in front of them. Caroline could make out the outline of his legs. She could hear him breathing. He was so close; he could have reached out and touched them. Did he know they were right beneath him?

Ava Dawn lifted her head. She scooted closer to Caroline and whispered, "Where did he go? I can't hear him."

Caroline froze as the butt of Roy's gun made a thud on the ground in front of them. "I've got you now," he growled.

Before Roy had time to react, Caroline reached out and grabbed ahold of his ankles, jerking his legs back towards where she was crouched. He lurched forward, and there was a sickening crack as Roy's head made contact with the stalactite in front of him. A gurgling noise emitted from his throat just before he hit the ground, and then it was quiet.

There was a chorus of shouts, and within seconds there were people in front of them, shining lights down into the terrified faces of Caroline and Ava Dawn. Caroline could see the outline of Roy's body on the ground in front of them. "Is he dead?" Caroline asked as Jep pulled her up. "Did I kill him?"

"Naw, he ain't dead." It was Silas. "He's knocked clean out, though. Gonna need a doctor, that's for damn sure." He kicked at Roy's body. "Son of a bitch deserves to be dead."

Caroline couldn't feel her feet, and she thought she might throw up. She didn't realize that Jep had passed her off to Noah until they were out of the cave and back in the fading daylight.

"Are you okay?" Noah was shaking her. "Talk to me, Caroline. Are you okay?"

Caroline blinked. A crowd had gathered outside. It looked like everyone from the station's grand opening had surrounded the mouth of the cave. There were shocked gasps from nearly everyone, and someone began to take pictures. "I . . . I think so."

Ava Dawn stumbled out of the cave, followed by Jep and Silas. She ran to Caroline and embraced her. "You saved our lives. My life," she sobbed into her cousin's hair.

"It's okay," Caroline soothed her. "It's going to be okay."

"Come on," Noah said, gently placing his hands on both their shoulders. "Let's get you two back to civilization."

Cranwell Station was lit up like a Christmas tree. There were flashing lights outside, and inside all the lights were on, and there were police, firefighters, and paramedics milling about. Caroline sat dazedly in a chair pushed up against one of the windows. There was a paramedic knelt down in front of her, addressing the wounds on her feet and knees.

"Some of these cuts in your feet are deep," the woman said, bandaging her up. "You may need a stitch or two."

"Okay," Caroline replied. She looked over at the doorway. Noah was guarding it, his arms crossed over his chest. He was watching the goings-on outside. Caroline managed to catch his eye and offer him a weak smile, but he turned away from her and went back to his watch.

"Caroline?" Max O'Conner brushed past Noah and into the station, followed by Court and Reese at his heels. "What in the hell happened? I got a call. Nobody would tell me anything." There was panic in his eyes. "Are you okay?"

"I'm okay," Caroline said.

"Where's Ava Dawn?"

Caroline nodded to the other side of the room where a deputy was interviewing her cousin. "She's okay, too."

"What happened?" Court asked. "We saw Roy's truck being impounded on the way here."

"He chased Ava Dawn out here," Caroline said. "Then he chased us to the cave, and we hid . . ."

"Wait," her father cut her off. "What cave?"

"The cave out past the station," Caroline replied. "Noah showed it to me a little while back. I thought we'd be safe there after he

403

cornered us on the road." She could feel tears welling up in her eyes. "I didn't know what else to do. I'm so sorry."

"What are you sorry for?" Court asked. "You probably saved both your lives." He patted Caroline's shoulder and headed over to talk to Ava Dawn.

Max O'Conner ran his hands down the length of his face and said, "I never thought Roy Bean would do something this stupid. I thought Ava Dawn was safe. I thought *you* were safe."

Caroline felt her shoulders slump, the tears flowing freely. "I was so scared. I thought he was going to kill us . . . shoot us. He tried to shoot us in the field. I was afraid we couldn't run fast enough . . ."

Her father sat down beside her. "It's okay. It's all going to be okay now."

Caroline took a deep breath. Her father was right. She was safe. They were both safe. She stood up when she saw the paramedics carrying the stretcher with Roy on it. She looked over and saw Ava Dawn staring out the window, too.

Ava Dawn caught her eye and mouthed, "Thank you."

Caroline smiled over at her cousin and sat back down. She glanced around the station for the first time. It looked amazing. The hardwood floors had been completely refinished. There were brand-new cases full of glistening food and beverages. Everything had a touch of shine with a bit of the old-fashioned flare that Noah had so admired in the pictures of the station he'd first shown her. She was so proud of him. She was proud of this place.

Max O'Conner stood up, helping Caroline to her feet, as well. "I think the officers outside have some questions for you," he said. "Maybe after that we can take you girls home."

Caroline winced as she walked across the floor and towards the door. She'd have her father look over her feet when she got home. She couldn't believe he hadn't demanded to give her a physical on the spot. It just proved to her how rattled he really was. Her heart leaped into her throat when she saw Jep Cranwell appear next to Noah. She watched as her father stopped in front of Jep.

"The police told me you found the girls," Max O'Conner said.

Jep nodded. "I did." He gripped his oxygen tank, and that's when Caroline realized he hadn't had it at the cave. He must've known it would slow him down.

After a few tense moments, Caroline's father stuck out his hand. "Thank you."

Jep Cranwell looked down at Max O'Conner's hand, astonished. He returned the handshake. The two men stared at each other, their eyes having a conversation that their mouths could not.

Caroline neared the door as her father walked

through it, and she saw Noah watching her. He still wasn't smiling.

"Wait." Noah grabbed her arm.

"What is it?" Caroline was hopeful. Maybe he'd decided he didn't want to be just friends with her. *Or maybe,* she thought, *he's angry that I ruined his big night.*

"Hang on just a second." Noah disappeared down the hallway. A few minutes later, he came back out with a pair of fuzzy house shoes. "I know they're too big," he said. "But it's better than walking on the dirt and gravel." He bent down and helped guide them onto her feet.

Caroline let out a sigh of relief at the cushion inside the slippers. "Thank you."

Noah nodded. He didn't say another word to her as she walked outside and into the blue and red lights of those waiting to see her.

Chapter 41

Caroline awoke the next morning to sunlight streaming through the windows of her room. She couldn't remember the last time she'd slept so well. When she rolled over, she realized that Ava Dawn was curled up next to her, still sound asleep. She didn't even remember her cousin climbing into bed with her.

She tried to slide out of the bed without waking

her cousin, her feet brushing against the slippers that Noah loaned her the night before. Caroline looked down at them, that feeling of disappointment creeping up from her belly and into her throat.

He'd seemed so worried about her once she'd got out of the cave, but he'd hardly spoken to her after that. Then he'd given her these house shoes to make it easier for her to walk. She couldn't understand what he wanted, but his words, "Let's just be friends," rang in her ears as if he'd said them seconds ago. Noah Cranwell just wanted to be friends. She'd missed her chance and probably made it worse the night before, ruining his party and practically showing the whole town the cave. She wouldn't blame him if he never wanted to see her again. At least the bait shop was closed. If she were careful, she wouldn't have to see him again for months. She slid her sore feet into his house shoes and padded into the living room.

She heard laughing coming from the dining room, and it didn't sound like her mother and father. Caroline was stunned to see Noah Cranwell sitting at the dining room table across from her father, drinking coffee and laughing like he was a long-lost friend. "What's going on?" she wanted to know.

"Oh, Caroline," her father said, standing up. "Here, have a seat. I'll get you a cup of coffee."

Instead, Caroline followed her father into the kitchen. "What's he doing here?" she asked.

"He wants to see you," her father replied. He pulled a cup from the cabinet. "He's been here since eight o'clock this morning."

"What time is it now?"

"Almost noon."

"You're kidding."

"I'm not," her father said. "Now go in there and try to be nice."

"I'm always nice," Caroline muttered, shuffling into the dining room, the cup of coffee burning her hands.

"Hey," Noah said when he saw her. He looked down at her feet. "I guess I won't be getting those back anytime soon."

"Not on your life," Caroline replied, sitting down.

"How are your feet this morning?"

"Sore, but my dad said I didn't need stitches. I guess I'm going to live."

"That's good to hear." Noah smiled over at her.

"So did you come all the way into town to collect your old house shoes?"

"Not exactly."

"I'm sorry about ruining your big night," Caroline said, her cheeks turning pink. "I didn't mean to. I tried to leave before it started, but then Ava Dawn showed up . . ." She trailed off. "The cave just seemed like the best place to hide from him. I didn't know it was going to turn out the way it did. Now everybody knows about it, and it's all my fault."

"Caroline," Noah said. "Caroline, I don't care about that. About any of that. That's not why I'm here."

"Then why *are* you here?" This was torture. What did he want from her if he didn't want an apology for exposing one of his family's well-hidden secrets?

"Can we go outside for a minute?" Noah asked. "Please?"

Caroline sighed. "Fine." She stood up and limped her way out to the front porch. "Okay, we're outside," she said once he'd shut the front door. "Now that I'm standing here in your stupid, smelly house slippers in my stained T-shirt and with my morning hair, what could you possibly have to say to me that you couldn't just say inside where there was air-conditioning?"

Noah cut her off with his lips on hers.

He was so forceful that Caroline almost lost her footing and began to stumble backwards. Noah grabbed her around the waist and brought her in closer to him. He didn't stop kissing her until they were both gasping and light-headed.

"What," she said, trying to catch her breath, "was that?"

"I don't want to be just your friend," Noah said. "I don't want to be your buddy, your pal, or any variation of that. I want to be with you. I want to be with you all the time, even when you're annoyed with me like you are now. I want to wake up next to you every morning, and most of all," Noah drew her into him again, "I want to kiss you whenever I want to kiss you."

"Okay," Caroline said slowly, attempting to take it all in. Her head was swimming. Her feet were on fire. Actually, every part of her was on fire.

"But if that's not what you want," Noah continued, "then you need to tell me. Because I'll sell Cranwell Station and go back to New Jersey. It's what I'll have to do if I have to look at you every day knowing that I can't touch you . . . that you don't feel the same way."

Caroline looked up at Noah. His dark eyes were clearer than she'd ever seen them before. He was telling her the truth and she knew it. Maybe he'd had selfish reasons for not telling her about the relationship between his grandfather and her mother, but he'd also been trying to protect her like he said, and she knew he'd been spending the last few weeks trying to prove it to her.

"Say something."

"You don't ever have to worry that I don't feel the same way." She pulled him down to her so that she could kiss him again. "The thought of being just friends and only friends with you made me sick to my stomach."

Noah brushed a piece of her curly red hair out of her eyes. "I *reckon* this means I'm here to stay."

Caroline grinned. That word suited him just fine. "Why yes, Noah Cranwell. I reckon it does."

Acknowledgments

It is with sincere affection and admiration that I'd like to thank the following:

PRIYA DORASWAMY—for taking a chance on me, always. For being patient when I scrapped the first draft at 50,000 words, and for being the best agent this Missouri Girl could ask for.

LUCIA MACRO—for being the best editor that anyone could ask for, and for always being enthusiastic about my work.

MY HUSBAND—for the Sam to my Dean, the Han Solo to my Chewbacca, the Jim to my Pam.

MY SON—for making me laugh all the time.

MY MOM AND DAD—for always reassuring me that I have a house in which to live if this "writer thing doesn't work out."

NICOLE HUNTER MOSTAFA—for being my Lucy Hanson forever!

BRITTANY CARTER FARMER—for being the Tom to my Mark.

About the Author

Annie England Noblin lives with her son, husband, and four rescued bulldogs in the Missouri Ozarks. She graduated with an M.A. in creative writing from Missouri State University and currently teaches English full-time for Arkansas State University in Mountain Home, Arkansas. Her first novel, *Stay*, was inspired by the year she spent teaching developmental English in the Delta of Arkansas, a place she says still has her heart. Her poetry has been featured in publications such as the *Red Booth Review* and the *Moon City Review*, and in 2006 she coedited and coauthored a coffee table book titled *The Gillioz: "Theatre Beautiful."*

Found

(or, How a Tiny French Bulldog Saved My Life)

I'd been in bed for a month. I got up occasionally to take the dogs out and to grab a Dr Pepper from the refrigerator, but for the most part I stayed under the covers watching reruns of *Gilmore Girls* and nursing a broken heart.

It was 2007, and I was twenty-five years old. My whole life, it seemed, had been turned completely upside down. I'd moved back home in January to take a job as the part-time writing specialist at Missouri State University–West Plains. The position allowed me to work with students on their writing during the day and teach developmental English classes at night, an arrangement that I loved. The university had given me the job temporarily until I finished my master's degree. However, when I applied for the full-time job that summer, I wasn't even given an interview. My boss in academic support called me in to her office, told me they'd hired someone else, and said that I needed to clean out my desk and make myself available to train my replacement.

That was it. I was out of a job, and if I didn't figure something out soon, I'd also be out of money and a place to live. Instead of looking for a job, I decided to do the next logical thing—buy a plane ticket and fly to Houston to meet one of my high school friends when he was released from jail. We spent three days in a downtown hotel and took a cab to Denny's for breakfast in the mornings, both of us pretending that our lives that existed outside of each other weren't complete and total disasters. He went home to his grand-mother's house broke, jobless, and on probation. I went home to Missouri broke, jobless, and in love with him.

He didn't love me back.

Even now, almost a decade later, that hurts to write. Up until then, in 2007, I'd always thought that he probably loved me too, at least a little bit. When it all came to an ugly end in August, via cell phone screaming matches and heated MySpace messages, I knew for the first time that it was never going to be anything other than a dysfunctional, one-sided obsession.

No job.

No boyfriend.

Cue the rolls of raw cookie dough and season after season of Rory and Lorelei Gilmore's witty banter. The dogs, at least, seemed content to be resting on the bed with me, snoring and farting their way through the days. Well, except for one of them. Tru, my little French bulldog, spent most of his time hiding *under* the bed. He would come out only if I left the room or was sleeping or pretended not to notice him.

I'd adopted him from an animal control department not far from where I lived after an afternoon of playing around on Petfinder. I noticed a listing for a French bulldog. I called my mom.

"You don't need another dog," she said.

"I just want to check it out," I replied. "Will you go with me?"

"Fine."

By the time we got there, the animal control officer was about to lock up for the day. He led us back to a shed behind the police station. Inside were two wire pens. Each pen held a dog, although it was so dark inside that I couldn't see anything. One of the dogs inside the pen was barking, high-pitched and panicked. I went inside that pen and scooped up the dog inside.

"Oh, you don't want to do that," the animal control officer said. "He's pretty dirty. He's been in here for a while."

"It's okay," I said, wishing I'd brought a nose plug. "I'll take him."

"You haven't even seen him."

"I don't care. I want him."

I didn't get a good look at him until after we'd filled out the paperwork and were back in the car headed home. "He's filthy," I said.

"He's tiny," my mother said.

"He's shaking," I said.

He *was* shaking. And panting. The moment we got home and his feet touched the carpet, he ran to my bedroom and hid under the bed. Nothing and no one could make him come out. My two other dogs, a Boston terrier named Lola and bulldog mix named Louis, didn't quite know what to make of this new dog.

Truthfully, neither did I. He'd been an impulse rescue. I'd scooped him up, paid the ten-dollar adoption fee, and taken him home. He was in pretty pitiful shape. His coat was dull and patchy. There were several long scars running the length of his back legs. His eyes were cloudy, his ears were tattered, and his belly was full of sores. The vet said most of his teeth were rotten and that he wasn't healthy enough to be neutered. The vet sent me home with antibiotics, medicated shampoo, and eye drops, and told me to wait it out. The dog might live if the infections cleared up and he started to eat.

And so I waited it out from underneath my covers while Tru waited it out underneath the bed.

Little by little, Tru got better, and the story of what his life must have been like before he came to live with me became more and more clear. His eyes were milky from ulcers that had never been treated, the sores on his belly were from staph infection, he had ear mites and fleas and ticks, and the scars on his legs, the vet said, were probably from being tied up and chewed on by other dogs.

He jerked away and barked violently when anyone tried to touch him during those rare occasions that he came out from under the bed. My other two dogs hadn't come to me this way. I'd read about abused dogs, but until now, I'd never had one. It didn't take long for me to figure out that Tru had probably been abused for a very long time before he was picked up by animal control. His wounds went much deeper than the physical, and although his body got stronger and stronger every day, his spirit remained broken.

By the end of the summer I'd managed to find a job teaching high school English, and I came home every day exhausted, ready to fall back into my routine of watching television in my room in my underwear. Sometimes I'd come home to find Tru at the water bowl, but most days he'd scurry back to his hiding spot before I saw him. I didn't blame him. I wanted to do the same thing.

One day I was cleaning my room when I leaned down and saw Tru staring back at me from underneath the bed. I lay down and slid under the bed next to him. He let out a yelp and army-crawled to the other end, where he watched me from a distance. I opened my mouth to tell him that it was okay, that I wasn't going to hurt him, but instead what came out was a sob. I was just so lost. I felt like I was suffocating. Everything was wrong, just so damn wrong. I couldn't believe that I had finished an M.A. in creative writing only to come back to my hometown and teach high school. I couldn't believe that I'd let some stupid guy destroy my self-esteem, couldn't believe how much it hurt every single day just to breathe and get through it.

I was lying there, face-first on top of dust bunnies and dog hair and God knows what else, wondering if it really and truly might be better just to die, when I felt something wet and rough slide across my cheek. When I looked up, Tru was right in front of me. He cocked his head to the side, his tongue hanging ever so slightly out of his mouth. We stayed that way for a long time until I collected myself enough to resume cleaning.

Neither one of us was magically healed after that moment. Tru stayed under the bed most days, and I still felt like my world was all wrong for a long time. But I think it's like many of those of us working in rescue say—the animals rescue us more often than we rescue them. My dog comforted me when I was feeling my lowest in the only way he knew how. He reminded me that even when you're sobbing in the middle of the afternoon in your underwear after crawling underneath your bed and you're feeling your absolute worst, there's a reason to keep going.

Almost a decade later, Tru's face is completely gray, and he's missing most of his teeth. He still has those scars on his back legs, but he doesn't run away when I or anyone else bends down to pet him. He sleeps on top of the bed instead of under-neath it, and if you're not careful, he'll lick your face before you've even had a chance to say hello.

I think about him every time I get a phone call or an e-mail from someone about an abused dog—a dog that is considered unadoptable, unlovable, too sick or too old to be of any use. I think about how I found him in the dark in that dirty pen and about how the animal control officer said I didn't want him. I wonder what might have happened to the both of us if I'd listened to him. More than anything, I think about that brokenness—Tru's and mine—the brokenness that we shared that summer and still carry around inside of us when things get tough, and I tell every single unlovable, unadoptable dog I meet that there is always a reason to keep going.

You Might Be from the Ozarks If . . .

1. You've ever ridden a tractor to a gas station for a snack in the summertime.

2. Your punishment as a kid was picking up rocks.

3. You can't throw one of those rocks you just picked up without hitting somebody you're related to.

4. You wave at everyone you meet on the road.

5. You are "fixin' " to do something.

6. "Hell" and "hail" and "think" and "thank" sound the same coming out of your mouth.

7. "A ways" is a fairly accurate measure of distance.

8. Your school lets out at least one day for deer season.

9. Your childhood swimming pool was a round stock tank.

10. You measure large weights in sacks of feed.

11. You can name the location of at least one permanent yard sale.

12. "He don't" and "I seen" are not improper grammar, but local vernacular.

13. You know how to get "ahold" of moonshine (and you talk about "getting ahold" of things and people).

14. You know how to get from one town to another without your tires ever touching a paved road.

15. You've ever been to a revival or a pie auction in your high school gym.

Center Point Large Print
600 Brooks Road / PO Box 1
Thorndike, ME 04986-0001 USA

(207) 568-3717

US & Canada:
1 800 929-9108
www.centerpointlargeprint.com